VANISH ME

LK MAGILL

FIRST HALE PRESS

Vanish Me/ LK Magill

Ebook ISBN 978-1-950928-00-2

Paperback ISBN 978-1-950928-01-9

Hardcover ISBN 978-1-950928-02-6

DEDICATION

For my Nonie and Grandpy.
When I was very little they allowed me to sit at the big roll-top desk
in their bedroom and play on their typewriter.
I'll never forget it.

ACKNOWLEDGMENTS

To God. Psalm 115:1

To my mother, Jan Koury-Hale. Without you, I would never have been able to get this far.

To my children, Jack and Molly, for living with a writer. To my father, Wally and step-mother, Kathy, who have shown me steadfast love and support. To my brother, Greg, no matter the time between talks, we're always the same.

To my early readers: Sara, Krystal, Jenna and Ali. Your input truly shapes each and every book, helping me to reach for depth when I'm lacking it and height when it seems too far.

Clutching at the gray leather of the steering wheel, Ava Montgomery's hands flexed involuntarily. Traffic was thick today, as it was every morning. Right foot hovering between the gas and brake pedal, she stole a quick glance at the dashboard's digital clock. The red block numbers displayed what she already knew: eight-seventeen a.m. They were going to be late, she hated being late.

"Alright Mason, we're almost to school," Ava said.

"Again?" Her son rolled his hazel eyes and huffed a breath. At six-years-old he was going on sixteen.

"Five days a week," Ava reminded him.

Trying to hide the smirk that wanted to play across her lips, she stole a look in the rearview mirror at him, but it was something more than his pouting face that caught her eye. There was a familiar black sedan lingering a few cars back.

Biting at her lower lip, Ava frowned. Was it the same one she had seen the day before? Giving her head a shake, she brushed off the rush of paranoia. Maybe she was just imagining things, after all, there had to be thousands of black cars in the Orange County area. What were the chances that this one in particular would be following her?

"Why can't I stay home with you?" Mason asked.

"I'm not staying home, I have to go to work," she countered.

"Again?"

"Five days a week," she repeated, but her former teasing tone was gone.

Putting on her blinker, Ava maneuvered her silver SUV into the right-hand turn lane, then slowed. Cars stacked up in front of her, everyone cramming into the entrance of Hudson Elementary at the last minute. Its freshly painted white buildings shone out amongst the flowing trees that dotted the green lawn. This was a nice neighborhood, one with good schools and clean houses. It wasn't how Ava had been raised, so she was glad to have Mason here, no matter what she had to do to accomplish it.

Sighing with impatience, she checked the rearview mirror once more. A lingering look revealed first one and then another black sedan moving over as well. The stop and go traffic made for a crawling transition and perspiration filled her itchy palms. Had she been found?

Ava's eyes danced back to her son. He fiddled with his backpack straps absently. No, she assured herself, tucking a shoulder-length blonde hair behind one ear. This was just her father talking inside her head again, more spillover from a lifetime of survivalist paranoia.

When the line began moving again, Ava bumped up into the driveway and pulled the car to a stop at the curb.

"Will you walk me in today?" Mason asked.

Shifting in her seat, Ava's bright blue eyes swept the line

behind her. The black cars were gone, she really had been imagining things. Nodding her head in acceptance, Ava maneuvered the SUV through the drop-off zone and found an open space in the school lot.

Jamming the vehicle into park, she released her belt and grabbed for the door handle. Better make this fast, she thought, or she wouldn't have time to hit the gym before work. As her feet landed on the black asphalt, she felt the cool brush of Autumn air swirl around her. Despite the temperate weather of Southern California, Ava was positively sweating.

"Backpack?"

"Got it."

"Lunch box?"

"Yep."

She fumbled with his booster seat straps as they echoed the familiar list of items. Standing aside, she held herself back from tousling his thick hair while he jumped out.

He looked so much like his father just then that the familiar pang of regret came to rear its ugly head. Had keeping Mason out of his father's life really been the best choice? In a perfect world she would have been given the answer before the decision was made, but this world was far from perfect, she knew.

Holding her son's little hand in her own, they weaved through the rows of parked cars and made their way steadily towards his school. Countless other children swarmed around them, they squealed and shouted, ran and walked. Some mothers appeared just as harried as she was, sweat pants stained with coffee or spit-up or worse.

Then there were others who were dressed to perfection in high heels and business suits with perfectly styled hair. She wondered absently how they did it. Giving Mason's hand a tight squeeze she smiled down at him. At least he didn't mind if she wore workout clothes to drop him off.

Crossing onto the sidewalk, they followed its path around the lawn. Mason's class was through one high archway and around to the left. Suddenly the school's bell began to clang loudly, announcing their tardiness to the world. Tugging at him, Ava hustled now. His classroom was just ahead, but she had to practically drag him there as he tripped and stumbled purposefully. Any other time she might have been angry, but his giggles had her smiling too.

His first grade teacher, Ms. Martinez, propped open the classroom door with a well-placed heel. She was one of the women Ava marveled at. Dark hair swirling down her back, her clothing fit perfectly, and the jade color of her blouse made her green eyes pop. On top of it, the woman was every bit the smart and engaging personality that you'd have to be in order to spend your day with thirty children.

"Sorry, again." Ava ducked her head in apology but saw no look of disapproval in the sparkling eyes.

"Welcome, Mason!" Ms. Martinez smiled warmly.

With one hand she waved Ava away, and with the other she swung the door closed behind them. Stepping back, Ava sagged in momentary relief, just glad to have made it in time. When she swiveled back around, however, the school grounds were a ghost town.

It was as if that bell had sucked up every human being and locked them tightly inside. Surveying her vacant surroundings, Ava suddenly felt very much alone. Palms sweaty, she swiped both hands down the sides of her yoga pants. The black spandex did a poor job of absorption.

Clearing her throat, Ava tipped her chin up and worked to keep things casual. The sun had moved behind a few drifting clouds in an otherwise blue sky, causing shadows to shift along the cement sidewalk. Ava followed its path back through the archway and into the open area in front of the school. Eyes darting right, she located her car still parked two rows back in the small lot. There were no black cars trolling, but her heart still fluttered inside her chest.

The real question was: should she make the particular phone call that was available to her, or not? Her brother had discussed it with her only once, but she was crystal clear on the rules. She should call in the event of an emergency only. And by "emergency" Clay had meant certain danger.

Keys gripped in one hand, Ava automatically reached for her cell phone before realizing that she had left it in her car. Bad move, she thought, and hurried her pace.

Internally, Ava began to struggle. One part of her, the new part, wanted to walk like a normal human being back to her car, get in and drive away. The other part, the old Ava, clamored for action, for self-preservation. Do something, anything, her father's voice haunted her. So, shifting her car keys around, Ava threaded them individually through her clenched fingers. It did little to dampen the rush of her heart.

Back in college she had often times walked alone to the far reaches of a vast empty lot. She never liked to do it at night, but class schedules sometimes made it a necessity. Positioning each key between her fingers like a weapon had made her feel better back then, although she wasn't sure how effective they would be in reality.

Of course, that was before Mason had come into her life and she had given everything up. College had ended before it had truly begun, and Ava had assumed the life of a single mother. Did she have regrets? When it came to Mason the answer was simple: none whatsoever.

Arriving at the curb, Ava held her free hand up to shade her eyes. The cloud cover from before had moved away to reveal a sudden burst of sunlight. Its beams glared off the window glass from the parked cars in the lot.

Frozen in place now, one foot hovering in the air, she was poised to step off the curb when she heard an unmistakable sound. The sudden screech of tires had her brain dialing back and her breath evaporating inside her lungs.

From just around the corner, a black sedan appeared. Its engine revved as it drew closer. She watched in slow motion as the vehicle whipped into the lot with its two masculine occupants filling the front seat.

They were wearing dark suits and sunglasses. Sunglasses that were focused entirely on her. Panic sent painful tingles to shoot through her system. She should have made that call.

Run.

All at once time caught up with itself. Adrenaline flooded her body, pumping through her system as she wheeled to take off. Veering at first towards the school, she crossed the strip of lawn, dropping her keys unknowingly in the grass.

Her breath came in harsh gasps as she sucked in oxygen, eyes wide, senses reeling. Don't look back, her father's voice sounded in her head.

Instinct had her moving past the elementary buildings. She headed for the nearest businesses, away from the school, away from her son.

Running shoes slapping hard against the cement sidewalk, Ava steered full speed into the street. Car horns blasted at her left side and she danced automatically away from them. She could hear the squeal of brakes, sense vehicles around her, but she couldn't afford to stop. Without looking, she knew that the men were behind her, gaining.

Yelling indistinctly, she could hear them, but her mind refused to translate what words they said. The sound of her own blood throbbing in her ears wiped away any details.

Focused singularly on the footing in front of her, the black asphalt roadway flashed under her feet as she made it through all four lanes of traffic without getting hit. A small miracle. The yellow and white painted lines had marked her progress. With any luck, a passing car would take out one of the problems racing just behind her.

Cresting the curb, she dashed onto the sidewalk, but stumbled just a little. Catching herself with an outstretched hand, she shoved back to her feet and increased her speed. There was an entire block of residential housing before the business district began and she simply had to make it that far. Had to.

Her toes gripped at the uneven gray cement of the sidewalk as her arms pumped, pushing her body to move even faster. Thank God she was a runner, she thought.

Small bungalow homes, old but in a well-kept sort of way, passed by on her right side. She knew this neighborhood from driving by it every day. She knew the baby blue one story with the ornate white trim. She knew the tidy tan house with the Great Dane in the front yard. She knew them all, but not well enough to know the names of the people living there. Not well enough to know who might be at home, who might be able to help her. So she tore past them, leaving her regrets to fly at their closed doors.

"Stop!" A male voice shouted.

He was so close now that she could understand his words, feel his presence like a weight pressing forward behind her. Just three more homes to go, she told herself.

Across the next street she could see the metallic pumps of a gas station. There were always plenty of people at gas stations, and surveillance cameras, but Ava would never make it that far.

The contact of the man's tackle had angry prickles shooting through her extremities. His long arms encircled her waist, wrapping themselves tightly around her body before the pivot of his weight had them listing to the side.

Tumbling over each other, they came to rest on the front lawn of one faded yellow house. Lungs burning, Ava wriggled uselessly underneath him, unable to roll him off, though she tried. He had her pinned effectively by his muscular body and her only reward was his equally labored panting. At least she had given him a run for his money.

Serious brown eyes stared down at her out of a chiseled face. He was appraising her, and in that moment, she watched a flicker pass in his eyes. Was there a look of recognition there? If so, then it was gone almost instantly as he transformed his expression into an annoyed frown.

"Why didn't you stop?" He demanded.

"Why should I?"

"Stop. FBI. Don't run. That mean nothing to you?"

"Let me see your badge," she said, tilting her chin up, undaunted.

Shifting awkwardly, he tried to get up without losing his grip on her. His dark suit jacket hung open to reveal a button-up white shirt tucked into a black leather belt. Around his neck hung a navy-blue tie that draped down between them, the end pooling itself on her chest.

He was young for FBI, maybe late-twenties, not that she was an expert. In truth, she didn't know how old she expected a Fed to be. The stare down between them lasted only a few seconds, but it had her pulse quickening.

It was obvious he didn't want to let go of her in order to retrieve the credentials that lay concealed in his pocket, but something inside of him pushed him to do it anyway. Watching him steadily, she observed him waging an internal war. Do the right thing and produce the requested badge but risk another foot chase.

As their breathing evened out, her ears picked up the sounds of an approaching engine. Breaking eye contact with him, Ava rotated her head up and watched as a black sedan pulled to a stop in the driveway of the little yellow home.

The front doors opened, unleashing more men in fitted suits to trample the lawn. Soon the man on top of her no longer had to make a decision. The others were grabbing at her as he shifted away. She could feel the wrap of their rough hands on her body. Hoisting her up, they practically carried her to the wide back seat and shoved her inside.

Before the sedan drove off, the young agent slipped in beside her and presented his identification as they reversed down the drive. Carefully she scrutinized the gold badge with its accompanying photo ID as he held them in front of her face. In typical black type, it read:

FBI Special Agent
Johnathan Finn

Though it appeared to be legitimate, she admittedly had no idea how to tell if it was fake. Seemed like something that should be taught in school, or maybe a lesson that her father overlooked.

Glancing from the unsmiling photo into the equally formidable face, she noted that they matched. Same thick crop of dark hair, strong jaw line and intelligent eyes.

"Satisfied?" Agent Finn's voice was gruff as he slipped the leather holder back into his pocket.

"Am I under arrest?"

"We just need to ask you some questions." The man riding shotgun spoke for the first time.

Ava leaned back against the cloth seat and tried to catch a glimpse of his face in the rearview mirror but failed. From behind, he appeared tall and slender, with salt and pepper hair, but his voice cut like glass.

"If I'm not under arrest, then I demand you release me," Ava countered.

"Consider yourself detained." He flicked his wrist but did not turn around.

Yanking at her passenger door handle, Ava hissed in frustration. It moved with ease but wouldn't open the door. The child safety locks must be on, she realized. She used them with Mason.

The window button was useless, too. Its fruitless clicking refused to roll down the glass. Huffing indignantly, she glared at the door. If the agents found her futile attempts at escape humorous, they made no mention.

"I want to call my lawyer," she said finally.

Not that she had a lawyer, but they didn't know that. What she really needed was access to a phone. She wished with every fiber of her being that she had made that call days ago, back when she had first noticed the black sedans. They had popped up at the grocery store, then again after work. If the Feds had discovered what she had done, then she might lose custody of Mason. Her insides quaked.

"We'll get right on it." The suit in front nodded, but Agent Finn shifted in his seat uncomfortably.

Pretending to look out her window, Ava studied him in the reflection instead. The expression on his face told her that the likelihood of access to a phone, let alone a lawyer, was slim to none. It was either the lie from the older agent, or the denial of her civil rights that had him squirming. He must be the rookie.

Squeezing her eyes shut for a moment, Ava fought with the heaving fear forming in her chest. She flashed back to one of her father's many lectures on the subject. If you show your emotion, then you give up your power. It's just a battle, keep your head for the war.

Exhaling a determined breath, Ava worked to quell the emotions that bobbed to the surface. Instead of losing her cool, she narrowed her eyes and kept vigil of the scene that passed by outside.

The suburbs faded, giving way to a vast freeway where cars zoomed unwittingly by them. Dark limo tint on the rear windows made the light of mid-morning seem dusky, almost purple. Traffic was light now, everyone was in school or at work.

Re-focusing, she tried to make note of their direction. They were heading south.

"I need to call work," she ventured.

"No."

"I'm a single mom, I can't afford to miss a day." She played every card she could think of.

"No."

The front seat was resolute, but Agent Finn's fingers tightened almost imperceptibly at his side. Clearly this situation wasn't by the book and he didn't like it. If her father hadn't raised her to tune in to this type of body language, she never would have noticed. He struggled with how this was playing out but hid it almost perfectly. She may be able to use that.

THE REST OF THE RIDE WAS UNEVENTFUL AS VARIOUS SCENARIOS ran through her head. She thought back to that fateful day so many years earlier, the one that had changed everything.

When the phone call had come in, she had been sitting alone in her college dorm. Still in shock from the death of her parents, Ava hadn't hesitated to answer her cell. Despite the years of estrangement from her older brother, Ava still missed him. He was all the family that she had left.

Even now she could hear the hitch in Clay's voice, the strain as he asked her for help. Someone else may have thought twice, but not her. Grabbing up her coat by the door, Ava had gone to her brother without a backwards glance. And she hadn't stopped looking over her shoulder since.

When the black town car pulled up to the FBI office building, Ava tilted her face against the window in an effort to see it more clearly. It was a fairly large structure, maybe ten stories high with massive gleaming blue-tinged windows lining the front. Palm trees ran down its length and three flags positioned at the top of silver poles flapped casually in the fall breeze. The FBI banner, the California State flag and Old Glory.

These were indeed legitimate agents, but their overall intention was suspect. Mind working quickly, Ava could think of only one thing they could possibly want from her. And she'd rather die than give it up. In a word, she was screwed.

TWO

They rolled up to a security check-point around the side of the building where a solitary guard reviewed the driver's credentials before waving them through. Slowly navigating the half-empty parking lot, the vehicle came to a stop at the curb just behind the imposing structure. Its engine was left idling and the driver did not move to exit. Ava tensed in anticipation of what came next.

"Better restrain her." The front seat instructed. "We already know she's a runner."

"Please turn towards the door and put your hands behind your back," Agent Finn began, retrieving a pair of shining cuffs from his waist. When she hesitated, he sighed audibly. "It's only for the walk in, I promise."

Gritting her teeth against his tone, she shifted around and pressed her palms together as he instructed. What was it that made her believe what he said?

Grudgingly, she submitted to the binds, feeling the heat of his hands moving over her wrists. The metal bit into her flesh but stopped a fraction before pain. When his fingers left her, a strange sensation remained. She shrugged it off.

Jogging around to her side of the vehicle, Agent Finn opened the door and steadied her elbow as she scooted awkwardly to the edge and got out. A brisk wind greeted her, she could feel its bite through the thin fabric of her mint-green workout jacket.

They were close to the ocean here; the smell of salt was clear on the air. The devil is in the details, she could almost hear her father chuckle softly. His memory made her ache, and for a brief moment she fought an unexpected flood of weakness. Agent Finn gripped her elbow all the tighter, his eyes darting across the side of her face once before glancing away. She didn't give him the satisfaction of looking back.

The rear entrance to the building was rather narrow. She watched as the lead agent waved his security ID card over an electronic reader. It made no sound, but the locking mechanism of the heavy door clicked before Agent Finn made a grab for the handle. It swung outward and he held it open as the lead agent moved through first.

Once inside, they traversed a well-lit hallway, arriving at a bank of elevators through which she could see the high ceiling of a lobby. Foot traffic echoed across the tile flooring. Anonymous men and women clad in more business suits crossed the space. Ava leaned back just enough to watch before the elevator doors slid open.

Once inside the box, Ava's eyes tracked the illumination of the buttons as they marked their ascent to the fifth floor. When the silver-hued doors opened once more, they revealed a wide hallway lined with doors on either side, all of which were closed.

Without encouragement, Ava followed the lead agent as he strode purposefully along the corridor. He stopped at an unmarked door. It was the eleventh one down on the left side.

After another electronic keypad was utilized, they arrived at their final destination, a single blank square of an interrogation room. And by square she meant perfectly square. Each wall was the same length as the other.

In the middle was a worn wooden table with three equally uncomfortable chairs positioned around it. Two were on one side, one on the other. She didn't have to guess which side she would be placed on.

Remarkably, Agent Finn removed the cuffs as promised. It took everything in her will power not to rub at her wrists after he was done. Taking a seat, she finally learned the name of the other man in the suit: Agent Palmer.

Positioned directly across the solitary wooden desk, she let her gaze flow over him now. His eyes were such a light shade of blue that they looked almost gray. A no-nonsense ferocity resonated from them. His features were angular and he appeared to be about mid-fifties in age, although men were harder to peg at this stage. There was a hint of salt in his short crop of mostly pepper-colored hair, so she thought he was probably too young to be in his sixties.

"Ava Montgomery." His voice was careful, everything that he said would be calculated. "I'm sure you can guess why we've brought you in today."

"Not a clue."

"We would like to ask you some questions concerning your brother," he continued, ignoring her remark.

"Clay?"

"Do you have any others?"

"No." Now it was her turn to shift uncomfortably. "When do I get to speak with my lawyer?"

"You don't," he admitted.

"Then I'm not saying anything."

She glanced over at Agent Finn seated solidly beside his seasoned counterpart. Scribbling long hand, his pen could be heard making copious notes across an old-style yellow note pad. No tablet for this guy, she thought, unusual.

"It would benefit you greatly to play along here," Agent Palmer persisted.

"How long will you hold me? I have to pick up my son after school."

It was then that Agent Palmer sighed and tilted back in his chair. Giving his head a slight shake, he pressed his lips together in an almost imperceptible smile. Her stomach did a flip when it finally dawned on her, they had no intention of letting her go get him.

"When was the last time you spoke with Clay?" Agent Palmer stared at her, gray-blue eyes steady.

"I haven't spoken with him in years," Ava lied.

"I'll try again. When is the last time that you spoke with your brother?"

The measured tone of Agent Palmer's voice had Ava considering. The last time that she had spoken with her brother... really and truly spoken to him... was when Mason was born.

Doing the math, she counted out six years. Had it really been so long? It wasn't by her choice, though she understood why Clay had insisted on the separation. He was getting involved in something dangerous. Something that put him at risk, and by extension, any family members. It was best for

Mason and Ava if everyone around Clay thought he didn't care about them, best if he pretended like they meant nothing.

It had been a hard pill for Ava to swallow but she had done it anyway. Throughout their childhood, though, she and Clay had been thick as thieves. If Agent Palmer had questioned her back then, she could have told him what Clay had chosen for breakfast, what clothes he liked to wear, what made him laugh, what made him cry.

Now all she was left with were monthly well-checks. He would call, they would talk about the weather, and he would know she was fine. After they would hang up, Ava would move on with her life.

Grinding her teeth slowly, she kept her hands still in her lap. "It's been years," she repeated.

"More like three weeks. Do I need to play the recording of your conversation?"

Ava blanched. What had Clay done to warrant the FBI recording them? Her thoughts drifted to that long ago conversation. The one where Clay had begged for her help. Did the FBI know? Would they take Mason from her?

Fear, came on fast. It was so deep and strong that it shook her core. If she didn't act fast, she would never be able to stop the trembling that threatened to take over.

"You wiretapped my phone?!" She shouted it, slamming her hands flat on the table. "Is that even legal? I should have known it was you guys following me for the past three days. What the hell do you want from me?"

Leaning forward, Ava raged at them, but the last question withered on her lips. A glimmer of surprise had sparked itself in Palmer's eyes. If she had blinked, she would have missed it.

Something she had said to him was unexpected. Though

he covered it well now, Ava felt a dull warning ring inside her head. Feeling out of her depth, she returned her hands to her lap and resolved once more to remain silent.

"You don't have much family, is that right?" Agent Palmer proceeded as if nothing were amiss.

She stared at him, making no move to answer.

"Both of your parents died in a car accident some years ago. Your extended family is scattered, you don't know them. Really, it's just your brother and your son, right?"

"What do you know about my parent's accident?" The question leapt from Ava's mouth before she could stop it, her heart leaping along with it. "Is the FBI looking into it?"

"The case file states that it was a head-on impact," Agent Finn recited. "On that long stretch of highway just outside of Vegas. The other driver was DUI and both occupants died on impact. Pretty straight-forward open and shut."

Ava nodded, eyes dropping to the tabletop. It had been the same answer that she had received from Clay, over and over. It was just a coincidence, her brother had assured her. Accidents sometimes happen. He had rubbed at her shoulder then, trying to offer comfort where none could be gained. Their parents had died just after her acceptance into college, Mason hadn't even been born yet.

Clay had been in the military for a few years by then and had flown back from the East Coast to help her deal with the funeral arrangements. Despite his assurances, she had always battled with her gut after her parents' crash, wondering if some sort of foul play was involved. With a father who didn't believe in coincidence, or accidents, how was she ever supposed to accept it?

"I need to go pick up my son." Ava tried to re-direct. "There's no one else to get him."

"What about Mason's biological father, is he around?"

"No."

"Well, you live in an awfully nice house in the suburbs. Who pays for it?"

"I do."

"No, you don't. What about your car? Who pays for that?"

"I do." Her palms grew slick, there was no way for them to tell where the money came from, she was sure.

"What about James Miller?"

"Who?"

Ava's heart skipped a beat, eyes darting to hold Agent Palmer's appraising look. Panic snaked quickly to her extremities before stoking a smoldering fire in her chest. They must have pulled the school paperwork, she thought. There was only one place that name was listed, just one extreme emergency form. Fingers digging into the edge of the table, she couldn't hide the dread that covered her face.

"Tell me you did not call that number."

"Is that Mason's biological father?"

Palmer remained calm in his questioning, one hand holding a ballpoint pen lightly. Every so often, he tapped it against the smooth surface of the wood. Agent Finn's eyes darted up from his note taking. She could feel the heat of his stare upon her skin, but she had eyes only for Palmer and his thinly pressed lips.

If the Feds had called that number, then Clay was on his way to extract her and Mason. The only problem was that right now she wasn't with Mason, so Clay would be left to choose between the two of them. Squeezing her eyes shut, she fought back vicious tears, they were supposed to be taken together.

Unable to hold it in any longer, she shot to her feet, the stiff-backed interrogation chair tumbled to the ground. Pacing now, she ran shaky fingers through her hair. That call was only supposed to be placed if she was dead or they were in danger. As a single mother, she had been able to submit the form to the school without any questions being asked, but she never thought that it would be used by someone other than herself.

"Despite our best efforts we have been unable to find a trace of information about Mason's father anywhere."

"James Miller is not Mason's father," Ava spat at them. He was no one. A ghost. A protocol.

"Who is he? A code name for your brother maybe? Will Clay be picking Mason up from school today?" Palmer showed her his cards, causing her to sneer in disgust. He was fishing for information and he had no idea just how right he was.

"That's what you think?" She forced a harsh laugh. "You set this whole thing up to flush out my brother? Did you even listen to our last conversation? He's harmless. He installs solar panels for a living and reads conspiracy theories online. Why don't you just pick him up at work?"

These were the lines that she had been given, and she delivered them well. Truthfully, she didn't know the details of Clay's work. They had agreed that it was best if she were in the dark.

"Clay Montgomery does not install solar panels, and try as we might, we haven't been able to convince him to come in for questioning."

"Let me go. Please, I need to pick up Mason."

"We have people at the school. Nothing will happen to him."

"You're using a six-year-old as bait. What kind of men are you?"

"The kind of men who get the job done." Palmer's face revealed its first hint of passion. "I've been doing this a long time now, Ava. I listen to the things that people say, but what I've found to be the most compelling is what they do not say. You haven't asked me why you're here. You haven't asked me why we want to speak with Clay."

Her father's voice sounded inside her head then, cautioning her not to step into the trap. Already, she had said too much, let them know too much, shown too much emotion. But she couldn't stop herself from defending Clay, he and Mason were all she had left.

"My brother is a good man."

"Your brother is the head of the Constitutional Militia."

"The what?"

Letting out an exasperated sigh, Agent Palmer threw a knowing look at Finn. Though Ava feigned ignorance, she had heard of it. Oh yes, she had definitely heard of it.

The Constitutional Militia was the most rapidly growing organization in the country. Comprised entirely of private citizens, the group focused on self-sufficiency, survivalist preparation and martial law enforcement. They were highly trained, deeply funded and attracting new recruits all the time. The source of constant media speculation, they did their best to fly under the radar, but with more privately owned weapons than most small nations, it was hard to remain unnoticed. Ava knew her brother was a member, she hadn't known he was the head.

"Clay Montgomery joined the military after high school. He was recruited, in fact. Did he tell you?" Agent Finn asked.

Turning away from his searching brown eyes, Ava hugged herself tightly and stared at the far blank wall. It was empty, as was every other wall in the room. She had expected a mirror which of course would actually be two-way glass. In the movies there was always someone on the other side, watching. But in reality, there was nothing.

Eyes darting up to the corner of the room, she studied the space carefully. No obvious camera with a blinking red light hung there. Shoulders tense with the strain of containment, Ava rotated back around to face the men. She reluctantly righted her fallen chair and took a seat heavily.

"I knew he joined the military," she admitted.

"Yes, but early on he was selected to participate in a special program. He underwent accelerated training. Did he tell you about it?"

"No."

"We can't divulge details, but he was privy to a great deal of sensitive information. All of the members of that program were expected to re-enlist, make it a lifetime commitment."

"But Clay got out after four years, right?"

Agent Finn's brown eyes flickered again, that same split-second of knowledge before shuttering closed. Watching his face, Ava noted he kept it purposefully blank.

In the ensuing silence, Agent Palmer's tapping pen was the only sound in the room. After a beat, the seasoned agent took over once more.

"Yes, something changed for him. Do you have any idea what it was?"

"No." Ava looked down, but inside her head she answered. *Oh yeah, I know what it was.*

Palmer and Finn shared another glance. The vet and the rookie, communicating in silence as she sat across from them. Narrowing her eyes, she lifted her head and folded her arms over her chest.

It was them. It was all them. They would decide how much she already knew, what more to tell her, and which one would do the telling. She had no control.

"Ava." Agent Finn reached his hand across the table towards her, fingers outstretched as he spoke. "We need to talk with him in person but we can't flush him out. You're his only living relative. He has no girlfriend. There isn't anyone that he seems to care about. Please, we need your help."

"Let me go," Ava reasoned, teeth clenched. "I have nothing to do with the Militia."

A brisk knock at the lone door had them all jumping. Palmer's once stoic composure dropped as he glared up into the corner of the room. So, there was a hidden camera there, Ava thought.

Metal chair legs scraped against the concrete flooring as Finn shoved back to standing. His large hands smoothed at the front of his navy jacket before he turned to open the door a crack. Ava was unable to see the knocker, but she could hear male whispering. Hushed insistence devolved into a harsh exchange. Something big was going down.

Tilting her head to the side, Ava maintained eye contact with Agent Palmer. He studied her as she did the same to him. *If my brother doesn't trust you, then I shouldn't either, she* thought. Because if there's one thing that I know about Clay, it's that he loves this country and would never do anything against it. Something is very wrong inside the FBI, Ava reasoned, if Clay went rogue.

The sound of the door forcefully clicking shut had her snapping out of their mutual trance. Agent Finn crossed to the older man and bent to whisper fervently in his ear. Nodding carefully, Palmer absorbed the information without providing a tell.

When Finn completed his message, he was gestured to resume his seat. Refusing to look at her, he did so.

"Ava, I need you to tell me everything you know about James Miller." Palmer was measured in his delivery.

"You've lost him." Ava barely breathed out the words. "Mason, he disappeared, didn't he?"

"Your brother never showed to pick him up at his school. When we sent one of our agents in to retrieve him, Mason was already gone."

THREE

S o hot.

The room that had once felt so cold was now unbearably hot. Ava worked to suck in oxygen, but her throat had constricted to the size of a straw.

This was the protocol, she reminded herself. This was how it was supposed to work. The number is called and Mason evaporates into thin air. Clay had him now, and he was safe. The only hiccup in all this was that Ava didn't know where they would hide. She was supposed to have been with them.

The anger she felt was unlike anything in her entire life. She imagined her hands wrapping themselves effectively around Agent Palmer's skinny neck. Tightening ever so slowly, her thumbs would apply pressure against his windpipe until they produced a satisfactory gurgle.

The one thing preventing her from reaching across the table was the knowledge that she would eventually regain custody of Mason. But when would that be? If the FBI couldn't locate Clay, then she certainly couldn't either. She would have to wait for his contact, and that could take weeks, maybe longer if the Feds kept her under surveillance.

Bottom line, Mason wasn't coming home to her tonight, or tomorrow, or the next day, or the next. Her chest heaved with the weight of it.

"Not only have you held me here against my will, but now you've cost me my son."

"We know this is difficult for you but we're going to do our best to recover Mason," Agent Finn interjected, drawing a warning look from his partner.

"No." Ava slammed a fist onto the wooden surface before her, wanting to make a point. "You've all done enough, expect a lawsuit."

Continuing on with his line of questioning, Agent Palmer would not be dissuaded. He tried his best to coax her into revealing more about James Miller, her brother, the Constitutional Militia, the list went on.

For a while she stared him down, willing him to drop dead by the sheer force of her mind. Eventually, she shifted to Agent Finn who held her eyes for only a few moments before looking away. At least one of them felt a twinge of guilt.

Beyond him, she studied the door with its silver colored handle and light leaking around the frame. Up in the corner of the room she scrutinized the area where the camera must be. How many people watched their conversation? From where?

For the first time she wondered what kind of manpower was being utilized to track Clay down. What exactly was he doing that had the Feds so stirred up? At the moment she could be thankful that she truly didn't know.

Hours passed, or maybe it just seemed like that. There was

no clock in the room. She had no watch on her wrist, no phone in her pocket, no way to tell time. Without a window, there was no sun to help her keep track. She was at a loss.

Her lips remained firmly sealed, but now and then a tear would fill her eye. Biting at the inside of her cheek prevented any from brimming over to run weakly down her face.

Another knock startled Ava out of her reverie. She may have jumped in her chair, but this time the agents didn't share in her alarm. They had been expecting it.

Agent Finn rose once more and shoved back from the table. She watched him stride to the door to retrieve several paper bags. The hand that passed them through was female this time, her copper nail polish stood out in the light. As the tantalizing scent of greasy drive-thru hamburgers wafted into the small space, Ava's stomach gave up a longing rumble.

Immediately her mouth began to salivate, her stomach churning in anticipation. It must be dinner time, she thought. Her mind shifted to Mason and where he would be getting his meal tonight. Where would Clay take him?

She had shown Mason photos of her brother and old family movies, so he knew what Clay looked like. Often her son had asked to meet him; how he hungered for a father figure. Well, maybe now they would have that chance. She only wished she could be there to witness it.

Agent Finn settled back across from her, the wooden seat creaking slightly under his fit frame. Shoving one wide hand into a bag, he began pulling out wrapped burgers and red cardboard cups of fries. There were even three large sodas, their straws still laying neatly packaged in white paper on the table.

Eyes darting to the mound of food, Ava came to a decision.

She refused to share a meal with Agent Palmer. He had become her scapegoat for all that had occurred and starvation was preferred to any positive interaction with him.

"Do you want some catsup?" Finn asked.

Refusing to acknowledge him, Ava stared at Palmer. She watched him casually select a straw. Ripping the paper wrapper somewhere in the middle, he slid off the end and pushed the yellow striped cylinder into his drink. Sipping quietly, he appraised her lack of participation. Her stomach protested, but her mind persevered.

"Hope you like Coca-Cola, they didn't have any Pepsi," Finn continued, shoving the last drink over to rest inches from her body.

Staring down at the soda, Ava observed tiny droplets of condensation slide down the outside of the cup. She studied their progress with rapt attention, but couldn't recall the last time she actually had a Coke. Soon a small water ring would be left on the table.

"She's not going to eat as long as I'm here," Agent Palmer announced.

Rising to his feet, he didn't bother to collect any food. Long thin fingers grasped his drink. That item, at least, he wouldn't leave behind. Finn rose too, hurriedly shoving his portion into one of the empty bags. He was a big guy, not heavy-set by any means, but his shoulders were broad under the suit coat. Ava realized how hungry he must be by the way he snatched at the food. He hadn't eaten since their chase and was likely as ravenous as she was.

"No, you stay," Palmer instructed.

Freezing mid-scramble, Agent Finn glanced over at her. He was thrown off guard and in that moment his face seemed hesitant, like a kid caught up in something he didn't want to be in. But just like before, it was only for a moment. Regaining his composure, the serious furrows returned to his brow as he settled back down. Ava continued to analyze his face, but Agent Finn kept his expression veiled.

Once Palmer had made his exit, Ava reached shakily across the table to select a hamburger. Hunger and stress had left her feeling unsteady. Surely Finn noticed her weakness, but to his credit he didn't push his advantage. Continuing to focus on his own food, he let her eat first one, and then another burger, sharing in her silence.

In between bites, Ava shoveled in French fries, still warm and dotted with salt. The combination was an old favorite. The taste brought her back to long road trips as a kid. Her parents would always stop at that special fast food restaurant just off the freeway, the one with an outside play area for kids.

She and Clay would rush through their nuggets before diving into the ball pit. Of course, now that she was a parent herself, Ava was reluctant to let Mason play in one. She'd never witnessed anyone cleaning them.

Back in the day, however, she thought they were heaven; a welcome chance to stretch little legs that were cramped from miles in the backseat. Clay would lead the way through the hot plastic tubes and down the swirling slide. Every so often, they were zapped by the static electricity that their shuffling caused. *I've been shot, have to keep moving,* Clay would call out. Always they would play soldiers. Back then it had just been pretend.

"I'm really sorry about your kid," Agent Finn began, his eyes seemed to hold true remorse.

"Do you have children?" Ava questioned.

"No."

"Then you don't understand."

"I promise that we will find him," Finn continued, his confidence unshakable.

"No, you won't."

"Don't you want us to bring him back? We need your help."

"Why would I want you to get him?" Ava was incredulous, dusting fry salt off on the leg of her pants. "So you can use him as bait again?"

"Look, even if you are involved with the Militia, we can get you out… with your son. We can keep you both safe." His eyes were earnest. He really believed what he was doing was right.

"I'll take my chances." She slurped up the soda, relishing the flood of dark syrup-laced liquid.

"Mason has been kidnapped and you don't seem all that concerned about finding him. Is that because you know where he is? Do you know who has him?"

She continued to eat but said nothing.

"This isn't a game, Ava. Some people think that you're intricately involved with the Militia. If you don't start cooperating, we're going to have to arrest you for conspiracy."

With a fry halfway to her mouth, Ava paused, eyes locking with Finn's. First, he pretended to be nice, then he made his threats. She almost wanted to laugh. Agent Finn could be both the good cop and the bad cop all in the span of one meal.

From what she could tell, the FBI didn't have anything on her. A conspiracy charge was a reach. As soon as they let her speak to an attorney, she would be out of their custody. Stretching both arms forward over the surface of the table, Ava offered him her wrists.

Arching one eyebrow, she dared him to cuff her. His dark eyes danced with a simmering frustration, but staring contests were her specialty, and she had all the time in the world just now. Even if she were released that very moment, she wouldn't be able to reach out to Clay for a long time. The Feds would tail her wherever she went, waiting. It could be awhile before her brother would be able to come for her, but he would come, eventually.

"Ava, stop making this so hard." Finn gritted his teeth, keeping his voice low. "I only want to help you."

"I don't believe you," she whispered.

The door swung open then without warning. Agent Palmer with all of his tall thin grayness walked resolutely back into the room, taking possession.

Finn got up and approached him, his broad back turned to Ava. More quiet communication transpired before Finn broke away to start cleaning up the discarded wrappers that were strewn over the table. Withdrawing her wrists, Ava observed him grip the pieces of paper, stuffing them roughly into one of the empty bags. He kept his eyes focused on the task at hand.

"We're moving you," Palmer announced.

"Where to?"

"To another facility."

Ava frowned up at him, studying the control that seemed to dictate every action Agent Palmer allowed himself. He hadn't given up yet, he hadn't even come close. Palmer's instincts had him zeroing in on her, and the information that he sensed she held so tightly in her grasp.

How long would it take for them to play this all out, Ava

wondered, eyes darting once more to the upper corner of the room. When Finn made his way around behind her, she knew what came next.

Standing without being asked, she placed her hands behind her back and held her palms together in compliance. Again, his touch was hot as he clicked on the metal cuffs. Adjusting her arms, she worked to rid herself of the uncertainty he caused.

They marched back down the hall but in the opposite direction from where they had come in. Twelve other closed doors passed by before they reached the end of the corridor. Counting gave her the illusion of control. It was the only thing she had left.

Opening the stairwell door, Agent Palmer lead the way through with Finn gripping her elbow all the while. They wound down, down, down; five flights exactly before pushing through a side door into the open air. It was nighttime, but no stars could be seen this deep in the city. Between street lamps and building lights, the darkness was well and truly squashed.

Another black sedan sat idling at the curb. At the sight of it, her insides revolted. Muscles twitching, pulse bouncing, she wanted to run, wanted to so badly.

But her moment's hesitation had Finn tightening his clasp on her right elbow, strong fingers depressing her skin. Agent Palmer had opened the rear passenger door, illuminating the dome light of the vehicle. Ava ducked her head to peek inside and noted an upright suit as the driver. It was another man, dark skin, unfamiliar. Briefly, she fought the urge to scream, and won.

Swallowing her terror at losing her freedom, Ava reminded herself that it was only temporary. She crossed the few steps to the car, then crouched down at the rear door in a feeble attempt to get inside. This was harder than it looked without the use of her arms.

Hovering just behind her, Finn gripped her waist and helped her to slide in. He followed closely behind with his bulk, encouraging her to scoot all the way to the end of the bench seat. Once she was settled, he reached across her lap and worked to fasten her seatbelt. When his hand grazed her hip inadvertently, he mumbled an apology.

Catching his eye then, Ava realized he would not be removing the cuffs for the duration of the journey. As the car started forward, she lay her head back against the seat, twisting strangely in an attempt to gain comfort despite her awkward arms. They exited the parking lot, leaving the FBI building behind them.

Shifting once more, Ava tilted her head against the window to watch the headlights of oncoming traffic. They were bright, blinding flashes in the surrounding darkness. Squeezing her eyes shut against the fear, she made an effort to control her breathing. In through her nose, out through her mouth.

When her thoughts raced ahead to Mason and Clay, she battled back to replace them with nothing. She couldn't afford to lose it just now. Weaving through surface streets she kept track as they entered a freeway, then merged with another. After an hour or so, it became apparent they were heading east, out of town, away from civilization.

"Another facility?" Her voice emerged finally as a croak after the long stretch of silence.

No one answered.

Classical music drifted softly from the radio, having been

long ago switched on by the nameless driver. Something by Chopin, she thought, reaching back in her memory for the time when melody was more than the Sesame Street theme song. She had a boyfriend once that lived for all types of music. He always had something playing and was forever naming the artist. Avery the musician, her mother had called him. It hadn't lasted long.

Twisting her body around, she leveled a searching look at Agent Finn. His face was obscured by the dim interior of the car. Once in a while he would become illuminated by an overhead light as they passed. It was difficult to judge his expression in the split-second frames that were then separated by minutes of darkness, but he was watching her, too.

The whirling rotation of tires over asphalt were interrupted by the ripple of a lane change. They were taking an exit off the freeway.

Her heart began to tap out a strenuous beat. This was pretty far out in the sticks and it was late. She wasn't familiar with the area but craning her neck, she could make out what appeared to be a series of industrial type buildings, all dark and imposing. Without a lot of vehicle traffic, she grew more concerned about the reality of where they were headed. If the FBI wanted to scare her, this was doing the trick.

Her body rocked with the gentle motion of the car coming to a stop. They were at a lonely intersection, waiting at a red traffic signal.

In the surrounding light, she got the opportunity to take a look at Finn, really look at him. His expression gentled, as if seeing the fear that radiated from her. Extending his hand, he patted reassuringly against her knee.

In that moment, he opened his mouth. He was just about

to speak when his expression transformed into one of horror. It was the last thing that she could remember before the other vehicle slammed into them. The side impact hit the driver side door with all the force of a heavy-duty truck, jolting her brain into immediate unconsciousness.

FOUR

wareness came in bits and pieces. The smell of smoke from deployed air bags. Shouting. The metallic sound of a van's sliding door. It was all background. Background to the throbbing of blood in her own head.

Taking center stage, it stole any sharpness of focus, replacing everything with a thick agonizing blur.

"You have to take her to a hospital, she probably has a concussion." It was Finn talking. He actually sounded worried which made her want to laugh.

When no sound emerged, she succumbed instead to the perpetual fog. In her dreams, she floated. There was no pain here. Holding hands with her mother on a summer day at the pool, she could feel the warm wrap of her palm. Together, they watched as Clay swam by. What a fish he was. On a laugh, her father grabbed her up, launching her high into the air.

Falling, falling towards the water, sheer joy filled her chest to bursting. When she took the plunge, the image, so vibrant a moment before, began to shimmer. Rippling unpleasantly, the memory melted around her.

Back came the pounding headache. Back came the sore body. Inhaling a ragged breath, the air was noticeably cold, icy even.

"There you are," Finn whispered, inches from her ear. "Come on back now, Ava."

"Is she waking up? It's been hours, they must have dosed her with too much." Palmer's voice grated against her senses, eliciting an answering groan of protest.

"She's coming around," Finn continued.

Stroking his knuckles down the side of her cheek, he encouraged her to open her eyes. It worked. The soft touch of this man was so foreign to her that it caused an inner struggle to break free of the unconsciousness. Blinking, the lighting in the room seemed garish to her eyes. When she tried to sit up, he quickly soothed her back to lying.

"What happened?" She moaned.

Slowly, his face came into focus and she caught his quick glance at Agent Palmer. When she turned her head to follow Finn's gaze, she noted the pinched expression of stress that covered Palmer's formerly composed face. He had a split lip, swollen with a bit of caked blood that he had failed to wipe away.

"There was an attack." Agent Palmer leaned forward, keeping his voice low. "Our car was hit by another vehicle and we have been taken."

"Taken." Her head still protested the interaction. Growing dizzy, she had to close her eyes.

"Hey. Hey, don't pass out on me." Finn insisted with a grip

on her hand. "Fight it, Ava. Take a breath and come through swinging. Get pissed at us. Come on."

Again, he made her want to laugh. Who was this guy, anyway? Sucking in a breath, she battled forward once more.

Searching for his face, she located his eyes, concentrating on them. They weren't so dark brown as she had thought before. She could see hints of lighter flecks here and there. It took a few moments for her brain to catch up. Bruising bloomed along the right side of his face, smears of dry blood trailed from a cut just above one eye.

Beyond his head, she could see the ceiling above them. Whisper white tiles with a strange diamond shaped pattern. Odd. She had never seen a ceiling like it before. Then realization came to sharpen itself against her brain, separating out the pattern from the background.

It wasn't a diamond pattern ceiling. They were in a chain-link cage and the white ceiling was far above it.

"Oh God." Writhing on her back, panic licked through her system.

"It's okay. It's okay. Try to stay calm." Finn coaxed her but released his hold on her body.

Sitting up quickly she gripped her legs to her chest, burying her face against her knees. Rocking back and forth, she tried to fight the urge to pass out, or scream, or both. This couldn't be happening. This couldn't be real. The pool with her family, that was reality, while this was the dream.

"Whatever you do, don't scream," Agent Palmer hissed.

"You son of a bitch," she seethed, looking up at him. "*What is going on?*"

"We were transporting you to another facility when they rammed our car. It was a hard hit, you were knocked out.

Agent Finn and I were stunned. They were on us before we knew what was happening."

"You expect me to believe that three FBI Agents were kidnapped that easily?"

"It wasn't without casualty." Palmer bristled.

"The driver?"

"He didn't make it." Finn shook his head, face drawn. "They injected us with some chemical cocktail to knock us out. You must have gotten too much because we've been awake for a while now."

Rubbing absently at her sore wrists, Ava surveyed their surroundings. The cage itself was situated inside a larger room. What she had initially thought of as chain-link was actually expanded metal.

This wasn't your flimsy backyard fencing material. It was rigid and solid, a formidable barrier to escape which surrounded them on all sides save for one where it was attached to steel posts that butted up against a wall.

Pushing up from the narrow mattress on the floor, she fought a stab of pain that persisted in her left leg. Limping lamely, she took awkward steps along the width and length of the cage. The men watched her quietly as she counted.

It was twenty-four feet square. She couldn't reach the roof section, but she judged it to be about twelve feet high. The room they were situated in could have contained at least one more full cage, but theirs sat centered along one wall; a box of loneliness in the otherwise blank space.

Lacing her fingers in the only door, she deliberately pulled it towards her, then pushed away. It gave no more than one quarter inch in either direction. Through the metal mesh, she surveyed two exit doors of the larger room itself. They were located on opposing walls, with everything painted a ghostly white. The flooring was linoleum, or something similar. Easy for cleaning up messes, she thought.

Capture, capture, what had her father ever said on the subject? Don't let it happen, was all that came to mind. Great advice Dad.

Turning inward, she surveyed the one thin mattress pushed into a corner of the cage. In the other corner sat a metal toilet much like the ones she had seen in television shows about prison. Nothing else, just her two companions.

Finn was casual, leaning against the far wall, head tilted back as he observed her. Palmer was sitting cross-legged a few feet from him, still appearing so severe in his way. Both were fairly banged up. She wondered how she must look, probably worse.

Knees buckling, Ava dropped like a stone to the floor.

"Shit." Finn cursed under his breath.

Bolting from his position, he crossed the space in a surprisingly short amount of time. Squeezing her eyes shut against the nightmare, she felt him scoop her up effortlessly. He carried her a few steps before lowering her back onto the mattress. Its four inches of padding did a poor job of providing comfort. Curling herself into a ball, she lay on her side, her back towards the men.

"She could probably use some water." Finn's voice remained close.

"We don't ask for anything." Palmer was hushed.

"We should have had a chase car," Finn whispered.

"Don't start again."

"She thought we had been following her for three days. We should have ordered the chase car," Finn insisted.

"It didn't sit right with me either, but it wasn't our call to make. No one thought the LO was after her."

Where had she heard that name before? The LO. The answer didn't spring easily to her mind so it had to have been in passing. She didn't get the chance to watch a lot of news programing on television. For her it was mostly cartoons and old-time family movies with Mason. Mason, the thought of him had her stomach turning.

Covering her face in both hands, she fought viciously against the threat of tears. She didn't want to give Palmer the satisfaction of seeing her cry. Steeling herself, Ava scrubbed roughly with her hands against her closed eyes before forcing the image of her son from her mind.

"What is the LO?" She asked.

Rolling over to face them, she battled for composure. The men shared another one of their famous looks. How much should they tell her? It grated on her last nerve but clenching her teeth, she waited. Finally, Palmer spoke.

"The Lockett Organization. Have you ever heard of them?"

"No, but the initials sound familiar. I can't remember where I heard it from," she admitted.

"They're a major player in the illegal weapons market. For decades they've sold to anyone willing to pay the price. Small arms, chemical weapons, incendiary, you name it. Recently, they expanded into the computer spyware game. Has your brother ever mentioned them?"

Palmer dropped the last sentence as innocently as possible, but it had a recoil effect on Ava. Warning bells went off in her mind, planting a tiny seed of doubt. This was still the same tired line of questioning from a seasoned FBI Agent trying to get at her brother.

"No, I don't think so." Reserved, she chose her words with care. "Why would they be following me? Why have they kidnapped all of us?"

"We don't know that for certain but I can make a good guess." Palmer's eyes darted about, but he kept his posture unchanged.

"Guess, then." Ava prompted.

"They were following you for the same reason that we were. They want you for the same reason we did."

"To flush out Clay," Ava finished for him. "Are you trying to convince me that my brother is a bad guy?"

"Your brother *is* a bad guy." Palmer was adamant, but Finn let his eyes drop to the floor.

The round of staring that ensued was broken by the sound of a far door swinging open. All eyes inside the cage pivoted away to track the newcomers to the pale room.

Agent Finn rose to standing, positioning himself between the cage door and Ava. Palmer too, got to his feet. Three men had entered, all wearing black military-type uniforms.

The first one was slender and tall. He walked like a bird, carrying three gallon jugs of sealed water. The second one was stocky, with a shock of red hair under his dark cap. He carried a tray with food on it. The third one moved like a cat, armed with a rifle which he held poised for use if the need should arise.

"We're going to give you this water and food, but then the big guy has to come with us without a fight." The tall one informed them when he got to the cage door.

"No," Palmer responded.

"The big guy comes over to this door, and he turns around

to get his wrists bound. He comes with us and then we give you the food." Again, the tall one spoke.

"No." Palmer was resolute but Finn was shifting on his feet.

"Okay, option number two. We get more guys. We go in there and take the lady instead."

From her seat on the mattress, Ava's insides began to quake. When Agent Finn moved to comply, she exhaled a long held breath. The relief she felt was mixed with dread, not wanting to imagine what he was about to endure.

Palmer gave no more verbal cues but she saw the look on his face when he turned to watch Finn's progress. He didn't want the younger man to go. Turning around at the cage door, Finn assumed the position that Ava had only hours earlier and submitted to the restraints through a small rectangular opening. The men then unlocked the cage door and shuffled him out.

True to instructions, Finn put up no protest. He watched calmly while the men shoved the tray of food and water into the cage before re-locking the door. Walking between the tall bird and the built redhead, Agent Finn disappeared through the far door of the room. The cat with the rifle followed close behind.

When they heard the final click of the door closing, Palmer made his way over to the food and water. He walked with a noticeable limp as well, more injured from the crash then he had let on.

Feeling a sudden flood of guilt, Ava rose to meet him half way. She bent to retrieve two jugs of water while he kept hold of the tray. When they settled next to one another on the mattress, she took stock of the provided food. A loaf of unwrapped white bread and one jar of peanut butter. No plates, no napkins, and certainly no knife. It was Skippy peanut butter, had to be. She loathed the stuff.

"We don't know how often they will be feeding us, so we have to be smart about our portions." Palmer unscrewed the blue plastic cap from his gallon jug. Tilting the heavy container up, he drank carefully, not spilling a drop.

"What do you suggest?" Ava strove to be equally polite in her drinking, but her parched throat relished a good chug. Water dripped unchecked from the corners of her mouth.

"We need to divide the slices equally in three, saving Finn his share. Let's start with a full peanut butter sandwich, then limit ourselves to one slice per meal until we know more." Palmer waited a beat for her to nod acceptance, then counted out the slices as described.

"Any plan for getting the peanut butter out of the jar?" Ava asked.

"No." Palmer hesitated, only just realizing there was no knife for spreading.

"I guess we'll have to use our fingers." Ava tried not to smirk at his grimace. He obviously didn't have kids.

The loaf, once separated into three parts, made for a pretty small amount of food. It wouldn't last them long.

Ava dipped her index finger into the jar first, then swiped it along one piece of bread. Palmer followed suit, awkwardly mushing the sticky substance onto a slice and immediately tearing a small hole in the bread. It would take another dip from each of them before there was enough peanut butter to make a proper sandwich.

Sucking at her finger, Ava rid herself of the leftover goo before drying her hand on her pants. Mason loved peanut butter and jelly sandwiches, but she had never been a fan. Again, she felt a quick stab of pain as the memories flooded her, but she battled back, knowing he was safe.

Alternating between bites and sips of water, Ava made quick work of her meal. Palmer, quite methodical, took his time, continuing to eat half a sandwich while she looked on.

"How long do you think we'll be here?"

"I'm not sure," Palmer responded, savoring the last bits of crust.

"Well, isn't the FBI going to notice we didn't arrive?"

"Yes, they will do their best to locate us, but it all depends on how well the LO has covered their tracks. We could be anywhere." Palmer scooted away from her to lean against the wall.

"When do you think Agent Finn will be back?" Ava whispered, dancing around asking a more direct question.

"Let's not focus on that, it's not productive." Palmer studied her before continuing. "Your brother must have some contact with the LO if you've heard of them. Does he purchase illegal arms? What types of weapons does he have?"

"Seriously, you're interrogating me again?"

Rolling her eyes, Ava got up to pace. She winced as she went, but made it to the far side of the cage before sticking her fingers through the diamond shaped holes. Squeezing her hands into fists once more, she pulled the metal towards her, then tried to push it away.

Barely any give whatsoever, like Agent Palmer and his singular focus. Was this whole situation beyond the possibility of an FBI set-up? Couldn't they have orchestrated the crash and capture in order to get her to talk?

When she really thought about it, aside from the obvious

injuries from the car accident, no one had gotten hurt so far. Agent Finn had been removed, and that was scary, but he hadn't been hurt that she could see. Maybe he was observing her from another room right now.

Considering, she looked up into the far corners of the ceiling. There were no obvious cameras, but there hadn't been in the FBI office either. Hobbling back over to Agent Palmer, she sat down to face him.

"I swear to you, I don't know anything." She willed him to believe her. "I didn't know Clay was involved with the Militia thing. I don't know anything about him anymore, or what he does. Please, just let me go."

"Let you go?" Palmer was incredulous. "You think we've set this up? You're as bad as your brother about conspiracy theories."

"What do you know about my brother and conspiracy theories?"

The click of the far door opening once more drew their attention away. Swiveling her whole body, Ava expected to see Agent Finn, but was disappointed by the reappearance of the other men without him. Three pairs of boots crossed the length of the floor, causing an eerie marching sound to fill the room.

"Okay, it's your turn old man." The tall one again did the talking. "Come over to the door to have your wrists bound."

"No." Palmer's familiar response was level, unperturbed.

"Come over here now, or we shoot the lady."

"You did all this to get the lady," Palmer answered easily. "You won't shoot her."

"Fair enough." The tall one gestured to the cat-like one

who aimed his rifle at Palmer. "Miss, come over here to get your wrists bound, or we shoot the old man."

Shifting to catch her eyes, Agent Palmer stared at Ava, willing her to understand his silent communication the way his partner so easily did. Heart pounding in her ears, it was hard to tell just what he wanted her to do. Obviously, he didn't want to be shot, but she wasn't sure if this was a bluff or not.

Although it seemed real enough when the sound of a bullet racked into the rifle's chamber. The menacing echo made the choice for her. She would go.

Agent Palmer's eyes registered their disappointment as Ava brushed past him on the way to the cage door. Not able to withstand his judgment, she looked away.

Turning her back to the men, Ava grunted involuntarily as she crouched down, her hip and leg screaming out in protest. She placed her wrists through the small rectangular opening and felt the plastic zip tie bite harshly against her skin. This was not the careful cuffing of Agent Finn.

Once she was secure, the cage door was unlocked and pushed inward. She felt the reaching hands of the men clasp her arms but she was willing when they walked her to the end of the room. Apprehension coursed through her system. She didn't know what was beyond the threshold of the solid white door and a nervous feeling crept slowly into her face, causing it to feel strangely numb.

Without the use of a key, the redhead twisted the knob deftly. It opened onto a well-lit hallway that somehow still managed to give a stark and vacant impression.

Fighting her flood of terror, Ava was marched down the corridor, passing three closed doors along the way. After about twenty feet they veered to the right and pushed through another doorway into a bathroom. It was moderate in size, being longer than it was wide, with one small window. The sun's yellow light shone through the thick glass blocks which were placed high up on one wall. It wasn't the kind that opened; there was no possibility of escape.

Glancing about, she noted a shower stall with no curtain or partition of any kind. In addition, there was a standard toilet that had a thread-bare white towel folded neatly on the back as well as a tiny porcelain sink. There was no mirror.

When the door snapped shut behind her, Ava realized that she wasn't alone. A pocket knife flicked open, causing her to jump slightly as the man behind her cut adeptly through her binds. Once free, she threw herself against the far wall; whirling to face him, breath hitching, eyes wide.

It was the red-haired man who looked back at her. Fear built itself quickly in her chest, squeezing all of the air from her lungs. Gasping, she struggled to gain oxygen.

"Easy now." The redhead made a calming motion with both hands, the knife having been returned to his pocket. "I'm not here to hurt you. Calm down."

Wedged against the toilet, she assessed him. Despite her terror, she noted the smooth lines of a pleasing face that gave the appearance of youth without being overly young. He was mid-twenties at most, she guessed.

Though he had no gun, he wouldn't need one to over-power her. Close to hyper-ventilation, Ava worked to control her breathing. Air came in through her nose, then exited slowly out of her mouth. What did he want from her?

"It's my job to watch you, so I have to stay in here, but I

promise I'm not going to hurt you, okay? You have to take a shower, clean yourself up. Can you do that?"

Nodding shakily, she remained crouched, leg throbbing. It would take several minutes before the fear settled itself into a solid unease. For a while the man waited, but eventually he insisted that she undress and start her shower. There was nothing else for her to do but rise and comply.

Keeping her lace bra and lavender thong on, she stepped into the hot spray as steam filled the room like a cloud. It provided her with at least some small measure of obscurity. Inside the shower stall were tiny bottles of shampoo, conditioner, and a box of bar soap. Reminiscent of hotel supplies, she scrutinized the labels, but found they were in another language. French? Italian?

As she scrubbed her body, she took the opportunity to clean her underwear as well. The bra would be miserably saturated when she was done, but it had seemed worth it to keep her private parts covered. Despite the thick fog, the man watched her closely. The moment her soaping and rinsing was complete, he bade her turn off the water and step out.

This wasn't the first time in the past twenty-four hours that Ava had been forced to do something against her will, and now she was sure it wouldn't be the last.

Complying shakily, Ava dripped water along the bleak tile floor before wrapping herself in the towel. A plastic hair brush was balanced on the edge of the narrow sink, and she reached for it automatically before stopping short with hesitation.

After a nod from the man, she picked it up and began to brush through her mass of blonde tangles. Without a mirror, she combed it until practice told her that it was reasonably straight. Once done, the man gave a few brisk knocks against the closed door. When it popped open a crack, a set of gray sweats were passed through.

Turning her back on the man, Ava appraised the outfit. Size small, her size. Already, her wet undergarments were beginning to chafe uncomfortably. The cotton material of the pants and sweatshirt would provide plenty of cover, she judged, plus the long-sleeve thermal shirt was black.

Making a final decision, she shimmied out of the thong and unhooked her bra before stepping quickly into the new clothes.

"All set?" The redhead asked, then continued. "Give me your wrists."

"Why am I here?"

Her question was futile, but she asked anyway. He provided no answer. The unease that had bobbled inside of her gave way to her natural tendency to question everything. Nothing about this experience lined up with a capture by some vicious organization.

No one had been beaten. No one had been hurt. They had been fed and given water. She even got to shower and change her clothes. She had to be in the possession of the FBI still. She had to be.

With her hands bound behind her, Ava was directed back out of the bathroom and down the hallway. They stopped at a door on the left where the redhead knocked and waited for a welcoming response before pushing inside.

When the door swung open it revealed a wide room full of high windows that let in the light. For a moment, Ava was blinded by the distraction of blue sky and puffy clouds. It took a nudge from behind to snap her awareness back.

Standing before her were the other two guards. They had Agent Palmer wedged neatly between them. He looked no worse for the wear, though both of his hands were bound tightly together, as was the custom.

Another shove at Ava's back had her lurching forward a few steps. There was an orange plastic chair with round metal legs positioned against a far wall. A black sheet hung down behind it. Yanking her to a stop just before the chair, the redhead cut her binds again, then spun her to face him.

Desperately, she tried to search his face for what came next but he was busy with his task. Gripping her wrists easily in one hand, he fished for another zip tie and snugged it down. Effectively, he tied her hands together again, but in front of her this time.

"Sit." A new voice had issued the command.

Ava hadn't noticed the man when she first entered, but he had been there the whole time, watching. Average height, average weight, plain face. He wasn't unpleasant to look at, but not handsome either. This was the perfect man to see, and then forget. The perfect man to blend into a crowd. With no distinct features, he would be hard to describe to a sketch artist. Brown hair, brown eyes, no facial hair.

"Who are you?" Ava's voice filled the space, coming across more boldly than she felt.

"Well, for our purposes you can just call me Aaron." The man gestured this time. "Please, have a seat."

So she did, with a little nudging encouragement. Aaron nodded tersely once which had the redhead retreating a few steps away. Casually, he approached her himself, a single sheet of paper held between relaxed fingertips.

"Today is going to be easy." Aaron's voice was as unremarkable as he was. "We're going to make a little video. Just read exactly what is on the paper and then you can both return to your cell."

Lifting her arms as one, she gripped the edge of the dangling white sheet in both hands and brought the writing up close to her face. Skimming through the material had her revolting. With a quick shake of her head, she released the page to waft its way down to the floor.

"No way, I'm not reading anything." Ava leveled her gaze at him, trying to take measure of this new adversary.

"Very well." Aaron sighed, almost bored. "If you don't read this for the video, then we will shoot Agent Palmer in the head."

"You aren't going to shoot anyone," Ava countered.

A new confidence had begun to build within her at the consistent level of decent treatment. Surely these were Feds playing one sick, sick game to get at her brother. If she stopped playing, then eventually so would they.

"Bring him over." Aaron gestured to Palmer. Instantly the two men picked him up, half-dragging, half-carrying him along. Agent Palmer struggled only mildly before being deposited next to her. "Look at him, Ava. Really look."

"Alright," Ava murmured.

They faced one another. Her eyes searched his gray-blue ones but she still couldn't pick up the message he was trying to send. Was there a hint of fear there?

"Will you read the paper for our video?" Aaron asked.

Hesitating a moment, Ava continued her silent query of Palmer. Would he just tell her what to do, already? Finally, after what seemed a long time, he opened his mouth to speak.

Click. Pop.

Before words could pass through his lips, the sound of a gunshot blasted mere feet from them. Eyes wide with surprise, they shared a last expression before Palmer collapsed in a limp pile on the floor. The hot spray of his blood was left to drip shockingly down Ava's face.

FIVE

S creaming.

It took several moments for Ava to realize that it was her own voice making that terrifying sound. Out and away from her body, she felt safely reserved. Everything was so simple as she watched the other woman losing her mind down there in that room.

The tiny blonde in the gray hoodie covered in blood spatter wasn't her, couldn't be. Calmly, she looked on as the redhead nodded once to Aaron. Coolly, she observed Aaron grimace just before slapping the woman open handed across the face.

Knocked to the ground now, Ava was stunned to discover that she was indeed that pitiful woman. Pain erupted, filling her left cheek and eye. Blinking in disbelief, she lay still on the floor, transfixed by Agent Palmer's empty gray-blue eyes. Those same eyes that had pierced moments ago with intelligent certainty were now distant, devoid, without.

"Take her back, Michael," Aaron instructed. His voice was

calm as he slipped the sleek handgun back into its hidden holster.

Grabbing her shoulders, the men hoisted her up to standing. She swayed on her feet. A last look down at Palmer's body, the blood pooling around him on the floor, had her knees buckling. It took two of them to haul her out after that.

The tall one hefted her upper body, while the redhead, Michael, supported her legs. She watched the ceiling tiles pass as they traveled out of the room and down the hall. The rifleman must have been opening doors because they didn't hesitate when crossing thresholds.

She knew the moment that they stepped back into the room that contained her cage. Mouth still hanging open, she noted the quality of the air was different, it was colder.

"Ava." Agent Finn called to her. Turning her head, she could see him get up from the ground and stride towards the cage door.

"Stay back." The tall man huffed before tilting her up to standing once more.

"What the hell did you do to her?" Finn fumed, pacing like a tiger that was caught, well... in a cage. "You feel like big men now? Beating up a woman?"

"Trust me, she didn't get beat up," Michael countered. Reaching into his pocket he fished out his knife, sharply severing the zip tie that bound her wrists. "Now stand back or she will."

Swearing, Finn stepped back. They made no move to open the door, so he took another step, then another. When his heels bumped the far wall, the tall one produced a key and opened the cage door.

When they shoved her roughly inside she staggered but

managed to keep on her feet while they worked the lock. Not wanting to look at him, Ava avoided Finn's questioning eyes. Face downcast, she listened while the other men left.

The snap of the outer door closing brought Agent Palmer's face to her mind. His expression of utter surprise after the shot, it was a memory that would never leave her. On auto pilot, first one bare foot and then the other shuffled haltingly to the edge of the mattress. Sinking down, she stared at the three piles of white bread.

"Hey, are you okay?" Finn eased down to sit beside her. "You're covered in blood. Are you bleeding?"

"No." Whispering it, she stuck out her hands and examined the speckle that had cast off onto her sleeves. "It's not my blood."

"Palmer?" Finn's voice cracked.

Shaking her head, the tears released from behind her eyes. Ava covered her face with both hands, sobbing as quietly as possible into them.

After a few minutes she pulled back to see that her palms were marked red with his blood. Wiping pitifully at her face, the blood only mixed with her salty tears, swirling and streaking instead of disappearing. Anger took over as she swiped again and again, trying to rid herself of the substance.

"Stop, stop." Finn shushed her.

Splashing a bit of water from his jug onto his sleeve, he knelt down before her. Cleaning her palms first, he moved on to dab gently at her face. He went slowly, rinsing his sleeve again and again, making sure to get her completely clean.

When he was done, she noticed that he had on sweats, too. Examining him more closely, she realized he must have gotten a chance to shower. The cut above his eye had been cleared of dried blood. His face was fresh.

"This isn't a setup." Ava choked on the words, then watched the pity fill Finn's eyes.

"No," he acknowledged. "We screwed up. It wasn't us following you for three days. We picked you up on our first morning of surveillance."

"They shot him," Ava stammered, but pushed on, feeling that Finn deserved to know. "They shot him in the head. He was a foot away from me."

"Why? Why did they shoot him?"

"They wanted me to make a video but I hesitated. I thought it was a setup." Guilt filled Ava's soul. "They killed him because I wouldn't read the damn statement for the damn video."

"What happened to your face?" Finn traced a light finger over the swollen area.

"I wouldn't stop screaming." She shrugged. "Aaron slapped me to make me stop."

"Aaron?"

"I don't know if you've seen him. He was in another room down the hall, on the left side."

"You notice details." Finn shifted to sit beside her. "That's good, Ava. I know you don't like answering questions but I need you to tell me absolutely everything that happened to you. Can you do that?"

"Yes."

Someone somewhere switched off the overhead lights in their room, causing it to fall to utter blackness. Not being able to see Agent Finn's face as they talked made things easier on Ava. Sticking to the details of the day, she told him the number of doors along the hallway, the size and position of everything in the bathroom, and the location of the far room where Palmer died.

Eventually she collapsed down onto the mattress, utter exhaustion overtaking her. Feeling that she owed it to Finn, she rolled onto her side and forced herself to keep whispering. She told him about Michael and Aaron. She gave him the details of the rifle that the cat-like man held, and the sheen on the handgun that blasted only a few feet away from her face.

Joints aching, her sentences slowed. Sleep crept towards her, it wouldn't wait much longer. His head lay on the edge of the mattress next to hers, but his body was positioned off on the hard floor. It would be an uncomfortable night for him. Her breathing relaxed, steady and shallow.

Quiet thoughts of Mason swelled her heavy heart. Would she make it out of here? Would she ever see him again? If she had tears left to cry, they would have spilled from the scrunched-up corners of her eyes, but instead she only felt the pain. The last question she recalled hearing from Finn went unanswered.

"What did they want you to say in the video?"

Eyes closed, she dropped into unconsciousness.

***

IN HER DREAM THAT WAS REALLY A MEMORY, SHE HELD MASON when he was just a tiny, tiny baby. Wrapped in a stiff cotton swaddle crisp from the hospital, he blinked up at her.

At the time, he had such deep dark blue eyes. But babies

always have blue eyes when they're born. It was the first time that she had seen him, and in that moment, she knew he would be the most important person in her whole life.

Clay had peered over her shoulder. She could *feel* the expanse of his smile. That was the last time that she had seen her brother in person. It was her first time with Mason, and her last time with Clay. In her life, they had exchanged places.

THE CLICK OF THE DOOR HAD HER EYES SHOOTING OPEN. Overhead, the fluorescent lights glared down. Someone had turned them back on, or perhaps they were on a timer.

Sitting up, Ava observed Michael and the rifleman cross to the cage door. Stomach pinching in on itself, Ava fought the impulse to throw up. Finn was already on his feet, broad shoulders tense under the hoodie.

"How's the eye?" Michael craned his neck to squint at her. Clutching a brown paper bag in one hand, his gaze popped back up to Finn, appraising and unafraid. "Come over here, Miss Ava."

"What do you want?" Finn questioned, but was ignored.

Ava got up to obey, not wanting him to get into an altercation with them. The floor was frigid on her bare feet. When she passed Finn, he reached out to grab at her sleeve, rotating her briefly to face him. Silently, she let her eyes plead with him. Did he want to get shot in the head, too? Face impassive, he released his grip.

"I need to take a picture of your face for Aaron," Michael explained, fishing in his pocket for his phone. "He needs to see how bad it is."

Nodding, Ava ran her fingers through her messy blonde

locks, holding them back to reveal the extent of swelling. She studied Michael as he brought the phone up to the cage, adjusting the distance, trying to get a clear shot through the metal.

He had light-green eyes to go with the red hair. This close up, she noticed the length of his eyelashes, and a hint of contrition hidden behind a well-controlled demeanor. Just a fraction on the short side, he was maybe five-foot-ten at the most. What he lacked in height, though, he made up for in muscle tone.

"It's not so bad as I thought before," Michael continued, his task complete. "Maybe two days at the most and you should be ready to shoot the video. I brought you these to put on your face. They should help with the swelling."

Digging into the brown paper, he produced a bag of frozen green peas. He took a few steps to the side and opened the small rectangle on the cage door. Sticking his hand through it, Michael held onto the bag and watched her expectantly.

When she realized that he wasn't going to simply drop it on the floor, she moved closer, reaching out to take it in her hands. Glancing up at him, she witnessed his careful nod. A hint of wanting flickered there.

After they had gone, she felt free to move, but the tension in the air remained. Finn had not shifted from his position. Lines of worry creased his face and she realized that he must be feeling even more helpless than she was. His partner was dead and he was likely next.

Hobbling back over to their shared corner, Ava lowered herself down onto the mattress. Pulling the bread and peanut butter over, she grabbed a slice for herself, then offered one to him. Taking it, he settled beside her, and they took turns dipping their fingers into the jar.

"How's the eye?" He asked.

"It hurts."

"You never answered my question from last night." Finn grabbed up the bag of peas in one hand and held it lightly against her face.

"I fell asleep," she countered.

Distracted by his closeness, she took hold of the bag herself. For a second, Finn seemed reluctant to let it go, eyes tracing over her face. But then he retracted his hand to his lap and leaned back against the wall. Ava felt the icy relief of the peas spreading their numbness over her sore eye and cheek. She let out a tiny sigh.

"You heard the question before you were asleep," Finn watched her through half-closed eyes.

"How do you know?"

"Because you haven't asked me what the question was, yet."

"Oh, you're good." Ava examined him, he wasn't the FBI rookie for nothing. "The message for the video, right?"

"That's right." Giving her a chance to collect her thoughts, he leaned forward, propping his elbows on his knees.

"They think Clay has stolen something from them." Ava wasn't sure how much detail she wanted to give. "They want it back."

"So, they want to trade you for it?"

"Yeah."

"Did they say what it was?"

"No."

"Do you remember the exact words they want you to say?"

"Not exactly," Ava lied.

"Will you do it next time?" Finn shifted, eyes locking with hers. "Will you shoot the video?"

"I will." Ava held his gaze, withstanding his scrutiny and the churning sensation that filled her gut. "I'll do everything they ask."

"Okay." Exhaling, Finn lay back on the mattress with a groan. "Keep ice on that and wake me if they come back."

Within five minutes, he was out cold. Ava listened silently to his steady breathing. He didn't snore. That was a plus since she didn't know how long they would be living like this together or living in general.

If Clay had in fact "stolen" what the LO thought he had, then he would never be able to give it back. Maybe no one else knew it yet, but she could guarantee there would be no trade. How long would it take for the LO to realize that there would be no exchange? What would they do with her at that point? With Agent Finn?

From her current perspective, escape seemed impossible, but it was her only hope so she kept her mind open to the possibility. Eventually, she would have to give Finn a heads-up as well, so that he could be ready to seize any opportunity that happened to present itself. For the rest of the day, she let him sleep. The guards didn't return and she figured he needed the rest.

Running her fingers along the metal cage, she counted the diamonds. Thoughts of Mason plagued her, causing her feet to wander, and her heart to twist. After several tours around the tight space, her leg began to cramp up.

Using the heels of her hands she bent to rub at the bunched muscle, working at the pain in deliberate strokes.

The aching persisted, so Ava eased over to stretch, wondering just how banged up her body was.

"That's a hell of a way for a guy to wake up." Finn's voice startled her, causing her to tilt forward awkwardly.

"You scared me." She pushed back and rotated to face him.

"How long was I out?"

"Seemed like a while." Limping over to the mattress, she sat next to him. "But it's kind of hard to keep track in here."

"Did you eat?"

"Yeah."

They hadn't touched Palmer's portion of bread but it wouldn't be much longer before they would have to start in on it. The peanut butter was practically gone and both of them had refilled their waters from his jug already.

"What are we going to do?" Ava sighed, tracing one finger along a seam in the mattress.

"Talk," Finn suggested. "Tell me about your son."

Getting up to stretch his legs, Finn didn't walk far, examining the cage as he went.

"He's like any other little boy." Ava studied the movements of Finn's back, the bunch of his muscles beneath his shirt. "He loves dirt, frogs, trucks and candy."

"Does he like school?"

"He does actually, and he's smart. Maybe too smart sometimes." It wasn't difficult to get a mom to brag about her kid, and before she knew it, Ava's guard had dropped.

"Must take after his Mama." Finn glanced back at her.

"That goes without saying." She bit at her lip subconsciously. What did he know of her intelligence? Holding eye contact, this time he was the first to blink.

"But he must look like his father," Finn continued causally.

"He doesn't look like you."

"Yes, he looks like his father." Ava was more measured now, sensing that the flow of conversation was turning towards interrogation. He was just doing his job, she told herself.

"Is James Miller his father?"

"No." Ava frowned.

"Who is he?"

"I can't answer that."

"Okay, can you tell me who Mason's father is?" Finn crouched down in front of her.

"I don't know who his father is," Ava lied.

"But you know that he looks like him?"

"I was at a party in college, got drunk and slept with some guy." Ava willed him to believe it. "I don't know his name but I can see his face when I look at Mason."

"I have a hard time believing you're that kind of girl." Finn scrutinized her.

"Oh, really? What kind of girl is that exactly?" Ava went on the offensive, causing Finn to stand up once more.

"I'm sorry, I didn't mean it that way."

Crossing her arms over her chest, Ava fumed silently as Finn turned his back on her and strode away. Angrily gritting her teeth, she tried to remind herself that the story she just told him was made up. How was it possible for her to feel so insulted over a fake one-night stand? She couldn't let him get to her that easily, she couldn't let the truth about Mason slip unknowingly from her mouth.

Without warning they were slammed once more into sudden darkness. You could hear a pin drop. Finn and Ava both froze then, listening.

The lack of windows in the room put them at a distinct disadvantage. It could be nighttime outside, or the LO could just be messing with their heads. When the far door remained closed, her pulse evened out. The guards weren't coming for them tonight at least.

Laying back on the mattress, Ava listened to Finn stalk about the cage. It was a sound that she had already become accustomed to, there was nothing else for them to do.

Mind heavy, her face throbbed and her stomach churned. She missed Mason, worried about Clay and did her best to shove Agent Palmer's dead eyes from her thoughts. Scooting to the far side of the mattress, Ava pressed her back against the wall and waved a hand absently in front of her face. Although her eyes had plenty of time to adjust to the dark, she still couldn't see anything at all. When there was no light source, it didn't matter how long you sat in the black, it was like being blind.

"You don't have to lay on the floor." Ava called to Finn. "We can share the mattress, if you want."

"Thanks, I'm just not tired, yet."

Finn's voice constantly shifted around the room, following his aimless wandering. He had slept the day away and was now wide awake. Curling into her customary ball, Ava tried to tuck her chilly feet up into her sweat pants. They were just a bit too short, exposing the small of her back in order to cover her feet. She had a newfound appreciation for socks. Socks and blankets. Keeping to one side of the mattress just in case, she instinctively knew Finn wouldn't be joining her on the bed. As she drifted off, she listened to his prowling movements around the room.

SIX

alling into a sort of routine, the next few days passed without incident. Finn slept mostly while the lights were on and Ava while they were off. Their tentative truce had evolved naturally into a guarded alliance. It was them vs the LO, or no one would make it out alive. Being in such close quarters, they were forced into almost constant interaction, so it was better to be friendly than otherwise. Soon the peanut butter ran out. It was not replaced. When the guards brought new gallons of water, Ava and Finn were forced to exchange them for any empty containers. During this time, no one stepped foot inside their cage, and they didn't step foot outside of it.

On the morning of the fourth day, Ava sat on the edge of the mattress examining the bottoms of her feet. Even isolated as they were in the room, dust seemed to collect on the surface of the flooring. Over time, her feet had been covered in grime, turning the bottoms an astonishing shade of near black. In short, they were filthy.

"Yuck." She made a sour face. "I can't stand dirty feet."

"They don't look so bad to me," Finn assured her, poking at the remaining slice of stale bread. "Shall we split it?"

"No." Ava's stomach grumbled. As the days had passed without a resupply of food, they had begun to cut their portions ever smaller. "You're bigger, you can have it."

"It's the last piece." Finn folded it in half in an attempt to break it, but only caused it to shatter instead. "Great."

Chuckling at his look of despair, Ava gathered the crumbles together on the barren tray. She scooted about one third of them towards her, then pushed the remaining portion at Finn. At some point, the LO would have to feed them again, she only hoped that it would be soon.

"Let's play fantasy food." Ava took her time, plucking each crumb individually, chewing the morsels to make it last.

"You're a glutton for punishment," Finn remarked, but then couldn't help himself. "Steak. Rib-eye. Rare."

"Good choice, but so... unimaginative," Ava scolded, but had him cracking the tiniest of grins. "Louisiana Chicken Pasta."

"Louisiana what?"

"It's amazing, a breaded chicken breast over a heaping bowl of pasta. The red sauce has chopped bell peppers, onions, and sautéed mushrooms in it."

"I hate you." He sighed.

"You only hate me because I win."

She bumped his shoulder with hers companionably, felt him sway in easy acceptance before bumping hers in return.

"You're right, you win that one."

The sound of the door opening had them both looking up but not getting up. Familiarity mixed with hunger had dulled their senses, so they watched the procession of guards with distant caution. Ava's stomach grumbled all the louder when she noted the full tray of food.

"The lady comes with us." The tall one spoke. "Come get your hands bound."

Finn's arm shot across her body like a barrier, preventing her from standing. The gesture had Michael frowning and the rifleman shifting in anticipation. Leaning close to his ear, Ava reasoned with Finn. They didn't have much of a choice as far as she saw it.

"If they kill you, then I'll be alone with them anyway," she whispered.

Offering no verbal reply, his arm retracted slowly, but his eyes never wavered from the other men. Pushing up, she brushed lightly at his shoulder before moving away. Her steps were almost imperceptible, bare feet meandering mutely across the floor. Dizzy from the lack of food, she worked to steady herself at the cage door before putting her hands behind her back and clumsily shoving them through the open slot.

Leaving the tray on the ground, Michael moved to secure her wrists before swinging the door inward. She felt his grip on her elbow as she skirted the doorframe and listened to it lock shut behind her. It wasn't until they started to march her away that she realized the food hadn't been placed inside the cage. Dragging her feet, she threw a glance over her shoulder. Finn was standing closer than she would have guessed, fingers interlaced through the expanded metal of the cage, watching.

"What about the food?" She asked, stomach a bundle of nerves.

"You'll get it later," Michael assured her, before they pushed her quickly through the outer door.

Down the familiar hall they went, stopping at the same bathroom door. Again, Michael accompanied her inside, slicing smoothly through her binds. It was daytime outside. The obscure light filtered in through the small block glass window. Another thread-bare white towel sat folded on top of the toilet, underneath it was a clean set of sweats. Turning to face him, Ava raised an eyebrow in question.

"Yes," Michael answered, nodding. "Clean yourself up."

Reaching for the faucet, she turned it to hot, hoping to cloud the air before undressing. He leaned back against the wall, eyes following her movements, arms folded across his chest. When the air seemed reasonably misty, she faced away from him, yanking the sweatshirt up and over her head.

"What did you say to the Fed?" He asked, causing a brief break in her stride.

"I told him that you wouldn't let them hurt me again." Ava pulled off her shirt, then shimmied out of her pants.

"Is he your boyfriend or something?"

"No," she answered carefully, stepping into the hot spray. "I barely know him."

Heart pounding in her chest, she struggled with a difficult decision. Should she face him, or not? If she kept her back to him, then she couldn't see what he was doing, which bothered her. If she turned so that she could watch him, then he would get a full view of her complete nudity. Peeking over her shoulder, she caught his eye.

"You won't, right?" She asked.

"Won't what?"

"Hurt me."

"I don't want to," he admitted. "Will you do the video today?"

"Yes." She turned back to the faucet, releasing a shaky breath.

"Just do whatever Aaron says, and no one will hurt you."

"Okay."

Pulse jumping, she tried to focus on the shower. Soap, hot water, clean feet, clean hair, clean everything. It was a warm relief from the cold monotony of the past days. He let her linger this time. When she was done rinsing, she stood still under the water, letting it run freely over her body and down her back. Finally, she shut the spray off herself, and stepped out.

To his credit, he tried to avert his gaze when she reached for the towel. But he was only a man after all, so she still felt his eyes absorbing her in furtive glances. Wrapping herself up, she took inventory of the new set of clothes. Her former bra and panties lay folded there, hallelujah. Once dressed, she stood in front of the sink, combing her hair, then cleaning her teeth. They had provided toothpaste, but no brush, so she scrubbed as vigorously as possible with her finger.

"All done." She turned to face him, damp hair shedding droplets of water on the floor.

Holding her wrists out in front of her, she blinked expectantly, waiting for him to retrieve a zip tie from his pocket.

"I'm going to do these loose." He looped the plastic carefully around her bruised wrists before softly cupping her hands. "But you have to promise not to slip them off. Don't do anything stupid, okay?"

"I promise."

She ducked her head, avoiding his gaze the way she wished she could avoid his touch. A rapid knock on the door had his hands dropping away. Opening it, he pushed her gently out in front of him. The rifleman waited. Making their way to the room of Palmer's demise, Michael tapped his fingers on the closed door. An answering assent sounded before they entered.

Same expanse of high windows, same plastic chair in front of the same black sheet against the same wall. This time there was no Palmer. Her eyes darted to the last place she had seen him, sprawled hauntingly on the floor. It was all clean now. No stain of dark blood marked the place.

"Good morning, Miss Montgomery." Aaron strolled into view, relaxed in his dark military fatigues. "Please, have a seat."

He followed her over to the chair where she sat heavily. The lack of food combined with the hot shower, and maybe some fresh anxiety, had the room spinning. Feeling weak, she took the single white sheet of paper that he dangled in front of her, clutching it with both hands. Reading through the words again, her heart heaved at the game she could no longer resist playing. A violent end seemed certain.

"So, this should be pretty easy. When I nod my head, you read exactly what's on the page. You don't add anything. You don't leave anything out. Do you understand?"

"Yes." She watched him pull a cell phone from his pocket.

Holding it up, he stepped forward, then back. He gestured for Michael to shift her and the chair, then adjust the black sheet hanging behind her. Once satisfied he waved Michael away. Swiping through the phone, he nodded at her once.

"Clay-" she began, eyes shifting down, reading from the paper. "I am in the custody of the LO. It seems that you have something that belongs to Mr. Lockett, and he wants it back. As you can see, I have been treated well."

Glancing up momentarily into the camera, she paused for only a second before looking back down. Her brother would know that was a lie.

"Mr. Lockett hopes that you have treated what you have taken with the same respect. He is willing to make a trade but warns you that the longer it takes for you to return what is missing, the worse my treatment will get. Hurry brother."

Aaron's fingers tapped away on the phone. Lowering it, he paced the room, reviewing the footage. She could hear her own voice echoing back the words, sounding so tiny on the recording. The rifleman watched him expectantly while Michael, instead, watched her.

Tilting her face towards the windows, Ava marveled at the blessed bits of blue sky that gleamed through. Why had she never noticed its striking beauty before? White clouds moved swiftly by. There must be a strong wind wherever they were, she realized. Straining, she could hear what sounded like the distant noise of traffic, of engines. They must be close to a highway, or a well-traveled road.

"This is good," Aaron announced. "Take her back."

Closing her eyes, she let the light from the outside dance across her face, trying to absorb the feeling for later. The tug of Michael at her elbow encouraged her to stand, and before she knew it, they were leading her out of the room once more. Guilt swirled itself around her chest. It had been too easy. If only she had done that before, then maybe Palmer would still be alive.

As they led her down the length of hall towards her cage, she heard the snap of a far door slamming closed. There were more people here than the four men she had seen. Kicking herself for losing focus, Ava had missed an opportunity to see the other people. Next time she would force herself to remain alert.

Entering their room, she saw Finn asleep on the mattress. The food tray had been placed inside the cage, as promised, and the sight of it caused her mouth to salivate. At the cage door, Michael cut through the zip tie, then held the door open while she walked through. Shutting her eyes for a moment, she listened to them lock the cage, then stomp out of the room, boots echoing off the walls. As soon as they were gone, she crouched beside the tray. It was piled high with boxes of crackers, a sleeve of salami, cups of pudding, apple sauce, and cans of corn. She couldn't believe the variety and amount of food. Grabbing at the crackers, she stopped short, noticing for the first time that it was unopened.

"Finn?!" She called over her shoulder. "Wake up, we've got food."

Why hadn't he eaten anything, she wondered. She had been gone for at least a few hours between the lengthy shower and the video shoot. No starving man was that polite. Worry tickled at her belly as she grabbed one package after another, finding them all untouched.

"Finn?" Getting up, she walked towards him. His position hadn't changed. "Finn!"

Breaking into a run, she slid down beside him, smoothing her hands over his limp body. Purple and blue bruises covered his face. Both eyes were swollen shut, and dried blood left a trail from his nostrils. Panic leapt inside her, making her hands shake as she checked for a pulse. It was there.

"Oh, Finn," she whispered. "Someone has beat the shit out of you."

His answering groan had hot tears coming to her eyes. As

gently as she could, she maneuvered his twisted body to lay flat on his back. His knuckles were raw and bruised as well. One or maybe two of his fingers might be broken. Lifting his shirt, she noted the expanse of purple spreading over his stomach. It flowed over his side, disappearing around his back.

Getting up, she retrieved the tray, then the fresh jugs of water. Using her sleeve this time, she dabbed at his face, wiping away the caked blood. She slid one hand beneath his neck and lifted his head up to pour just a little water into his mouth. When he gulped greedily, she slowly continued the process, careful not to let him have too much. Fighting the mix of rage and fear that swirled inside of her, Ava spoke soothingly to him as she broke up bits of cracker to slip into his mouth. He crunched haltingly before swallowing.

For an hour or more they ate that way together. She fed him manageable pieces but was unable to keep herself from shoveling the rest into her hungry mouth. This time there were no frozen peas, no bag of ice, nothing to provide him any comfort. He writhed and shifted, groaned and grimaced. His pain was hard for her to bear, for in a way she felt completely responsible. He would never have been here if it wasn't for her, so she gave him just a taste of what he had wanted all along, information. Keeping her voice low, she murmured, not sure how much he would remember anyway.

"James Miller is not a person. It's a code name for a protocol that my brother set up for me when Mason was born. If we were ever in danger, like serious fear for your life type danger, then I could call the number. I would ask for James Miller, like you Fed idiots did, and then Mason and I would be picked up. Only, I wasn't with him when you called, so I got left behind."

Lowering herself carefully beside him on the mattress, Ava positioned her body lightly along his, trying not to bump him unnecessarily. The overhead lights had been switched off, plunging them into perpetual blackness. It seemed early for bedtime, but she had lost track of the hours as she cared for Finn. One thing was certain, a long and torturous night lay ahead of them both.

Moving in his sleep, Finn would cry out suddenly, having inadvertently tweaked his injuries. At those times Ava would wake up and run her fingers lightly along his body, trying to assess his progress. Laying the back of her hand against his forehead she checked for a fever. Coming back cool, she would exhale with relief, no fever meant no infection, that was good.

When he seemed thirsty, she offered him sips of water. When he appeared fretful, she quieted him with more information. Head lying next to his, she smoothed her hand over his arm as she spoke, lips moving close to his ear.

"You were right about me in college. I didn't sleep with some guy and then forget his name. Although, looking back now I kind of wish that I had done that at least once." Ava chuckled ruefully, thinking about the last years of self-enforced celibacy. "The truth is, I knew Mason's father very well."

She told him what she felt she could but nothing more. Even so, it was a terrible night of interrupted sleep. Cramped and half falling off the edge of the mattress, Ava's back ached, muscles quivering in protest. When the lights finally flicked on in the morning, she was grateful to get up.

. . .

OVER THE NEXT WEEK, SHE PLAYED NURSEMAID. DESPITE HIS many protests, Finn needed her help to get to the toilet, eat, drink, stand up, and lay down. She suspected that he either had a cracked rib, or just severe muscle bruising, but she was admittedly no expert. When the swelling around his eyes eased so that he could see clearly, his ability to do things on his own gradually returned.

When Michael would come in to deliver their food and water, Ava kept her back to him, angry over what had happened to Finn. Despite the fact that he hadn't been the one to inflict the beating, she blamed Michael for it. For some reason, this seemed to bother him immensely. He brought her special food, lingering with it at the cage door. He would make her come take it from his hand, eyes stuck on her the whole time.

"If he had just shot the video," Michael protested one day. "Then he wouldn't have gotten hurt."

Refusing to respond, Ava gripped the bag of potato chips that he held through the slot in the cage door. Finn had told her that he was beaten for refusing to make an FBI ransom video. She had done her best to convince him to participate the next time around but so far, he remained unmoved. Keeping hold of the bag, Michael ran his fingers carefully over Ava's tense knuckles. Feeling his eyes upon her, she kept her gaze averted, lips pressed together in a firm line.

"Ava," he continued quietly. "What can I get you? What do you want?"

"Something for the pain."

Eyes popping up to search his, she could see his inner

calculations. Relinquishing the bag, he closed the hatch and left the room. Something told her that he would find a way to smuggle her some medication. It wasn't much but it should help. Rotating around to face Finn, she was startled to see him sitting up, appraising her. Making her way over, she crouched down, ripping open the bright yellow bag.

"Bet you can't eat just one." She smiled at him, trying to lighten the mood, but he didn't return it.

"He likes you." His expression was serious. The bruising had turned his skin a sickly greenish-yellow.

"I guess," she acknowledged.

"He's the one that watches you shower, right?"

"Yes." Ava could see where this was going and rolled her eyes.

"Don't brush this off, Ava."

"If I'm nice to him-"

"Nice or not, that man is bad news." Clutching at her with his hands, he jerked her closer, eyes willing her to see the danger. "The next line to cross isn't that far off."

"What am I supposed to do?"

Her proud exterior broke for just a second, exposing her underlying fear with a tremble in her voice. Softening, he encircled her body with his arms, drawing her protectively against his chest. "I can start teaching you self-defense." He spoke into her hair. "Or, you can seduce him into helping you escape."

"I don't know if I can do it." She breathed into his neck, noting the smell of his skin.

"I'm sorry that I can't protect you the way that I should, the way that I want to."

Closing her eyes, she listened to the thud of his heart

inside his chest. His breathing was steady, like the stroke of his hand that ran along her back. For several minutes, she leaned against him, while the terror at their situation thrummed through her mind. How would they ever get out of here? When he began to shift uncomfortably, she remembered his injuries and sat back. Biting at her lip, she peered up into his face, wondering if she should be embarrassed by the embrace. Veiled brown eyes studied her. His expression was impossible to read but reaching out with one hand, he ran tentative fingers through her tousled hair.

"Thank you," he said finally, retracting his hand to rest in his lap.

"For what?" Drawing her knees up to her chest, she looked away.

"For telling me about James Miller and Mason's father."

"I wasn't sure you would remember."

"Has he ever met his son?" Finn scooted over towards the wall and tilted back against it.

"Once," Ava admitted. "He was there when Mason was born."

"He's a fool." Finn grimaced as he continued to shift, searching for a comfortable position.

"Oh?"

"To let you and his son go. Is he a bad guy?"

"No, he's not a bad guy. We just agreed it was best for Mason if he wasn't around, that's all. It's not that he didn't love him, or want to be with him," Ava said, then wondered if she had divulged too much.

"Were you in love with him?"

"Who, Mason's father?" Ava stifled a laugh. "No, I was never in love with him."

"I was raised by my stepdad," Finn reminded her. They had talked at length about his family, his Mom, Dad, and three sisters. They lived on a farm in rural Utah. He rarely saw them anymore. "He's the best dad that I could ask for, but even so, I wanted to know everything about my biological father. Will you tell Mason who he is when the time comes?"

"I would have to ask his father first." Ava hadn't thought about it before.

"So, you're still in contact with him?" Finn's eyes narrowed.

"I could be."

A warning rang distantly inside her head. Standing up, Ava walked away, fingers twisting themselves together with nervous energy. It was all too easy to forget who she was talking to. This was Agent Finn, the investigator, and he was getting a little too close for comfort. As she paced, she could feel his eyes scrutinizing her. A new tension filled the space between them.

At the sound of the far door opening, the strain broke, and they watched Michael push through alone, toting a fresh jug of water. Looking her way, his pale green eyes communicated success. This time she met him at the cage door while Finn remained tucked away in the corner, observing.

Setting down the water, Michael opened the cage and pushed the door inward several inches. Using his foot, he slid the jug just inside, then reached out for Ava, pulling her close by the arm. Fear bubbled at the surface but she managed to remain calm as he quickly stuffed a handful of pills into the front pocket of her hoodie. She felt his breath exhale against the side of her face, making her hair sway slightly. Before releasing her, his lips glanced softly against the side of her cheek. Heart thumping crazily against her ribs, she took a step back and watched him adeptly secure the cage door.

"Thank you," she mouthed, then watched the kindness in his eyes mix with desire.

Bobbing his head once, Michael turned on his heel, boots tromping a straight line back out the far door. Bending over, she grabbed the water and shuffled it back over to Finn. He was on his feet now, looking every bit as uncomfortable as she felt. Coming in close, she stood toe to toe with him. His instinct had him grasping her shoulders, but she resisted when he made to pull her against him. Producing the ten white pills from her pocket, she cupped them in her open palm between them. Slowly, he lowered a hand to pluck one up, rolling it carefully between his thumb and forefinger.

"What are these?" He asked.

"Something for the pain." She pocketed the rest once more.

"Did he bring you these on his own, or did you ask for them?"

"He wanted to get me something. This is what I asked for." She could tell by Finn's furrowed brow that he was not as grateful as she had hoped.

"You shouldn't have done that." His hand shook her shoulder just a little.

"Why not?"

"Because this is going to cost you a lot more than you might be willing to pay." His eyes searched hers, a new fear present in them. "Don't do things for me, Ava. It's not worth it. If you're going to get something from him, then get yourself out of here."

"And to think that I expected a thank you," she huffed, shoving away from him in frustration.

. . .

LATER THAT NIGHT, OR DAY, SHE COULD NO LONGER TELL which, she lay down next to Finn in bed. The lights were still on, but they were both worn out, and his admonition had begun to tick inside her like a clock winding down to zero. He had taken the pills and she could tell that they made a difference for him. Even now his breathing was more regular and calm than it had been in over a week.

Shifting onto her side, she analyzed the profile of his face. Flat on his back, he lay with both arms crossed over his belly, so careful not to touch her unnecessarily. He was so reserved, so professional. She didn't know how he did it because she felt at any moment that she would fly all apart.

Her thoughts wandered, as they often did, to Mason. She missed him terribly and wondered what Clay had told him. Why did Mason think she wasn't with him anymore? What explanation had Clay used? Suddenly, Ava broke, she just couldn't hold it in a second longer. The pain and fear that was all twisted up inside her filled her eyes as she choked on the sound of her own sobs.

"I'm sorry," Finn mumbled sleepily. "It's going to be alright."

She hadn't meant to wake him. Rolling over onto his side, he kept his eyes closed but let his arm drift over her waist. The pain meds had relaxed him, his movements were slow and heavy. Pulling her up against him, he let his hand stroke comfortingly down her back. She listened to his quiet murmuring as tears continued to streak across her cheeks and the pain pounded like a drum inside her chest.

SEVEN

Time grew increasingly difficult to keep track of. With no way to write, they were left to guess. Had it been another two weeks, or three? It had to be somewhere in there but they couldn't say for certain. Finn's face looked normal again and his limp was gone. There had been no more videos, no more beatings. Killing time was currently the biggest challenge that they faced.

"Hand slap?" She asked.

"You'll just lose again." Finn plucked kernels of corn out of a peel-top metal can.

"Best two out of three?"

"More like best five out of seven, but okay."

He stood up, then stretched this way and that, she frowned at his mockery. Standing before him, she looked decidedly up into his face. He held his hands out between them, palms up, waiting. Carefully, she placed her hands over his. Staring down hard, she tried not to blink. Quick as anything he moved, flipping his hands up and over hers, slapping the tops before she could scoot them away.

"Dang," she cried, rubbing her hands together. "My turn."

Switching positions, she waited for him to place his palms gently against her own. He stared into her eyes, not bothering to watch her hands. Biting her lip in concentration, she held his gaze, refusing to be the first to look away. Wriggling her fingers, she got him to flinch only slightly. A knowing smile crept over him.

"What?" She asked.

"You're really terrible at this, you know that?" Laughing, he easily dodged her slap attempt, then the next, and the next.

"How do you do it?!" She cried at last, giving in to his obvious superiority.

"I watch your eyes," he admitted. "They get a little wider right before you're going to make your move… every time."

"That's cheating!" She cried in false protest. Pushing at his chest with both hands had him backing a step, but the smug look was fixed firmly to his face.

"It's the same with self-defense." He began a now familiar lecture. "Watch your opponent's eyes, always. They will tell you when the next hit is coming. Let's practice."

"Not again," Ava sighed, but there wasn't anything else to do.

Removing their hoodies, they went through a few of the easiest moves first. He would demonstrate, posing her as the aggressor before switching positions. She was able to unbalance him once in a while, but the size difference between them made it a challenge. As they went through the motions one thing became abundantly clear.

"Let's be honest." She panted after half an hour. "In a real fight between a man and me, I'm screwed."

"You just have to keep practicing," he pleaded. "With some confidence you could do some real damage."

"Damage," she repeated. "What good is that going to do me in the end?"

Nodding, he acknowledged her comment. With both hands resting on top of his head he breathed in air steadily, then stepped away, seemingly to think. When he turned back around, his eyes were closed. His mouth moved slightly, like he was talking himself through something, instructions maybe.

"Okay." Laying down on his back in the middle of the cage, he beckoned for her to walk over. "Get on top of me."

"You've got to be kidding." She came to stand over him.

"Ava, this is serious." His eyes grew frustrated, brow furrowed. "Get down on all fours on top of me. You're the guy, and I'll be the girl."

Throwing her head back she let loose a few whoops of genuine laughter. Over six feet tall and pushing two hundred pounds, the idea of wrestling successfully with Finn had tears of good humor coming to her eyes. Catching her breath a moment later, she stared down at his unamused expression. Maybe it wouldn't hurt to play along, she thought, she didn't want to really upset him. Rolling her shoulders, she tried to shake off her nerves and crouched down as instructed, lowering herself to straddle his body.

"Really?" He asked. "You're the guy, put your legs together. Mine go on the outside."

"Sorry." She swallowed in embarrassment as they shifted clumsily around.

"So, you want to do more than damage, right?"

"Right."

Nodding solemnly, she let her eyes travel over his face. He had a beard coming in and a mustache to match. For a split second her fingers itched to touch it, feel the bristle that stood out there, but then she realized what she was thinking and a flush crept into her cheeks. His frown deepened.

"More than likely if you're being attacked, then it would come down to this position. He will probably still be wearing a shirt, that's the key."

"Okay," she whispered it.

Eyes growing wide, she sucked in a breath as he reached an arm up and over her right shoulder. Hiking up the bottom of her shirt, he gathered it together, holding it in his hand.

"I'm going to walk you through the basic steps first, but in reality you two would be fighting. Maybe he's hitting you, so you would want to wrap your legs around his body and keep as close to him as possible. Bury your face in his neck. The closer you are, the less damage he can do."

Adrenaline pumping, she fought the rush of heat as his legs encircled her waist, bringing them fully against each other. Her shirt was gathered in both of his hands now, poised just at the top of her shoulder. She could feel the cold air tickling the bare skin of her back.

"Ava," he whispered. "Stop looking at me like that."

His face was so close that she could feel the warm pant of his breath on her neck.

"Why?" She exhaled the word, fighting the mix of embarrassment and wanting.

"This lesson is really important, and if you keep looking at me like that, then I'll never be able to finish it."

With a sudden jerk, he straightened both of his arms. Looping one around the opposite side of her head he brought their bodies back in close. Deliberately he squeezed his forearms into her neck, using her own shirt as a noose to effectively cut off her air supply. Gagging, Ava's expression revealed her utter shock as she stared into his dark eyes. His experienced eyes. It was only a split second before he released her completely, but in that moment, she knew he had done this before, had done this for real. Sitting up, she sucked in air, hands braced across his chest.

"Whoa," she said.

And then a new understanding dawned within her. With hardly any pressure she could strangle a man of considerable size. That's if she could hang on long enough.

"Whoa, is right." He nodded, still lying there. "Want me to show you, again?"

"Yeah."

Hunkering down, she began to pay attention.

OVER THE NEXT HOUR HE DRILLED HER IN THAT ONE MOVE. Jitters and tension evaporated; they were quickly replaced by focused memorization. It would take many more sessions of practice before she could perform the move as smoothly as Finn, but she was determined to perfect it. Finally calling for a break, they both panted with exhaustion. Rocking back on his heels, Finn eased himself to sit on the floor. Arms quivering like jelly, she propped herself up on her elbows to watch him. Every muscle burned, but it was nothing compared to the sliver of hope that fired within her. If he had let her, she would still be practicing.

"Clay never taught you any of this stuff?" He left to fetch their water.

"No." She shook her head, watching him move, a triangle of perspiration stained the back of his shirt.

"Your dad either? He was military, right?"

"Nope. I can shoot, though. I guess they figured I wouldn't ever be at close range without a gun." Gulping from the jug he handed her, a nagging thought surfaced. "How do you know my dad was military? I never mentioned it."

"FBI, remember?" He brushed it off. "We do a lot of research."

"Right." It was a believable explanation but still made her uncomfortable. What else did he know about her? About her family? "Did the FBI teach you all that stuff?"

"I'd rather not talk about it in here," he said, stalking the perimeter of their cage.

She frowned. There were secrets circling but she let them slide. Apparently, she wasn't the only one hiding something.

Moving to sit on their mattress, she examined the small supply of rations that remained. Four slices of stale white bread, half an open can of yellow corn, and one semi-cool piece of string cheese. During the past five days or so the portions had grown smaller. Conspiratorially they had whispered together, guessing that something new was going to happen soon. It was easier to manage them if they were weak and hungry. Ava knew that was especially true of Finn, who was still insistent on not participating in the ransom video. The LO would want him on the edge in order to get him to comply.

Carefully, she did her best to limit her food intake so that he would have more. Whenever Finn caught her doing it, an argument ensued. He wanted the food split evenly in half, dismissing her desire to dole it out based on their size. Today was no different. Meticulously, he came over to count out kernels of corn, placing them systematically into her hand.

After the workout, she didn't have the energy to fight him. Each yellow squish of kernel in her mouth was an explosion of delicious nutrients. How had she not realized canned vegetables tasted this good? Shaking her head slowly, she eyed the cheese. Following her gaze of longing, Finn grabbed it up, handing the whole thing over.

"You worked hard today," he explained. "Your body needs this."

"So does yours," she protested, unwrapping the cheese before tearing it in half.

Rejecting the offer, he gently pushed her hand away.

"Finn." She inched closer and turned towards him, hoping to persuade him to accept it. "Please, just eat this."

"No."

He shook his head but didn't retreat from their closeness. Reaching out, she took his fist in her hand. Setting the cheese aside, she worked his fingers open before retrieving it and placing it decidedly into his palm. When he closed his fingers around it, she smiled, then peered up into his face. Steady brown eyes locked on hers, causing a rush of heat to flood her system.

"Ava," he said, but the rest died on his lips.

The outer door snapping open had Finn shoving away from her before rising to his feet. Michael and the other two guards strode in. No food tray accompanied them. This was a business visit. Ava remained seated on the mattress, wondering which one of them would be called out. Fear leaped for Finn, knowing that he would surely be beaten again if he refused to participate. Underneath that lived a small sinking sensation. It could be her turn as well, if Clay hadn't come through.

"Stand back against the far wall, Agent Finn." The tall one pointed. "It's the lady's turn for a shower."

"I can't let you take her out of here anymore." Finn's jaw clenched.

"You don't have a choice." The tall one countered, as the rifleman swung up to take aim.

"I'll go," Ava said, and rose from her seat.

It was the same scenario every time. If they wanted her, then they threatened to kill him. If they wanted him, then they threatened to kill her. It was a simple and predictable tactic, but it worked, each one refused to be the death of the other. Defeated, Finn hung his head as she brushed past him, finger tips catching at her shirt as she walked by.

The guards were nothing if not consistent. She offered them her wrists behind her back and felt the snug plastic against her flesh. Cage door opened, cage door closed. Boots sounded in the otherwise silent room as they marched her out. Same hallway with its garish lighting. Same number of doors fastened shut. Same room for her shower. And of course, same Michael with his shock of red hair and questing eyes. Once alone in the bathroom together, he helped her to slip out of her binds. The plastic was just tight enough to stay on, but if she had really tried, she could have wriggled free.

"I got you a present." He smiled at her, rummaging through a pocket of his fatigues.

"A razor!" She practically salivated over the tiny blue disposable. She had requested it from him over a week ago.

"You can shave with it in here, but then you have to give it back." He handed it over easily. "Don't try to cut yourself, or me either, okay?"

"I won't," she assured him.

Stepping out of her clothes, she hopped into the stall before turning on the spray. Although Finn had warned her, she had let her guard drop around Michael. He watched her shower every few days, but never did anything to alarm her. Maybe he was working for a bad organization, but despite that, she thought he must be an okay guy. He didn't bring her everything that she asked for, but he tried his best to get some of the things that she wanted. While she washed, he watched through the steam and talked.

"Negotiations with your brother have broken down," he informed her. "It's becoming clear that Clay isn't going to trade you for Sophia."

"Sophia?"

Her heart raced. She knew that name, it clanged like a bell inside her head. This was the first time that Michael had told her exactly what they were after, and it suddenly made everything in her life click together in perfect sense.

"That's Mr. Lockett's daughter." Michael explained.

"He can't seriously think that Clay kidnapped her." Ava shifted to face him and had to work to keep her expression veiled as the water soaked down her hair.

"Not kidnapped exactly." Michael's eyes roamed her body but he didn't move from his position. "He was definitely the last one with her before she dropped off the radar."

"Well, what is he supposed to do?"

"I don't know. Find her. Bring her back. I'm worried about what happens next for you. Clay can't stall any longer." Michael's expression was grave.

Nodding, Ava turned back into the spray, switching the water to hot. Letting the droplets sting her skin helped to calm the spread of tightness that creeped across her chest. If Michael was concerned, then so should she be. Taking her time, she shaved, rinsed, and stepped out, leaving the razor for him in the stall. He handed her the threadbare white towel, which she wrapped carefully around her naked body.

Despite supplying fresh clothes, the LO did not provide her with new underwear. As an unspoken agreement, Michael had taken to washing her only pair and bra. In this way she had clean ones every few days, but then had to go without the next time. Today she left them in a pile on the floor as she slipped into the new sweats and long sleeve thermal top.

Brushing her hair and teeth over the sink, she was consumed by her own thoughts. Upon turning back to face him, she swallowed nervously. When he saw the fear in her eyes, Michael closed the distance between them and took her into his arms. His press of contact had surprise shooting through her system. He had never done this before. Gently, he cupped her face with one hand, rubbing at the small of her back with the other. Raising her hands between them, she spread her palms over his chest in defense.

"Michael-" she began, but was cut short.

Lowering his face, he kissed her. Stiffening, she hesitated, wondering just how to get out of the situation. When his lips parted her own, she pushed decidedly away from him, but only managed to separate their bodies by a few inches. He was strong, very strong.

"You're scaring me." Her whisper was harsh as his mouth traveled down the length of her neck. "Michael, I'm afraid!"

"I'm sorry." Jolted by the call of his name, he stepped back, studying her reaction. "I don't want to frighten you."

The knock on the bathroom door had him rolling his eyes but he answered. Exhaling her relief, she offered her wrists in front of her body which he bound loosely once more before following her out of the bathroom. Behind the rifleman, they walked until they reached the video room. Palmer's face came unbidden to her mind.

Entering, she noticed Aaron was waiting on them. His pinched expression was one of frustration. He wasn't the big boss, so whoever was above him must be unhappy. That wasn't good for her, Ava guessed. The line of high windows along one wall framed a blazing orange sunset that resonated over numerous puffy clouds. For a moment, she stopped in awe, appreciating what she hadn't seen in a very long time. How many weeks had it been since she tasted the outdoor air?

"Your brother hasn't returned what we asked for," Aaron said, as she settled into the plastic chair. "You can guess what happens now."

"What if he doesn't have what you want? If you let me go, then I promise I will find it myself and bring it to you." She pleaded as he crossed in front of her.

"Not possible." He sighed. "We need you to make another video, but this time you have to really beg him. He has to know that his lack of participation has real consequences."

"I will." She nodded eagerly.

"That's good," he said. "But words alone, I'm afraid, won't do the trick."

"What do you mean?"

Trying to buy time, she glanced fearfully at Michael, who refused to meet her gaze.

"Michael," Aaron said. "It's your turn, tune her up a little. Make sure it will show on the video."

"Please." Ava shot to her feet. Running to Michael, she clutched at his chest with her bound hands and whispered to him. "Michael, please, Michael."

For a moment, he fought with himself. Dropping into silence, the room awaited his move. She kept her body snugged up close to him, repeating his name over and over. Eventually he just shook his head and stepped away.

"Damn it," Aaron cursed. "I knew you were getting too close."

Closing the distance between them, Aaron shoved Michael aside with one hand and struck Ava hard across the face with the other. Stunned, she tilted off balance, arms bound together awkwardly. Bracing for the next blow, she squeezed her eyes shut and ducked low, but the next hit never came.

Instead, she heard the sounds of a fight. There was shouting, then flesh striking flesh. Blinking in shock, she opened her eyes to take in the scene. Michael had recovered from the shove, and much to Aaron's amazement had come through swinging. The two men twisted, rolling together along the floor as the tall man moved fast to separate them.

"Get her out of here!" He shouted.

Still crouched on the floor, she didn't have time to look over her shoulder before the rifleman wrenched her up by the hair. Crying out in pain, she stumbled ahead of him, his fingers laced at the base of her skull. Shoving her out the doorway they veered down the long hall. He made no sound. When they were almost to the end, a door to their right flew open. Two other men jogged past, heading in the direction of the commotion. She had never seen them before.

Stopping at their cage room door, the rifleman tilted her forward, indicating that she should twist the knob. It wasn't locked, so opened easily. When they entered, Finn sprang to his feet, running the length of the cage as the rifleman marched her in. Unceremoniously, he held her against the expanded metal while digging for his keys.

"Get back," he warned.

When Finn hesitated, he jerked Ava's head and slammed her face into the cage. This had Finn backpedaling rapidly, screaming insults all the while. Unperturbed, the rifleman waited until Finn's body hit the far wall before opening the door and releasing Ava to fall through it. The lock was clicked while she still lay on the ground. Before Finn could slide to a stop beside her, the rifleman disappeared out the far door.

"Ava." Finn gathered her up to sit on his lap. "What happened? Are you okay?"

"Michael-" she began, but he cut her off.

"I'm going to kill him." His voice heaved but he scooped her up without effort, carrying her back to the mattress.

"No." She shook her head, face stinging and sore. "He wouldn't do it. He couldn't hit me, so Aaron did, but then Michael attacked him."

"He what?"

"Michael attacked Aaron. They were still rolling around on the ground when the rifleman pulled me out. Negotiations with Clay haven't gone well. They wanted my face messed up for the next video, but I never got around to shooting it."

"That means they'll come back for you." Finn traced his fingers along the side of her cheek, inspecting the swelling. "I can't let them take you again."

"What are you going to do? You can't get yourself killed, Finn." Worry consumed her.

"I'll think of something."

His eyes darted across her face as his fingers continued to brush against her skin where the bruising had already begun. Heart pounding in her chest, she studied him. Her eyes were drawn once more to the short stubble that had risen along his chin and jaw. It gave him a rugged appearance, he hadn't benefited from her smuggled razor. Though his shoulders were still broad with muscle, his waist had narrowed from the sharp drop in their diet.

Eyes lowering, she wondered what would become of them. Clay did not have Sophia Lockett, of that Ava was certain. How could he trade her for someone he didn't have? The truth of their circumstance hit her like a ton of bricks. They were never going to make it out of here. Gripping his grey shirt in her hands, Ava clung to Finn, and buried her face in his chest.

"It's alright," he whispered into her hair, rocking her body slowly. "We're going to be alright."

"No, we're not." Ava's mouth moved against his shirt, her voice thick. "We're never going to get out of here."

"Shhhh," Finn soothed, wrapping his arms more tightly around her waist.

While he rocked her, she shifted her face against his chest, keeping the uninjured side resting against him. Blinking back tears, she watched the far door through the expanded metal of the cage. But then the lights in their room flicked decidedly out, sending them into unending blackness. For a few moments, they didn't move. The flat of his palm slid around to the middle of her back, and he held her against him, waiting, listening. When the door failed to open, she felt him let out a sigh of relief. They wouldn't be coming back for her tonight.

The caress of his hand still lingered over her back, and she became gradually more aware of the sound of his steady breathing. Heat, like the kind that had always accompanied his touch, bloomed all over her body. Clearing her throat, Ava purposefully released her grip on his shirt and pushed away to sit back. They were still close, she could feel the touch of his knees against her own.

"I wish it wasn't so dark," he whispered. "I can't see you."

Blowing out a breath, she felt him reach for her, then tentatively run his fingers up the length of one arm. Biting at her lower lip, she waited, everywhere he touched was left with tiny vibrations. Lightly, he traced the line of her throat before retreating away into the darkness. It left her aching.

"We shouldn't do this," he murmured.

And he was right, of course he was right. But she was so scared just then, and so tired of the incurable feeling. She wanted to escape it, to replace it. Tilting towards him, she let her hands meet with his chest, spread over his shoulders and up the sides of his neck. He was even closer than she had realized. Feeling the bristle of his cheeks pass under her palms, she let her thumbs glide over the smoothness of his lips. Nerves fluttering, she leaned in, brushing her mouth lightly over his once, then again.

"Forget the rules." Finn's voice was thick, he was on the edge.

Suddenly, his arms snaked out to encircle her body, gathering her up close against him. He applied deep slow kisses to her lips, drawing her in and igniting a spark that burned low in her belly. Shifting her body in response, she moved to sit astride his lap, wrapping her arms about his shoulders and neck. His large hands welcomed her, traveling across her upper back and down her sides to grip impulsively at her hips.

As his mouth left hers to seek the bare flesh along her collar, she let out a tiny gasp. She wanted to feel his skin, to run her hands over the muscles that she had only seen through his shirt. Yanking on the bottom of the fabric she sought his flat stomach, running her palms up to his chest. He released his hold on her long enough to help get the shirt over his head. When his hands returned, they raced underneath her own top.

Murmuring her desire into his neck, she trailed hurried kisses first along the line of his shoulder, then up under his chin. He made quick work of her shirt after that, tugging it off easily. Pressing her bare chest against his, she felt him reach between them and smooth a hand over her breasts. Mouth seeking hers once more, he let a thumb brush casually over first one nipple, then the other. Working her hips over him, she elicited a low moan from his throat.

When his hand dipped down between her legs, he slipped a testing finger inside. Finding her already damp with wanting, he cursed quietly under his breath. For a few moments he fought to slow things down but eventually lost. Tipping her onto her back, Finn continued to rub her, causing her to arch in encouragement beneath him. She grabbed for his waist and barely managed to work his pants over his hips before he slid himself fully between her legs. Crying out, she moaned her pleasure into his neck, letting each stroke he made build sensation inside of her.

As she clung to him, the sound of his harsh panting next to

her ear sent a thrill along the length of her spine. Coming close now, she bit gently at his jaw and squeezed her eyes shut as her climax rocketed through her body, sending tiny convulsions to hug tightly around him. Holding on then, she buried her face in his neck as he pumped quickly to follow.

EIGHT

A slight headache woke her the next morning. Groaning, she sat up, easing the tips of her cold fingers over the hot swelling that ran along the left side of her face.

"Looks worse today." Finn came to kneel next to her, examining the bruising with a careful eye.

"Thanks." Sarcasm dripped from the word. "Do we have anything to eat?"

Stomach rumbling, she sat up, gathering her knees to her chest. Pulling over the sparsely populated food tray, he handed her two slices of stale bread. Biting into them was like chomping on crumbling air.

"I've made you scrambled eggs, breakfast sausage, and the pancakes are almost done," he teased, counting corn kernels into her hand. This was the last of their food.

"Did you sprinkle the eggs with cheddar?" She played along, what else could they do?

"Absolutely."

"Can we switch the pancakes for Belgium waffles?"

"What?!" His shock was genuine. "How dare you try to trade in my pancakes. The answer is no Ma'am."

Laughing, she shook her head, which caused the ache to increase. She wasn't sure which hurt worse, the hit from Aaron or the feel of her face being smashed against the cage. Sitting together, they ate in silence, finishing every last morsel of food. It didn't take long to consume, and it didn't do much to battle the incessant weakness that caused her to tremble.

Over a month ago she had worried about calories, making sure to work out a few days each week. Now she was on the crash diet of the century. There was no telling where her weight was at this point. On the plus side, if she ever got out of here, she would be able to eat an entire cheesecake by herself without an ounce of guilt. When she glanced over at Finn, she caught him studying her. Warm prickles turned to goosebumps that rippled down her arms. Reaching out, she traced her fingers over the knuckles of his hand. After a beat, he pulled away, causing her stomach to trip uncertainly.

"I've got to talk to you about last night," Finn began.

"I don't think I want to hear this," she mumbled, returning her hand to her lap.

"No," he spoke quietly, looking past her shoulder at the far door. "It's not that. Last night was good, really good, and I wouldn't be telling the truth if I said that I didn't want it to happen again. It's just that we can't let the LO know. If they find out, then it will make us both more vulnerable than we already are."

"Okay." She scrutinized his face. "So, no touching or whatever while the lights are on. Is that what you're saying?"

"Yes." He bobbed his head, then went on. "Have you told me everything that happened to you yesterday?"

"Yeah." She was careful now, sensing a trap.

"Everything with Michael?"

"Yes, everything."

"You're clean shaven and you no longer have underwear, Ava. How did that happen?"

"Oh, you noticed."

"Yeah, I noticed. How much did that cost you?"

"Are you jealous?" Her mouth dropped a bit in surprise, examining his reaction.

"No, but I'm worried about you taking these extra risks."

"You can relax. I asked Michael to bring me the razor a while ago and yesterday he did. As for the underwear, he gets them washed for me and returns them the next time I shower."

"And you've given him nothing for all this?"

"Well, he kissed me yesterday, but when I told him that I was afraid, he stopped. He's really a decent guy," she protested.

"A decent guy? Ava, you've got to be kidding me. First, your brother, then Mason's father is some dead beat, and now Michael? I'm starting to think your judgment is pretty screwed up."

"Hey, my brother is not a bad guy." She pushed up to standing but the head rush was too much, causing her to sway.

"Damn it," Finn muttered, getting up to help steady her. "How bad is your head exactly?"

"It hurts," she admitted, letting him sit her back down.

In silence, they sipped water for several minutes while the angry words dissipated around them. When you're trapped twenty-four-seven in a cage with another person arguments happen. Unlike in normal life, they weren't able to walk away. It was moments like this that made their lack of freedom all the more acute. She longed for the chance to go for a walk outside. For the ability to breathe the fresh air, clear her head. She knew that Finn was wrong about Mason's father, but how was he supposed to know that?

"Mason's dad is not a dead beat," she offered.

"He abandoned you and his son," he countered.

"He didn't abandon us, he's just not physically around."

"Is he the one that pays for your house? Gives you the extra money?" He circled back to the original round of FBI interrogation, such a long time ago now it seemed.

"Yes," she admitted. "He pays for mostly everything."

"Why isn't he around, Ava? What kind of man is he?"

"I can't tell you that."

"Is he married? Is he famous, or some politician? Give me something," he pleaded.

Ignoring him, she laid back down on the mattress, shutting her eyes. This was one of many things that she would never, ever, be able to share with him. And all this talk of Mason had her heart squeezing into a tiny ball in her chest. Finn was right, someday he would ask about his dad. She only hoped that she was there to explain herself. Keeping her eyes closed, she rolled away, and drifted in and out of sleep. At times she listened to Finn's incessant pacing, then let it fade.

Voices. Raised voices inside their room is what finally caught her attention. Groggily, she shifted onto her side. Three new guards stood at the cage door having words with

Finn. Absently, she wondered what had happened to Michael and hoped that he was okay.

"We're going to come in there and get her whether you like it or not." One of the men was saying.

"I'm willing to make you guys a deal," Finn responded. "Give you something that you've wanted."

"And what's that?" The man asked. Interest piqued, Ava sat up, wondering what Finn was up to.

"I'll make the video that you wanted, but you have to swear not to remove her from this cage again. Not for a shower, not for a video, not for anything. Then I'll make as many videos as you want."

"What if we don't agree?"

"Then you'll have to kill me to get to her," Finn said simply, making Ava's heart jump. "And we all know by now that your boss won't let you kill me."

"Alright." One of the guards nodded. "Deal. Put your hands behind your back."

Finn complied. Keeping his face downcast, he refused to make eye contact with Ava. She remembered what he had said about not wanting the LO to know they had slept together. It would make him more vulnerable and she knew it, but watching him give himself up now was even harder. Determined to support him in the only way possible, she lay back down. Rolling over on the mattress, Ava stared at the white wall.

Footfalls bounced through the stark space, pounding at her ears. Holding her breath, she listened to the door snap shut before letting it shakily back out. The overhead lights were unyielding. Pulling her hoodie over her head, she cinched it down tight and curled her body into the fetal position. This was the most privacy that she could hope for in here so she let herself cry. Cry for Finn and for Palmer. Cry for Mason and for herself. Cry until all of the feelings had leaked out of her, dripping themselves onto the worn mattress. Cry until she passed out from it.

It couldn't have been more than half an hour later when the guards returned. Again, she slept through the opening of the outer door. The twist of the cage lock also failed to rouse her. Unfamiliar hands gripped her shoulders and rolled her roughly onto her back. That's what had her eyes finally shooting open. That's what had her pulse skipping crazily. That's what had her struggling.

Before she had the wherewithal to fight, however, they had her wrists bound in front of her body. Yanking her up to her feet, the men seemed unruffled as Ava tripped clumsily between them. They marched her out the same way Finn had gone. The plastic ties that now bit painfully into her skin made her miss her mild interactions with Michael. It was clear that he wouldn't be back.

Down the hall they moved fluidly past the bathroom. No shower today, she thought. At the end, a few knocks on Palmer's death room door elicited an answer of assent. When the door swung open, they shoved her unceremoniously inside. Finn was seated in the orange chair, hands bound in front of him now. His hair was damp and skin fresh, they had let him shower first. In his hands he clutched a single sheet of white paper. Upon seeing her, he leapt to his feet, letting the paper coast away forgotten through the air.

"We had a deal!" He shouted his outrage. "I won't read this with her in here."

"You can and you will," Aaron countered.

When he turned to face her, Ava could see that he sported a bandage over a split lip and mildly swollen right eye. Michael must be a lefty, she thought, at least he had gotten some punishment in. Sweeping his arm across the room, Aaron gestured for the guards to bring Ava closer to Finn. She planted her feet in an attempt to resist them, but it was almost laughable. Tip toes dragging across the floor, they deposited her easily in a heap.

Turning her face, Ava could see the ferocity build in Finn's eyes as his instinct had him moving toward her. But it was the placement of a single black boot on the side of her neck that had him stopping short. Stepping down firmly, the tread pushed into the skin along her cheek. Ava stopped struggling. Hands raised together now, Finn spread open his palms, trying to ease the tension.

"Alright." He backed the few steps to the chair. "Alright."

Sitting heavily, his eyes locked on hers. Aaron grabbed up the discarded paper, its crinkling sound was the only one in the room, and handed it back over to Finn. Briefly Finn looked down at the words, causing him to break eye contact with Ava. She could tell that he didn't want to read it aloud, the way his jaw clenched. Aaron held up his phone, shifting his body a few feet to the left before taking a step forward.

"Read," he commanded.

"Clay," Finn began. "Things are not going well for me or your sister. The beatings are happening more often now, and the food supply is running low. The LO knows that you have the ability to give back what you took. They will not accept anything less. Your offer of money and favors are an insult. If our time together in the service meant anything to you, then as a friend, please help us."

At this, Aaron swung the camera around. Lowering it slowly, he zoomed in on Ava's face. He wanted Clay to see the battered state of his sister. Head held firmly against the floor, it was only her eyes that registered surprise at the information contained in Finn's last sentence. He knew her brother. He knew him well.

Reeling from the shock of it, what happened next was a blur. The guards picked her up and she walked willingly back to their cage. Finn was returned as well. Having gotten what they wanted, the LO shoved in a fresh tray of food. It was another loaf of bread and plastic jar full of peanut butter. Ava felt faint. Sinking to her knees just inside the cage door, she refused Finn's offer to make her a slice. He did anyway.

"You have to eat." Finn held the fresh bread slathered with peanut butter under her nose.

"I'm not hungry." Shaking her head, she pushed his hand weakly away.

"Ava." His whisper came close to her ear. She felt his presence crouch down beside her. "Eat."

"There was no FBI ransom video." Thoughts tumbled out of her mouth. "They didn't kill you because they needed you. You're leverage against Clay, too. You know my brother. You're his friend."

"We were friends but not anymore," Finn corrected. "I haven't seen him in years."

"When you took me into custody, for a moment, it looked like you recognized me."

"Only from photos that Clay used to have," he admitted.

"You lied to me."

"I withheld information, it's different."

"That's a cop out."

"Everything that I've kept from you is for your protection," he seethed. "Look around you. Do you think this is torture? It's not even close. This is a hostage negotiation, so they don't care about what we may know. If at some point they realize they won't be getting what they want, then that could all change. When that happens, it's better not to have any information to tell."

"You should have told me that you knew Clay. Is there anything else?"

"It's not like you aren't keeping things from me, Ava," he reminded her.

"The special program, the one that made Clay get out. You stayed in. You're still a part of it."

Setting the slice of bread on her lap, he got up and walked away. He wouldn't continue the conversation, just like she wouldn't tell him the truth about Mason's father. Laying down on her side, she let his offer of food slide to the hard floor. Focusing her attention on the thin bread spread liberally with a much-needed boost of protein, her face soured. If she ever got out of this situation, then she swore she would never eat peanut butter again.

Poking the crust with one finger, she toyed with the food, shifting it this way and that along the floor. She was beyond caring about germs. When it was all said and done, she would eat it. Across the space, Finn sat on the mattress, leaning back against the wall. His eyes were narrowed, observing her. Fighting the unwanted spark of attraction, she succumbed instead to the sharp pangs of hunger. After finishing one slice, she sat up, feeling the shock of energy coursing through her veins. With a shrug, she scooted over to the tray and served herself up another, then another.

"You're going to make yourself sick," Finn warned, but didn't stop her.

Washing it all down with water, she swiped at her mouth with her sleeve. The silent treatment would do nicely, she thought, still wanting to punish him for transgressions she too was guilty of. Ignoring him until lights out proved easy. He gave her the space she required, making no attempt to engage her further. Once engulfed in the blackness, however, their chosen corners seemed decidedly to his advantage. She was left with the cold hard floor and he had their only source of relief, the mattress.

"Why don't you switch with me?" Finn's voice called out to her. He hadn't moved. "It's not good being so close to the cage door."

For a brief moment, she battled her own pride. She had chosen to make a stand against him, but now her butt was numb, joints achy, and stomach jumping. The last time she had fallen asleep in here she was woken by the guards grabbing her. Standing, she stepped one tentative foot in front of the other. It was dark as pitch, so she counted her footfalls, hoping to get close before tripping.

"Over here." His voice was close.

"Where?" She called.

"Here," he managed before she bent down to crawl the remaining few feet.

Curling up beside him, she listened to his quiet breath exhaling into her hair. She closed her eyes against the unyielding obsidian and felt the beat of her own heart instead. This man. What was it about this man that had her so churned up? Pulling her in tighter, he trailed soft kisses along the back of her neck.

"I'm still mad," she warned.

"Noted," he whispered and stopped.

Sometime in the night, he shook her awake.

"Do you hear that?" He hissed, already pushing away from her.

Adrenaline shot through her system as she recognized the sound. It was the distant thrum of helicopter blades, and they were growing ever louder. Over a month had gone by with them living crammed together in their cage, in this room, inside this building. Never once had they heard this particular sound. In the game of survival new could be good, but it could also be bad. Very bad.

"Get off the bed and lie flat on the floor," Finn whispered. She moved to comply. "I'm going to cover you up with the mattress, so keep as still as you can. Don't move unless I tell you. Got it?"

"Got it."

Her answer was muffled as he was already shifting the bed on top of her. Turning her head to face the wall, she kept one ear to the ground and worked hard to control the hitch in her breathing. Don't panic, stay aware; her father's voice offered comfort.

Inhaling through her nose, she listened to the thump of landing. The whirling blades were now a constant pulse that filled her head. Finn was utterly quiet, although he would have had to yell to make himself heard over the rush of blood in her ears. Distant shots were fired, there was yelling, and the pop of far off doors slamming. They were so vulnerable, trapped with nowhere to run. Closer and closer the ripple of noise approached them.

Click. Their door cracked open. She heard the sound of metal rolling, rolling, rolling.

Boom.

The room was illuminated by a brilliant flash. Smoke spewed forth to fill the small space, causing her to hack uncontrollably. Underneath the mattress, she gagged, fighting with every impulse inside that screamed for her to run. Run for air. Seconds stretched out as she fought the primal urge for survival. She hardly noticed the eerie silence that now surrounded her. She couldn't hear a thing.

Blinding light ripped into her eyes as the mattress was dragged off of her. Men obscured by helmets, eye gear, and half masks peered down. Nodding, they gestured, pointing at her, then turned to call over their shoulders. She couldn't hear what they said, nor could she read their carefully hidden lips. A dim ringing in her ears hailed the return of sound, but it grew until it dominated the landscape, pushing everything else into the background.

Starting to struggle, she sat up, scooting away only inches before her back came hard against the wall. Behind the soldiers and through the smoke, she observed Finn. Pinned down by two more men, his face was turned away from her, arms wrenched up behind his back. The cage door had been blasted open. It hung grotesquely on what was left of metal hinges.

For the first time in over a month freedom was possible, but still too far away. Eyes watering from the smoke, she hacked and coughed, tasting irony in its most bitter form. She was finally clear to get out, but there was also no protection from the geared-up soldier that now jogged in. Sliding to a stop on his knees, he yanked down his face cover and pulled up on his eye mask.

"Clay!" Throat erupting with the scream, she had never felt such elation at seeing him in all her life.

"It's her," he confirmed. "What do you say we get out of here, Sis?"

Unable to speak further, she threw her arms around his neck and sobbed.

"No time for this crap," he grunted. Tossing her body over his shoulder, he packed her out past Finn. "Grab that guy, too, let's go!"

NINE

Wedged between her brother and another soldier, Ava rocked with the motion of the helicopter. Across from her, Finn's bare feet tapped an excited rhythm along the floor. Where she had been content to sit back, he had immediately grabbed for a headset and proceeded to grill Clay in an old childhood game of twenty questions.

By tilting her head to the side, she was able to listen to her brother's one-sided responses. It didn't take much to guess what Finn must be asking. The helicopter itself was indeed government property, but Clay had called in a favor. Apparently, Finn knew the pilot too because he leaned up to shout some profanity at him, tapping the guy briefly on the shoulder before resuming his seat.

The LO had been holding them in Canada, so Clay had been forced to wait until the pilot was scheduled to make a training run in that direction before detouring for their rescue. Now they were headed to the Constitutional Militia Regional Headquarters located in the Pacific Northwest. Clay had been holed up there since Ava had been taken, working on pinpointing her exact location. Though he was unwilling to divulge how he actually found them, he did admit to knowing their whereabouts for at least the past two weeks.

As their conversation grew more coded, Clay fished around in his pocket and shoved a four-by-six photograph into Ava's hand. With once glance, her chest heaved. Gripping the tiny image of Mason, she stared. Healthy, happy and bright, he was aglow in a sea of Lego blocks and army men. Smudges of what must have been chocolate ice cream creased the corners of his upturned mouth. His mischievous hazel eyes flashed in the picture. Her little boy was alright.

There were a million questions she wanted to ask of Clay, but with the crowd of men surrounding them, she knew it wasn't the place or time. She had always prided herself on being fairly tough for a girl, but in the past month, she had never wanted to cry so much. Squeezing her eyes closed, she buried her face in her brother's shoulder in an attempt to hold back an emotional outburst. As brother's go, Clay offered comfort in the way most natural to him. He pinched her hard on the leg, then kissed the top of her head. Giving him a good elbow jab in return brought a smile back to her face.

By the time they landed, Ava was spent. Between the midnight extraction and roughly four hour flight, sunrise was not far off. The men headed towards a remote two-story building with Ava and Finn padding after them. The icy chill of concrete soaked into the souls of her feet as she listened to the whirling blades of the helicopter lift back into the air. The area surrounding them was heavily wooded with old growth pine. Trees towered all around, dark swirling figures that swayed with the winter wind. This could be Washington State, or maybe Oregon, she wasn't sure.

Pushing through a simple wooden side door, the stomp of boots and shedding of gear began. The narrow hallway was stuffy, full of warmth that flowed down from a nearby ceiling vent. How long had it been since she felt the comfort of such a luxury? Forced air heating. While the men murmured and shuffled about, she stood completely still, face upturned to the vent, inhaling.

"Who's hungry?" Clay's voice rose above the din but the question was rhetorical.

Almost reluctantly, she followed the push of taller, bigger people. Feeling very much how a small child might amongst a throng of busy adults, forgotten. Eyes darting about, she wondered if Mason was here even now. The hall gave way to a meeting room of sorts. Mismatched tables and chairs were shoved together, creating a space to gather and in this case, to eat.

Hanging back, she observed her brother's interaction with the other men. Joking together, they talked easily. To them, this was just another successful mission. Taking a seat at a table, they ranged around him as the head. It was clear to her that they regarded him with trust as a leader and also as a comrade, a friend. He belonged here with them, and although jealousy tickled her senses at being left out, she was happy for him.

Creeping up beside her, Finn's fingers encircled her elbow. He whispered in her ear, encouraging her to sit with him and to eat. Food was being brought in by the cart load, wheeled to the room from a nearby kitchen. Glancing at her brother, Ava saw his watchful eyes tracking their interaction. She had made a promise to him after Mason that there would be no men in her life. They ask too many questions and pose too great a risk, he had reasoned. At the time, she was willing to sacrifice anything, but this thing with Finn had just fallen into her lap. Now that it was here, she wasn't sure what to do about it.

An empty plastic plate was tossed unceremoniously on the table in front of her. The guys here ate family style, with a variety of large serving dishes lining the center of the table. If you wanted something, then you leaned up and dished out a portion onto your plate. If not, then leave it be. The smell alone was overwhelming. Spaghetti with giant meatballs, fried chicken wings, mashed potatoes, green beans, bread sticks, salad, meatloaf. Everything looked amazing and revolting at the same time.

Shock had her hesitating, watching the others dig in. They slopped heavy portions onto their plates, laughing, teasing, chugging soda, and chewing. Suddenly, she realized that she was at nothing more than a glorified frat party and had to stifle a smirk.

"What's the matter?" Clay called from a few seats away.

"You guys are a bunch of pigs," she replied, and had them all hooting.

"Don't make me tell stories about you as a kid," Clay warned, but there was no seriousness to it.

Blinking innocently at him, she selected a few pieces of the chicken first. After breaking the ice, so to speak, her stomach clamored for more. Spoonful after spoonful of mashed potatoes and green beans heaped high onto her plate only to disappear into her ravenous mouth. When she made a move for more, Finn stilled her hand.

"This time you really will make yourself sick," he told her, and brushed an errant hair back behind her ear.

The intimate gesture had her brother shifting. She could see him out of the corner of her eye. Nodding to Finn, she withdrew her hand, scooting a few inches further away from him. When he raised an eyebrow in question, she did her best to ignore it. If he thought the LO knowing they had slept together was a vulnerability, then he had better watch out for Clay.

"So, Finn." As Clay's voice sounded out, all others dropped away. "What do you think of your first interaction with the Constitutional Militia? Are we the boogie men your superiors make us out to be?"

"I'm grateful to each and every one of you for saving our ass back there." Finn took his time, looking each man directly in the eye. "As to the rest, I guess it depends on what your overall plans are."

"Overall plans?" Clay asked, wanting Finn to be the one to put words on it.

"Well, this many civilians banded together with this much fire power would make any government nervous."

"Maybe they should be nervous," Clay observed.

"Word is that your numbers nationwide are up near a million. That rivals the current military. Some wonder if you aren't planning to take over for yourself."

"Absolute power corrupts absolutely, is that it?" Clay set down his fork.

"Something like that, yeah." Finn nodded, not one to back down.

"I can assure you that we, and it is a 'we' in the Militia,

have no desire to take over the government. We have no intention of ruling."

"Then what are you doing, Clay?"

"Our mission is simple. We only want our current government to uphold the Constitution. That's it. Things out there are getting so corrupt, we figure a little back pressure to play it straight is the only way to encourage rightness."

"Who's definition of rightness?"

"It's a shared definition, the same one in the Constitution. If the government stays on the straight road, then we stay out of it. You can tell your superiors at the FBI and elsewhere, that they have nothing to fear from us, other than that."

"Elsewhere?" Finn's expression was reserved.

"You know what I'm talking about, Johnny. I know you don't want me to go into more detail here." Clay's face was dead serious.

"When will you be releasing us?" Finn deflected.

"Us? First of all, my sister isn't going anywhere with you. Secondly, now that you've been here, seen some of our mutual friends, I'm not at all sure that I can let you go. I'll need some time to think on it."

Clay rose from the table, which caused the other men to stand as well. Their meal was at an end even as the dawn light began its subtle illumination through an outside window pane. In the shuffle that followed, chairs scraped against the worn floor and men began to move about. Finn reached under the table and gave Ava's hand a brief squeeze. Heart beating fast, she ran her fingers over his knuckles. He wasn't free, yet. Maybe she could convince her brother to let Finn go. After all they had been through, she trusted him. And the man could keep a secret. If she asked him not to say anything about the Militia, she bet that he wouldn't.

As the men from the rescue crew dissipated, another stepped into view, taking his place beside Clay. His dark skin and almond eyes were striking. Dressed neatly, his military-style clothing fit over strong shoulders and long limbs. The handgun, that she could see, was displayed casually in a holster at his hip. This must be her brother's right-hand man because together they crossed the room to address Finn and herself.

"Ava, this is David Laurel." Clay tipped his head towards the man but didn't take his eyes from Finn. "You'll see a lot of him. I trust him with my life, so anything that needs to be said can be said in front of him. Okay?"

"Okay." She nodded, but knew he meant almost anything.

"I expect you are both tired, and in need of some sleep," Clay continued. "Maybe you're even up for a shower?"

"Yes," Ava replied. "I would love a shower."

Finn remained silent, still in the presence of captors.

"Let's set you up for that, but after I'd like a nurse to check you out. You're face looks awful and you can talk to her about girl stuff."

"Girl stuff?" Ava had to bait him, they both knew what she really wanted to talk about and it wasn't with a nurse. Where was Mason? When would she see him? But their present company prevented her from discussing it.

"I don't know what the hell happened to you in there," Clay huffed. "You're such a pain in the ass."

Reluctantly, Ava left Clay and Finn behind to follow David into the hall. The building itself appeared to be two stories, although there could have been a basement. It was large, with multiple doors leading to multiple rooms, all of them left open. Glancing in as they walked by, she glimpsed a kitchen, office, storage area, bunk room, and bathroom. Up the stairs to the second level, she marveled at the expanse of windows that let in all kinds of natural sunlight. The day was upon them now, with the lush evergreens sprawling over hillsides in the distance. For a moment, she paused at one, staring out. David let her, his energy a quiet patience at her back.

"It's beautiful isn't it?" She asked.

"What is?"

"The trees, the ground, the sky, the air." She held her palm up to the glass, felt the cold of the outside.

"Yes," he agreed. "We should keep going."

Towards the end of the hall they ducked into a bedroom. It had two twin beds arranged next to one another. Mismatched nightstands flanked either side, each one was made up of a different style of old wood. The eclectic look was completed by cheap ceramic lamps. Walking ahead of her, David pulled open the accordion door of a small closet. Inside there was a white dresser and several empty clothing hangars dangling from a bar.

"Your brother had a few of your things brought up here. Grab a change of clothes and then the shower is two doors down on the right. I'll be hanging out in the room just across the hall. Holler if you need anything."

His boots were cushioned by the thick brown carpeting as he let himself out. Pulling open the top drawer, Ava found a few bras, underwear, and a set of pajamas. The next drawer down stuck slightly when she tried to pull it open. Leaning into the dresser, she was able to bump it back onto the track and reveal a few sets of jeans and handful of folded shirts. The bottom contained white socks and a thick red jacket.

Scanning the floor of the closet, she spied a pair of her running shoes and her favorite black boots. There was only one problem. Spinning slowly on her heel she double-checked the space. None of Mason's things were here.

"Hey, David." Ava called through the still open door.

"Yes?" The tall man poked his head around the frame.

"Is my son here?"

"No kids."

"Can you tell Clay that I need to speak with him when he gets a chance?"

"Sure thing."

David bobbed his head before fading back into the hallway. Running her fingers over the pale pink flannel of her pajama pants, she tried not to feel concerned. It would be best now just to focus on getting through the shower and into bed. Once inside the bathroom, she twisted the brass knob lock on the old oak door. This would be her first private shower in so long that she almost forgot what it felt like.

Turning on the faucet, she let her hand dangle under the spray, waiting for it to warm up. With winter outside, the pipes took a bit of time to heat. Glancing over her shoulder, she spied her reflection in the large rectangular mirror. The side of her face was discolored by purplish-yellow bruising. Her cheek was swollen, blonde hair stringy and split. This was like that dreaded three a.m. bathroom break at a club. The one where you drunkenly survey your reflection in the mirror and wonder how anyone could find you attractive.

As steam took to the air, she climbed in and slid the shower curtain closed behind her. There was bar soap, shampoo and conditioner stuffed into a metal holder that dangled from the shower head. The space seemed narrow, almost claustrophobic after her forced open showers with Michael. Taking her time, she scrubbed at her tangle of greasy hair, applying shampoo twice.

Halfway through the process, she noticed a long thin window above her head that ran the length of the stall. Gasping, she reached up on her tip toes to slide it open. To her amazement a rush of cold air flowed briskly inside, swirling to push at the steam. Gulping it in, she laughed, almost hysterical. The luxury of opening a window was something that she would never take for granted again.

Finished with her shower, the adrenaline that had kept her going through this ordeal quickly began to wane. Exhaustion, both emotional and physical crept up behind her, licking decidedly at her heels. Dressed comfortably in her own pajamas, white tube socks encasing her aching feet, she crossed back to the little bedroom. Although she hadn't noticed him, David must have been on watch for her because no sooner had she sat on the edge of one mattress then he appeared.

"Clay wants our nurse to take a look at you," he reminded her.

"Now?" It was hard to keep the whine from her voice.

"Then we will leave you alone, I promise."

"Okay, send her in I guess."

As she waited Ava spread her hand over the worn quilt comforter. It was made up of blue and yellow squares, one positioned right on top of the other then surrounded every so often by a white strip border. Pretty, she thought, peering closer at the stitches, must be handmade. It was light outside, mid-morning, she gauged by the way the sun shone through the slats of blinds. Although the room itself was quite small, the lone window was a decent size, maybe four feet high and five feet across. She wondered if she would be cursed to forever keep track of windows from now on, having suffered in their absence.

"Hello." The woman who entered was taller than Ava but not by more than a few inches. A short bob of auburn hair was pinned back from her steady eyes, and her nose boasted a dusting of freckles.

"Hello," Ava answered.

"I'm Nurse Harper." Closing the door behind her, she turned back to Ava and extended a hand. "It's nice to meet you. Ava, right?"

"Yes, nice to meet you." Ava rose to shake hands briefly, then settled back on the bed.

"It sounds like you've been through a lot." Placing a small bag next to Ava, Nurse Harper pulled out a jar of ointment, bandages, and a bottle of pills. "Do you have any injuries aside from this one on your face?"

"No." Ava frowned as the nurse began to smooth the cream on her skin.

"Anything you would like to share with me? It will be just between us."

"Nope."

"I'm here to help."

Finishing up with the cream, the nurse shook several unmarked pills into Ava's hand. From her bag, she retrieved a bottle of water and unscrewed the cap. Offering the drink, Nurse Harper motioned for Ava to swallow the medicine.

"What is this stuff?" Ava speculated over the oblong white pills, there were no customary letters or numbers on them.

"It's for the pain." Nurse Harper fixed her face into an easy smile.

"Well." Ava's stomach churned. "I don't think I want to take them. Thanks, anyway."

"They will make you feel so much better. You should really just take them."

Holding the pills out towards the nurse, Ava waited for her to jerkily reopen the bottle and dump them back inside. Something was off here, Ava thought. Nurse Harper was a lot more torn up about the medicine then one would expect. Senses prickling, Ava watched her pack up the remaining contents into the brown leather bag. The pill bottle rattled as it hit bottom, then the snap of the ointment jar, rustle of bandages, and thunk of the untouched water bottle.

"So, thank you, anyway." Ava spoke carefully, watching the nurse's hands fumble for a moment inside the bag.

"No, thank you," Nurse Harper spat.

The odd change in tone had Ava tilting away ever so slightly. It was this instinct, in the end, that saved her. Faster than she could have imagined, Nurse Harper swung her hand up from the bag, a loaded syringe held tightly in her fist. Already shifting away, Ava was able to duck the downward blow that would have made easy contact with her upper arm.

Letting out a short cry, Ava scrambled off the bed, with the nurse in pursuit. As she tried to get away, Ava kicked out with her legs, causing the nurse to trip forward. They both watched as the needle flew through the air, bouncing to a stop in the thick carpet across the room. Adrenaline rocketed through her system as both women dove for the syringe. Coming up short, they wrestled with each other instead.

Pulling hair, grunting, and rolling about, the nurse was a

great deal heavier than she had appeared at first glance. In the background, Ava heard shouting, and a solid thump against the locked bedroom door. Using her superior size, the nurse leveraged herself over Ava, pinning her wriggling body against the floor. Hanging on, Ava tucked herself in close, preventing the other woman from crawling away to grab the needle.

As the door continued to take a beating, Ava's heart raced, and her eyes shot wide. Jerkily, she gathered the material of Nurse Harper's shirt, hiking it up to just behind the other woman's neck. As she had practiced with Finn, she sucked in a breath before pushing violently away. In one fluid movement, she flipped her off hand around the other side of the nurse's head.

Snapping her back in close, Ava pressed her forearms against the pink flesh of the other woman's neck, using the shirt to complete the circle of strangulation. Struggling, the gurgling sounds sputtered close to Ava's ear. She knew what this felt like, knew the terror. Squeezing her eyes shut against the nurse's panicked pupil stare, Ava held on.

TEN

ursting forth like a flood, the door finally gave way.
In tumbled Clay, David, and Finn. Blinking up, she
could see their faces circle strangely in the air just
above her, shouting down. She could hear them calling for her
to let go as they tried to drag the nurse off. Despite her brain
sending signals to her body, Ava's arms just wouldn't release.
It wasn't until Finn tapped her hurriedly on the shoulder, his
sign for defeat when they practiced, that she felt safe enough
to give in.

Dropping away, she was sucked back into her own body
just as the nurse was hoisted up into the air. Gasping, choking, sputtering, the nurse drew oxygen into deprived lungs.
Scooping Ava up, Finn cradled her against him before sitting
heavily on the edge of the bed. Arms wrapped around his
neck, she clung to his body, refusing to look at anything but
his chest. She had done this thing, this bad thing, but she was
alive. Because of what Finn had taught her, she was still alive.

"What the hell happened?!" Clay yelled.

"The nurse went inside and closed the door," David

explained, panting. "She must have locked it. I heard the sounds of a struggle but couldn't get back in."

"Is she one of yours?" Finn accused.

"She's supposed to be," Clay answered, then addressed the woman. "Who do you work for? The LO?"

Ava listened as the woman spit into her brother's face. He had his answer.

"David," Clay instructed. "Take her downstairs. Put her in the holding room that Finn was in. I'll be down shortly."

"You've been infiltrated," Finn spoke through gritted teeth after David and another man had hauled the nurse out. "What in the hell did you take from these people, Clay?"

"Not what," Ava murmured, turning her face to look at her brother. "Who."

Grimacing, Clay paced the room once before attempting to swing shut the battered door. The lock was splintered at the frame and so wouldn't catch to hold. The door itself was largely intact, so he satisfied himself by propping it up as best he could. Running stressed fingers through his thick chestnut hair, her brother's hazel eyes took on a stressed appearance.

"I didn't take her, exactly," he admitted. "More like she wanted to get out, so I helped."

"Who?" Finn was still in the dark.

"Sophia Lockett," Ava whispered.

"Robert Lockett's daughter?" Finn was incredulous. "You aren't serious."

"The last time that I saw her, she chose to stay in. She couldn't leave her father and the empire he built. So, six months ago when she showed up on my doorstep, it was a surprise, but I couldn't refuse her. I only gave her what she needed to disappear. If I would have known that the LO would trace her back to me, then..." he trailed off.

"Then you would've done it anyway." Ava finished for him.

"I don't want a war with the LO." Clay pinched the bridge of his nose.

"Well, now you've got one," Finn countered. "And you can't keep your own sister safe."

"Yes, I can." Clay glared at him. "I just need to clean house."

"That could take months." Finn pointed out. "What about tonight? Tomorrow?"

"Clay-" Ava blanched. "Where's Mason?"

"He's safe." Clay waved her off.

"If he's not in this house, then you better get a hold of him right now!" She yelled, pulse jumping.

"He's not here," Clay admitted. "But I'll make a call."

"I want to talk to him."

"You will." Clay's eyes darted to Finn, then back to her, a warning.

Ava tried to stand, but Finn held her in place. She felt the dread of not knowing, and the flood of outrage at her brother's behavior. In his defense he felt that they were still in the presence of an FBI Agent, one whom he did not trust. It took all of her self-control to stop struggling and bite her tongue. For a moment, Clay went to walk out, but at the door he hesitated. Surveying Finn, he clearly had reservations about leaving them alone in the room.

"Give me a gun," Finn persuaded. "I'll protect her."

"Yeah right, like I'm going to give you a weapon so you can blast your way out of here using my sister as a shield."

"Fine, no weapon, but I'll stay with her. What do you think I've been doing this past month?"

"It's okay, Clay, I trust him. He could have killed me a million times before now."

"You have no idea who he really is," Clay reproached her, but then shoved out of the room.

Left alone, Finn cupped her face and applied a soothing kiss to her lips. The warm rush of feeling that he kindled in her helped to distract from worry over Mason's well-being. Frowning now, she gave her head a slight shake. Pieces of a long ago puzzle were finally clicking into place. She remembered what Clay had said at the hospital so many years ago. At the time, Ava had agreed that she shouldn't have more details, but now that seemed like a poor choice. Mind jumping to the present, Ava flashed to the nurse once more, she could almost hear the sound of her wheezing.

"I hated it. I hated doing that," Ava mumbled.

"You had me scared. It took way too long to break down the door." Finn closed his eyes, trying to rid himself of the feeling. "All we could hear was someone dying."

"If you hadn't taught me that stuff-"

"Shhh," he whispered. "It's not safe for you here or anywhere that you've ever been. You've got to disappear."

She was too tired just now, strung out on anxiety and stress. The idea of running seemed an impossible hurtle to leap. All she could hope for at this point was to hear that Mason was okay. Only then would she be able to sink into an all-encompassing sleep. Minutes later, Clay reentered the room. Mason was perfectly fine, missing her, but thinking he was on the vacation of a lifetime. Ava's heart pitched with a mix of relief and concern. Where was he? Who had him? She thought she could venture a pretty good guess. When she got her brother alone, she would get answers.

For a few moments, she listened as Clay and Finn argued. Her brother insisted that Finn leave the room, and of course, Finn refused. Finally, they reached a compromise. The door would remain open and Finn wouldn't leave the other bed. Surrendering to the inevitable, Ava crawled under the quilt of her mattress and groaned as her head hit a real honest to goodness pillow.

Watching her for a beat, Finn spread his palms over the blanket, smoothing down the fabric around her. When he shifted to turn off the lights, she stopped him. They had spent too many nights sleeping in the dark, light was welcome, light was good. Seeming to nod in understanding, Finn sighed as he slipped into the neighboring bed.

It came on quickly then, a deep abiding sleep, one that belonged to a journeyer upon reaching their far-off destination. No thoughts rushed up to meet her. No dreams disturbed the trance. It engulfed Ava with its consuming, gentle embrace. They say you cannot fully appreciate the good until you've endured the bad. Ava appreciated this sleep more than any in her life.

WHEN SHE WOKE, THE LIGHT THROUGH THE WINDOWS WAS waning, but the lamp at her bedside burned bright. Sitting up, she felt groggy from too much sleep, although it appeared to be dusk, which meant she hadn't slept for more than a few hours. Looking over at the other bed, she noted that Finn was still out cold. The steady rise and fall of the blankets draped across his bare back were comforting.

Swinging her feet over the side, Ava relished the soft squish of thick carpeting through her white socks. Shuffling slowly, she crossed the threshold of their open door and peered down the hall. It was empty, devoid of human traffic. Making her way to the bathroom, she flicked on the light, then locked the door. The window above the shower was still open, letting in its rush of cold air, just the way she had left it. Somewhere in the building, the heater cycled back on, pushing warm air out of the ceiling vent. After using the toilet, she examined her face in the mirror. Longing for makeup, she ran her fingers over her cheek, noting that the swelling was going down somewhat.

Back in the hall, she encountered David. His lanky figure leaned causally against the wall.

"Rise and shine," he said. "How're you feeling?"

"Good, thanks," she replied. "Have I missed dinner?"

"Dinner?" He chuckled. "It's dawn. You missed the rest of yesterday, but breakfast should be served soon."

"Oh, wow." She paused, thinking. "Clay up yet?"

"His room is at the end." David gestured.

"He sleep alone?"

"Always."

Nodding her thanks, she walked past him towards the appointed door. It didn't hurt to ask, after all, she didn't know what his current dating status was. Sophia had popped back into his life, but it sounded brief. Men dealt with their failed relationships a lot differently, so it was entirely possible that he drowned his feelings in the company of other women. Sophia, Sophia, he had mentioned her only once back when they had first started dating.

Breaching his closed bedroom door, Ava didn't bother to knock, never had. Although it was unlocked, Clay still shot upright in bed, swinging a dark handgun to level at the intruder. Raising her hands simply, Ava froze. A blink or two later, he threw out a string of curses before shoving the gun back under his pillow. Laying down, he attempted to bury himself deep in the covers, hoping she would go away. This was a familiar game they had played for as long as she could remember.

"It's morning," she said, sitting heavily on the edge of the bed.

"Go away," he grunted.

"But it's morning, the sun is coming up." She bounced on the edge, sending uncomfortable ripples through the mattress.

"Ava." He sighed. "You may have slept the entire day, but I didn't have that luxury."

"We need to talk, Clay." Her voice grew serious. "She has him, doesn't she? Sophia Lockett."

Groaning, he rolled over to face her. They appraised one another. In this way, they had woken each other for nearly every day of their shared lives until he left for basic training. Sometimes it was him up early, other times it was her. This was when they had shared their secrets, told the truth, asked for help, planned their day.

"Yes," he admitted. "She has him, but he couldn't be safer with anyone else right now."

"Will I ever get him back? I'm his mommy now, Clay. I love him." Her heart tripped fearfully.

"Yes," he assured her. "You will get him back, when it's safe."

"How can you be sure that she can protect him? Her father and the whole LO are looking for her."

"She learned a thing or two from her dad and I set her up with everything they'll need. In a few months, we'll transfer him back to you. It's just that right now, you aren't safe either," he reasoned.

"I don't know how I'm supposed to do this." Her voice pinched with emotion.

"Hey-" He shook her shoulder a little. "She's supposed to send little videos and pictures of him once a month. I'll send them to you, too. This is what's best for him. That's the goal in all this remember?"

"Yeah." She nodded, steeling herself. "That's the goal. But why can't I hide with them? Can I call him? Talk to him?"

"You are a target now and the LO will be looking for you wherever you go, not to mention the FBI. We can't risk having you around Mason, drawing attention to where they are. As for calling him, it can't be too frequent. I can't risk having someone trace the lines. I never thought it would play out this way," he acknowledged finally. "I'm sorry."

"I can't do this!" Ava shouted suddenly, tears welling in her eyes, her heart breaking in her chest. "You're asking me to be away from him for months!"

"Mason is safe." Clay's hazel eyes searched Ava's, willing her to understand. "People in the military leave their families for months at a time, sometimes years. If they can do it, so can you. It's what's best for Mason."

"Damn you, Clay." Ava wiped at her eyes, sucking in a shaky breath.

"How do you think we've done it all these years? Because we put his needs before our own. You can do it, too. I know you can."

Unable to talk further, Ava rose to leave. She heard her brother's frustrated sigh as he sank back into his bed. Angry and hurting, she shut the door on him, not bothering to look back. Weaving down the hall, she felt dazed and raw. At the threshold to the small bedroom she stopped and watched Finn sleep. He had shifted his position, but his breathing was still regular, shallow. Glancing down at her pajamas, she tugged absently at the fabric, then decided to change into some real clothes as quietly as she could. A walk outside was the only thing that sounded good to her.

Not wanting to wake him, she eased open the various drawers of the dresser, pulling out a pair of skinny jeans, lace thong, matching bra and long-sleeve blue shirt. Stepping out of her pajamas, she hopped on one foot, trying to regain her balance. Naked and close to falling over, she steadied herself on the dresser just as Finn's voice broke the silence.

"This is a pretty good way to wake up." His voice was husky.

"You're supposed to be sleeping," she admonished, but swiveled around to face him as she finished getting dressed. The look of misery that filled her was plain.

"What's wrong?" His eyes were thoughtful, roaming her face for the answer. "Something happened."

"I can't have Mason back." Ava's voice cracked and she turned away, wanting to hide the tears that threatened to fall.

"Who says?" Finn's voice was gentle as he threw back the covers and approached her.

"Clay."

Still facing the closet, Ava felt his hands come to rest on her shoulders. He rotated her around, then pulled her in close against him. Applying soft kisses to the top of her head, Finn worked to comfort and soothe.

"Who has him?" He murmured.

"I can't tell you." A sob hitched in her throat. "I can't tell you anything."

"Alright. It's alright."

Falling silent, Finn simply stood, keeping his arms wrapped around her while she fought the flood of sadness. Clay was right, of course. Things were all messed up, and she was suddenly in the middle of a war game she knew nothing about. She didn't want Mason anywhere near it, and by extension that meant near her. Now the only option available to Ava was to wait. Clay had mentioned a few months, so she clung to that timeline and worked to calm herself down.

"What can I do?" Finn asked finally.

"I want to go outside."

"Outside sounds good, just let me get dressed."

Managing a nod, Ava watched him paw through a black duffle bag that had been shoved in the corner of the room. The guys must have found him some extra clothes because Finn pulled out a pair of military style pants and long-sleeve thermal shirt. Following him down the stairs, she glanced absently at the trees through the windows. His hand still holding hers felt natural, it felt right.

The scent of cooking had them detouring from the hall to linger in the kitchen. A short woman with pleasant rolls and jet-black hair hovered over the stove top. Hair piled atop her head in a tight bun, she introduced herself as Rhonda, and offered them each a seat at the bar. On the refrigerator just beside her hung a sign that read:

Never trust a skinny cook.

Tongue tucked in her cheek, Ava thought that this woman was everything she could ever want for in a chef.

A lone coffee pot dripped and sputtered. The sound was like a siren song, calling them closer. When was the last time she had a cup of coffee? Too long, Ava thought, her mouth watering. The kitchen itself was average in size, comparable to one you would find in any large home. Formica counters colored a speckled shade of brown stretched along two walls to form an L shape.

Rhonda worked happily over the older model stove top; the propane burners had strips of bacon crackling in a cast iron pan. As she cooked, she chatted amiably about her work for the Militia. She told them that the building they were in was a headquarters of sorts, but this was the busiest she had seen it. Mostly the local guys used the facility for training and monthly meetings. When the word had gone out that Clay Montgomery himself would be occupying the property, the local chapter had buzzed with excitement. They were all eager to contribute in any way possible.

"Any chance for waffles?" Finn asked sweetly, and had Ava smiling. He remembered her request from inside the cage.

"Nope, sorry." Rhonda didn't break stride. "We don't have the griddle for it. I can make you some pancakes instead."

Rolling her eyes at Finn's little victory fist pump, Ava took the liberty of searching through the oak cabinets. Coffee cups, Ava frowned, no sane person stocked a kitchen without them. She hit the motherlode on the third door she opened, it housed a sea of thick white mugs. Selecting three, she strummed her thumbs impatiently along the counter. Ava watched the dying sputters of the full pot of coffee with unwavering lust. Just tell me these people have French Vanilla creamer and I'll die a happy woman, she thought.

Pouring the dark liquid into the three cups, Ava set the first one next to the stove for Rhonda, who bobbed her head appreciatively. Sliding in next to Finn, Ava handed him another. He had pulled up a stool at the bar that ran along the edge of the center island sink. Feet now laced up in hand-me-down boots, he sipped at the black swirl of heaven, moaning out his ecstasy.

"Rhonda." He breathed between gulps. "You have no idea what this single cup means to me."

"Well, honey," she huffed, before cackling. "I can think of a few ways for you to thank me."

Finn's mouth dropped open in surprise and Ava couldn't contain the swell of laughter that erupted from her lips. Without batting an eye, Rhonda laid out two plates on the bar. They were heaped generously with bacon, eggs and hash-browns. Tucking in, Ava and Finn dropped into silence, enjoying their first real breakfast together. It was the one that they had debated so often on the inside.

"I see you've met Rhonda." Clay's voice had them jumping.

Ava scowled, still upset by their earlier discussion. Although deep down she knew Clay was right, admitting that fact was going to be hard for her. They all had to make sacrifices for the benefit of Mason, and now it was her turn. Though she wasn't sure exactly how she was going to bear it, she recognized that other people did it every day.

Pouring his own cup of coffee, Clay was already alert and dressed for the day. He rooted around in the refrigerator for a few moments before selecting the milk, no French Vanilla after all. Exchanging pleasantries with Rhonda, he helped himself to a plate of food, then swung down to sit beside Ava. Determined to prove she could handle anything, she listened in subdued silence to his absent talk of the weather and local fishing prospects. It wasn't long before he had her flashing back to their childhood. Their father loved to fish. A mild ache formed, then dissipated.

Much to Ava's surprise, Clay and Finn conversed easily. They talked football, traded jabs about opposing teams, and reminisced on a friendly game of touch they had won together when they were back in the service. Throughout the conversation Ava remained reserved. Sitting between them, she hoped they could reach some sort of understanding wherein Finn would be released, but not cause Clay any harm.

As more men wandered in to grab a bite, Ava got up to clear her plate and make room for the hungry guys to sit. Finn followed her lead, dropping his dish into the sink next to hers. Grabbing a dry towel, he stood waiting while she scrubbed the dirties with a soapy sponge. Just when she thought she was done, Clay handed over his plate, too. Complaining loudly, she snatched it from him, but continued to wash.

"When you two finish up in here," Clay directed. "I need to speak with you in the office. It's just down the hall."

"Got it." Ava nodded her head, not watching him walk out.

Over the next half hour, the dirty dishes dropped steadily into her soapy hands. To his credit, Finn never wavered in his duty. Calmly, he rinsed and dried the plates, setting them carefully back into the cupboard. When the last man had his fill, Rhonda released them to go. Ava offered to start on the pans but was waved away. Rhonda explained that she appreciated the relief in the dish cleaning but was content to do the rest by herself.

Not one to beg for extra work, Ava took Finn's hand in her own and booked it out of there. She steered them towards the office she had spied the night before, or had it been the previous day? Prior to entering, Ava wriggled her hand away from Finn's, causing him to give her another questioning look. With everything that was going on with Mason, Ava felt it would be better if Clay didn't know the level of connection between them just yet. He had wanted her to remain single until Mason was out of the house, and she understood why.

Still simmering with resentment towards her brother, Ava knocked rapidly against the closed office door. Clay hated the incessant tapping, always had. Anything that caused irritation to him, had her smirking in sisterly triumph.

"Come in, already!" Clay shouted through the oak. "I swear you are the most annoying person on the planet."

"Right back at you!" She called, as Finn twisted the brass knob and swung the door wide.

The office was larger than she had expected. It was about twice as long as it was wide with several desks, each topped by a computer. Positioned at the far end, one long conference table had eight identical chairs ranged evenly around it. Unlike the rest of the building, which contained a mish-mosh of various furnishings, the desks, table, and chairs were all new and they all matched. The laptops were sleek and modern. A large television monitor hung from the far wall but was switched off.

Swiveling around in the leather office chair behind the nearest desk, Clay clicked a few times at the keyboard before rising to greet them. He indicated that they should sit together at the conference table, but in typical fashion arranged the seating according to his liking. Ava would be sitting by Clay's side, with Finn directly opposite, interrogation style.

"So, let's address the elephant in the room," Clay began, leveling a steady look at Finn. "The FBI picked up my sister, triggered my nephew into going underground, and then got her kidnapped by the LO. When I say the FBI, of course I mean you."

"Clay, that's not fair." Ava leapt to Finn's defense, but was silenced with a formal look.

"I accept responsibility for all of that." Finn nodded. "We should have been more aware of the situation revolving around Ava before we moved on her. In our defense, you hid how vulnerable her circumstances were very well. So well, in fact, that she wasn't even aware of them."

"Her best chance for a normal life was to be in the dark," Clay objected.

"Well, I'm not anymore," Ava ventured, but drew no confirming looks from either of the men.

"The problem I have now," Clay went on. "Is that you're still an FBI Agent, and they're going to want you back. I couldn't just leave you in the custody of the LO, but now you've seen too much."

"What if he promises not to say anything about the Militia?" Ava ventured hopefully, but Finn wouldn't meet her gaze.

"Are you kidding?" Clay actually laughed. "Old Johnny Rule Book is going to go against regulation? That's never happened."

"Johnny Rule Book?" Ava questioned.

"That's what we called Finn back in our Program days. He never met a rule he didn't like." Clay leaned back in his chair. "Isn't that right?"

"That's right," Finn acknowledged.

"Speaking of which," Clay went on. "You're still in the Program, which means the FBI was your designated target. What's the end game for you? Director?"

"You know I can't answer that." Finn's face remained cool.

"I'm so confused." Ava's eyes darted between their faces.

"The Program isn't a military training tool," Clay explained, making Finn shift uncomfortably. "They assign each member a target career. With years of work, the member could become a judge, a governor, a senator, you get the idea. The end goal is for almost every major player in our political system to be a member of the Program. It would give the overseers an unprecedented amount of power."

"What?" Ava breathed, searching Finn's face for confirmation.

"You should never have told her that," Finn accused. "You've put her at serious risk."

"No," Clay countered. "You've put her at serious risk."

"I'm not the one who's rival organization just tried to kill her," Finn seethed. "What are you going to do about that?"

"I can keep her safe," Clay countered. "I just need a few months to clean house."

"And during that time?"

"I'll stash her," Clay frowned. "What do you care?"

"Alone? She doesn't know the first thing about staying hidden, she'll be a sitting duck. Let me hide her."

"Let you?" Clay was incredulous. "So you can march her back to the Feds? Not a chance."

"He would never do that," Ava protested. "I trust him, Clay."

"You trust him? You keep saying that." Clay turned his

attention to her for the first time since sitting down. Looking her over, he analyzed her face carefully. "What could he have done to make you trust him with your life?"

"I just do." Ava glanced away from her brother's prying eyes, but he knew her too well.

"No." Clay shifted to look at Finn, then back to Ava. "There's no way. You're his witness, he would never break regulation, it would compromise his whole case."

When no one spoke, Clay slammed his hands down on the table. Standing up, he leaned across the breach, staring at the other man. After a few seconds, Finn was forced to look away as well.

"Come on Clay," Ava protested. "I'm not a sixteen-year-old girl, anymore."

"You son-of-a-bitch!" Clay pointed angrily. "You put your hands on my little sister, I should have left you with the LO!"

"It's not like that," Finn replied weakly.

"Not like what?" Clay was outraged, pacing the room in an attempt to burn through his fury. "You took advantage of her while she was scared and being abused. There are only two reasons that you, of all people, would do that. Only two."

"Stop it!" Ava interjected, but was ignored. "He didn't take advantage of me."

"Reason number one." Clay sat back down. Propping his elbows on the table, he leveled Finn a steady look. "You didn't break any regulation because she is the assignment. The Program ordered you to seduce Ava to get to me."

"Is that true?" Ava's heart thudded painfully as she searched Finn's face.

"No." Finn shook his head.

"I'm supposed to take your word on that?" Clay pressed,

then went on. "Okay, fine. You've accomplished your mission. We can set up a video conference with the FBI or the Program overseers. I'll answer their questions, return you to them, and designate you as the only one that I'll work with. It would make your career. The only catch is, you can never see Ava again. You don't look at her, don't touch her, don't know where she is, don't hunt her down. Deal?"

Holding her breath, Ava watched Clay extend his hand to shake over the table. Tears welled at the back of her eyes and her heart beat in a pitiful fashion. Could it actually be possible that Finn had used her? That she was nothing more than a means to an end? They had only known each other for a relatively short time, so why did this feel so much like betrayal?

Refusing to meet her gaze, Finn focused all of his attention on Clay. The former teammates examined one another as Clay's hand hovered in the air between them. Remaining perfectly still, Finn's eyes never wavered. After what seemed a long time, he folded his arms defiantly over his chest. He couldn't shake on it. Ava exhaled.

"That leaves reason number two." Clay withdrew his hand. "You've got feelings for her."

"Stop, Clay." Ava clutched at her brother's arm, but he shrugged her off. Finn gave no verbal answer, but his eyes darted to Ava once before shifting away.

"The problem with feelings," Clay continued. "Is that they are so damn hard to prove. If I'm going to let you hide my sister, then I've got to really, really believe you'll put her ahead of your mission. That is so hard to swallow, knowing your history."

"I can promise you that I'll keep her safe." Finn's voice remained steady.

"That's not good enough."

"I trust him," Ava persuaded.

"You trust him?" Clay spat, turning his head to stare into her eyes. "You think you know him?"

"Yes."

"Did he tell you that he's married?"

ELEVEN

"You can be a real prick, you know that Clay?" Finn shot him a dirty look.

"You're married?" Ava's jaw hung slack with the shock of it.

"It's not what you think."

"Are you, or are you not married?!" Ava shouted it.

Shoving up to standing, her heart pitched with a sudden rage that seemed to burst from every pore. After all of the time spent talking in the cage, all of the information that had been shared between them, he had never, not once, mentioned another woman. Reaching out with both hands, he leaned across the wooden surface between them, imploring.

"Legally, yes," he admitted. "But I had to be as part of the Program."

"A good candidate for FBI Director has a wife, right?" Clay interjected.

"Shut up, Clay," Finn growled, his nervous eyes tracking Ava.

Leaning back in his chair, Clay observed the fallout from

the bomb he had just released. His face was cool, this was clearly a strategic move on his part. If you want to know how a man feels about a woman, watch what he does when you try to take her away.

Pushing down on the sorrow that threatened to take over, Ava covered her face with trembling hands. Slowly, she blew out a breath. She wasn't sure if she hated him or the strength of her reaction more. How could she have let this man get under her skin so easily? Clay had been right all along, there should be no men while she had Mason, ever. It was not worth the risk, and it certainly wasn't worth the devastation that now filled her chest. While she struggled, Finn crept slowly around the side of the table. Lightly, he let his fingers curl around her upper arms.

"Do not touch me," she said, shrugging away.

"Ava, please," Finn pleaded. "We've never even slept together, okay? She's part of the Program, too."

"You expect me to believe that?"

"I expect you to believe the truth." Finn's eyes searched hers. "She means nothing to me."

"Said every cheating husband ever," Ava seethed. "Clay, I'm not going anywhere with this man."

Skirting around Finn, Ava made tracks for the door. She didn't want him to see just how badly this hurt. Pushing past leather office chairs and tripping around a desk, her vision narrowed on the singular brass knob. Escape. Behind her, she could hear Clay get to his feet and Finn quicken his steps to catch up.

Just before she got to the door, she felt the brush of a hand at her elbow. Gripping her adeptly, Finn spun her around and forced her to glance briefly into his face. It was filled with panic. Planting both of her hands firmly against his chest, she shoved him once, hard. At first, he rocked back a step, but it was only to gain better footing.

"Get away from me," she demanded, and pushed him again, but he clutched at her wrists, pinning her arms easily at her side.

"You can hate me all you want." Finn's voice was low. "It still doesn't change the fact that your life is in danger. Your brother can't protect you and you can't hide yourself. Do you ever want to see Mason again?"

"Yes," she hissed, the last sentence getting her attention.

"Then let me do this," he reasoned. "Let me keep you safe. It's only for a few months."

"No."

"Actually, yes." Clay reached between them, releasing Finn's hold on her arms. "You will be going with Johnny, after all."

"What?!" Ava railed at her brother.

"You may not be convinced," Clay continued. "But now I am. With my help, he will make you vanish until all of this blows over."

"Screw you both," she fumed.

Reaching a hand behind her, Ava grasped blindly for the door handle. Upon finding it, she twisted firmly and sprinted to make her escape. Except, now she didn't need to run, they made no move to follow. Racing up the staircase anyway, she took the steps two at a time before launching herself down the narrow hall and into her bedroom. When she slammed the crooked door, it ricocheted off of the disjointed frame, causing her to jump back. She had forgotten that it was broken. With a door that wouldn't shut there could be no privacy, and it was privacy that she desperately needed.

Running frustrated fingers through her hair, she turned on her heel, lungs heaving from the quick ascent to the second floor. Clouds shifted in a stiff wind outside the window, throwing shapes across the carpet. If she was outside then she could actually go for a run. Then it dawned on her, there wasn't anything stopping her.

Tearing through the dresser drawers she discovered one errant set of black yoga pants. As fast as she could, she changed into them, then laced up her running shoes. Jogging back down the way she had come, she noted David's lifted eyebrow as she cruised by him on the first floor. Picking up to a run, she tore past the doorway where Finn and Clay's voices could be heard drifting out.

"Where do you think you're going?!" Clay called.

Refusing to break stride, she slammed through the side door and into the open. Lungs pulling in the shock of icy cold air, Ava sped over the concrete driveway. A quick survey of the tree line had her spying a well-worn path. Checking her speed, she entered the thick cover with a hint of caution, footfalls slapping against the uneven dirt footing.

The trail was narrow, but well traversed by the men that worked there. It must lead to something, she thought, and she intended to find out what. Muscles that hadn't been used in over a month screamed their protest, but she relished the burn. Constructive pain like this helped to dominate the destructive kind that now coursed through her veins. Pumped by a jilted heart, her blood ran hot. For a while, murderous thoughts threatened, but the further she got into the thick of forest, the better she felt. Her body strained, dragging in each breath to fill laboring lungs. Pushing past the initial round of dizziness, she began to even out, regain awareness and strength.

After a mile or so, her pace slowed. Dialing it back, she took notice of the change in slope. The trail tilted forward, winding its way down through the forest. As it began to snake and twist, she was forced into an easy jog. Just as a hint of trepidation gathered itself in her mind, the tree line gave suddenly away.

Stopping short, she surveyed a small lake, its beautiful expanse of blue water was so clear that it reflected the clouds like a mirror image of the sky. Tall pines covered the hill sides, coming all the way down to the water's edge. Panting, she put her hands on top of her head and resumed a brisk walk.

Beside the shoreline, she paced back and forth, giving her body a chance to cool down. This must be the fishing spot her brother had been going on about that morning. It was isolated, pristine in its sanctity. Bending low, she traced her fingers along the still edge. Cold. The water was very cold.

Ears tingling, she heard the jogging footfalls of another person making their way down the path. Ava could only guess which one of them had come after her. Refusing to acknowledge the newcomer, she kept her back to the woods. Underneath the water, old fallen logs lay haphazardly along the floor. It was so clear that she could see a few fish swim by.

"You can really run." An unfamiliar voice intoned.

"David." She glanced over her shoulder, then rose to face him. "They sent you?"

"An uninvolved third party." He smiled. "Peace negotiator."

"Ha, ha, ha," she mocked, but couldn't withhold a return

smile, he seemed like a nice enough guy. "Sounds like dangerous work."

"You fish?" He asked.

"Not since I was a kid," she replied, thrown off balance by the change in topic. "You?"

"Oh, yeah." He nodded, eyes surveying the water. "My dad and I used to go once a month."

"Used to?"

"Well, now we've cut it down to twice a year. But since I've been up here, I've gone almost every day. I wish I could take him."

"Why can't you?" She watched his eyes dance as he crouched at the shoreline.

"Because he thinks that I'm a stock broker living in New York," he admitted.

"You're in the Program, too?" She was surprised.

"I was in the Program, but your brother got me out."

"You've known Clay for a long time."

"And Finn." He glanced up at her. "If Johnny Rule Book went against regulation, then it must have been for a pretty amazing reason."

"No comment." She didn't want to think of him.

"Look." David stood to face her. "Everyone who joined the Program did so because they take the protection of this country very seriously. We were all prepared to give up our lives for the sake of doing what was best for our people. Sometimes that meant fashioning fake lives in order to accomplish the ultimate goal. In Finn's case, and some others, it meant having a spouse."

"Don't try to defend him."

"It's not like he got to pick her out. She's in the Program, too. She needed a spouse, too. I can't speak to what happened between them, but I can tell you that it wasn't either of their idea. It's just part of the job."

"Did you get married?" She asked, hoping to pin him into a corner.

"Almost. I probably would have, but then I ran into Clay. He'd been out for a year but I still trusted him. In the end, your brother convinced me that the Program overseers have ulterior motives. Since then, we've turned a few more. They've agreed to stay in, work a double-shift so to speak. Johnny isn't quite there, yet."

"What are you trying to say?" She studied him. "You want me to try to turn Finn? I'm no spy."

"No." He laughed. "You're no spy, but Johnny is as close as it gets. Maybe you could cut the guy some slack for what he did before he met you."

"I think it would be easier to simply not like you, either," she mumbled, not wanting to give in.

"Fair enough."

"You're pretty good at this, though," she admitted, before he turned to walk away. "Are you the designated negotiator of the group?"

"Something like that." He cracked a small smile as she moved to go with him.

ONCE THE SHOCK OF EMOTION HAD WORN OFF, AVA'S BODY trembled with overexertion. A workout that would have barely fazed her before practically blew her over now. Feeling faint and hungry, she followed David to the meeting room where they had eaten that first day. Finn and Clay were already sitting, heads together, discussing something over lunch. Purposefully ignoring them, Ava chose a seat at the far end of the table. David pulled up a chair across the way and engaged her in friendly conversation.

Lunch was again served family style. Selecting a roast beef sandwich, Ava helped herself to a double side of French fries. David looked impressed. Fixing her face with her most charming smile, they chatted together about the upcoming holiday season and the best toys for little kids. Apparently, David had three nieces and one nephew that he was desperate to buy the most annoying things for.

It wasn't hard to convince him that if he wanted to be the best uncle, but the worst brother, he should get them a puppy. He was sold on the idea, and they laughed companionably. In the back of her mind, Ava could almost hear Mason's pleas for a puppy. Now she wished she had gotten him one after all. Stomach turning, Ava excused herself and rose to leave. She could feel Finn's eyes follow her to the exit. Let him look, she thought ruefully.

Rhonda was busy in the kitchen when Ava stepped up to scrub her own dish. She was already prepping for dinner, despite having just served lunch. Rhonda claimed that she didn't mind the work, insisting that cooking was her passion. When Finn eased up beside her with his dirty plate, Ava sighed and shoved back from the counter. Listening to his dish clatter clumsily into the sink, she felt his presence behind her as she crossed the threshold into the hall.

"Not you again." She gritted her teeth, refusing to stop her forward progress.

"Yes, me," Finn insisted. "We need to talk."

Ignoring him, she took her time climbing the stairs. Maybe

the run had been a little overzealous in her current physical condition. Her thighs quivered with each additional step, but she refused to let it show. Pausing at the second-floor window, she pretended to look out, but really just needed the time to let her muscles settle. Even with the full plate of food, her body trembled.

Finn leaned against a nearby wall, surveying her in silence. Ava hoped he didn't notice her weakness. With a sigh, she finally left the window, and walked carefully down the hall into their shared bedroom. Once inside, she sat gingerly on the bed, kicking off her running shoes with first one toe, then the other. Before he could say anything, she lay down on her back and threw one arm across her eyes.

"Are you feeling alright?" He asked.

"I'm fine."

"You can't run off like that when we leave here together."

"I'm not going anywhere with you."

"Yes, you are."

"What was it you told me back in the cage?" She tossed the words up in the air, not bothering to uncover her eyes. "Oh, yeah. I only withhold information from you to protect you, Ava. That was it."

"I couldn't tell you about Stephanie because then I would have had to tell you about the Program," Finn explained.

"Stephanie." She rolled the name around in her mouth, wanting to feel the taste of it. "You expect me to believe that you married a woman and then never slept with her."

"We have to stay married for the Program, we figured the best way to do that was to not let sex cloud our mission," Finn said. "It's a piece of paper, Ava, that's it."

"Honestly, I hate that it bothers me so much, I don't understand why," she admitted.

"Because you feel it, too." Finn's voice was urgent. "Don't you?"

"I feel like I don't know you, that's what I feel."

"You're pissed because you've spent the last month with someone, only to find out that person doesn't exist."

"That sounds about right."

"What if I could prove to you that's not true? What if I could show you that you're the only person who really knows me? Would that change your mind?" Finn had moved closer, easing himself to sit next to her on the bed.

"Are you legally married to Stephanie?"

"Johnathan Finn of the FBI is legally married to Stephanie," he qualified.

"Are you Johnathan Finn?"

"Yes."

"Do you work for the FBI?"

"Yes."

"I hate you." She scooted away from him.

"You'll have to see it to believe it. Just give me a chance, let me hide you," he persuaded.

"Fine." She briefly moved her arm to look at him. "But until then, get off my bed."

"Deal."

She wished he would just leave the room but instead he flopped down on the mattress across from her. Thoughts jumbled themselves inside her head, clamoring for position. David had said Finn was as close to a spy as it gets, but David had been out of the Program for years by his own admission. On the other hand, these guys all seemed to know each other really well. Whatever training they had undergone for the four years they were together had really created a bond. Now Finn himself had become a riddle, hinting around his fake marriage with bogus legalities. She hated riddles.

Eventually, the war that raged in her mind was overpowered by the level of fatigue in her body. She thought of Mason and Clay, then wondered where her son was. Shifting on her side, Ava reached for the picture of him with that Cheshire Cat grin on his face, the one Clay had given her in the helicopter. Running her fingers over it, she pressed it to her chest and exhaled a shaky breath. She could do this... for him. Floating on her back, she felt sleep swimming towards her from deep underneath. Easing its arms around her body, it carefully sucked her under, and she succumbed.

An hour later she woke to the harsh knocking of her brother on the doorframe. Feeling the most rejuvenated she had in a long time, Ava propped herself up on an elbow to glare at him. Clay's hair was mussed and his eyes were bloodshot. He must have been staring at a computer screen while she napped. When they were kids, he could play war games online for days on end. Ever the enabler, she had fetched him snacks and drinks in exchange for being allowed to watch. In those days, it had been an honor not to get booted from his room.

"I need a word," he said.

"I think you've had too many of those with me today," Ava informed him. "My quota has been reached."

Hovering just beyond Clay's figure, she could see David stifle a laugh, covering his mouth with one hand. Frowning,

Clay sucked in a breath, then glanced over at Finn. His eyes were open, but he hadn't bothered to sit up. His nap could have gone on for hours, she suspected, having watched such events during their days in the cage. The man could sleep. Anywhere. Anytime.

"It's not a request." Clay gritted his teeth in frustration.

"Say it," Ava commanded, unperturbed.

"Get out here, Ava."

"Say it."

"Please." Clay finally acquiesced.

Smiling now, Ava threw back the covers, jumping daintily to her feet. A chuckle escaped David's mouth, causing Clay to turn ever so slightly and glare in his direction. Ducking his head, David did his best to sober up his expression, but lost the battle.

"It's just-" He panted between fits of laughter. "I've never heard anyone talk to you like that. It's pretty awesome."

"Finn." Clay ignored his right-hand man. "You, too."

"Sure thing." Finn groaned before rolling out of bed.

Back down in the conference room, the four of them sat. This time Ava and Finn were seated next to one another, with David and Clay across. Evening was steadily approaching, she could smell the homemade lasagna baking just down the hall. Mouth watering, and mind distracted, Ava couldn't figure why they were back here. Boring blank walls surrounded them. The room was devoid of any pictures or decoration. Now that she thought of it, the entire building hadn't contained one such item. Was it frugality or lack of a woman's touch? She thought the later.

"So, the best I can figure is that when Sophia made her

break from the LO, they began their infiltration into the Militia," Clay began.

Handing them a few photographs, David took over. "Five months ago, Nurse Harper applied for her position with our Northwest Chapter. She passed all background checks, maintained her duties, and gave no reason to suspect she was an operative. Do either of you recognize her now that you've had time to think?"

"No." Finn studied the pictures, head bent in towards Ava.

"Me either." Ava was quick to add, but then something gave her pause. "But Michael told me that they knew for certain you were the last one Sophia was with before disappearing."

"Wait." Clay and David exchanged a look. "Did you say Michael?"

"He was one of our guards at the facility in Canada," Finn answered for her. "She was close with him."

"Close?" Clay was measured.

"Not that close, jeez," Ava rolled her eyes. "Why are you and Finn so weird about it?"

"Finn advised you not to interact with him?"

"Yes," Ava admitted. "But like I told him, Michael wasn't really a bad guy. He only let them hit me the one time."

"Oh, is that all?" Clay kept his voice light but it had deadly undertones. "Can you describe him?"

"He tried to stop it the next time," Ava reasoned, then realized how she must sound. "Look, just trust me on this one. I'm doing an awful lot of trusting with you guys."

"Alright." Reluctantly, Clay moved on. "What else did he tell you?"

"That they wanted Sophia back and that you were for sure the last one with her. That was all."

"Okay." David nodded. "We still don't know how they knew that, but unfortunately for us, they've had a head start. Since that time, they've probably sent out any number of employees to join the Militia. We fear we may have a case of a large sleeper cell imbedded in our organization."

"What that means is," Clay elaborated. "We've got to do a wide scale re-screening of our members. I'm going to start in this region but will need to move on soon. You can both stay for a few more days but then it's time for Ava to go underground."

"No problem." Finn nodded.

"Here is a burner phone for each of you." Clay slid two sleek black cells across the table. "Yes, everything you say on there is recorded. And, yes, I will review every word. Ava, mainly yours is to receive my calls. I'll send you the photos that we discussed once a month. If anything, and I mean anything feels off, then call me right away. Got it?"

"Got it," she echoed, pocketing hers.

"Johnny, you will contact your supervisor at the FBI. Tell him that you're going undercover to infiltrate my organization. Tell him that I'm still unsure about you and it will take at least six months before you can gain my trust. I don't know how often you have to check in with the Program, but my assumption is that you won't want that call recorded anyhow, so that's your problem."

"Okay." Finn nodded, running a finger over the screen. "You know that I'm going to make that call and then toss this into the nearest river, right? Hers, too."

"Fine," Clay acknowledged. "Then you need to use some

cash and buy her an untraceable phone so that she can contact me."

"Agreed." Finn held his open palm next to Ava until she relinquished the cell phone to him. He shoved it back at Clay.

"Next order of business." Clay bent out of sight for a moment. When he sat back up, he scooted a tan purse across the table towards Ava. "I'm going to say this in front of everyone so we're all on the same page. There is twenty-five thousand dollars cash in that bag. The money is for the both of you to survive over the next six months. Cleaning house shouldn't take any longer than that. If it does, then make contact and we can resupply."

"That's a lot of money." Ava leaned over the purse, eyeing the stacks of green bills that lay neatly bound inside.

"Ava," Clay continued. "Do not let Finn use any credit cards, bank cards, or checks. Don't even let him withdraw cash from his own account. He isn't to sign his name on any hotel register, apartment lease, or car rental. Nothing. He isn't to give his name out at any time to anyone, and neither should you. If he does any of those things, then it could be a tip off to your location. Do you understand?"

"I understand." She scrunched up her fingers, this was starting to feel real.

"What about weapons?" Finn asked.

"What about them?" Clay huffed indignantly, but then nodded in assent. "I can give you one."

"Three," Finn countered. "I get to choose them. Two for me and one for her. She said you taught her to shoot."

"My dad did," Clay corrected. "Fine, three of your choice."

"Transportation?" Finn asked.

"Well, I would start you guys off with a decent car, but we

all know the first thing that you're going to do is ditch it," Clay responded. "So, David is going to buy a cheap truck off of a local guy and strip the vin. You'll start out with that. It should get you a few hundred miles at least."

"Sounds good." Finn nodded.

"Great. Fuel up, rest up," Clay finished. "You've got to be out in three days."

TWELVE

"You hungry?" Finn asked.

Shrugging, Ava kept her gaze focused on the coastline as they drove past. Overcast and cloudy, the ocean was a melancholy blanket. Speckled with white caps and wind, it matched her mood perfectly.

Rubbing her hands together, she held them out, testing the air that flowed from the navy-blue vents in the old Jeep. It was lukewarm at best. The heater had been notoriously unreliable over the past few days, causing them both to bundle up. Beyond the sea, winter filled the sky with a thick swirling mass of clouds, the cold churning colors had her overthinking.

"You can't play the silent treatment game forever," Finn cautioned.

"You have sisters, you should be used to this," she mumbled, but had to admit that it was getting old.

They had used the full three days that her brother had given them before setting out on their journey. Taking their time, they had weaved their way down and out of the southernmost mountains of Washington state. True to his word, Finn made a phone call to the FBI, persuading them to let him go undercover to infiltrate the Militia.

Overhearing the conversation, Ava had listened to him give notice of Palmer's death, detail their time in the possession of the LO, and provide an overview of their recent recovery by Clay. Finn was careful not to commit to the location of Militia holdings or members. Staying vague, he claimed to have been blindfolded and only recently able to convince Clay he wanted to become a member.

Lastly, he placed a call to his wife. Trapped in the same car together, Ava gritted her teeth, belly somersaulting as she listened. If she was being fair, she would have to admit that the call sounded like one between old friends. He told Stephanie that he was going under for several months and wouldn't be reachable. There was no fuss, no lengthy explanation, and no terms of endearment as the call ended. The most uncomfortable aspect was the explosion of jealousy that Ava had to work to control. It wasn't like her to get so wrapped up in such a short period of time. The emotional pull grated on her.

Removing the SIM card and battery, Finn had chucked his cell into a river just before they ditched the first vehicle that the Militia had set up for them. The Jeep they now occupied had been purchased several cities away, after two separate bus rides, both paid for in cash. It was clear that Finn intended for no one, including the Militia, to know where Ava was. Hell, at this point she didn't even know where she was, and so far she had refused to ask him where their final destination would be. Still feeling the sting of his double life, she hadn't wanted to engage him in lengthy conversation.

When he was hungry, they stopped to eat. When he was tired, they stopped at nameless motels to sleep. When two beds weren't available, he kept to his side of the one they shared. At night she tossed and turned. Sometimes she was plagued by flashes of memory from their cage. Other times she woke startled. Sitting up in bed, she was unaware as to the cause, having had no bad dream. On those nights, it was all she could do not to scoot closer to Finn, pressing the fitful length of her body comfortingly against his. In the cage, the mattress had been so small that there had been no choice about touching. She missed that.

He had stopped and picked up two burner cells when they entered California. Hugging the coast, she found it increasingly difficult not to ask him to share his plan. But it didn't take a genius to notice that they were heading perpetually south. The only thing still holding her back was her own damned pride, and even that was slipping.

"Um-" He glanced over at her, large hands gripping the steering wheel. "About the sisters."

"You've got to be kidding me." She shifted in her seat to examine the side of his face as he focused on the road. "No sisters?"

"Nope." He cracked a grin.

"Why are you smiling?" She fumed.

"I'm sorry." He worked unsuccessfully to straighten his face. "You're right, it's not funny."

"Let me guess, no Utah?"

"I've driven through it a few times," he admitted.

"Is anything that you've told me over the past month true? Who the hell are you? Where are we going?"

"Come on, Ava. You know the kind of food that I crave

when I'm starving. You know my favorite color, the type of music that I listen to, that I like dogs, and kids. Every crazy quiz game that we played to keep from dying of boredom was completely true. You know all of the important stuff about me and I know it all about you, too."

Blowing out a frustrated breath, Ava leaned back in her seat, trying to ease the numb feeling of her body caused by days on the road. Finn dropped into silence. She knew that he would let her wrestle with what he had said on her own. It was true and not true at the same time. They had shared all of the tiny pieces that make up the personality of a person, but not the big chunks. She knew the way his muscles twitched just before he dropped into a deep sleep. She knew his workout routine and had laughed uncontrollably when he had attempted yoga. He was generous with food, was the first to make a sacrifice, was intelligent, patient, and always leapt to her defense.

Turning to rest her back against the passenger window, she stared again at the side of his face. It was smooth now. As soon as he had access to a razor, he had shaved away the scrub of bristle that had populated his cheeks and chin during their confinement. Her fingers itched to touch the clean skin.

Frowning, she held his eyes as he stole quick glances at her while trying to maintain focus on the road. He had a politician's way of not quite answering the question. Finn still hadn't told her where they were going, and a nagging fear began to form under the surface of her frustrated anger. Up until this point she had assumed that his plan was to go into hiding together. It was possible, though, that he intended to stash her somewhere alone, making return visits to check up instead of staying. The idea of him leaving her made her heart beat uncomfortably.

"In a way, I do know you, but then again, I don't. It's like we've done this backwards," she said finally.

"Fair enough, let's start over. Can I take you out to dinner?"

"You're asking me on a date?"

"Yeah."

"I don't date married men."

"It was never consummated. So technically, I'm not married, or at least I think that's true in some states," he protested.

Flipping down the ripped blue visor, she used the sleeve of her red jacket to wipe away a layer of dust that had built up to cover the tiny mirror. Her face had almost completely healed, but without makeup, or a decent hair brush, she certainly didn't feel very date-worthy. The next major town was Santa Barbara. She was sure there was a mall nearby where she could buy some fresh clothes and other necessities.

"If you're asking me out." She pushed the visor back up to the ceiling. "Then I'll need to go shopping first."

"Shopping?" He was incredulous.

"That's right." She narrowed her eyes at him.

"Shopping it is then."

Later that evening she leaned close to the hotel's bathroom mirror as she applied a layer of crimson lipstick. There was nothing quite like a new set of clothes and arsenal of makeup to make a girl feel good. The hot shower with its imposing granite walls and plush white towels had helped, too. Smiling to herself, she recalled Finn's exasperation at her insistence on choosing a nicer place to stay. Why not splurge a little on her brother's dime? After all, it was his fault that she was in this mess to begin with.

When they pulled up to the hotel and surveyed the sweep of smooth white walls topped by an expanse of red Spanish tile, she released a slow heavenly sigh. No more fear of bed bugs, or rodents, or whatever else scurried out of no-tell motels in the night. To his credit, Finn bit his tongue when she flirted with the front desk clerk, making a point of ordering two adjoining rooms. A little privacy wouldn't hurt, either. Speaking of which, his brisk knock could be heard firing rapidly against their shared door.

"Just a second!" She called.

"I thought we agreed that you wouldn't lock it," he grumbled loudly, twisting the door handle with no success.

Let him wait, she thought. Crossing to the closet, she pulled the new little black dress from the dark wooden hangar. Ripping off the white price tag, she unzipped the back and stepped inside. The fitted satin of the empire top gave way to a chiffon fabric that flowed with her body before ending abruptly at her thighs. It was short. Oh yes, it was short. But there was a see-through lace border around the bottom that added a respectable inch or two.

Doing a quick twirl in the silver framed full length mirror, she rolled her eyes at his second knock and slipped into a pair of new three-inch black pumps. It seemed ridiculous to feel excited about this, but the last date she had gone on was before Mason had arrived, so maybe it was just because she was out of practice. Balancing carefully on the new heels, she held herself back from doing a sexy strut before casually opening the door.

"Whoa, you clean up good." Finn's brown eyes flashed in quick appreciation before resuming a determined frown. "But you can't lock this door, Ava, for any reason."

"Okay, I get it," she placated, before turning away to grab her clutch.

A quick rush of heat had begun to work its way into her cheeks. The outfit that he had begrudgingly allowed her to choose for him looked great. Really great. The light green color from his collared shirt complimented the brown of his eyes, and it was hard not to notice how the sleeves accentuated his well-muscled shoulders. Maybe she should have chosen something a little easier to look at. It hadn't been hard for her to stay mad at the soldier boy in his hand-me-down clothes. The handsome man standing before her was another story.

"Ready to play fantasy food for real?" Finn asked as he opened the door.

"Oh, yeah."

Cruising down the hall, jitters had her biting her lip and tucking carefully curled blonde locks behind her ear. His hand brushing the small of her back as he ushered her into the elevator, caused a low warmth to spread. It wasn't like she hadn't already slept with him, but for some reason it all felt so new. A quiet tension filled the space as they watched the little round lights signal their descent to the lobby. For a brief moment she caught his stare in the gold-tinted reflection of the elevator doors just before they slid open. Her reason for keeping distance between them was quickly dissolving.

Crossing the threshold into the lobby, she felt the bite of

the nighttime wind and absently wished for a coat. Heels clicking against the marble floor, Finn caught her hand in his own, causing her to glance back and share a soft smile. The hotel boasted its own waterfront restaurant, and fortunately for them it was the off season. Reservations were not necessary.

When the maître d began to escort them to a table over-looking the expanse of dark water, Finn quietly intervened. Instead, they were placed in a far corner where he could sit with his back against the wall and survey the activity in the room. He was still the FBI Agent after all. His order of a ribeye, rare, with a twice baked potato did not surprise her. What did cause her to raise an eyebrow was the bottle of red wine. In the cage he had always opted for a fantasy beer. Eyes twinkling, his expression was anything but innocent.

"What's the matter?" He asked. "Don't you like wine?"

"You know I do." She laughed. "But I didn't think that you did."

"It goes great with steak."

"Of course it does."

The basket of warm freshly baked bread that was placed before them had her salivating. Politely, Finn doled out a piece to her first, then took one for himself. It had been like that in the cage, too, even at their most hungry. Fingers biting into the roll, she pulled it gratefully apart, then noticed his eyes constantly tracking the room behind her. Ever vigilant, he had appraised every fast food restaurant since they hit the road in the same way. The last time she recalled him eating with ease was in the company of the Militia.

"Is it always like this?" She ventured. "Watching everything while you eat?"

"It is when I'm alone. You know, without a partner." He paused, seeming to think before going on. "Although, I guess then I'm still watching his back while he watches mine."

"I'm sorry about Palmer." Old feelings of guilt floated to the surface. "It's my fault that he died."

"It wasn't your fault."

"If I had done the video the first time they asked-"

"Then they would have found another excuse to shoot him in front of you. He was unnecessary to their purpose and used most effectively to manipulate you."

"It worked."

She could still see Palmer's grey-blue eyes lit up with surprise the moment before they turned off forever. A brooding silence settled on their table. Ava picked at the crumbs of bread left on her tiny white dish. Finn drank deeply from the wide glass of shimmering wine. After several minutes, their waiter fluttered over and deposited two Caesar salads neatly on the table. Silver forks clinked lightly against the porcelain plates as they ate. Ava listened to the soft notes of classical music that floated throughout the restaurant.

"So, where are we headed?" She asked.

"Southeast," Finn answered between bites of crouton.

"Seriously? That's all you're giving me?"

"Yup," he said, then laughed at her huff of exasperation. "Arizona. We're going to Arizona."

"What's in Arizona?"

"Warmth, safety, anonymity."

"Are you dropping me somewhere, or..." she trailed off, not able to meet his eyes.

"Do you want me to drop you off?" His gentle tone had her glancing up.

"Not really," she admitted.

"That's good because I can't leave you."

He didn't elaborate, although she wanted him to. Their salad plates were cleared, making way for the heavy meal they had ordered. Though in the cage she had opted for the pasta, in reality the red meat on the menu just couldn't be denied. Prime rib, dripping in au jus with the sting of straight horseradish was cooked to perfection. Each bite that she placed into her mouth melted, just the way it had in her daydreams.

Deliberately pacing herself, she observed Finn while sipping on her second glass of wine. He had stopped after one, waving the waiter away when he attempted to pour another. Now his focus was split between enjoying the bloody steak that dwarfed his plate, and the more than occasional eye sweep of the room. Even her father, with all of his prepping and paranoia, had never been this keen.

Drink held loosely in one hand, she let her gaze drift to his strong jaw, then travel down to the collar of his shirt. The alcohol relaxed her just enough to let her mind wander unbidden to old memories. Giving her head a slight shake, she came back to herself, realizing it was that slip of awareness that had him stopping at one glass. He was good at this. Whatever this was.

"Don't look at me like that, Ava." Finn's voice was low.

"Why?" She whispered the familiar response.

"You know why."

She managed to hold his searing look for a few moments, but eventually let her eyes fall to her plate. This tension, or whatever there was between them, pulled at her. Clay had trusted Finn enough to send her away with him, but had still taken Ava aside, reminding her not to divulge too much. It was hard to keep her wits intact with her body so constantly yearning to betray her.

When the waiter came back around to offer dessert, Ava welcomed the interruption. Ordering strawberry cheesecake, she couldn't resist clapping her hands together in anticipation. This was the skinniest that she had been since high school, so she could eat the entire slice herself with absolutely no remorse. Finn was shocked when she seriously refused his request to share.

"You're not going to let me have even one bite?" His tone registered shock.

"Fine," she relented. "One bite."

Reaching over with his fork he scooped up a giant man-sized portion, shoveling it quickly into his mouth before she had a chance to protest. He groaned happily as he chewed, taunting her until she giggled.

"So, are you missing Mason a lot?" Finn asked.

"Yeah, I think about him all the time," Ava confessed. "He would love the road trip and the beach. He's a car guy."

"You're sure he's safe?" Finn was measured.

"He's safer right now than I can make him."

"Do you know who has him?"

"Remind me again who I'm talking to. Is it Johnny Rule Book from the Program, or Agent Finn with the FBI?"

"Give me a break, Ava," Finn shot back. "It's just me."

"Who is me exactly?" Ava mocked half-heartedly. "Is John Finn even your real name?"

The look he gave her had her laughter fading.

"It's my legal name," he told her. "But it's not the one that I was born with."

"What does that mean?"

"Ever since I was a kid, I've wanted to join the service, but it wasn't until high school that I realized simply joining wasn't going to be enough. I knew that I had to do covert work, special operations, something like that."

"Spy work." Ava studied him. "David told me."

"I'm not a spy," Finn corrected. "The point is that what I wanted to do with my life wasn't just dangerous for me. Same as Clay, it can get dangerous for anyone you care about."

"Your family."

"My family," he nodded. "So right before I enlisted, I changed my name to Johnathan Finn. With the help of a little tech class and an old friend, I buried the records of who I was before. It's possible, but someone would have to hunt really hard to make the connection."

"So, the military thinks that you're John Finn from Utah with three sisters?"

"Yes."

"The Program thinks that, too?"

"Yes."

"Stephanie? Clay? The FBI?"

"Everyone." He nodded. "Everyone, but you."

"What about your family? What do they know?"

"I don't get to see them much but my family thinks that I'm a software engineer living in San Diego."

"Holy shit." Ava let out a barely audible whistle. "I thought you were living a double life, but this has got to be like a third life, or fourth, or I don't even know. I don't know what to think Finn. Is that even right? What's your real name?"

"Finley Moore."

"John Finn. Finley Moore. You kept something."

"Yeah, I kept something."

THIRTEEN

Lying alone in her bed, Ava tossed and turned. They had propped the adjoining door open, but in the dark, she struggled with sleeplessness. What he had confided to her over dinner had turned the mood serious once more, reminding them of the reality of their situation. This wasn't some romantic first date between new lovers, they were on the run. People wanted her dead, she had lost custody of her son, and Finn was so deep in the system that it was hard to see the truth.

Head reeling, she slipped in and out of twilight sleep. It was the kind of sleep where you think you're awake, until something actually wakes you up. The last red numbers she could recall seeing on the bedside clock shone three a.m.

In her dreams she held Mason's hand. They were walking together, surrounded by green grass. Her heart was at ease just being beside him, listening to his nonsensical chatter. When the talking stopped, he was gone, replaced by Agent Palmer. She looked into his intelligent eyes. He had something to say. Her insides yearned to hear the words, so she waited expectantly until the hand she held grew icy, stiff, and cold.

Stifling a cry, Ava sat up in bed, gasping. Finn was there in an instant, checking the room with swift efficiency in the semi-dark. Light seeped in from around the curtains drawn over large windows. Dawn was approaching. Finding nothing out of place, he took a seat next to her on the bed and looped his arm gently around her waist.

"You okay?" He asked.

"Just a bad dream."

"Want to talk about it?"

"It was about Mason and then Palmer." She offered no more.

"I'm sorry."

"What time is it?" She groaned, flopping miserably back onto her pillow.

"Five-thirty," he answered. "Rough night? You can go back to sleep."

"I haven't been able to sleep."

Nodding, he raised the corner of the blankets and scooted her towards the middle of the bed. Creeping in beside her, he lay down and pulled her body alongside his. She listened to the easy rhythm of his breathing, felt him exhale over the back of her neck. Within seconds, her tight muscles relaxed. Whoever he really was, this Finn made her feel safe.

"Why did you tell me about your real name?" She whispered sleepily.

"Because that's the guy you spent a month in a cage with," he confessed. "When I'm with you I remember who I was before, and I miss it."

"But you've put your family at risk now." Her eyes fluttered once, then remained closed.

"I trust you," he whispered, just before she succumbed to an enduring sleep.

HOURS LATER SHE WOKE TO THE SNAP OF A GUN BEING assembled. Opening her eyes, she observed Finn hunched over the little corner table. The handguns that he had selected from Clay's stash lay carefully arranged on the surface in various stages of cleaning. Yawning, she sat up in bed, arranging the pillows behind her before leaning back against the headboard. She didn't feel groggy at all. In fact, it was the best rest she had gotten in a long time.

"Aren't you concerned that Clay may have placed a tracking device in one of those?" She teased.

"Nope," Finn answered seriously. "I checked all of them before leaving Washington."

"Of course you did."

Shaking her head, Ava fought the smile of approval that wanted to form on her lips. Stomach growling, she threw back the covers and stood up to stretch. She didn't need to glance at Finn to know that he had stopped to watch. Making her way to the bathroom, she closed the door and twisted the lock. Ever since Michael, she hadn't felt comfortable taking a shower with an unsecured door. Even with Finn just outside, something about the process now made her feel vulnerable.

Inhaling the clouds of hot steam, she stepped into the spray, refusing to leave until every last bit of hotel shampoo had been squeezed from the tiny tube. When she was done, she could hear Finn's voice carry from the other side of the door. He wanted to get on the road soon, this was their last day of travel.

Curious, she wondered what part of Arizona they would be going to. Rushing through her routine, she blew her hair dry and applied a light layer of makeup. Still wrapped in a fluffy white towel, she opened the door to find Finn leaning against the near wall, tapping his foot with impatience. While she had showered, he had packed all of their things, so she had to rifle through her new suitcase to select an outfit for the day. It would be warm in the desert, but still cold in the Jeep, so she opted for tight jeans, a white tank top, and light sweater.

"What about breakfast?" Ava asked, as she grabbed up her purse, following Finn out the door.

"We can drive-thru."

He lugged his own duffle bag while wheeling her suitcase behind. The thought of another fast food meal had her revolting, but his determination to get on their way outweighed her need for real sustenance. She would just have to suffer through one more day of greasy faux nutrition before they were able to stop. Bright blue sky peeked out from behind a shifting cover of grey clouds. Winter winds blew in from the sea, whipping her hair before she slipped into the shotgun seat.

By now she was used to the Jeep's plethora of clunking noises. Unlike newer model vehicles, this one seemed to have an air gap for every door frame and an odd squeak for every wheel. Finn was unperturbed by the sounds, having assured her that it was safe enough to see them through to the end. Only once had he pulled over to examine the workings underneath the heavy metal hood.

This choice of transportation was two-fold. It was cheap but also so old that it had no modern electronics. No GPS, no fancy radio, nothing with a computer sophisticated enough to keep track of where they had been or give information as to their current location. He had thought of everything, or he had done this enough times that covering his trail was second nature, she couldn't be sure which. Oddly, she found it intensely attractive, his proficiency at disappearing. Looking over at him now, with his drive-thru egg sandwich gripped in one hand, she had to smile. The glance wasn't lost on him, things rarely were.

"What?" He asked between bites.

"How many times have you done this?"

"Run away with a beautiful woman?"

"Real cute." She fought the blush. "You know what I mean."

"Vanish?" He checked his blind spot before changing lanes, the highway had become congested. "A few times. Mostly as part of the Program training. We played a six month game of hide-and-seek at one point. It was a blast."

"Who won?"

"Can't say his name." He chuckled. "They still haven't found him."

"How do you know he's not dead somewhere?"

"He checks in every once in a while, to see if they want him to come back." He crumpled his empty wrapper, tossing it into the back seat. "Now that's a spy."

"My brother thinks that the Program is dangerous," Ava ventured, having nibbled at some sorry excuse for hash browns before polishing off her fruit parfait.

"I know what Clay thinks," Finn grumbled. "But it's not

like that. He's just too steeped in conspiracy paranoia to see it."

"Well, what do you think the Program's goal is?"

"The goal is to give highly-trained, dedicated patriots an opportunity at long-term career positions throughout our government. Why shouldn't like-minded service members hold power? It would be a stabilizing force."

"That sounds like a politically correct explanation," Ava commented. "Are you still beholden to the overseers? Will they have a say in the choices that each member makes while in their final career position?"

"You make it sound like some dark enemy is trying to execute a coup d'état."

"Couldn't it be?"

"No."

"Does the FBI know that you're a Program member?"

Picking up his long ago drained coffee cup, Finn took a testing sip, then tossed it over his shoulder restlessly. She watched his fingers tense on the steering wheel. The curl of stress worked its way up into his arms, but his mouth remained sealed. His silence spoke volumes. Of course the FBI didn't know. She could guess that the members assigned to become congressman, judges, and governors also kept the true nature of their affiliation to themselves.

As they traded the idyllic views of the coast for the crush of Los Angeles traffic, they worked their way ever east, towards the nothingness that filled the desert. Grubby grunge towns populated the sides of the highway, popping up more infrequently as the hours passed. She never thought that they would travel so closely by the area that dominated her child-hood. But now, as an anonymous passenger, her observations were once removed. This had been her hometown, but no more.

Somehow, she didn't feel the sting of loss at the place, or even of who she was before. If any sadness permeated, it was solely about Mason. Without him, she didn't know who she was anymore. How long would she have to wait before she got to see a picture of him again? Heart thumping out a jumpy rhythm, Ava rolled down her window to let in the warm desert breeze.

"You okay?" Finn had to raise his voice to be heard over the whoosh of wind.

"Just a little car sick," she lied.

"We're almost there."

"Almost where?"

"Lake Havasu, ever heard of it?"

"Only that it's the place to go for a party." She let her hand float in the open air, enjoying its hot push against her palm.

"That's during the summer," he agreed. "This is winter, it's different."

"Spoken like a local," she commented.

"You could say that."

Their approach had them driving through the river enclave of Parker, following the curve of the Colorado River as it snaked north to the bottom of the lake. After a last span of lonely highway, businesses began to pop up along the road. Clusters of homes stretched out to the right, filling up the barren expanse with a flourishing suburb. A few signals in, they turned up a road, twisting casually by a variety of one-story houses whose attached garages towered over them in height.

Each one was slightly different, some adobe, some

hacienda-style, some with smooth beige stucco. All had multi-colored rocks peppered with succulents and cacti instead of green lawns. Ava had thought they would be spending their first few nights in a local hotel before securing nondescript housing of some sort. Their winding pace through the neighborhood grabbed her attention, but reality failed to click into place until they pulled to a stop in one stone driveway. When the engine shuttered to a halt, her eyes snapped to Finn.

"Where are we?"

"This is my parent's house." He gestured at the large ranch-style home before them.

"Finley Moore's parents?"

"That's right." He smiled.

Getting out, he left her staring dumbfounded in the Jeep. For a moment, she didn't know what to think and simply watched him walk around to retrieve their luggage from the back. During the last hour of their drive she had left the window down, enjoying the swirling warmth of the wind. With the welcome heat, she hadn't needed her light sweater, shedding it in favor of the tiny tank top underneath.

Grumbling, she ran her hands over her bare arms, wishing for something a bit more appropriate to wear. Quickly she combed through her mussed hair with her fingers, then, exasperated at the lack of progress, gave up altogether and shoved out of the vehicle. Finn waited for her halfway up the concrete walk, his black t-shirt falling untucked over casual blue jeans. She had just caught up behind him when the massive glass and wrought-iron front door burst open.

"The prodigal son has returned!" A short man in his late-fifties called, arms stretching wide to receive Finn.

"Dad." Finn dropped the bags to clap the man heartily on the shoulder.

"You didn't call us back so we assumed you wouldn't be making it for Thanksgiving this year either," his father continued.

"Thanksgiving?" Finn shot Ava a worried look, they had both lost track of the days.

"Yes! You know, the one where all the family gets together except for you." The man stepped back to survey his son before his eyes came to rest on Ava. "And who do we have here?"

"Dad, this is Ava." Finn shifted to introduce them. "Ava, this is my dad, Paul."

"It's nice to meet you." She shook his hand warmly, noting the twinkle of good humor in his eyes.

"Please, come in," Paul beckoned.

Sandals flapping against the concrete walk, Ava followed him through the high archway of the front door and into the cool dimness of the home. Large travertine tiles set on a diamond pattern swept out from the foyer into a vast open-concept living room. To the left, an enormous flat-screen television mounted above a fireplace flashed with a game of football. Arranged for best viewing, several brown leather recliners and one long sofa surrounded a Persian-Style area rug, rich with red earth tones.

The kitchen was situated against the far wall with a long high-top bar that separated it from the living room. Delicious smells permeated the air, filling it with the scent of baking turkey, mashed potatoes, and stuffing. The house overwhelmed Ava's senses. Petite and busy, a woman, brown hair swept up in a loose pony tail, scrubbed vigorously at some dishes in the apron-style sink. Her back to them, she didn't notice their approach over the sound of the game blaring on the television.

"Olivia!" Paul shouted. "You won't believe who showed up on our doorstep."

"Finley!" Olivia cried, not bothering to dry her hands on a towel before skirting the granite bar, she threw herself at her son.

"Hi, Mama." Finn returned her fierce hug. "Sorry I didn't call first."

"I've been trying to get a hold of you for weeks now," she scolded. "If it had gone on one day longer I was going to call the police."

Ava swallowed a smile, the idea of Finn's tidy mother reporting him missing was endearing. Of course, doing that would have created all kinds of extra trouble for her son. After a few moments, Olivia pushed back to hold Finn at arm's length, examining him with a mother's sharp eye. Discovering nothing out of place, she glanced around his bulk and her eyes came to rest with surprise on Ava.

"And you've brought home a friend," Olivia remarked, sharing a brief look with her husband. "Welcome."

"Thank you." Ava offered her hand but was pulled in for a tight hug against the woman. "I'm glad to be here."

"Oh, we don't shake hands in this family, dear." Olivia gave Ava an extra squeeze. "We're huggers."

"Alright you huggers," Finn interjected. "We need to stay here for a few days. Got any room?"

"Absolutely!" Paul clapped him heartily on the shoulder. "We converted your old bedroom into a guest room. Your girlfriend can stay in there."

"Um… she's not exactly my girlfriend," Finn attempted awkwardly.

"Sorry," Paul laughed. "Your friend, who is also a girl, can have your old room. You can sleep on the couch."

"What about Andrew's room?"

"He'll be here any minute," Olivia jumped in. "I guess you guys could share a bed."

"No." Finn made a face. "I'll take the couch."

Leading the way past the kitchen, Finn halted at the end of a short hallway containing three doors. Gesturing to his left, he pointed out a bedroom and bathroom that Ava had to assume belonged to this Andrew person. On the right was another well-lit bedroom of average size. Plush grey carpeting cushioned her steps as she entered. Skirting the queen size bed with its brick-red comforter Ava made her way to the walk-in closet.

Trailing behind her Finn hefted her suitcase before setting it gingerly on an old cedar chest just inside the closet door. Empty plastic hangars occupied half of the railing, while the rest was stocked with what appeared to be Olivia's extra clothing. Swiveling around, Ava took a survey of the neat room. It had a dark-colored wooden headboard with two matching night stands.

A few picture frames holding family portraits dotted the top of a long dresser. Running her fingers absently over them, Ava could easily spot a youngish Finn, his formerly serious expression was softened by a mischievous grin. It was a sneaky smile that was shared with the two other boys who filled up one of the photos. Each brandishing a fishing pole, a serene body of water stretched out behind them. Eyes darting,

Ava evaluated the collection of pictures in turn and found the same boys in various stages of aging.

"You have brothers," she finally commented.

"Yes." Finn nodded, sitting just behind her on the side of the bed. "Mark is the oldest, he's the one with the lighter hair. Andrew is the classic middle child, the one with the dimples. I'm the youngest."

"You grew up here?" Turning to face him, Ava leaned back against the dresser, their knees touched almost casually.

"We moved here when I was about three, so I don't remember anything before. The real estate market was way down and my parents bought a duplex on the cheap. That first rental turned into another, and then another. I think they own something like twenty houses now."

"Wow." Ava curled her fingers subconsciously over the edge of the dresser. "They're landlords."

"Yeah." Finn bobbed his head. "And it's a giant pain in the ass. The second we were old enough my dad took us out to help fix any complaints. If I never repair a leaky toilet again, it will be fine with me."

"Oh, you're a handy man, too?" She joked.

"Not anymore, I'm not," he protested, then added. "I'm a software engineer, remember?"

"Right." Ava blinked at him, not quite able to make that title fit.

"And, I'm sorry about the Thanksgiving thing," he went on. "I guess I've completely lost track of time. Looks like you'll be meeting the whole family."

"This will be my first Thanksgiving without Mason." Ava's throat went dry with the realization. "I missed Halloween, too. He wanted to be a firefighter this year. I wonder if she took him trick or treating."

"She?" Finn caught every detail.

"When do you think it would be safe for me to call Clay?" Ava ignored him. "I need to set up a way for him to send me monthly pictures of Mason. You said you don't want anything going to the burner cell."

"Yeah, don't open any files on it." He paused, thinking. "Let me get a computer first, then we can set up an email account for him to send the stuff to. I can create a path for you to access it without getting hacked."

"Hmmm." Ava eyed him. "Software engineer isn't sounding so far off anymore."

Shrugging, he pushed to his feet before encircling her in his arms. The already narrow space between the dresser and bed had them snugged up close. Feeling the gentle stroke of his palm against her back, her vulnerability about Mason had her burying her face in his neck. They fit together all too well. A persistent longing worked its way through her blood stream. In this emotional place, she would have accepted his kiss with equal wanting. But this was Finn, and her brother's recent accusation about him taking advantage still stung. Holding back, he instead contented them both with the calming strength of his embrace. His lips brushed lightly against her hair, no more.

It was the clamor of an entering horde of children that had them breaking apart. They could hear the calls of greeting through the closed bedroom door. Finn's boisterous family of brothers was home for the holidays, and apparently that included young kids. It made Ava ache for her own noisy boy all the more.

Letting go, Finn maneuvered around Ava to head for the exit. Before he could grasp the silver knob, the door flew open, admitting two rough little boys to tumble crazily into the space. Ava judged them to be about four and six-years-old. Each one had sandy blonde hair and twinkling brown eyes. Behind them, a handsome man with matching hair and a rogue grin leaned casually against the threshold.

"Holy shit, it is a real girl!" The man called over his shoulder, attracting the attention of a tall brunette.

"Hello to you too, brother." Finn answered the cock-eyed smile with one of his own as they clasped hands.

"Mark, what are you doing?!" The beautiful woman had closed the distance in record time before shifting her apologetic eyes to Ava. "I am so sorry for my extremely rude husband and equally rude children. Boys!"

"It's okay." Ava's heart melted for the rowdy kids. "Boys are so impossible to control at this age, or any age really."

"You have kids?" Elbowing Mark out of the way, she extended her hand. "I'm Brooke."

Shaking warmly, Ava felt the sassy strong energy that radiated from the other woman. As the boys ran out to circle around the living room, the adults followed. Brooke uncorked a bottle of Chardonnay and Olivia hummed happily in the kitchen. Pulling out a tall stool, Ava settled herself at the bar, glass in hand. Brooke did most of the talking but worked in an unending line of questions causally. It was easy to understand the curiosity of the Moore clan at the arrival of a new woman.

Playing along, Ava confirmed that she did have a son, but that he, unfortunately, was spending this holiday season with his father. Chestnut hair flowing in graceful cascades down her back, Brooke chattered openly about the local elementary school options, swimming lessons, and her lack of a personal life. Like any stay-at-home mom, she thirsted for adult female companionship and jumped at the chance to swap war stories with Ava. Not having allowed herself a good girlfriend in years, Ava enjoyed Brooke's endearing humor.

She was a local, having gone through school with the Moore boys. She fell for Mark fairly early on, but it took him a little while to notice her. Apparently, it was something that he was never going to live down, but by the way he pinched her butt as he walked by, Ava could tell he was smitten. Even at the far reaches of the room, as Brooke joked unawares, his eyes would dart to her every once in a while.

It had Ava wondering if she herself would ever have something like that. She thought the answer was probably no. With Mason, dating was impossible. Perhaps if she had chosen a more traditional lifestyle, then things would have played out differently. Would she have a tidy little family? Would she have a devoted husband?

Taking another sip of wine, Ava acknowledged a slight twinge from deep inside. She watched Brooke referee a dispute between her sons, then swoop in to help Olivia with the turkey. Envy, not of the nice woman who was working hard to make her feel included, but at the honesty of Brooke's life itself, tickled her quietly. But when Ava thought of Mason, the feeling was decidedly snuffed out. He had been worth the sacrifice.

A few hours later, Ava found herself crammed in next to Finn at his family's long mahogany dining table. Aside from his parents, there was Mark's little family along with Olivia's father, who was affectionately termed, Grandpa Jack. Somewhere in his late-eighties, the man appeared spry, with sharp eyes set in a wrinkled face topped by silver-soft hair.

The middle brother, Andrew, had arrived late, as was his custom. They had all teased him mercilessly, but like his brothers, Andrew remained unruffled by the attention. Dimples flashing, he was clearly the entertainer of the group. Regaling his young nephews with tales of his travels across the globe, Andrew emanated a mysterious air. Leaning close, Finn informed Ava that his brother was a free-lance photographer. Andrew didn't stay permanently in one place for very long, so had no home of his own. When he was in town, he stayed in his old bedroom. Ava detected a note of disapproval in Finn's tone, but inwardly she thought his brother's vagabond lifestyle quite mirrored that of Finn himself.

"Ava." Olivia's voice lifted over the din of her progeny. "Tell us how you came to meet our Finley."

"It was through work," Finn supplied. "Her office needed help troubleshooting a new computer system that we installed."

"Yeah, he's really great at his job," Ava added, remembering the foot chase and subsequent full body tackle that was their actual first encounter.

"Oh, come on now." Grandpa Jack rattled his fork against the fine china plate before him. "None of you actually believe that crap, do you?"

"Oh, Daddy," Olivia crooned affectionately. "Not in front of our new guest, please."

"She's in on it!" Grandpa Jack pointed at Ava. "Software engineer my right eye."

"I'm sorry, Ava," Olivia addressed her worriedly. "My

father has always insisted that Finley is actually a military operative of some sort. Crazy, right?"

"Crazy," Ava echoed, trying not to smile broadly at the keen old man. He was right.

"Grandpa Jack." Finn winked at Ava. "You're blowing my cover, as usual."

"Sorry about that kiddo." Grandpa Jack let loose a gruff laugh. "Mums the word."

FOURTEEN

The crashing sounds of punk rock music blaring from down the hallway had Ava's eyes opening wide. For a moment, she thought she was back in middle school during Clay's "nobody understands me" phase. Grabbing for a neighboring pillow, she rolled onto her side and smashed it down over her exposed ear. When the lead singer began his unintelligible screaming chant, she knew it was time to get up.

"I give in," she muttered to herself, swinging bare legs over the edge of the bed.

Yawning, she stood up to stretch and adjusted the position of her cotton sleep-shirt. Overnight, the temperature in the desert had dropped drastically, but the house remained pleasantly warm. Male voices lifted briefly in a fit of laughter during a lull between songs. It was then that the wafting fragrance of freshly brewing coffee snaked its way under her nose.

Twisting the knob of her bedroom door, Ava left the comfort of carpeting for the cool hardness of tile when entering the small hallway. Andrew's door was flung wide, letting the music emanating from inside carry throughout the entire house. She could see Finn lying across the foot of his brother's bed, gesturing wildly at Andrew, who absorbed the story with interest. Deciding to make a detour, Ava leaned against the threshold, arms crossed casually in front of her body. For a few minutes, they continued to dialogue, but had to yell at each other to be heard. Shaking her head, Ava sighed. It was Andrew who noticed her first.

"Hey!" He called. "You know you're way out of his league, right?!"

"What?!" Ava shouted back, tapping her ear with one hand. "Can't hear you!"

"Oh, sorry!" Andrew laughed before Finn reached to turn down the music.

"That's better." Ava exhaled. "Good morning, gentlemen."

"Good morning," they echoed in union, eyes dancing.

"What are you two boys up to today?"

"Well." Finn glanced for confirmation from his brother. "I think we'd like to take you for a little boat ride."

"You have a boat?"

"Mark does." Andrew smiled happily. "We're gonna steal it."

"Oh, great." Ava blew out a breath. "I want no part of it."

"Not steal," Finn corrected. "Borrow without permission."

"Yeah, that's it." Andrew bobbed his head. "Borrow."

An hour later, after a breakfast laced with leftover turkey, Ava found herself wedged into the middle seat of Andrew's single cab pickup truck. Legs positioned uncomfortably in an unsuccessful attempt to avoid the gear shift, she swayed to tap shoulders lightly with Finn as Andrew made a sharp left turn. The mid-morning sun was subdued by a pair of cheap sunglasses that Finn had tossed at her after their stop at a gas station. Meandering towards the lakeshore, the rumble of the engine could barely be heard over the steady bump of hard rock.

They were heading for Mark's shop, where the object of their desire was stored. Being the eldest, Mark was the steady, responsible sibling. He graduated with a Bachelor's Degree in Business from Brown University, then returned to open his own boat sales and repair store. Ava had been suspicious of this simple explanation at first. Her experience with the Moore brothers thus far had her asking what the catch was. When Finn had admitted that Mark actually raced boats as a hobby, it made more sense. The three of them were a bunch of adrenaline junkies as far as she could tell.

"Why don't we just ask him to take out his boat?" Ava reached to lower the volume of the radio.

"Because then he'll insist on driving it," Andrew explained. "Plus, this is way more fun. He's going to freak when he sees that it's gone."

"I don't know," Ava wavered.

"Oh, come on." Andrew glanced at her. "The software engineer and the administrative assistant have got to learn to have a little fun. Time to ditch the boring day jobs and enjoy some excitement."

"You may be right." Finn elbowed Ava mid eye roll. "Show us how it's done big brother."

After pulling into the parking lot, Andrew came to an abrupt halt that had Ava and Finn bracing open palms against the dashboard. The sign in the window glowed with the blue word OPEN, and the security fence that ran along the back was pushed wide. An older model maroon SUV was parked in front. Ava recognized it from the day before.

"What kind of person works the day after Thanksgiving?" Andrew asked.

"Mark," Finn answered the rhetorical question.

"Well," Ava chirped with relief. "I guess that means the plan is ruined."

"No, no." Andrew shook his head. Putting the car in gear, he inched forward into a nearby space. "You go distract him while Finn and I hook up the boat in the back. When you hear a honk, then meet us out front."

"Seriously?"

"Seriously," Andrew answered, as Finn stepped out to let Ava crawl free.

"I hate you guys." Ava swore under her breath as the sounds of their snickering followed her towards the building.

Chiming pleasantly, the glass front door admitted her with its welcoming tones. The shop was well organized and inviting. Tall metal shelves ran down the length of one wall, dividing half of the store into aisles. In the middle were several circular racks filled with bathing suits, coverups, and lifejackets. The other half had no less than three full size boats gleaming under the bright overhead lights. The space was a lot larger than she had estimated from outside.

"Ava." Brooke's voice beckoned her from behind the long expanse of counter. "What are you doing here?"

"Hey, Brooke." Ava's stomach dropped, she hadn't expected her to be working. This mission just became impossible.

"Andrew and Finn wanted to take me on a little tour. Your store is great."

"Oh, thank you." Brooke beamed. "Mark is great with sales and repairs, but a miserable mess when it comes to design. That's my end."

"The layout shows off the space well, really inviting." Ava twirled a little, admiring the room.

"The brothers are up to something." Brooke smiled knowingly. "And you've been suckered into it. Am I right?"

"I'm so not good at this," Ava admitted, shrugging apologetically. "They're stealing your boat."

"Those bastards," Brooke hissed. "Going on an adult joy ride?"

"I am so sorry, Brooke." Ava's embarrassment bloomed.

"Screw it," Brooke whispered. "I'm going, too."

"What?" Ava's mouth dropped in shock.

Watching in wonder, she followed Brooke's casual path toward her husband's office. Inside, their two sons were absorbed in a full screen video game. Mark's eyes lit appreciatively when he spied his wife. When he caught sight of Ava, he rose to greet her warmly.

"Hey babe." Brooke let her fingers play lightly against her husband's collar. "Would you mind watching the kids for an hour while I grab a cup of coffee with Ava? She's so lonely, being new here and all."

"Only an hour, right?" Mark's eyes darted to the two barely tamed children sprawled at his feet.

"Of course," she crooned.

"Well, alright." He kissed her lightly on the cheek before she scooted away, narrowly missing his booty grab. "Have fun ladies."

"We will!" Brooke called, linking arms companionably with Ava.

Scurrying quickly, Brooke grabbed a swim suit off the rack on their path towards the exit. The sound of a honk had them both picking up speed until they hurled their way through the front door and into the cab of the truck.

"You brought this traitor along?!" Andrew laughed as Brooke took over the middle seat, forcing Ava to sit hunched on Finn's lap.

"It's like old times though." Brooke's smile was broad. "A day without freaking kids! I could faint."

The launch ramp wasn't far off. Andrew backed the trailer down expertly, dropping the sleek powerboat into the calm water. Finn helped Brooke and Ava climb aboard, careful to show Ava where not to step. The gleaming white boat was accented with burnt orange and red striping. It's clean upholstery and spotless interior shone with the effort of a devoted owner. This was clearly Mark's beloved mistress. In fact, the name on the back echoed the sentiment, **The Other Woman**, it said.

Andrew took over the captain's chair, while Finn hopped back into the truck. Switching on the engine, it roared and rumbled smoothly before Andrew motioned with his hand for Finn to lower them deeper into the water. Floating now, the boat backed away from the truck and trailer, leaving Finn to pull forward and park in the lot just above the ramp.

Idling slowly, Andrew spun them in lazy circles while they waited for Finn to walk down the length of the nearby dock. Brooke settled herself in the shotgun position, leaving Ava to sit alone on the wide bench that ran along the back. Although it was nearing December, the air was warm. It was about eighty degrees already and it wasn't even mid-day. Glancing around, Ava could see that the lake wasn't crowded, only a handful of boats motored further out.

As they bobbed comfortably in the water, Brooke chattered happily, snapping open an ice-cold beer from a cooler Andrew had hefted aboard. Ava watched Finn approach them along the dock. His dark hair was mussed, a tad longer than when they had met. Cheap shades on, towel hanging casually over one shoulder, he looked good in his blue and gray striped board shorts.

Steering expertly, Andrew teased the boat over towards the dock, then kept it steady while Finn jumped on. Giving his brother a thumbs up, Finn settled next to Ava on the bench seat, one arm slung over her shoulders. Biting her lip subconsciously, she tucked an errant hair behind one ear. Giddy tingles filled her suddenly and she found it hard to look at him. When he leaned down to whisper in her ear, the feeling spread.

"Ready?" He asked.

Before she could respond, Andrew had made it to the buoy line that signaled the end of the no wake zone. With a hoot of approval from Brooke, the boat shot forward, cutting deftly through the water. Ava's hair whipped mercilessly around her face as they picked up speed. Smile broad, she helped Finn grab at her locks, pulling them down to her neck with one hand.

The acceleration continued as the boat bumped lightly through oncoming waves. Beyond the far edges of the water was a rise of rocky hills that towered several stories high in the distance. Other boats cruised along, all crisscrossing in their choice of direction. Some were heading the opposite way, some were chasing along with them. Letting herself lean into Finn, Ava enjoyed the ride.

After a sweep around the edge of the lake, the boat slowed as it entered a cove surrounded by high cliffs. Idling further in, Ava saw two other boats anchored, their occupants lounging comfortably. Relaxed and accepting, everybody offered a welcoming wave. One rock formation stood out, jutting away from the others to form a perfect jumping spot. Well-traveled foot paths could easily be seen wearing down its side.

"This is Copper Canyon." Brooke turned to inform Ava as Andrew cut the engine. "You're not a member of the Moore family until you've jumped from that rock."

"I see." Ava gulped, eyeing the three-story high tower. "Good thing I'm not a Moore."

"Afraid of heights?" Finn asked, as he tossed an anchor into the water. "It's no big deal."

"Said the boring software engineer." Ava arched an eyebrow at him in mock warning.

"You don't have to put up with their crap, Ava." Andrew rid himself of his shirt before cracking open a beer. "If you were my girl, I'd never pressure you like this idiot."

"Very funny." Finn punched his brother affectionately in the arm. "You still can't get over that thing with Theresa? I said I was sorry."

"Bullshit." Andrew turned a face full of glee towards Ava. "This kid stole my girlfriend and I swore to him that one day I would return the favor."

"We were in middle school!" Finn cried.

"It doesn't matter." Andrew began lifting cushions to sift through the hidden compartments underneath. "The only trouble is, I have been unsuccessful to this day. So, what do you say, Ava? Help me pay him back?"

"As tempting as that offer is." Ava played along as Brooke slathered on sunscreen. "I'm going to have to pass."

"Oh." Finn feigned relief. "So close this time, brother. So close."

"Yeah, yeah." Andrew found what he was looking for and straightened. "Want to dive for treasure?"

"Always." Finn bobbed his head in acceptance.

Both men spit into their eye goggles, then bent over the edge of the boat to swish them clean with water. Fastening their masks on, they dove head first over the side, leaving tiny splashes to ripple the water behind them. Ava moved to lean over the side, watching their occasional air bubbles float to the surface. Glancing up, she accepted the bottle of sunscreen from Brooke, who had expertly changed into the stolen swim-suit using a discreetly wrapped towel.

"Why do they spit in the masks?" Ava questioned, stepping out of the crochet cover up she wore to reveal an arctic-blue polka dot bikini.

"It helps keep the mask clear of fog," Brooke replied.

Every now and then the guys would surface to catch their breath before swimming back under. As Ava watched, they swam further and further out. Brooke explained that so many people come to swim in Copper Canyon that a lot of valuable jewelry, watches, and sunglasses were often lost to the water. Growing up, the guys always dove to search for such items. When Brooke offered her a beer, Ava turned up her nose, waving it off.

"You don't day drink?" Brooke asked.

"It's just that I don't care for the taste of beer," Ava admitted. "If I was to take one, I'd just be wasting it."

"Do you like sangria?"

"Yeah." Ava nodded, curious.

"Looks like Finn bought some girly drinks for you because there's a few cans of carbonated sangria in here," Brooke observed, pulling one from the ice.

"Wow." Ava took it. Popping the top, she sipped the contents with a smile. "I didn't realize he did that."

"He must really like you," Brooke commented, sitting sideways in the captain's chair with her feet propped up.

"Why do you say that?"

"He's picking out special drinks for you, bringing you to Thanksgiving dinner." Brooke bobbed her head happily to the pop music bumping in the background. "You know, you're the only girl that he's brought around this family in a decade."

"Really." Ava contemplated the information as the sun stroked her skin with waves of heat.

A sharp piercing whistle rang through the air catching the women's attention. Brooke's return catcall had Ava following her line of sight across the stretch of water and up the rock line. At the top of the jumping cliff, she could make out the two figures of Andrew and Finn. Standing side by side, they waved casually, white teeth glinting from afar.

"They aren't going to-"

"Oh, yeah." Brooke grinned.

Twisting to get a better view, Ava shifted to balance on her knees, leaning forward over the back of the bench seat. Heart skipping a beat, her stomach dropped. It wasn't that she was afraid of heights exactly, it was the falling that had her turning squeamish. A split second later the two men launched themselves out, somersaulting once in the air before straightening to enter the water feet first. Their twin splashes sent ripples emanating out from the base of the rock.

Applause from a few of the other boats greeted them as they surfaced. Ava hadn't known she was holding her breath until just then. Exhaling slowly, she tried to push aside her rattled nerves. Clearly they had both done this countless times before. Cutting through the water with practiced strokes, their cocky grins could be seen plastered across handsome faces.

"Ready for your turn?" Finn was left to tread water while Andrew hoisted himself up using the rear swim step.

"Not a chance." Ava shook her head. "You guys are nuts."

Climbing aboard behind his brother, Finn dripped cold water along the upholstery covering the rear engine compartment before tossing his abandoned goggles on the floor. When Ava scooted away to avoid getting wet, Finn made a dash for her. Wrapping her in his strong arms, he pressed the length of his body against her back, turning her squeals of protest into a bubble of laughter.

"You're so cold." Ava reached to pinch at his side. "I didn't think the water would be that cold."

"Well." Finn refused to release her. "It is November. Speaking of which, I think it's time for you to go for a swim."

"No you don't." Ava's eyes grew wide as he lifted her up. "Put me down, Finn. I mean it!"

"You can swim, can't you?" He asked casually, stepping up to balance precariously on the side of the boat.

"Of course I can." She clung to his body, her grip fierce. "If I'm going down, then you're going with me."

"Deal," he agreed.

Andrew reached out to give his brother a helping shove, tipping them both over the side. The icy bite of water was shocking as it swallowed Ava. She sank fully underneath it before kicking for the surface. Finn had let go of her on impact, so she floated up easily before sputtering. Treading water, she absorbed the good-natured shrug from Andrew, still comfortably standing in the boat. Brooke winked from her seat, giving Ava a little wave.

"Come on!" Finn called.

He had surfaced about ten feet away. Rotating around, Ava swam after him. He headed to a nearby rocky shore, hugging the edge until a low point emerged. The coldness of the water melted into the background of her mind as the simple act of swimming worked to warm her muscles. When she drew close, Finn crept up the side of the rock, placing his feet and hands carefully. Treading water, she waited for him to vacate enough space before crawling up behind him.

Several yards up, the rock flattened out, providing a comfortable sitting spot to dry out in the sun. Sprawling on his back, Finn shaded his eyes, but kept watch on Ava. She sat shivering for a minute before the warmth of the hot rocks absorbed into her body. From their position, she could see the boats drifting in the cove, listen to the mix of music that vibrated from each. Studying the water below, she judged them to be about ten feet off the surface. Across the expanse rose the cliff that the guys had just jumped from, it towered at least three times as high.

"Mark races boats, Andrew steals things for fun, and you live a secret life," Ava declared. "How did the Moore brothers get this way? How can I keep Mason from becoming like you?"

"He's a boy," Finn explained, reaching out to run the tips of his fingers down her arm. "We like to do dangerous stuff."

"You guys take it a step further." She eyed the cliff across from them meaningfully.

"You wouldn't ever jump?"

"No." Ava thought a beat before adding. "At least I don't think that I could."

"What if there was something really great at the bottom?"

"I don't know."

Falling into silence, Ava lay down beside him, letting the sun tan her skin. A slight breeze blew, shifting a few thin clouds that marked the bright blueness hanging high above them. It was a perfect day, a beautiful day. How many times had they talked about doing this exact thing from inside the confines of their metal prison? Turns out that he had been honest with her when it came down to the details of his life, just the names and places had been changed.

If Clay had chosen a new name, maybe she and Mason would still be together. But she couldn't let herself think like that. She had to be strong, she would see him again, when she was no longer a danger to him. Unable to shake the creeping sadness, Ava sat up, drawing her knees to her chest.

"Listen." Finn rolled onto his side to face her. "I wanted to talk to you about what happened between us when we were on the inside."

"Do you regret it?" Ava's heart gave a quick dip.

"You must have been scared out of your mind, and I shouldn't have-" Finn hesitated, searching for the right words.

"Is this about what Clay said?" Ava shifted to examine him critically. "Because you didn't take advantage of me, Finn. I'm a big girl."

"Yeah, but maybe you feel that way because I still have custody of you." Finn looked worried. "You haven't had a break from me. The life and death stuff is still real, it can twist how you think."

"You know what I think?" Ava frowned. "I think that you've gotten too close and now you're looking for a way to back out."

"That's not true." Finn sat up, cupping her chin with one hand. "I don't want you to look back and wish this never happened."

"I wish that my brother had been honest with me. I wish that Mason wasn't taken from me. I wish that the LO never kidnapped me. I don't wish that I never slept with you."

"What if someday you do?"

"How long are you going use that as an excuse?"

In response, his hands smoothed around the back of her neck, lips descending to consume her own. His tongue teased against hers lightly. Running her palms up to feel the smoothness of his bare chest, she felt her own hunger spread along with his fingers as they left to trace down her sides. Stopping at her hips, he tugged gently on the ties of her bikini.

"Hey!" Andrew's shout could be heard from only a few feet below. "You two love birds wanna grab some lunch?!"

Forcing himself to pull away, Finn looked down at his brother motoring gradually by. The boat had started without either of them noticing. Ava had to smile at Brooke's innocent eye wiggle. Standing up, Finn gestured for her to jump into the water below, but after a quick shake of her head, he changed his mind. Going first, he supported her back as they carefully picked their way down the side of the rock's crumbling surface.

Back in the boat, they resumed their seats along the rear bench. Andrew directed the bow towards the open water and waited for the no wake zone to clear. Just before pushing forward on the throttle, his phone began to ring. Glancing at the display, he gave up a small "uh-oh" that had Brooke giggling.

"Hello!" Andrew answered. "Yes, big brother. Well, it's possible that I am in possession of both items."

Pausing to listen, he let the boat drift out lazily. It tipped in rhythm with the waves that were built from other boat wakes and the wind.

"That depends, which one are you most concerned about? Of course, the boat is doing just fine, not a scratch on it, I swear."

"Hey!" Brooke called out in mock indignation. "Don't you care about your wife?"

"He says Mom is willing to babysit the kids." Andrew's eyes beamed. "Want to go pick him up?"

"As long as my day without children continues." Brooke cracked another beer. "Then let's go get the hottie."

FIFTEEN

"And then Henry asks me, where is your go-fast boat Daddy?" Mark gestured to his youngest son, now wiggling restlessly at the long dining table. "That's when I knew that I'd been played."

"Well, in Brooke's defense, the original plan involved ditching her, too," Andrew interjected between bites of spaghetti.

"A fine excuse," Mark cried, feigning his outrage. "Betrayed by my own wife and two brothers."

"Don't forget to blame Ava." Finn leaned back, patting his full belly in satisfaction. "She helped steal it."

"I saw Brooke and confessed." Ava pointed her fork accusingly at him. "A lot of help I was."

"Sounds a lot like the time you boys got caught moving that statue in front of the high school." Paul chuckled, cradling a sleeping Caleb in his arms.

"No one was ever formally caught for that Dad." Andrew stared pointedly at Brooke, who blinked innocently.

"Oh, right." Paul nodded, the smirk still lingered on his

face.

After they had picked up Mark at the dock, the rest of their day was spent simmering in the sunshine, sipping adult beverages, and taking lunch at a restaurant that overlooked the lake. Now back in the comfort of Paul and Olivia's home, they had gathered once more for a giant meal. Green salad, breadsticks, spaghetti with sausage, Olivia simply shined in the kitchen. Despite her repeated efforts to assist, Finn's mother had waved Ava away, insisting the rare opportunity to feed all of her boys again was something she treasured.

With the meal complete, Ava was determined to contribute this time by scrubbing up the dirty dishes. Rising swiftly, she began to clear plates, laying a calming hand over Olivia's shoulder when the woman attempted to stand. A murmur of surprise rippled through the crowd as Finn joined Ava to wash in the sink. She had a sneaking suspicion that he wasn't the first to clean up under typical circumstances.

Elbows bumping, he joked quietly with her as she applied a soapy sponge to a large silver pot. This wasn't the first time that he had helped her at this task. Living with the Militia, the two of them had often pitched in for Rhonda in the kitchen. When his hand grazed hers while accepting another plate to rinse, she felt her heart thump at the glance of his touch. Taking his time, Finn used a brick-red towel to dry before replacing each item in the walnut cabinets.

"It's time for us to pack these kids up and head home." Brooke came up behind Ava to give her a farewell hug.

"Hey-" Ava smiled at the other woman. "That was fun today, thank you."

"No." Brooke grinned. "Thank you for stealing me a free day. Let's do it again, soon."

"Let's."

Resting back against the kitchen counter, Ava watched the close-knit family say their goodbyes. Finn swooped in to lift a slumbering Caleb from Paul's numb arms, carrying him out the door to the waiting SUV. Olivia hugged her eldest fiercely before kissing her daughter-in-law on the cheek. Henry gave Ava a wave before following his parents out. Such sweet boys, it was impossible not to acknowledge the sadness that formed at the absence of her own.

"Hey, I think we're going to hang out back by the fire-pit if you're interested." Andrew snagged a bottle of soda from the stainless-steel refrigerator. "It's a nice night for it."

"Alright." Ava sighed, jerking her hand haltingly through terribly tangled hair. "I think I'd like to clean up a bit first."

"That's cool." Andrew nodded. "See you out there."

Exiting the kitchen, Ava traveled down the short hall before turning right to enter her bedroom. Just past the closet was the door to an attached bathroom. It was already stocked with clean towels in Olivia's most loved accent color, burnt red. Twisting on the silver faucet had lukewarm water pouring down to fill the standard sized tub. Flipping a switch, Ava listened to the transfer of water spritz upward until it fell down from the showerhead above.

Shedding her coverup and bikini, she stopped to analyze her reflection in the massive mirror hanging above the single sink. Aside from the messy hair, her face glowed with health, kissed by a day spent in the light. All of the swelling was officially gone and even without makeup, no discoloration remained. Blue eyes questing, for a moment she flashed to Agent Palmer. The instant memory had her stomach twisting before she was able to force his face from her mind.

Stepping into the spray, she let the hot water cascade over her hair, soaking it thoroughly. Why had she thought of him just now? Maybe it was that his eyes had been blue like hers. Or, maybe it was that she had been seeking an answer from him when he died, staring so intently at one another just as the gun had gone off. She wondered if Finn struggled with the loss of his partner. He never mentioned it, but that didn't mean it didn't bother him as it bothered her.

Rubbing the water out of her eyes, Ava examined the various bottles lining the rim of the tub. Olivia kept the guest bathroom stocked with all of the essentials. She was a very efficient hostess. Selecting the lavender bottle of shampoo first, Ava squeezed a copious amount into her hand, then lathered her hair from scalp to tips. After a rinse, she repeated the process before moving on to the conditioner. With her head held directly under the water, Ava didn't hear the door swing smoothly open to admit Finn. It wasn't until he slid the flower-print curtain open a few inches that she even suspected another presence.

Naked and caught off guard, Ava's first glimpse of him merged in her mind with that of Michael, blending Finn with the other man who had always watched her shower. Fear mixing with shock had her stumbling backwards. A brief cry ripped from her throat as her feet slipped out from under her. She went down hard.

"Ava-" Finn's quick reach to steady her had missed, his eyes flooding with concern. "I'm so sorry. Are you okay?"

"I'm fine." She put up both hands defensively, freezing his outstretched hands in place. "Just go, please."

"But, I didn't mean for-"

"I can't have you in here." Ava's voice cracked. Despite her best efforts, her pulse raced with adrenaline. "Not while I shower. Okay?"

"Okay." He turned quickly on his heel, shutting the door solidly behind him.

Water continued to spray down as she sat at the bottom of the tub, catching her breath. It was the first time that she had forgotten to lock the bathroom door. The day had been so relaxed that it had slipped her mind. Pushing herself to her feet, she rubbed at her newly sore backside, letting the conditioner rinse itself out under the showerhead. In an attempt to collect her thoughts, Ava focused on her breathing and let everything else even out.

She had never been attacked in the shower, so why was it such a sensitive issue for her now? Gritting her teeth, she recalled Finn's expression full of surprised worry. Embarrassment at her overreaction had her scrubbing rough hands over her face. Another time in her life, she would have welcomed a shower with Finn, but now that seemed impossible. Shaking the trembles from her hands, she resumed her routine.

Lathering rich soap over her skin, she washed methodically, ending with her feet. The water had begun to run back from hot to warm, so she twisted off the faucet and stepped out. Trying not to drip unnecessarily onto the tile floor, Ava wrapped her body in one brick-colored towel, while dabbing at her hair with another. She couldn't see her reflection, as the mirror was enveloped in a fine layer of steam. Not wanting to leave a mark, Ava held herself back from wiping a quick slash to clear the tiny droplets.

Brushing blindly through her layers of wet locks, she figured it was probably for the best, not willing to risk seeing another set of grey-blue eyes staring back at her. A quick survey under the granite counter revealed no blow dryer. Contenting herself with damp hair, Ava opened the bathroom door and crossed the threshold into the empty bedroom.

At this point she would give almost anything not to go out to the backyard and face Finn. He would need an explanation and she honestly didn't know what to say. Selecting a pair of black leggings, she topped it with a soft cream-colored sweater. After the LO, she would never own a set of matching sweats again.

The Moore's backyard was expansive. Pretty twinkle lights hung from the wooden pergola with matching strands wrapping a pair of slender palm trees in the far corner. Stone pavers stretched out from French doors to spread around a pool and Infiniti-style jacuzzi. Olivia and Paul sat in Adirondack chairs, feet propped up against the stone ring that comprised their fire-pit. The murmur of their voices could be heard locked in effortless conversation.

Flames danced, casting welcoming shadows over the space, complimenting the cool flow of nighttime air. Off to the left, Andrew stood ankle deep on one shallow step of the pool, talking quietly to his brother. Finn sat with his back to her, legs dangling in the cerulean blue water. Hesitating at the edge of the patio, one meandering walkway led her to the fire, while the other led her to the water. She chose the safety of his parents and veered right.

"Ava." Olivia smiled up at her on approach. "I didn't get a chance to thank you for cleaning up after dinner."

"You're very welcome." Ava returned the smile and settled into her own matching chair. "I'd love if you'd allow me to help with the cooking, too."

"You've got it." Olivia chuckled. "So, you must be missing

your son something terrible. Custody exchanges can be so hard."

"Yes," Ava admitted, propping her bare feet against the warm rocks. "This is actually the first time that I've had to give him up for even a day."

"Really? Doesn't your mom ever take him for the weekend? You know, give you a break? Brooke and Mark love it."

"No." Ava gulped down the flood of emotion. "My parents died before Mason was born."

"Oh." Olivia glanced fretfully at her husband before continuing. "We didn't know, that must have been horrible."

"What happened dear?" Paul leaned forward to pat kindly at Ava's knee.

"They got into a car accident right after I graduated from high school. My brother was still in the service at the time, but he made it back within a few days."

"I just lost my mother barely a year ago," Olivia offered. "It's still so hard. I can't imagine going through pregnancy and birth, let alone raising my boys without her help. Dad's still lost."

"It was a rough time."

Ava tried to be honest but thought about her answers carefully before uttering them. It was impossible not to wonder what life would have been like had her parents survived. Everything would be different. They would have raised Mason, there would have been no hiding the truth then.

"Well, if you ever need a babysitter, we would be more than happy to oblige." Olivia tried to lift the dark mood.

"We're hoping someday that we'll get to meet him," Paul ventured.

"I hope so, too."

Ava nodded along but felt the pressure of Finn approaching. The two brothers stood, hovering on the outskirts of the fire.

"I'm going out." Andrew announced, giving them all a brief salute.

"Where are you off to so late?" Olivia questioned.

"Got somewhere to be, Mom." Andrew gave her a lopsided grin before bending closer, kissing her lightly on the cheek. "My flight leaves tomorrow, so..."

"So..." Paul bated him.

"So, I'll see you next time." Andrew winked at Ava before giving Finn's hand a shake.

"Till next time." Paul rose, walking his son back towards the house.

"At least I have one that sticks around." Olivia huffed, wiping at her eyes. "That's why you need more children, Ava, because they all leave you."

"I don't want to think about Mason being old enough to leave me just yet." Ava grimaced, eyes tracking Finn as he took a seat next to her.

"How long do you two think that you'll be sticking around?" Paul had returned.

"Awhile longer if that's alright." Finn glanced sideways at Ava but his gaze didn't linger.

"What about your jobs?"

"I can work from here," Finn answered easily.

"I'm taking a leave of absence," Ava lied, knowing that her employer would be reluctant to let her return, having not heard from her in almost two months.

"We have some work you guys could do, if you're up for it," Paul ventured.

"Let me guess." Finn sighed. "Rental repair?"

"Hey, it's put food on the table all these years."

"We'd be happy to help out." Ava silenced Finn with a stern look.

"What about Mason?" Olivia asked. "When will you be picking him up?"

"Um-" Ava hesitated, not sure how to answer.

"It's a six month on, six month off agreement," Finn supplied.

"That's unusual," Olivia pointed out.

"Mom, enough with the third degree."

"I see where you get your interrogation skills," Ava commented, causing Olivia's gaze to flick to her husband.

The spark of suspicion that hung briefly in his mother's eyes was a small warning to Ava. Even though the indulgent laugh that circulated amongst them was effective in changing the subject, a mother's instinct tickled at the older woman. Ava recognized it well, having experienced the sensation herself. If Olivia hadn't wondered at her youngest son's very distant life before, she was beginning to wonder now.

Apparently not sharing in his wife's concern, Paul listed the array of problems that faced their various rental homes for several minutes. A family had recently moved out of a two-bedroom house, leaving it in need of new paint, new carpeting, and a severe cleaning. Finn twisted in his chair, sighing audibly, but agreed to take care of it and any other problems that he would happen to discover once there.

The wind picked up, blowing ripples across the surface of the pool. Ava hugged herself tighter, suddenly sagging from the activity of the day.

"I'm going to turn in." Ava rose to her feet but avoided Finn's upturned face.

"Goodnight, dear," Olivia chimed. "We won't be far behind you."

"Goodnight."

Ava pattered back down the stone paver path. The hard surface against the pads of her feet reminded her of the cement floor in the cage. Through the French doors, she skirted around the kitchen, veering towards the little hallway off of the living room. Andrew's bedroom door was open, the expanse beyond was silent and dark. He's no freelance photographer, Ava thought with a slight shake of her head before entering her own room.

Closing the door behind her, she purposefully didn't turn the lock, thinking that Finn would definitely be visiting her tonight. Too much had gone on for him not to seek her out. And she felt that she owed him a discussion, he was an investigator, after all. Changing into her pale blue nightdress, Ava adjusted the slim straps that fit over her shoulders before it transitioned to loose cotton material that drifted down to mid-thigh.

Flicking on her bedside lamp, she pulled back the covers and climbed into bed. The mattress was soft, the sheets cool and comfortable. After a few minutes, she heard the rap of his knuckles against her door. She had left the light on so that he would know she was awake but after the incident in the shower, he wouldn't be pushing through unannounced.

"Come in," she called.

Sitting up at his entry, Ava curled her legs underneath her, then tilted back against the dark wood of the headboard. It gave up a slight creak as he let himself in and shut the door.

The temperature drop outside hadn't seemed to affect him. Still wearing his board shorts from earlier in the day, he had thrown a white t-shirt on, but nothing heavier. Pacing a few steps in the small room, he shifted around awkwardly, as if unsure where to stand. Ava watched his appealing face crease itself with seriousness. Fingers twitching, she longed to run them through his dark hair, but instead kept them at rest in her lap. All the ease that they had built between them had vanished.

"You don't actually believe that Andrew is a photographer, do you?" Ava decided to break the ice with a little distraction.

"Yes." Finn frowned at the thought, before continuing. "You should see his work, it's really great stuff."

"Finn." Ava managed to catch his wandering eyes for a moment. "He's exactly like you, only two years older. Same anonymous drifter, same bullshit explanations, same vibe. You're sure he's not in the Program?"

"He's absolutely not in the Program," Finn was adamant, but then hesitated. "I've never looked into anything else, though."

"Might be worth a peek," Ava ventured.

"Listen, that's not what I want to talk to you about." Finn gestured to a spot on the bed next to her. "May I sit?"

"You don't have to ask permission to sit next to me, Finn." Ava started to laugh, but let it fade at his pained expression.

"Maybe I do, though." He held her eyes with a searching soberness she hadn't seen in a while. "Part of this is my fault. You're a civilian, and I'm not. I've been trained for this, but you haven't. I should know better but something about you clouds my judgment." He paused, watching her a few moments before continuing on. "You see, every time that

Michael would come to get you out of the cage, I saw the way he looked at you. He wanted you, and I knew that it would only be a matter of time. I've never felt so out of control in my life."

"Nothing happened-" Ava interrupted, but Finn waved her off.

"I kept telling myself that if they did anything to you, then I would be able to tell. I was so full of myself, Ava, but it was a way for me to cope. When they would bring you back to me, I would hold my breath, waiting to see some sign. But I never saw any, and like an asshole, I didn't question it. What I realize now is that it's entirely possible you hid it from me. So, I'm asking you, did anyone force themselves on you at the LO?"

"No." Ava shook her head.

"But today in the shower," Finn pressed. "You were terrified. It was the look that I expected back in the cage, but never saw."

"I admit that I have had issues with taking a shower." Ava sighed, leaning forward. "Ever since we got out, I've locked the door. The idea of anyone watching me... I just get panicked for some reason. I don't know why it upsets me so much."

"You've been through a pretty serious trauma, are still going through one. A man was executed inches from your face. You can't walk away from that without some repercussions."

"But it had nothing to do with the shower," Ava protested.

"Trauma can leak out in different ways. Sometimes it's something that you would never think of that turns out to be a trigger point. When you get back to a normal life, you need to see a therapist about it."

"I can't do therapy." Ava shrugged, causing a slender strap of her top to slide off of one shoulder. "It only works if you can share all of your secrets and I'm only getting more of those lately."

"We can't be physical anymore, we've got to keep it professional." Finn paused, eyes coming to rest on the loose strap. "And that's why I need you to tell me to leave now."

"Leave?" Ava watched him struggle as he extended his fingers to pluck carefully at the strap, returning it slowly to its place.

"I'm a trigger for you." His eyes shot up to hers once, then back down to where his hand rested against her skin, one thumb tracing lightly along her collar bone.

"You aren't," she whispered, absorbing the sensation he created.

"I recognized the way Michael watched you, because that's the same way that I watch you. That's why you lost it in the shower. When you saw me, you saw him, and you were afraid."

"I'm not afraid of you."

"It would be better for you if we weren't physical and I've tried, I swear that I've really tried, but I can't seem to keep a clear head around you. I've lost my discipline, and that's never happened to me. So, I need you to tell me to stop."

"Don't stop." She breathed. "What if I don't want you to stop?"

Purposefully, Ava shrugged her shoulders, causing both straps to fall loosely around her arms. She watched his eyes track downward as he tried to withdraw his hand from her skin. That look of wanting he had spoken of brewed, causing his already dark eyes to deepen in their intensity. He was right about so many things, but not about how he made her feel. The truth was that Finn was far from a trigger for her trauma. When he was near her, she felt safe and steady and alive, so very much alive.

For a moment, he had almost mastered himself. His fingertips that brushed whisper soft circles over her skin nearly returned to his lap. Just before withdrawing completely though, his heavy hand betrayed him, dragging downward to take the remains of her top with it. Soft material pooled at her waist, sending a scatter of goosebumps to dance over her exposed skin. In the partial light of the bedside lamp, she listened to his sharp intake of breath, watched his eyes dart up to meet hers, then back down.

Leaning forward, his mouth took hers, one hand reaching to cup the back of her neck as the other left to cruise lower. Slow, deep kisses drew heat to her cheeks, igniting a fire within her that burned with longing. As his hand worked to stroke and cup each breast, she let a low moan work itself from her throat. His response to the sound was unmistakable, whatever misgivings he had started with evaporated.

Tipping her back under the press of his weight, Finn pulled on the loose material at her waist, scooting it over her hips, past her thighs and away. Grabbing at his shirt, she tugged it up and over his head. For a moment, she let her eyes roam his bare chest, let her hands caress his tight stomach. His eyes burned into her, his breathing ragged with wanting, but he waited.

Reaching up then, she looped her hands about his neck, applying kisses to his mouth until he collapsed heavily onto her. Moving beneath him, she rubbed her breasts against the skin of his chest, causing him to let loose a groan of protest. Between her legs, she could feel him already hard behind his board shorts, the silky-smooth fabric was the only barrier left to separate them. Sliding her hand into his shorts, she found him ready for her.

"Wait." He managed to breathe out.

"No waiting," she teased. "Can't wait."

"Wait," he insisted.

Taking her mouth with his own, he silenced any further protest. When his lips moved off down her body, they lingered over her breasts, then her belly. As he continued to travel down, his tongue cruised along the inside of her thigh, finally settling between her legs. Purring her pleasure, she arched against him. With each passing minute sensation built within her until she clutched at his shoulders, biting her lip in an effort to keep quiet. Under his expert attention, she whimpered and bucked until finally she cried out. When his hand shot up to cover her mouth, the muffled sounds of her climax were trapped against his palm.

Panting, she lay well and truly spent beneath him. Her mind was dizzy, her lungs ached for air. Taking his time, she felt him crawl back up over her body and wait. Patiently, he applied soft kisses to her chest, neck, and cheeks as she worked to catch her breath.

"Ready to go again?" He whispered finally, after she had recovered.

"Again?" She was incredulous. "I don't think it's possible."

"Again." Finn's voice was husky.

As he pushed himself slowly inside of her, she gave up an answering moan.

SIXTEEN

Over the next several months, there wasn't a night that passed without him lying beside her. During the first several weeks, they fell into a familiar routine, having decided to remain living with his parents. In the morning, he woke her early. Before the heat of the day was cast over the desert, they went for a run. After breakfast with Olivia, the pair would set off with Paul to work on rental houses.

Ava learned the names of tools and sizing of wrenches so that she could pass them to the men when they were trapped in tight spaces. She fetched ladders, hauled paint buckets, and filled black plastic bags with mounds of trash. After the first month passed, they began to teach her various skills, causing her once delicate hands to toughen with calluses. Filled with a sense of pride at her small accomplishments, she could now change a showerhead, lay tile, and even fix a leaky toilet.

The time with Finn and his dad was well spent. Quick to make a joke, Paul's full laugh echoed down empty hallways, never failing to spread a smile across Ava's face. The work load served to keep her occupied during the day, but the melancholy that plagued her at the absence of her son hovered forever at the back of her mind.

Finn had secured a computer from which Ava checked each month for news of Mason. Clay never failed in his promise to forward a detailed email of his progress, along with photos. Mason was being homeschooled but participated in a playgroup with other children twice a week. His new best friend was named James, and they were having a sleep over soon. He wanted a new race car toy. He missed her. Somehow the information only made Ava ache all the more.

Christmas had been especially hard. Surrounded by the Moore family, Ava suffered quietly at the giddy swirl of Brooke's two boys. Caleb and Henry's joyful rush around a towering tree, trimmed with multi-colored lights, had her heart swelling and breaking at the same time. Finn's gift to her had been a carefully arranged phone call from Mason himself. Though Clay had been reluctant to agree, with pressure, he had eventually set it up. Ava had never been more grateful to Finn than in that moment. Hearing her son's voice soothed her very soul. When the call was over, however, she raged against her utter lack of control. Murmuring promises to her that he could never keep, Finn held Ava tightly, laying reassuring kisses along her forehead.

January came and went and Ava was happy to see the holiday season go. In the midst of February, there was a shift in routine as the Havasu area flooded with vacation rental requests. The city was gearing up for its annual fireworks display and would be bustling with activity. Most of the Moore rentals were long term, but they did keep a handful for vacationers. These homes had stood vacant since the end of the summer season, so Finn and Ava were kept busy hopping from house to house. It was time-consuming, good work, that had both of them feeling extra tired in the mornings.

On one such day, Ava opted to sleep in, so Finn decided to go on their run alone. After he had gone, Ava tossed restlessly, reaching out to stroke his empty side of the bed. The sheets were still warm from his body. Grunting unhappily, she found that she couldn't get back to sleep without him. Finally giving up, she shoved at the covers and headed for the shower. The water only served to perk her up all the more, so by the time she was done, her eyes were wide and mind alert. Getting dressed in jean shorts and a fitted shirt, Ava walked barefoot out to the kitchen where Olivia was frying up some bacon.

"How do you want your eggs?" Olivia asked.

"Over easy, please." Ava retrieved a cup of coffee for herself before pulling up a stool at the bar.

"No run today?"

"I had high hopes of sleeping in." Ava sipped her coffee, cradling the warm mug in her hands.

"It always seems that you can never sleep in when the opportunity presents itself," Olivia agreed.

Setting down two plates, she took a seat next to Ava. Forks clinking occasionally against their plates, the two women ate companionably together. From their position at the bar, they could see through the large French doors and into the backyard. The sunlight reflected off of the surface of the pool, causing sparkles to dance on the walls of the kitchen. Though Olivia was Finn's mother, she was an easy person to get along with. Ava marveled at the other woman's welcoming nature and was forced to acknowledge that they had developed a quick closeness. When their conversation on this particular morning turned serious, it came as a bit of a surprise.

"Is my father right?" Olivia asked. "About Finn?"

"What?" Ava tried not to choke, grasping at her coffee to wash down her last bite.

"Finn isn't a software engineer, is he? Since you've been here, he has only used the one computer a handful of times."

"Well-" Ava was at a loss for words.

"Just tell me." Olivia's eyes bore into her. "Is what he does dangerous?"

"Finn is very good at his job," Ava answered as honestly as she dared. "He's a good man."

"He's in love with you." Olivia's look softened. "Do you at least feel the same way?"

"Mom." Finn's warning tone had them both jumping, they hadn't heard him come in.

"Oh, you scared me." Olivia breathed, sharing an embarrassed blush.

"Ava, you don't have to answer that." Finn's face was stern. "And if you don't mind, I'd like to speak to my mom alone for a minute."

Nodding her head, Ava slipped down off the bar stool, clearing dishes as she went. Heart thumping loudly in her chest, she thought that it was probably the only sound in the room. She didn't want Finn to be mad at Olivia; after all, it was only natural for her to wonder. Someday, if Ava was in the same position, she probably wouldn't be able to hold herself back either. Clattering the plates into the sink, she deposited them before turning to go.

"Olivia-" Ava stood facing them both, poised to exit through the wide doors. "I can't answer the first question because it's not my business to tell. But as to the second, the answer is yes."

There was time only to see the flash of grateful understanding emanate from Olivia's eyes before Ava pushed her way out into the backyard. Snapping the door closed behind her, Ava's brisk walk took her to the edge of the pool. Had she really just confessed that she was in love with Finn? It was something that she hadn't even allowed herself to dwell on. Jittery tingles reached into her hands, causing a strange numbness.

The morning was calm, with minimal cloud cover dusting the vivid blue sky. Dipping a testing toe into the water, Ava found it to be remarkably cold. She had learned that it was a rare house that heated their pool in Havasu. During the summer, it was hard to keep the water below ninety degrees. But in the winter, the chill air at night kept the temperature low. She wouldn't consider swimming in it just now.

Before long she heard the gentle push of the French doors swinging open. Glancing over her shoulder, she spied Finn, turning his back to secure it shut behind him. Pulse quickening, Ava focused on the water. Although she couldn't hear his barefoot approach, she sensed him drawing steadily closer. Refusing to look, she felt his arms encircle her waist; the exhale of his breath caressed the side of her neck.

"Don't be upset with her," Ava whispered, laying her hands over his as they rested against her stomach.

"I'm not," he said. "It was time that I told her the truth and now she's the one mad at me."

"She flipped it around on you, an admirable quality in a mother."

"Takes one to know one I guess."

"Something like that."

"So, are we going to talk about the other thing?" His lips brushed the side of her cheek.

"Let's not," Ava pleaded, but had to smile as his kisses trailed down to her neck.

"Okay," he murmured against her skin. "But the feeling is mutual. Just so you know."

"Okay."

"Hey, there's someplace I'd like to take you." His voice brightened as he straightened up, rotating her around to face him.

"Oh? We don't have to steal anything do we?"

"Not this time," he chuckled.

Taking her hand in his own, he led her back through the house and out the front door. Absently, he gave a farewell shout to his mother as they passed. The old Jeep that they had used to get to Arizona was parked in the driveway. Guiding her to the passenger seat, he opened the door. It had never even been locked.

"Where are we going?" She asked, watching his face shine with mischief.

"To the Desert Bar." Finn jogged happily around the front of the vehicle before darting into the driver seat.

"You're taking me to a bar before noon?"

"Not just any bar." He turned the key. "You'll see."

Hours later, she found herself bumping along a dirt road, rock music blaring from the old radio. Sparsely covered mountains surrounded them with patches of mesquite and other cacti dotting the hills. It was pretty, in the way that any barren place was. She could tell by the way Finn shouted over the speakers, that he had driven this way countless times. He wasn't hardly paying attention to the road. One hand working at the gear shift, the other balanced casually on top of the steering wheel, he described the history of the place that he was taking her.

The bar itself had been built on an abandoned mining camp that was way out in the middle of nowhere. It had to supply its own electricity using solar panels and pump its own water from a nearby well. There were no paved roads that reached it, only dirt paths would take you there. The structure itself had been built with mostly recycled materials, even the windows were taken from old glass refrigerator doors. It had a stage, horseshoe pit, outdoor bar, and saloon. Ava rolled her eyes a time or two, wondering at how dilapidated the place was going to turn out until the cluster of buildings rose up before them.

"Wow," she said, mouth dropping for a moment.

"And you doubted me." His grin was priceless.

Parking next to several other trucks in the dusty lot, they left the Jeep to walk across a covered wooden bridge that dumped them in the heart of the structure. Inside, the ceiling was lined with stamped tin.

Waiting beside Finn at the bar, she ran her hand along the smooth brass. It was unique, larger than expected, and in its own way, beautiful. Music pumped from a live band outside. People milled about, talking and laughing. Handing her a fruity cocktail, Finn guided her back out by the elbow. They grabbed a small table and sat in mismatched plastic chairs, listening to the music as it threaded itself through the air.

"Pretty sweet, right?" He kicked back, sipping on a frosty beer.

"Yeah, pretty sweet." Her eyes cruised over his smug face. "How many innocent girls have you taken for a ride out here?"

"I plead the fifth."

"Wise choice." She ran her hand along his forearm absently. "Have you heard from Clay at all?"

"No." He frowned. "Why do you ask?"

"Because he's late on sending the Mason email."

"How late?"

"A few days," she said, not wanting to confess that she had counted a total of seven.

"I'm sure he's just distracted, you know how guys get."

"Will you call him? Or, can I?"

She knew how guys could get, but that didn't apply in this situation. Her brother would be on top of this, especially because Mason wasn't just some kid to him. Fighting the nagging feeling that something was wrong, she shifted her gaze around the bustling bar. This was a good distraction, for now.

"I'll call him when we get back." Finn bobbed his head. "I'll bet he forgot."

"Yeah." She forced the fear from her mind. "Does this place have anything to eat?"

"I'll grab us something."

She watched the way his body moved off through the bar, so confident and relaxed at the same time. Since they had lived here together, he had lost the tense watchfulness that marked his persona before. Not that he didn't choose a corner table, because he did. And it wasn't like he ever sat with his back to a crowd because he didn't. The anxiety was gone, though. His eyes were alert, but not fierce.

When he returned, she almost laughed. The juicy burger and hot fries reminded her of their first meal together. It hadn't been more than a few months ago that she had sat across from the rookie FBI Agent, watching him unwrap greasy fast-food burgers to shovel into his mouth. The hungry man who now sat before her was considerably more polite.

Taking her time, she nibbled on a French fry, enjoying the dusting of salt left between her fingers. Even back then she had fought her attraction to him. And what was different now? Only the fact that she had lost herself completely, so wrapped up in this alternate life. Frowning at the thought, she tried not to let herself picture the outcome. Best case scenario, she got Mason back and returned to their former existence. What would become of Finn then? He was still in the Program, still an FBI Agent. Try as she might, she didn't see a way for those two lives to blend. The realization sliced at her heart more than she would have liked.

In the background the band kicked down into a slow tune, the melody seeming to dip with her mood.

"What's the matter?"

"Nothing." She shook her head slightly, trying for a sure smile.

"Do you dance?"

"What?"

"Will you dance with me?" He rose from his seat and offered her his hand.

"Seriously?" She half laughed as he helped her up.

Pulling her in close, he swayed slowly along with the music. The spread of his hand against the small of her back had her leaning against him. With one hand on his shoulder, the other clasped tightly in his palm, she let her body move in time with him. Looking around the bar, she noticed that other couples had joined in. She had to smile at that, shifting her head to peer up into his face. The look he gave her took the breath from her lungs. Before she could glance away, he kissed her, releasing a ripple of heartache to chase through her bloodstream. For the first time since they had been together, she recognized that what they had built together was going to come to a crashing end.

It hurt badly, more than she wanted to admit, but she forced herself to hide the pain. She didn't want him to suffer now, there would be plenty of time for that. Breaking the kiss, she lay her head on his chest, listening to the pump of his beating heart. She closed her eyes as he pressed his lips along the top of her head, then reached up to smooth a hand through her hair. In that moment, she wanted to tell him the truth; wanted to confess the most important secret in her life. After all, he had done the same for her.

Risking everything, he had taken her into his family's home and given her access to information that could destroy him. Didn't she owe him that same power? When she was gone from his life, then he would know that she had truly loved him. If she returned his trust with her own, then what they had now was equal, and real.

But then the song ended. The mood was broken and the time to confess seemed over. Beating out a fast melody, the band transitioned back to an upbeat tune. Leading her over to their table, Finn had to shout over the music to be heard. She plastered a fake smile across her face, nodding an assent at his offer of another drink. Walking away through the growing crowd, his step was light.

Dusk approached steadily, its reaching arms of grayness streaked and blurred in the sky. The sun set early this time of year. Despite the bustle and roar of a Saturday night, the bar began to warn its patrons that closing time loomed. Sucking down her last drink, Ava used the haze of alcohol to erase her inconvenient sadness. Finn explained that the bar didn't stay open past six o'clock. If she wasn't ready to quit, he would be happy to take her to another.

Linking her arm in his elbow, they strolled back over the pedestrian bridge to the dirt parking lot. She sat a bit heavily in the passenger seat, her head swimming with the help of booze. As he started the engine, she shifted to analyze him. Even in the company of his brothers, Finn never drank more than two beers at a time. She assumed it was because he didn't want to drop his guard, but she had never asked.

The bumpy dirt road that had snaked them along the way to the bar was now a vacant blackness, illuminated by the pass of weak headlights alone. She couldn't tell where they were heading, or if it was even the same path as before. Finn seemed sure though, twisting the wheel this way and that. He made no attempt at conversation, instead letting the radio's mix of songs fill the cab.

Soon the lights of the city could be seen in the distance. Suddenly, she felt like a silly girl, playing a silly game. Tilting her head back against the seat, she stared at the twinkle of humanity that awaited them. Part of her never wanted to return. It was the selfish part. The part that longed to steal a life with the man seated beside her. Closing her eyes against the pull of that wish, she let her head rock with the movement of the vehicle. She didn't open them until the last harsh bump marked their transition back onto paved asphalt.

Traffic signals blinked brightly; overhead lamps shone down. Several quick turns had them pulling into the driveway of his parent's house. The Jeep rumbled pleasantly to a stop but they lingered for a moment in silence.

"You're upset," he said, turning to run his thumb down the side of her cheek. "I know you're really missing Mason. I bet the email is there now."

"I don't know how much longer I can live without him," she confessed.

"Let's go check." Finn's eyes searched hers for a moment before leaning over to brush his lips against her own.

"Finn-" Ava struggled, wanting to tell him the truth, but the words just wouldn't pass. "I bet you're right."

For a moment, his gaze pierced her, like he could tell that there was something more she wanted to say. When nothing came out, he nodded his head finally and popped open his door. She did the same. Grabbing at his hand as they walked towards the house, Ava held on tight, wanting the reassurance of his affection, even if it wouldn't last forever. Before them, the home appeared heavy and dark. Twisting his key in the lock, Finn swung the ornate glass door open and called briefly for his parents.

He flipped on the lights in the living room and strode over to search the granite countertop in the kitchen. Finding a square of small yellow paper, he relayed that Paul had taken Olivia out for dinner. They had the place to themselves. Walking back to their bedroom, Ava pulled the silver laptop from one dresser drawer and flopped down on the bed. She sat cross legged and turned the power on, waiting while the machine whirred its familiar warm up. When Finn came in, he crawled beside her. Lying flat out on his stomach, he buried his face for a moment in a pillow before rolling onto his side.

"I'm so tired," he sighed. "That beer was like giving milk to a baby."

"That's what happens when you only drink two," Ava chided. "It puts you to sleep."

"That and the burger." Finn groaned. "The glorious burger."

"It was good." Ava agreed, tapping swift fingers over the keyboard.

Scrolling, she clicked here and signed in there. A tiny circle rotated and rotated. Gritting her teeth, she tried to wait patiently for the final screen to load. When it did, the empty inbox sent a sick certainty up her spine. Still no email. Something was definitely wrong.

"Anything?" Finn shifted to look.

"No." Ava's voice strained with the weight of anxiety. "Call him, Finn."

"I'm sure it's fine." He tried to assure her but rolled away to retrieve his burner cell.

Watching him pace was reminiscent of their time on the inside. His shoulders were hunched as he gripped the black phone, holding it pressed up against his ear. She couldn't hear the sound, but she knew that it rang, and rang, and rang. Just when she was about to scream, Finn ducked his head. Clay had picked up.

"Hey." Finn never used names. "Everything is clear here, but we're missing some things."

Stopping dead in his tracks, Finn turned quickly away,

giving his back to Ava. Her heart dropped as she watched him listen to Clay in silence.

"How long?" Finn's voice was low, measured. "You know I'm not going to be able to do that, she's right here."

Stress had built like a boiler within Ava's skin. Instinct. She should have trusted her own damn instinct and called her brother seven days ago. Listening to this one-sided conversation was torture. Without thinking further, she leapt for the phone, snatching it from Finn's hand.

"You've lost him!" Ava screamed into the receiver, terror licking at every inch of her body. "Tell me the truth!"

"They haven't checked in," Clay admitted, voice tight with his own version of despair. "I'll find them."

"You're holding something back." Ava's eyes darted once to Finn, who hovered close, face stricken. "I know it's the truth, like I know you."

"Ava-" Clay's voice pleaded.

"Damn it!" She seethed. "If you don't tell me everything right now, I swear that you won't like what comes next."

"I've had contact from Robert." Clay had never sounded so beaten. "He's got them both. He knows."

SEVENTEEN

"How long?!" Ava shrieked, as she clutched at the phone. "How long has he had them?"

"I don't know." Her brother sucked in a ragged breath. "Maybe three weeks."

"Where are you?" Ava glanced at Finn, who's brow creased into a frown. "I'm coming to you."

"Oh no we're not." Finn yanked the phone from her grasp.

Fending her off easily with one hand, he took control of the conversation. Frustrated tears began to seep from the corners of her eyes as she struggled against his dominance. Peppering Clay with questions, he exchanged snippets of information. The last contact from Mason was the email packet that Clay had forwarded over a month before. Having no idea where they were located, Clay hadn't even realized that they had been picked up until the LO made contact several weeks ago. He hadn't planned on telling Ava until he had located them.

Sagging against Finn, Ava resorted to begging. She

wrapped her arms around his waist, stared up into his serious face and pleaded.

"Let me go to him." Ava held the back of his cotton t-shirt tightly in her fists. "Please, Finn. Please."

"Can we do anything?" Finn's resolve broke finally. "Where can we meet you?"

As the conversation continued, Ava relinquished her grip on Finn and set to flying about the room. Yanking out her suitcase, she tossed it on the bed and opened the black zippered flap. Coat hangers clattered and clicked together as she ripped her small collection of clothes from them. Some tumbled noisily to the ground, but she didn't care. Dresser drawers slid open sharply as she piled underwear, bras and socks in a great mound on the bed behind her.

When Finn ended his call, he followed behind her into the bathroom doorway where she hurriedly slammed cosmetics into her makeup bag. When he attempted to block her progress with his body, she wriggled around him, ignoring his call for her to stop. Mason was in the possession of the LO. This was the one eventuality that she and Clay had worked so hard to avoid and now it had come to pass. She had failed, utterly failed, at her duty as Mason's mother.

"Stop for a minute." Finn kept pace with her as she swept back into the bedroom and threw the toiletries into the suitcase.

"Where are we going?" Ava asked in passing, trying to get around Finn.

"Nowhere until you stop and talk to me." Finn was adamant, so she stood straight to face him.

"How long will it take us to get there?"

"We've both been drinking and we've been up all day. It's

going to take some time for Clay to get his stuff together. What we need to do now is sleep, then pack tomorrow morning and go."

"There is no way that I can sleep now." Ava gritted her teeth. "And you haven't answered any of my questions."

"Clay isn't willing to let us go to where he is," Finn elaborated. "I'm still FBI, and he doesn't want me to see any more of the Militia's holdings or members than I already have. He's going to meet us back at the headquarters in Washington state, but it will take him a day to fly there and settle in."

"So, we should get on the road now. It will take us two days to drive there."

"At least two days." Finn rested his hands on her heaving shoulders. "I promised you that we would get Mason back before and I will keep that promise. What I need you to do is trust me."

"I can't sleep. I can't-" Ava's voice hitched with pent up pain.

"We need to report Mason as having been kidnapped. We need the full force of the FBI working on this."

"No Feds." The vehemence of Ava's refusal cut through her emotion.

"Why not?" Finn searched her eyes, catching her chin in his hand. "Clay refused too, but you're Mason's mother. You need to report this."

"Let me see my brother first," Ava reasoned.

This fresh need to strategize had Ava dialing back her initial panic. Finn's request to involve the authorities reminded her that she was playing a long-term game. She had to keep her wits, she had to focus. Failing Mason a second time was not an option.

"Every minute counts when it comes to a kidnapping." Finn looked perplexed, then suspicious. "If there's anything else that I should know, now is the time to tell me."

"There's nothing else," Ava lied. "Clay is my only family. I need to make this decision with him."

"Okay," Finn relented, pulling her in close. "Let's get in bed and make an early start tomorrow."

Nodding her head, Ava watched him turn to heft the suitcase that overflowed with haphazard clothing, moving it adeptly to the floor. Bending to pick through the mound, Ava shakily snagged her pajamas and changed into them. Finn waited patiently as she slipped into bed before clicking off the bedside lamp. She lay prone for several minutes, blinking into the dark, before he reached out to pull her against him.

Fighting the comfort, Ava stiffened, her throat constricting from the developments of the evening. Finn's warm palm stroked up and down her arm. The gentle puff of his breath caressed the skin of her neck. Eventually, her tense muscles relaxed, her busy mind grew fuzzy. Despite her anxiety, her body dropped into a fitful sleep, overpowered by the stress and subsequent soothing.

Waking just before dawn, she sat up suddenly in bed. The light was on underneath the bathroom door and she could hear water running through the pipes in the house. A quick glance to her side revealed Finn's absence. Jumping up, she flicked on the bedside lamp and changed into warmer clothes. It was February in Washington, that meant winter weather. Skinny jeans, boots, and a fitted long-sleeve thermal would be a decent start. She could keep her red coat in the backseat for later.

Briefly, she surveyed the havoc that she had wreaked in

her attempt to pack last night. With the quick efficiency of a mom cleaning up her child's mess, Ava folded, arranged, and re-packed every item. By the time Finn completed his shower, the bed was made, room tidied, and she was running a brush through her hair.

"Whoa," Finn commented upon opening the bathroom door. "You work fast."

"Want me to pack yours next?"

"No." Finn shook his damp head, the brick-red towel tucked around his waist. "Why don't you get us a quick breakfast to-go?"

"Alright," she agreed.

Leaving him in their room, she entered the kitchen and stood, hands on hips. She wasn't hungry but knew they both needed food to sustain them. Opening the refrigerator, she stared at the contents vacantly. A fried egg sandwich was relatively easy and could be eaten one-handed while driving. As quietly as possible, she selected a pan, and cracked eggs into it. Out of the refrigerator she fetched shredded cheese and butter. Turning to the toaster, she shoved in slices of wheat bread, then rifled through the cupboards for any sign of paper plates. There were none. Spying a roll of paper towels, she tore off a handful, then smoothed them flat on the counter.

When breakfast was done, she washed the dirty pan, spatula and knife in the sink, leaving them to dry on a kitchen towel. While she had worked, Finn crossed back and forth, traveling from their room to the outside. Before they left, he wrote his parents a brief note of thanks. Ava signed her name, too. A reluctant sadness loomed as she gripped the pen, knowing that she would never see the Moore family again.

Settled into the Jeep, Ava held both sandwiches in her lap

while Finn turned the engine over. It had been cold the night before, and even with the sun rising in the eastern sky, the air remained brisk. The old motor cranked and sputtered for a minute until it rumbled haltingly to life. Finn's quick grin at his success softened the sharp edges around Ava.

Handing him his breakfast, she took a tentative nibble of her own. A long drive lay ahead of them. They would be traveling north, tracking the path of the Colorado River until they were forced to cross it. There they would enter a snippet of California before moving on up to Nevada. This wouldn't be the rambling coastal excursion of several months ago so they agreed to take shifts driving. With any luck, they hoped to tackle the nineteen plus hour drive time in less than two days.

Rays from the freshly risen sun lit the right side of Ava's face. The cheap sunglasses from Finn shaded her eyes, but she tilted her head away from it, instead looking past his profile into the distance. Flashes of the wide lake, its blue water glittering, could be seen. Brooke's honest laugh, hair streaming in her husband's stolen boat, came to mind. Goodbye friend, Ava thought, goodbye life that I never had.

Hours passed with the spin of their tires. Conversation was sparse, the task ahead of them preoccupied both their minds. The radio spurted music, then crackled with static, alternating between little known stations as they moved through the reach of various towers. Stopping only for fuel, food, and bathroom breaks, Finn and Ava switched driving every few hours.

By the time the sky was streaked with the dying orange and pink rays of a setting sun, Ava was numb. Extremities prickling, she felt like she practically vibrated with exhausted tension. Finn had laid the passenger seat as far back as it would go. Eyes closed, he appeared to sleep, legs sprawled awkwardly against the dash. It was technically his turn to drive, but she wanted him to rest if he needed it. Glancing at the gas gauge, she figured they had another few hours to go before being forced to refuel. Biting at the inside of her cheek, she gripped the wheel tightly in both hands and motored on.

When she eventually pulled off the highway in search of a gas station, he woke, scolding her thoroughly when he noted the time.

"Wake me." Finn rapped his fist lightly on top of the center console. "Wake me, wake me, wake me. How many times do I have to say it?"

"Alright." Ava exhaled shakily as she stopped the Jeep next to a pump.

Trading places, Finn left to obtain coffee, water, snacks, and pay for the fuel. The seat he had so recently vacated was warm from the press of his body. Bundled now in her red coat, she fastened the gray safety belt across her lap before settling in. Eyes fluttering, the last thing she could recall was the sound of the pump clicking on just before unconsciousness took her. She slept almost the entire rest of the way.

Waking in the wee hours of the morning, she witnessed the last winding curves of a black two-lane road in the pine forested mountains. They had stopped to fuel more than once while she was out, but she hadn't stirred. It wasn't like her to sleep so heavily. Ever since Mason was an infant, Ava had become a light sleeper, moms have to be.

"Almost there," Finn murmured.

"Wake me, wake me," Ava taunted him, but ran an affectionate hand through his rumpled hair.

Thanks to him, they had made the drive in just under

twenty-four hours. Nearing her brother, the barely controlled panic began to subside. From this place, they could work together to get Mason back. It gave her the illusion of control.

Giant trees towered overhead, and Ava had to hold her face close to the window to see them in the pass of headlights as they wound by. It was foggy up here. Thick, cold, remote. Rubbing her hands together, Ava huffed her hot breath at them. The damn heater in the old clunker had quit entirely. Braking hard, Finn stopped the Jeep in the middle of the asphalt. His eyes scrutinized an obscure dirt road that cut off to their right but it was difficult to see it clearly in the dark. After a beat, he reversed a few feet before making the turn onto it.

Bumping slowly down the path, they came to a halt as a large man dressed in starched blue jeans and a tan canvas jacket stepped in front of them. He carried a shotgun slung back over his shoulder, a black ball cap was pulled low over his eyes. Ava watched Finn's hand move deftly to his hip. Lifting up his coat, he flipped the release snap on the holster that lay hidden there.

For a moment, the two men simply watched each other. The stranger made no move to swing his gun around, so neither did Finn. Casually, the other man walked up to the driver side window. Finn rolled it partially down.

"He's been expecting you." The man peered at Ava through the crack in the glass. "I'm sorry about your little boy."

"Thank you." Ava ducked her head.

Relief flooded her system as the man stepped back. Finn shifted the Jeep back into gear and bumped the remaining mile down the rutted road. When they finally reached the large house, Ava sagged for a moment in the passenger seat.

Eyes closed, she felt Finn reach over to take her hand in his own. Sitting there together, her heart beat for him.

"Let's go."

Finn gave her a parting squeeze before relinquishing his hold. The windows of the second story were all dark, but the open side door flooded with internal light. Approaching the familiar entrance, Ava could see David's figure illuminated on the threshold. His welcoming smile helped to set her at ease.

"Didn't think I'd be seeing you again." David stood aside to admit them. "Sorry about the circumstances."

"Me, too," Ava responded.

Warmth hit her like a wave slamming against the shore. A few steps inside had her shrugging out of the woolen coat. She placed it on an empty hook. It was one of many that lined the hallway. Finn murmured to David who stood just behind her, but Ava was too distracted to catch their words. Just where was her brother exactly?

"Clay's still asleep." David answered her silent question. "Why don't you two get settled back in your old room? I'll wake you when he's up."

"Sounds good." Finn jumped to respond before Ava could protest.

They worked their way up the familiar staircase and down the corridor to the small room. The door had been repaired since the last time they had stayed there. Twin beds, made up with the same blankets as before, were a welcome sight to Finn. He had just driven straight through the night and tipped face forward onto one mattress heavily. Ava, on the other hand, had slept that entire time. So close to her brother now, she felt the pull of a job that was just about to begin. A mother's sustaining drive to secure her offspring nagged at her, so she was unable to rest.

Contenting Finn, Ava lay next to him on the bed. She ran her fingers through his crop of hair, stroked his broad shoulders, and felt the inward sigh of his release. Down into slumber he tumbled. She knew the moment the last muscle twitched in his arm that he would be out for hours.

Sitting up in bed, she leaned against the headboard, legs stretched out straight next to Finn's body. In the darkness, she watched David come to fill the doorway. From the light of the hall, she saw him crook his finger at her in silence. Time to go. Carefully, she peeled away from Finn and crept out.

"There are some things that you need to see." David's pace was brisk as he jogged down the stairs.

"Clay up?" Ava asked, following him.

"He hasn't hardly slept in weeks," David confided.

They stopped in front of the office. David knocked gently but didn't wait for a response before opening the door. Clay looked up from his computer when she entered. His hazel eyes were bloodshot, brown hair buzzed short, skin pale. Her brother suffered cruelly. The scruff of a forgotten beard worked to hide some of the drawn lines that riddled his face. From the full plate of untouched food that sat next to him, it was apparent he wasn't eating well, either.

"Clay," Ava breathed it. "My God, you look terrible."

"Nice to see you too, Sis." He laughed a little, but not with his whole heart. "It's the hair, right? Too short?"

"He wasn't washing it," David spoke up. "So, I cut it off."

"Of all the pathetic excuses." Ava mustered some much needed intensity. There was only one way to snap Clay out of this. "How dare you waste time feeling sorry for yourself?"

"What?" Clay registered shock as Ava came to shove the plate of cold lasagna that sat beside him.

"You promised me that you would find them! How can you do that if your mind is soft from hunger and sleep deprivation?"

"You think that I've done nothing?! You think I'm just sitting here twiddling my thumbs?!"

"You're worthless to me right now," Ava spat, sending the dish clattering to the floor. "Get your shit together, this isn't about you."

"Screw you, Ava!" Clay shot to his feet, hands slapping down against the desk. "You think I don't know that?"

"Do you have a sleeping pill?" Ava had turned to David, who nodded his assent.

"I don't need any pills," Clay seethed.

"Eat a full meal, take the damn pill." Ava stared down her brother. "When you wake up, get in the shower. Then come ready to play because we need the best right now and you're not it."

Shoving past her, Clay made a fast exit. Just before disappearing into the hallway, she heard him instruct David to wake him as soon as Finn was up. Listening hard, she heard the sounds of him rummaging through the nearby kitchen. Step one, whip her brother back into shape, check. It had only cost her a little slice of dignity and a floor covered in cold cheese and red sauce.

Crouching down, Ava righted the plate, then used her bare hands to scoop up the sloppy mess. After the big chunks were cleared away, she spied a roll of paper towels and bottle of cleaner set neatly on the far end of the table. David was a sneak, she thought. By the time the carpet had been doused and scrubbed, she heard her brother's heavy footsteps ascending the stairs.

"Don't be too hard on him." David's voice came to fill the room. "His only son has been absorbed by the LO."

"He told you." Ava turned to watch David shut the door carefully behind him.

"Clay Montgomery and Sophia Lockett." He shrugged. "I was surprised at first, but only because he hid it so well."

"This is worst case scenario." Ava tried to keep her insides from quaking. "They both gave up Mason so that he wouldn't end up in the LO."

"I know, but there are new developments. Let me show you what we've been working with."

Gesturing for her to sit, David moved around behind Ava. He clicked a few times on the laptop, closing some files, and opening others. Ava leaned back against the leather office chair, trying to give him room to work. Kneeling down next to her, he pulled up a video file and pressed play. Ava shifted forward, watching with rapt attention.

The blank screen blipped, then filled with a man's face. He was handsome, but severe. Short gray hair was styled neatly, blue eyes shone with intelligent calculation. Though his full body could not be seen, he gave the appearance of height. He was thin, but not overly so. The expensive grey suit that he wore fit him perfectly, helping him to exude complete power. Ava gauged him to be somewhere in his late sixties. This was Robert Lockett, head of the LO.

"Clay Montgomery-" Robert began. "I always respected you as the head of a worthy organization. Though we were never able to conduct business together, I had high hopes of securing supplies for you in the future. You were young, but impressive in your quick rise to power. Apparently, I underestimated you.

Imagine my surprise when my only daughter simply dropped off the map one day. It took more than a bit of doing, but my people were able to trace her back to you. Not the Militia that you run, not the cause that you champion, but you. When I succeeded in obtaining proper leverage against you, I thought surely you would make an even exchange. My daughter for your sister. After all, what was Sophia to you?

You must think me a simple old man. But I assure you that, though I may be getting up in years, I am far from stupid. Maybe that's when you began to underestimate me. Maybe that was your first mistake. You see, with the proper time and resources, I have found my daughter, and guess who she had with her? Guess."

The screen blacked out once more, the video ended. Ava held back a scream.

"So, that was the first one that we received." David resumed his clicking on the computer.

"When was it?"

"It was three weeks ago. Must have been right after he got them because you can tell that he didn't know who Mason actually was at that point. It sounds like he thought he was Clay's nephew, still valuable, but not in the same way. Here's the next one."

Ava leaned into the screen, blinking hard. Her heart beat faster and faster, causing the blood in her body to rush through her system. When the video began to play, Robert Lockett had returned. He was relaxed this time, less superior, more in control. There had been no background beyond blackness in the first video, that remained the case now.

"Clay-" Robert nodded slightly. "As a father, part of me wants to kill you. Not only did you date my daughter without my permission, you put her in a very compromising position. I'm still trying to wrap my head around the idea of her hiding an entire pregnancy from me, but she is a Lockett, so I must give her credit in that regard.

On the other hand, I have to admit that I am overjoyed to learn of the existence of my only grandson. Mason is a fine child, but he's never met his own father, can you imagine that? I'll be happy to step in and foster a positive male role model in your absence. You can rest easy knowing that I will provide the lifestyle for both he and his mother, that you were unable to. Any ideas of an exchange can be safely put to rest. Don't try to recover them, you will fail."

The video stopped and the screen returned to black. Choking on the rapid intake of air, Ava rose to standing, the office chair rolled back abruptly. David stood too, clapping her hard on the back. The force of the slaps had her shaking off the oxygen deprived sensation. As she resumed normal breathing, the two eyed one another.

"Is that it?" Ava managed.

"There's one more." David tilted his head to the side as if wondering whether she could handle it.

"I want to see it."

"This one came in a week ago." David stared at her. "Clay stopped eating after he saw it."

"I can handle it." Ava sat back down in the chair, scooting it close to the desk. "Show me."

Kneeling beside her once more, David worked the controls with efficiency. The video popped up, and he pressed play.

Robert filled the screen, his superior face had settled into a calm directness. The flare of victory was gone.

"Clay-" Robert folded his hands in front of him. "Mason has had some recent trouble transitioning into his new home here. Despite the best efforts of Sophia and my staff, he remains… inconsolable. I must admit that I sympathize with his situation. You see, for the first six years of his life, the role of his mother was played by your sister. He misses her, and I don't blame him.

I have always counted myself as being a very open-minded man, and by all accounts Miss Montgomery was a loving and secure force in his life. Why can't Mason have two mommies? He has no father, and lots of kids have different parenting structures these days. So, for the sake of your son, I must make the request that you give Ava up to the custody of the LO. I can promise you that she will live a comfortable life in my own household along with Sophia and Mason.

As she is the only remaining relative in your possession, I know that this decision will be hard for you. I'll give you time to consider it, but in the end, I think we both know what you'll do. Send us Ava as soon as you can."

EIGHTEEN

"No." Finn sliced his hand angrily through the air. "It's not an option."

"It's the only option," Ava countered. "I can do this."

"You couldn't even steal a boat!" Finn shouted. "How do you expect to play super spy?"

"Steal a boat?" Clay looked perplexed.

The three of them had been round and round like this for hours. When the two men had woken in the middle of the day, David had escorted them down to Ava in the office. Sitting around the conference table, they had discussed the LO's request for custody of Ava but left out the true parentage situation with Mason.

"I want to see the videos," Finn demanded again.

"That's not possible." Clay shook his head.

"You can't actually be considering sending your sister back to the LO." Finn was incredulous. "It was hell. It's dangerous. They will hurt her."

"They won't treat her the same way this time and it would

only be long enough for me to find their location and orga-nize a rescue," Clay reasoned. "I'll inject her with a tracker. She will lead me right to them."

"What if they find the tracker on her? What if they kill her?" Finn strode away, agitated waves emanating from his body. "We need to report this to the FBI."

"No Feds," Ava and Clay said in unison.

"Why not?!" Finn whirled back around. "We can keep the Militia and Clay completely out of it. Just Ava will report him kidnapped. He's her son, it won't affect anything else."

"It's too risky." Ava went up to Finn, spreading her palms across his chest. "No FBI."

"Is there a ransom? Can't you afford to pay it?"

"No ransom, he doesn't want an exchange," David supplied.

"Why would he want to keep your nephew? What's in it for him?" Finn looked over Ava's head, zeroing in on Clay. "You're leaving something out."

The room fell into silence as the door was pushed slowly open. Rhonda poked her head in, hefting a brown plastic tray laden with food. Waving her in, Clay blew out a frustrated breath and folded his hands behind his head. David held the door while Rhonda moved to deposit the tray on the long conference table before walking back out. Ava's stomach growled unhappily.

Leaving Finn's side, she plopped down at the table and began sorting through the food. She selected a cold corned beef sandwich and took a massive bite, groaning with mild contentment. Unlike her brother, who had lost his appetite at the thought of sending his sister to Robert Lockett, Ava had grown ravenous. For the first time in many months, she would see Mason again. Her mind wouldn't allow her to think past that point.

Drawn by Ava's feasting, the three men succumbed to the table. Chip bags ripped, ice tinkled inside water glasses. The sounds of quiet chomping resonated throughout the room for several minutes. Reaching satisfaction, Ava kept her gaze on the table. She wasn't sure of the details of this plan, or even if it would work. What she was sure of was that she was going back to the LO, even if the men in the room did not agree. The finality of that choice calmed her.

"Where were you guys this whole time?" Clay asked. "You look almost tan."

"New Mexico," Ava supplied. "Winter is pretty nice in the desert."

"I couldn't locate you," Clay admitted. "Did you learn anything about hiding while you were gone?"

"A few things." Ava bobbed her head.

"Could you do it again?" Clay asked cautiously. "If you needed to?"

"Absolutely, I could hide Mason too, better than..." Ava trailed off, catching herself at the last moment.

"Wait." Finn sat up, causing Ava to cringe with her slip. "Who was hiding Mason when the LO grabbed him? Can I speak to them? They may have valuable information."

"Not possible." Clay shook his head.

"Why not?" Finn's frustration began to boil over. "How do you expect to find Mason like this? I can help but you have to give me the full story."

Taking his time, Finn analyzed each face in the room. Clay held steady, fighting fire with fire. David shrugged casually before folding his arms across his chest. Ava looked away, unable to keep the misery from contorting her features.

"Ava." Finn crouched down before her, sensing the weak link. "Don't you remember what it was like in there? Aren't you afraid that they are going to hurt Mason? Let me report this to the FBI. We need the full resources of the government to get him back."

"Robert would never hurt him!" Ava cried, trying to keep her face averted.

"What makes you so sure?" Finn whispered, fingers brushing gently against her face as he held her chin, forcing her to look into his eyes.

"He wouldn't hurt him."

"Robert Lockett would kill that boy without a second thought. Unless-" Finn's eyes popped wide with the realization. "Unless he was related by blood. Ava, did you sleep with Robert Lockett?"

"No." Clay stood now, taking the heat off of his sister. "She's never even met the man. Mason is my son. Mine and Sophia's."

"Mason is your son." Finn rose to face his old friend, his voice jumping with each progressing sentence. "Your son with Sophia Lockett? Your son that you had your sister raise as her own?! My God, you could not have fucked this up any worse!"

"Finn-" Ava pulled at his arm. "You have to understand."

"Oh, I understand." Finn leveled an accusing finger at Clay. "You let them keep your name, you didn't hide them, you didn't prepare Ava for anything. How could you be so sloppy?"

"It was last minute!" Clay shouted. "I dropped out of the Program, I was ready to run, but Sophia backed out at the last possible moment. Ava didn't know anything about my life. She didn't know about the LO or even about Sophia. I was left holding Mason in one hand and a blank birth certificate in the other."

"So you shifted the burden to Ava?"

"I called the only person that I could trust," Clay seethed. "She came, took her nephew as her son, and started a new life. Under the circumstances I thought that her lack of knowledge would be enough to protect them. I never thought that Sophia would come back but then she just showed up and convinced me to make her the James Miller contact. She had no intention of returning to the LO. They ran her down, simple as that."

"You are in way over your head," Finn exhaled, running his hands through his tussle of dark hair. "You need the Feds more than ever."

"If we report him as kidnapped to the FBI," Ava interjected. "Then they will find out that Mason is Sophia and Clay's son."

"Johnny-" David offered his level voice. "Mason is the only direct heir to the Lockett Organization as well as the Constitutional Militia. What will happen when that becomes common knowledge? His chance for a normal life will evaporate entirely. He will be a pawn in the games played by bloated governments and bad men."

"All the more reason for Ava not to go back." Finn gripped her shoulders, bringing her face close to his. "Ava, don't do this. After everything that we've been through, you have to trust me. You didn't trust me with the truth about Mason, but please, believe me now."

"I have to go to him." Ava's eyes searched Finn's, trying

desperately to convince him. "Mason needs me and I love him. I'm going back."

"No." Finn shook her gently. "I won't let you go."

"She can do this." Clay's eyes had narrowed, watching the subtleties play out between them.

"She has no training." Finn glanced over at him, refusing to release Ava's arms. "She's not a damn operative, Clay. She doesn't know what she's doing."

"She knows what she's doing... she seduced you, didn't she?"

Clay dropped his last sentence on Finn as if pulling a pin from a hand grenade. The first few beats of silence that filled the room were like the seconds when the little bomb rolls and tumbles into place. Reactions are slow, drawn out. Finn's eyes darted to lock with Ava's, shock registering on his face. Clay crossed his arms confidently over his chest while David braced for impact.

The explosion of emotion itself sent shock waves of speed and sound to ricochet off the walls.

"Why would you say that?!" Ava screamed at her brother, breaking free as Finn's arms fell limply to his sides.

"Is it true?" Finn whispered, senses dulled by the possibility. "Did you set out to seduce me? Are you working for them?"

"No!" Ava shouted, grabbing for Finn, panic licking at her heart. "It's not true. It's not true."

But Finn melted away from her. She saw the shift of uncertain agony in his eyes just before they clouded over. Shoving past her, he stormed from the room. The door slapped open violently on his way out. Clay hurried around the side of the table, catching Ava around the waist as she made to follow. Holding her in place, he called to David.

"Let him go!" Clay instructed. "Let him go."

"Why would you say that?!" Ava cried, turning to pound her fists against her brother's chest. "It's not true!"

"You made up your mind, right?" Clay questioned. "You decided that no matter what, you're going to Mason?"

"Why would you?" She continued to moan, sagging against him.

"It was the only way to get him to leave." Clay wrapped her in a brotherly embrace. "As long as he was with you, he would have made sure you didn't go. Trust me, I know John. Once he gets a hold of something, that's it."

Chest heaving, she worked hard to calm herself. Clay knew nothing about Finn, at least not the real one, and she resolved to keep it that way. Wiping at her eyes, she pushed back from her brother, who released her to sit in a nearby chair. David poked his head back in briefly.

"He take the Jeep?" Clay asked.

"Yeah, he's gone." David nodded.

"Alright, so let's assume that we have at least a few hours head start while he collects his thoughts." Clay shifted to sit at a computer. "We've got to vacate, asap. Call in a clean team to wipe down everything. I don't want one hair, one finger print, nothing left. List the property for sale."

"On it." David disappeared from sight.

Sitting by numbly, Ava watched as the Militia swung into action. Within half an hour there was a crew of no less than a dozen men on the premises. Methodically, they emptied every room, took boxes upon boxes of weapons, ammunition, kitchen wares, and clothing. Furniture came next, followed by bags cinched tightly around bedding, pillows, towels, and rugs. Computers and electronics of every sort were packaged carefully before being hauled away. Outside, two huge moving trucks had pulled up to sit, engines idling in the driveway. The sun had set by then and the darkness covered the details of their activity.

Standing alone as a witness, Ava hugged herself, the red woolen coat did little to warm her icy insides. She had known the relationship with Finn would have to end, but she hadn't wanted it to go in quite this way. Bitterness against her brother's intervention, though, had begun to fade. She understood why he had made the cut. If she could change anything, it would be that Finn thought she had betrayed him. That reality burned in her already anguished soul. Shifting her thinking, she focused instead on Mason. Nephew or son, she didn't care. He was hers, she loved him more than anything, and she would be joining him soon.

"Ready?" Clay had come to stand beside her.

"What's next?"

"The clean-up crew will be arriving shortly, but David will stay to finalize that. You and I have a plane to catch."

"Plane?"

"Come on." He grabbed at her arm to start her moving.

Skirting the heavy trucks, she followed his lead. A dark sedan was parked just beyond, headlights shining brightly against the black night. Momentarily, her feet stilled. The last time she rode in one of these, all hell had broken loose. Of course, it ended with her in the hands of the LO. That's exactly where she was going to end up again, only this time by choice.

"I hate black sedans," Ava snarled, causing her brother to laugh.

Clay rode shotgun while Ava settled herself into the back seat. Sliding her hand over the smooth leather, she inhaled the scent of new car. Glancing at the driver, she saw a pair of brown eyes reflected in the rearview mirror. Another anonymous man taking the wheel to steer her through life. She had learned not to care.

Winding out of the mountains, they sought the speed of a highway. Ava rocked with the gentle motion of the car as its tires absorbed the asphalt that passed below. Talking rapidly on his cell phone, Clay ordered a private plane, rearranged a few meetings, and issued a series of coded orders. When the lights of a city approached in the distance, Ava took little notice. Sucked down into turmoil, she fought herself.

On the one hand, her heart soared at the prospect of reuniting with Mason. On the other hand, it bled slowly inside of her, leaking out its contents with every beat that reminded her of Finn. Closing her eyes, she refused to witness the rest of their journey.

THE AIRPORT WAS BUSY BUT THEY HAD NO LUGGAGE. TRAILING Clay, she weaved behind him through the crowd. They passed unchecked through security and ducked into a small terminal off to one side. When they boarded the tiny jet, Ava's eyebrows raised in question. This was expensive, no doubt.

"You're wondering where the money comes from," Clay supplied, settling into a wide leather seat.

"I didn't ask." Ava shrugged.

"It's clean, if that's what you're worried about."

"That's not what I'm worried about."

"I really could use you, Ava." Clay was intent. "To help run the Militia. It has assets, property holdings, membership dues, you'd be great at that kind of thing."

"Stop talking, stop talking, stop talking," Ava commanded, pushing her hand against the side of Clay's face.

"Fine." Clay changed seats with a huff. "But think about it."

Turning her back on him, she watched the brightness from the airport buildings flash past them through the jet's oval window. Faster and faster they went, until everything blurred and the nose of the plane lifted high into the air. Ava pressed her fingertips against the cold glass, and thought of Finn.

When they touched down in Texas, a blue pickup truck waited to escort them to a nearby hotel. Painfully, it reminded Ava of Andrew's, although this one was much newer and a size or two larger. She had nodded off for several hours on the flight down but felt oddly disconnected from her body somehow. In the past forty-eight hours she had traveled through no less than five states.

Counting on both hands, she settled on six. Texas was the sixth state, and now she felt them all. When the truck ceased its rolling, Ava found herself staring up from their position in a circular hotel driveway. It had been the middle of the night when they left Washington, but with the time change, dawn was just on the edge of bursting. Still, lights from the neighboring high-rise buildings illuminated the area completely. They were in the heart of downtown Houston.

"This place looks nice," Ava commented.

"Thanks." Clay bobbed his head before shoving open the heavy door.

"Thanks?" Ava moved to follow. "Kind of a weird response."

"Not really." Clay glanced back as he crossed the threshold into the expansive lobby. "I own it."

Stopping short, Ava blinked a few times before regaining her composure. It was the end of the graveyard shift at the hotel, but still a handful of employees stood expectantly behind the sleek front desk. Its wide white counter was set off by a large blue background that housed the emblem of the establishment. Clay didn't pause, but simply waved in greeting as he veered towards a bank of elevators.

"You do not own this place," Ava hissed, finally catching up to him.

"Well," Clay elaborated. "Technically the Militia does and I'm something between a President and CEO, so I guess you're right. I don't own it, I run it."

The pleasant ding of an elevator sounded, distracting the siblings from their dispute. Quietly they loaded into the shining gold box, its reflective interior wiped impressively clean. Clay depressed the button for the third floor which had the elevator jumping only slightly before sliding its doors open once more.

"What?" Ava teased. "No master suite?"

"I've had them convert several rooms into a small apartment for me. The lower the floor, the better." Clay was casual.

Following him down the well-lit hall, Ava noted that the hotel looked completely normal. There were numbered rooms, a few Do Not Disturb placards hanging from silver door knobs, and one abandoned room service cart. Near the stairwell at the far end, Clay stopped and used a regular key to unlock his door. This one had no number.

Upon entering, he pushed at some buttons on a keypad located just inside. Silent alarm, Ava realized. Flicking on lights, he moved further in and let the door slam shut behind them. There was a small kitchen off to the left and a living area with a couch and television on the right. It had standard hotel furnishings, the cherry colored cabinets matched the coffee table, television cupboard, and barstools. Pale tile flooring transitioned into tightly woven dark-blue carpet.

"It's remarkably clean in here." Ava ran her finger over the white granite that comprised the kitchen counters.

"I use the maid service, same as everyone else." Clay's voice dropped as he disappeared down the hall.

"You trust them?" Ava followed behind.

Down the short corridor Ava passed the bathroom, then leaned against the threshold of an open door where her brother rummaged about just inside. It was another nondescript hotel bedroom, complete with queen mattress, dual nightstands, and a flat screen mounted against the far wall. Closet door hanging open, Ava noted a small dresser, again in the Cherrywood color, along with men's clothing hanging from a silver rod.

"I only use a select crew to clean and they aren't allowed in my office." He gestured back down the hall. "I keep that one locked. There's another bedroom on the other side of the living room, that's for you."

"You've been living here?" Ava turned back down the hall and walked to inspect her own quarters. Clay shifted to dog at her heels.

"I don't live anywhere for very long," he admitted. "But this is where I most often stay. I'd like to slow down a bit, but I need more help running things. I wasn't kidding when I asked you to come work for me."

"You mean not as a super seductive operative?" Ava glared over her shoulder before opening the bedroom door.

"I said I was sorry about that," Clay protested. "Do you really think Johnny would have let you go?"

"No." Ava acknowledged her defeat.

"I took the liberty of moving the rest of your clothes here from the Orange County house." Clay sat on the edge of her bed while she ran her fingers over the full hangars in the closet.

"Mason's clothes, too?" She was desperate to bury her face in the little boy's shirts, inhale his scent.

"Yeah, I sold the property. Hope you don't mind but you can never go back there anyway."

"I understand." Ava turned to face him, though there was a twinge of sadness that grew at the thought. "Do you ever regret it?"

"Regret what?"

He was being facetious, Clay knew exactly what she meant. Withering under her pointed stare, he relented.

"Every day of my life. There, you happy?"

"Not really," she sighed, sitting beside him. "Is there a way to fix it?"

"I could never make up for the years that I've missed."

"No, but you could spend the rest of them together. If you really wanted to."

"What are you suggesting?" Clay studied her face.

"I'm going back to the LO, right?" Ava clasped his hands in her own. "They'll take me to Mason and Sophia, and then you'll track our location. When you recover us, then what? What comes after that?"

"I hadn't thought that far," he admitted.

"If Mason can have two moms, why not a dad, too?"

"You want us all to live together?"

"You and I both know that Sophia will not want to give him up." Ava gave him a little squeeze. "Is there anything left between you?"

"It was a long time ago." Clay withdrew his hands abruptly and stood. "We just need to focus on the next steps right now. Get some rest little sister. Within the next three days, we're going to deliver you to Robert Lockett, and you'd better be ready."

NINETEEN

Alone, she sat on the hard floor and surveyed the scatter of paper fanning out around her in the shape of a noonday sun. Systematically, she had separated, sorted and stacked the never-ending business documents that made up the last several years of her brother's life. Hands clasped briefly behind her neck, she arched her back, trying to stretch out the dull ache that persisted. Why had she volunteered for this again?

"It's a mess isn't it?" Clay poked his head through the open door of his office.

"That's an understatement." Ava sighed, feeling overwhelmed. "Why haven't you hired an assistant?"

"I've interviewed but could never find anyone that I could trust." He smoothed at the army green jacket he wore. "This room holds every move the Militia has made since I took over. It lists every bank account, every business investment, membership rosters-"

"I get it, I get it." She held up her hands to cease his listing.

"Well, I'm off." Clay gave her a quick nod.

"Where to this time?" Ava complained. "It's been three days, you said I would be going to the LO by now."

"I have a strategy meeting that I can't miss." Clay straightened impatiently. "We are negotiating with Robert on how best to deliver you and I don't want to rely on the trackers alone. If we can set up surveillance, then a team could follow you."

"Alright."

She waved him off abruptly, causing his face to twist in frustration before he stomped out. Rubbing absently at the base of her skull, she tested the injection site for the hundredth time. Even though she knew exactly where to push, her fingers still failed to sense the tiny electronic device.

That had been the first order of business when David had arrived two days previous. Together, the two men had debated over and over the exact placement of the trackers. The plan was to have one tracker be live and functioning when she was transferred to the LO, while the other would lay dormant for ten days. Only a fool wouldn't search her for electronics, so it would be better to give them what they wanted up front and hope the second would get by under the radar.

Willingly she had submitted as David held up her hair to expose the back of her neck. Hands steady, Clay had pierced her sensitive skin with the injector. A few drops of blood had squeezed out, no more. It reminded her of her eleventh birthday, when her mother had taken her to the mall to get her ears pierced. It wasn't terribly painful; the anticipation was the worst part. The second tracker was placed neatly between the index and big toe of her left foot. Purposefully now, she gave them a wiggle. Still nothing. If all went according to plan, that one would never be detected. Grimacing, she tried not to think of them being cut out, but it was inevitable.

Shaking her head, she refocused on the mountain of documents before her, and got back to work. Since her arrival, Clay had insisted on her isolation inside the hotel. In order to stave off boredom, she had agreed to organize his office, but it was a decision that she soon came to regret. Not only was it an inordinate amount of work, but the knowledge of critical Militia practices washed over her in waves. They owned a chain of hotels throughout the country, large parcels of rural land in almost every state, training facilities, weapons caches, vehicles, and equipment; everything a doomsday prepper could lust for. Plucking up the next manila envelope, Ava laughed out loud. Mentally, she added a water treatment facility to the list of assets. Clay was brilliant, truly. Their father would have been proud.

Several hours later, her stomach rumbled, though Clay had not yet returned. Bracing her hand on a nearby filing cabinet, Ava stood up and propped herself against it. He had taken her to the hotel restaurant twice and the food had been delicious. The other option available to her was room service, but she had already ordered everything on the limited menu.

Stepping carefully between stacks of paper, she skirted the large mahogany desk and sat down. The brown leather office chair enveloped her, giving much needed support to her lower back. Letting out a quiet sigh, Ava flipped through the laminated room service menu once more. Pasta? No. Salad? Maybe. She was just about to pick up the hotel phone to dial, when her eyes were drawn to a half opened brown box. It was haphazardly wedged amongst more envelopes and an array of other boxes, but the contents of this one caught her attention. Burner phones. The box positively overflowed with them.

Since leaving Washington, Ava had relinquished hers to Clay. Up to this moment, she hadn't thought twice about it. Fingers itching, she dropped her hands solidly back into her lap. Is it still considered drunk dialing if you aren't drunk? Thoughts of Finn came to wrap around her body, making her remember the steadiness of his presence. Throat a little tight, she fought the impulse to contact him. She didn't know if he still had his burner cell or not, but the number was etched into her memory.

Heart beating with a distinctive thud, she recalled the way things had ended between them. The look of betrayal that had filled his eyes still seared its brand on her chest. She hated to leave it like that. She hated the thought that he was left to wonder at the truth of the past few months. What could one call hurt? Just one call to give a proper explanation. Just one call to say goodbye. After all, she was about to disappear yet again, this time under the control of Robert Lockett himself. If all went well, then she would return shortly with Mason in tow. If all did not go well she might never return at all. Better to sew up any regrets now, while she still had the chance.

Before she could change her mind, Ava snatched a cell from the box. Powering it on, her eyes lit along with the tiny rectangular display. These were older model flip phones, not capable of email or so much as a text. Still, Clay would not appreciate this move on her part. Shoving the contraband into the back pocket of her tight jeans, she left the office to slip into tall black boots and a heavy woolen coat. When she crept into the hallway, not a face was to be seen.

Following the geometric design on the carpet, Ava told

herself to walk normally. Rushing only attracts attention. She depressed the elevator button and didn't have to wait long before the ding of arrival sounded. Golden hued doors slid open with no one waiting inside. How could one girl get so lucky? Resolving to stay in the lobby, Ava's hands shot to the phone, checking that it was still there, of course it was.

Mind racing, she shuffled through what it was that she wanted to say to Finn. She was in love with him, she missed him, she was sorry. Nothing sounded right as it formed itself into sentences that ran like ticker tape through her head. Better to just wing it because the desire to hear his voice had come to overpower any logic. When the elevator released her into the lobby, Ava noted the curious stares from the check-in desk. These employees knew nothing of the Militia, but they were aware that she was a female guest of the hotel's owner.

Offering them a lopsided smile, Ava suddenly felt the pressure of an audience. She couldn't call Finn under such scrutiny. Deciding that a brisk walk around the block couldn't hurt, Ava stepped through the front door which was held open by a doorman dressed in a midnight-blue uniform. He didn't say anything to her, but her heart raced all the more.

Cold air whipped about, tossing her loose hair briefly into her face. It was still winter here, but the days locked inside had made her forget. A cement sidewalk skirted the circular driveway before hugging the side of the building and continuing on along the busy street. She let her feet travel over it as it guided her through the heart of downtown. Hotels, offices and skyrise apartments shot up to tower overhead, blocking the afternoon sun.

Trembling now, she pulled the phone from her pocket, and quickly dialed the digits. It rang, and rang, and rang. With each extended chime, her nerves ratcheted up a notch until finally there came the familiar click of an answer. Exhaling slowly, Ava waited, fingers tingling. It was like him not to say hello. It was like him not to say anything at all. She had to smile.

"Finn," Ava began, slowing her pace to meander along the sidewalk. "It's me-"

"Don't hang up." Finn's voice was gruff, causing her to frown.

A muffled sound covered the receiver; he had placed his hand over the phone. She heard him speaking in the background, excusing himself from a group of people, one of which he addressed as "Sir." For a moment, she wanted to hang up, but something kept her there, holding the line.

"Still there?" He was back, walking now. She could tell by the huff of his breath.

"Are you working?" She was tentative, asking for cues.

"Yes."

"Can you talk?"

"I can listen."

"Alright." Ava squeezed her eyes shut for a moment before resuming. "I called because I wanted you to know that what my brother said was not true. I wasn't working for him and I didn't set you up."

She waited a beat, but he failed to respond. His breath kept coming like a man in a rush, so short of cutting the call, she resumed speaking.

"I thought that I owed you an explanation and I wanted to tell you goodbye. Maybe I'm just being a silly girl, but I'm in love with you, Finn. I'm going to miss you."

"Then don't go," Finn whispered.

"I've already made my choice. I've got to see Mason."

"There's another way to make that happen," Finn hissed. "Don't hang up, I'm almost outside."

Wandering along beside the reflective windows of another building, Ava approached an intersection. Traffic zoomed through a green light. Distractedly, she turned the corner, keeping her steps slow.

"Finally, I'm free to talk." Finn breathed. "Look, I should never have left you in that house. I should never have driven away. What Clay said got under my skin like nothing in my whole life, and I lost my head. By the time I figured he was full of shit, the house had been cleared and you were gone. Where are you, Ava?"

"You know I can't tell you that."

"Let me come to you. Wait for me to get there, please. We can do this another way, a safer way."

Finn did his best to persuade her, each sentence gathering speed as he went. The desperation in his voice ran clear. Head down, one hand shoved into her coat pocket, Ava's eyes tracked the various cracks that ran along the path before her. It was so hard not to give in. Finn had done everything for her over the past few months, and she had grown reliant on him. A part of her desperately needed to lean against him now, but she knew that if he were here, she would never be allowed to leave with the LO.

Just before her resolve solidified, Ava ran headlong into a fellow pedestrian. Instantly embarrassed, she began to utter an apology. Those words evaporated from her mouth the second she looked up, shock filling every aspect of her face.

"Michael?" Ava asked, as the phone dropped from her loose grasp to clatter noisy on the ground.

"Ava." Michael smiled easily, stooping to retrieve the cell. "Surprised to see me?"

"Yes, I was afraid that Aaron had you killed for defending me."

"Oh, they can't kill me." Michael shook his head, flipping the phone closed with a decided snap. "Uncle Robert wouldn't stand for it."

"Uncle?"

"Afraid so." Michael joked as he offered his arm. "So, are you ready to see Mason?"

"Um-" Ava hesitated as the burner cell began to ring, and ring.

"I know this isn't the way that your brother wanted to do this, but it avoids a lot of potential bloodshed. Anyway, this is your decision, so I can walk away if you'd rather." Michael extended the ringing phone, offering it in his open palm.

"No." Ava shook her head at the cell, then looped her hand through Michael's elbow. "I'm ready to see Mason."

Together they walked along the sidewalk until Michael reached a trash can. Casually he held his hand to hover above it, relinquishing the phone to fall down and ring amongst the icy garbage. At the next corner, a sleek white town car sat purring along the sidewalk. As they approached, the driver exited and held open the rear passenger door. With all the courtesy of a gentleman on a date, Michael helped to settle her inside the plush interior before scooting around to slide in on the other side.

Subtle music drifted from the speakers, filling the car with quiet luxury. If Ava hadn't been aware of the danger of her situation, she might have exhaled in relief. Pulling out into the flow of traffic, the driver steered them north before seeking the entrance to a nearby freeway. The rear seat was spacious, but even so, Michael's presence felt close, though not overbearing. Flicking his wrist, he gestured to the driver, who reached for a small black case on the front seat.

"Even though we've caught you a bit off guard." Michael unzipped the bag. "I'm going to need to give you a quick scan. It won't hurt."

"Okay."

Ava turned to look at him, keeping her face relaxed, the way she had practiced with Clay. Flashing her a quick smile, Michael made no effort in hiding the contents. He drew out a thin black rectangle, it was no bigger than a cell phone. Methodically, he moved the device just above the surface of her skin. Beginning with her forehead, he took his time scanning each and every inch of her body.

The device beeped plaintively only once, when he passed it behind her neck. Eyebrows shooting up in mock surprise, he made a scolding tsk sound, and bade her turn away from him. Cool fingertips probed gently along the hairline at the base of her skull.

"I can't even feel this one," Michael commented. "When I extract it, I'll do my best not to cut any of your hair."

Another beep from the scanner sounded, then another. He was doing his best to locate its exact position. After a beat, she felt a cold alcohol wipe swabbing the back of her neck. Heart jumping, her fingers gripped the seat leather nervously. The trace of an ink pen circling against her skin sent goosebumps cruising down her arms.

"Ready?" Michael asked.

"Yes," Ava whispered.

She felt the careful slice of a thin knife pierce her. Biting back a cry, Ava squeezed her eyes shut, trying to focus on something else. The insertion had been easy, direct and quick. Extracting the tiny device was more difficult, requiring Michael to be deliberate, and slow. For longer than she wanted, he probed her flesh.

"Got it." His voice came out behind her. "Sorry about that."

"It's okay," Ava lied, hoping this would be the only violation she would endure.

Cleaning her up, Michael applied a bandage over her wound before letting her hair back down. He passed the tracker up to the driver who unceremoniously rolled down his window and tossed the device onto the rushing asphalt below. Shortly thereafter, the car exited the freeway only to get back on heading in the opposite direction. South, towards the border, just like Clay had predicted. Ava kept her face impassive, hoping against hope that in ten days' time, the other tracker would flip on and ping her location for Clay to see.

"There aren't any other tracking devices that we need to be worried about, are there?" Michael asked.

"None," Ava replied confidently, the practiced lie seemed well received.

The drive itself rolled smoothly along, all five hours of it. Michael set her up with a few movies to watch on an old DVD player and made certain to stop for meals. When she turned her nose up at fast food, he directed the driver to call ahead for take-out from a sit down restaurant, then went in himself to fetch it. Reminding herself to keep her guard up, Ava was admittedly impressed by his expensive suit, gentle manners, and casual conversation.

Outwardly he was a far cry from the conflicted man in

military fatigues who had watched her shower one day, then smuggled her contraband the next. Underneath the change in exterior, his quick smiles and stolen glances were the same that she recalled before. Now freed from the confines of their prior interactions, Michael was relaxed, open, and often funny. He explained that his mother and Robert Lockett were brother and sister, but that from an early age he had been raised in his uncle's home.

By the time they reached the border crossing, Ava had learned that Michael traveled wherever Robert sent him and did exactly as he was told. It was expected that members of the immediate family take part in the business, and now that Mason had come along, his education in that regard would likely start right away. Despite the boy's young age, Robert had every intention of full integration. Ava's insides quaked at the notion.

When they pulled in line behind dozens of cars to be checked by a border guard, she was surprised when the driver produced three passports. Seeing her curious stare, Michael handed hers over. It looked as real as any she had seen. Her driver's license photo stared back at her, and the name Ava Anne Montgomery was followed by all the correct particulars, even her date of birth was accurate. After a few moments, it dawned on her that the LO wanted there to be a record of her crossing into Mexico. They wanted that information to make it back to Clay.

Cruising easily through the checkpoint, the border guard examined each passport briefly, scanned them into a database, then waved them on. White car glinting in the bright overhead lights, the dark night of a foreign country accepted them greedily. The car made its way only a few additional blocks before pulling to a stop at a broken down gas station. Jittery nerves collected in her extremities as both the driver and Michael made to exit. Gathering up a few small bags, Michael visibly checked a matte black handgun that had been hidden in a holster at his hip. Ava gulped audibly, then squinted through the deep night, trying to make out their location.

"Where are we?" Her voice cracked.

"Hey-" Michael reached to soothe a comforting hand over her knee. "I promise that no one will hurt you, okay? If you keep your head down around Uncle Robert, then everything will be fine."

Searching his pale green eyes in the dome light from the town car, Ava saw nothing but honesty there. She bobbed her head in acquiescence before stepping a boot out of the open door held steady by the silent driver. The gas station was abandoned, or at least it appeared to be. No bulbs burned from inside, no clerk worked the dusty counter. In the back storeroom, there were shelves and shelves of expired food products. Boxes of crackers, unopened bags of chips, and cans of soda.

The three of them crowded into the narrow space, flashlight beams tracking across the floor. Wedged between Michael and the driver, Ava's mouth went dry. Of all the neglected items scattered about, one shiny new metal lock reflected in the gradual pass of illumination. It was a padlock. A padlock that secured a cellar door. Kneeling with key in hand, the driver twisted his wrist. The faint click of the releasing mechanism echoed dully.

Down the darkened steps they went, sinking into a carved-out cavern that was barely tall enough for a man to pass through unhunched. A braided wire ran the length of the tunnel. Every so often it powered a lantern, casting their shadows on the walls as they walked by. They were traversing an illegal tunnel underneath the border and its silence swallowed them whole, the reverence of the place seemed to demand it.

Ava plodded carefully along. The ground was uneven; its occasional rubble left them all a bit unsteady. The LO sought to lead the Militia out of the country, while keeping she and Mason securely inside of it. Over and over, she repeated her thanks in her mind. Thanks for the other tracker, her only hope of eventual freedom.

After what seemed like a few miles, they came to a sudden stop. Abrupt though it was, she was grateful to climb the equally haphazard steps up into the light. Blinking through momentary blindness, Ava instinctually braced herself against Michael's arm. He steadied her hand with his own. The room they found themselves in was dimly lit with no windows along the walls. They were still underground, more than likely in the basement of a building somewhere back in the US.

A new man was present. He was bulky and short, with a fitted grey suit and iron dark eyes. Furnishings were sparse, with a row of chairs lining one wall and a simple wooden table along the other. In the middle of the room stood a sleek white machine, its pristine condition, electronics aglow, meant it was new and well-tended. She recognized it immediately. It was a full body scanner, like the ones used by so many airport security lines. Eyes widening in reflex, Ava worked to still her rapid pulse. Clay hadn't thought of this.

"Take off your boots, please." The man spoke, stepping forward to tweak at the instrument panel for the machine.

Ducking her head dumbly, Ava braced herself against

Michael. Hopping on first one foot, and then the other, she tugged at the low heels of her tall boots. When she straightened, she could feel the deep cold that permeated the wooden floor rising up to inhabit her black stockinged feet. When she walked into the archway of the scanner, she felt her own body trembling, but hoped it was imperceptible to the men observing.

Air puffed out at her from tiny holes, causing her hair to toss quickly before laying back down. Out of the corner of her eye she spied Michael's head shake from side to side as the man at the controls frowned. Gesturing him over, the man pointed to the small screen he held in his hands, circling an area for Michael to scrutinize. After several moments she knew for certain they had found the second tracker. What would the consequence of her subversiveness be?

"Ava." Michael spoke as a father to his naughty child. "Come sit down over here."

Obeying, Ava left damp foot prints as she walked across the floor. The warmth from her feet caused momentary condensation tracks to collect on the wood. When she sat in the grey plastic chair with its silver metal legs, she listened to its creaking complaint with trepidation. Michael knelt before her, his short red hair the only indication of color in the room. His eyes, at least, remained kind.

"You have another tracker," he commented.

"I do." She gulped.

"I'll have to cut this one out as well."

"I know."

"But there's no reason for you to suffer."

Michael pushed up the sleeve of her coat, exposing the flesh of her forearm. Ava frowned, wondering why he cleared an area so far from the location of the second tiny device. When he held out his hand palm up, she blanched as the driver placed a single syringe into it. Before she could open her mouth to protest, before she could question the contents, he expertly slipped the tip of the needle beneath her skin.

As the plunger depressed, so her awareness filled with the warm flood of liquid. After that, came the sensation of nothingness. It was like an old friend, walking her towards the hazy all-encompassing blackness.

TWENTY

The room was filled with light. It was expansive, fitting the queen size bed easily along with two pale blue sitting chairs nestled close to a crackling fire. Wide windows lined one wall, their sheer fabric curtains hung lazily to pool on the plush beige carpeting below. Eyes fluttering open, she absorbed the radiant warmth with a deeply inhaled breath. Sounds stirred at the edge of her consciousness. The sound of voices, footsteps, and doors.

"You're awake." A female voice was close.

Turning her head to the left, Ava blinked into the familiar face. Waves of dark brown hair cascaded down to frame glittering green eyes. The petite figure of Ms. Martinez stood quietly beside her. What was Mason's teacher doing here?

"Did they kidnap you?" Ava's voice was hoarse as she attempted to clear it.

"Yes and no." Ms. Martinez's expression was kind. "I'm afraid that I didn't come here of my own will, but it was my fault entirely. You see, I wasn't honest with you about who I was when we first met."

"I don't understand." Ava's brow furrowed, trying to make sense of so many words.

"My real name is Sophia Lockett. I purposefully took a job as Mason's teacher in order to be close to him. I'm sorry."

Ava gaped. Mind still fuzzy from the drugs, she struggled to form a reply. Thoughts that normally whirred quickly, were sluggish, taking too long to form coherent ideas. In the distance, she heard the tumultuous thunder of footfalls. Rushing feet and a tiny shouting voice overpowered any reaction Ava would have had concerning Sophia's admission. Mason was coming.

"Mommy!" The door burst forth as Mason launched himself onto Ava's bed.

"Mason!" Ava cried, clinging to her little boy with steadily strengthening arms.

"I've missed you." Mason buried his face in her neck, snuggling close.

"I've missed you, too, baby." Ava breathed, trying not to let the tears show. "I've missed you, too."

For a long while they clung to one another. Running her hand along his back, she comforted them both with her reassuring presence. Her boy was resilient, though. Before long he had climbed under the covers next to her and began chattering away. He told her about his adventures with his second mommy, and the past month of living with his new grandpa. There was a pool that he loved to swim in, and a new puppy to play with. He had a nanny, lots of toys, and his own bedroom.

Pretty soon, Mason was tugging on her, urging her to get up and see all that he had to offer. Nodding slowly, Ava held a hand to her own forehead where a dull headache had begun.

During their initial exchange, Sophia had stepped away, leaving them alone in the room. With Mason's raised voice and excited banter, she returned to offer her assistance. Tucking her flowing hair behind an ear, Sophia worked expertly to calm Mason, before retrieving a glass of water for Ava.

"Thank you." Ava accepted the cup gratefully, her throat was so dry.

"You're welcome." Sophia smiled as Mason raced circles around the large room. "Are you feeling well enough to take a little walk around?"

"Sure." Ava couldn't deny the look of longing in Mason's eyes.

"This is a guest room in our section of the house." Sophia gestured. "You're welcome to choose this as your own, or we have one more available. This one is right next door to Mason's, so I figured it would be a good option."

"Alright." Ava swung her bare legs over the edge of the bed and tugged absently at the long sleeve nightdress she wore.

"It's cold outside, but warm throughout the house." Sophia offered an arm, leading Ava patiently towards the walk-in closet. "We've stocked this closet for you, but you're welcome to order anything online or from a catalog. Only, my father prefers that the women in his household wear dresses or skirts."

"No pants?" Ava's eyebrows shot up in question.

"He prefers not." Sophia bobbed her head.

All the doors in the house were made of solid knotty pine, the light-colored wood was sealed clear to show its character. Ava traced her fingertips around and around the occasional circles as she leaned against the open closet door, surveying the sweep of expensive clothing. If you were going to eliminate pants, this was the way to do it.

"Wow." Ava plucked a hangar off the rack, eyes absorbing the formal dress that hung there before replacing it.

"I selected the wardrobe personally when my father informed me that you had agreed to come."

"He made it hard to refuse," Ava continued, drifting deeper into the room. Mason kept close at her heels.

"I wasn't sure if Clay would let you." Sophia's expression betrayed her at the mention of her former lover.

Ava paused, studying Sophia's gaze as it shifted nervously away. The smoothly tan hands wrung themselves together, folding and unfolding until a tiny sparkle of gold caught Ava's eye. It was a ring, and not just any ring.

"Did my brother give you that?" Ava knew the answer but asked anyway.

"Yes." Sophia glanced down at the small diamond that winked back at her.

"That was my mother's ring."

"Oh." Sophia gulped, twisting the jewelry briefly before slipping it off and handing it to Ava. "I didn't know that."

"He asked you to marry him?" Ava placed the ring gently on her own finger, sighing as she tried to absorb her mother's energy.

"Once upon a time, yes." Sophia rubbed at the empty spot it had left. "But we never did get married."

"I know." Ava watched the other woman carefully. "If you had, then he would have given you the matching band. It's gold, with tiny leaves etched on it."

"It sounds lovely."

"When I was a little girl, my mother used to let me try it on while she got ready to go out." Ava smiled at the memory. "It was too big then."

"I'm sorry." Sophia's look was genuine. "That she died."

"Did you know Clay then?"

"We had just met."

The two women eyed one another for a few minutes, Mason lay sprawled at their feet, messing around with the rows of neat shoes. Only a year ago, Ava would likely have handled the whole situation differently. Back then she wouldn't have recognized the shadow of desperation that hid itself so well behind a layer of expert makeup and reserved expression. This woman was still very much in love with Clay. Ava could see it so clearly now, because a part of her carried that same lonely hunger for a man she also couldn't have.

Closing her eyes briefly, Ava did her best to inhale the peaceful love that her mother's ring brought to her soul before removing it. With a measured smile, she handed it back over to Sophia.

"Are you sure?" Sophia's hand trembled slightly as she grasped the ring.

"She would want the mother of her only grandchild to wear it." Ava relinquished the gem with a last nod. "But let's agree to one thing."

"What's that?"

"If you ever stop loving my brother, then I'd like it back. Agreed?"

"Agreed." Sophia slipped the ring back on.

In the center of the room was a stand-alone dresser made of the same light-colored pine as the doors. It was wide, with several drawers lining each side. Sliding first one and then another open, Ava inspected the carefully arranged undergarments, sleep clothes, and stockings. The items were clearly new but had all been laundered and were in her correct sizes. Luxury with attention to detail, it was difficult not to be impressed.

With Mason's patience growing short, Ava selected a wispy dress that contained a mix of sapphire and sky-blue hues. It had a V-neckline with spaghetti thin straps. Its silky material fell in light layers that ended in mismatched triangle tips at her ankles. Rubbing at her bare arms, she matched it with a chunky cable-knit sweater, the material was so soft and warm that it reminded her of cashmere. Glancing at the tag, she saw that it was. Figuring that she didn't need shoes, Ava gestured for Mason to lead the way. Sophia walked companionably beside her.

Just outside her doorway was a large central room. It contained two extended leather sofas, a flat screen television mounted above a massive stone fireplace, and a small wooden dining table situated underneath a far window. In a semicircle to her left were several doors spaced apart from one another. Following Mason's excited bounce, Sophia explained that the first door led to Mason's room, the second to her own, the third to the nanny's room, and the fourth was another guest room.

When they pushed open the door to Mason's bedroom, it overflowed with boyish energy. There were brightly painted model airplanes hanging from the ceiling, a carved wooden race car bed in one corner, and a puppy kennel tucked into another. Happy yips of greeting emanated from the large crate. Ava could see a tiny black nose pressed through the slats of a wire door, the soft yellow head of a Labrador just beyond.

"Want to see my puppy?!" Mason shouted, not waiting for an answer before rushing to release his companion from his cage.

"You guys really did try everything," Ava commented, bending low to run her hands over the wiggly warmth of the dog at her feet.

"We did," Sophia admitted. "This is Hank."

"Hello, Hank." Ava chuckled.

"Can we take him for a walk, Mommy Sophia?" Mason asked, eyes wide and appealing.

"Are you up for it Ava?" Sophia searched her face.

"Sure." Ava fought the sudden pang that the new title caused in her chest. After all, it must be hard for Sophia to hear him call Ava mommy as well.

On the far side of the common room, next to a bank of expansive windows, stood a large French door. Its gold handles dipped easily, opening onto a lush green courtyard with a rectangular pool just beyond. Cobblestone pavers, chill like the breeze, guided them out. Hank the puppy raced ahead, Mason, pumping little boy legs to catch up, shouted all the while.

The courtyard itself was covered by an extension from the massive house. Its high arched ceiling offered protection to the entire pool along with a section of manicured green lawn that was bordered by pruned bushes. Ava had no time to inspect the outdoor kitchen, fireplace, and furniture as the boy and his dog soon reached the end of the grass.

"Did you grow up here?" Ava asked, panting a bit as the women walked.

"We moved around a lot," Sophia explained. "But of all the houses that we ever lived in, this was my favorite."

Ava had focused on her feet plodding through the icy cool grass, so hadn't noticed the view until Sophia stopped at the edge of the lawn. When she looked up, her breath caught in her throat. The stormy grey-blue water of the ocean stretched out before her, its color affected by the cloud cover that hung low in the sky. Before them, Mason and Hank careened down a slight incline onto the sandy white beach, howling together as they reached the water's edge.

"Where are we?" Ava whispered it, wondering at the soft lap of too small waves that licked the shore.

"We're in Texas." Sophia gestured up and down the beach. "My father owns this peninsula and all of the homes on it. You can interact with anyone you happen to see on the beach, they are all business associates of the LO."

At the mention of the LO, Ava's mind was sucked back to the original reason for her coming here. Wiggling her toes, she grimaced at the sharp pain that sprang from the small incision where the second tracker had been removed. Stomach sinking, Ava wondered at the gravity of her predicament. She hadn't listened to Finn and she hadn't waited for the final okay from Clay. Now, she and Mason may be lost to them forever.

Fighting back the surge of guilt and fresh fear, Ava marched through the uneven sand, her feet sinking with each new step. It wasn't far to the lap of the tide. With Sophia lingering safely on the dry shore, Ava kept moving forward until she was knee deep in the sea. The tips of her dress soaked in the water. Facing the horizon line, Ava watched, and watched. She could just see the casual drift of a far-off sail boat, nothing more.

The puppy yipped and Mason laughed as he splashed by,

no one caring that he soaked his pants. It wouldn't be impossible for her to escape by herself, but with Mason, there just wasn't any way she could do it without help.

"Uncle Mikey!" Mason shouted from behind her, causing Ava to turn her head.

Over her shoulder, she saw Michael crossing the sand towards them, the smile on his face spreading along with his arms to welcome Mason. The boy didn't hesitate to throw his body at the man who scooped him up easily, tossing him briefly into the air. He was Sophia's cousin. Raised in his uncle's home, Michael had spent the last month with them both. Catching her son on his way back down, Michael set him onto the sand before tousling the little boy's hair with affection. Ava turned her face away, but not before catching the look that Michael threw her, it was one of questioning desire, an expression she knew well.

Hugging herself tightly with her arms, she listened half-heartedly to the murmured conversation between adults. He had seen them leave their quarters through his window and wanted to check if they would all be making it to dinner. It was clear that Sophia loved her cousin, the trust and mutual affection in her voice echoed back to her in his. Bringing a tennis ball out of his pocket, Michael kept the puppy busy with a game of fetch. Mason ran too, until he plopped in the sand, panting his exhaustion.

After a while Ava's feet became numb and the silky material of the dress was likely ruined. But at that moment, she simply did not care. Eventually she was forced to move by Mason himself, who tugged incessantly at her hand. She left her post in the sea to walk back to the house, his little fingers clasped loosely in her own. One thing was clear, Mason had no intention of letting her out of his sight.

"I'm sorry, Ava." Michael fell into step beside her. "I know that this is hard for you."

"You have no idea," Ava corrected.

"You're right, I don't," he admitted. Sophia said nothing.

At the courtyard, they went their separate ways. Michael retreated to his own quarters across the way, while the women, boy, and puppy returned to their suite. At once the nanny appeared, a pretty young thing with a French accent and short bob of dark hair. When she attempted to lure Mason in for a bath, he staunchly refused, pitching a classic category four fit. Ava watched in measured fascination as the nanny and Sophia only went so far as threatening in an attempt to calm him down. He flopped on the floor, screamed at the top of his lungs, then shed real tears at the prospect of cleaning up. No wonder they had sent for her, Ava gritted her teeth. He was spoiled beyond all measure.

"Time out!" Ava barked, making the other women jump. "Now!"

Before Mason could wriggle away, Ava scooped up his thrashing body and carried him into his bedroom. She did her best to set him gently on his mattress, which was a challenge considering the full body gyration that was occurring. Without further comment she left him to wail, shutting the door solidly behind her.

"Sophia," Ava scolded. "You were a teacher, you should know better. You're letting him get the best of you."

"You're right." Sophia blushed. "I guess I just feel so guilty about everything, I don't want to upset him."

"Well." Ava looked to the nanny. "We need to get a set of

ground rules together so that we're all consistent. This is going to take a few weeks before he's normal again."

Between the three women and several additional time outs, Mason finally submitted to a bath before dinner. Washed and dressed, he reclined on the sofa while a cartoon played on the common room television. This gave Sophia and Ava time to prepare as well.

When Robert was in residence, dinner was held at six-thirty each evening, with all immediate family members expected to attend. The most difficult part for Ava was the shower. Her room had an enormous ensuite bath, but Mason refused to let her out of his sight. Normally, him hanging out while she cleaned up was no big deal. But as irrational as it was, Ava's body twisted with anxiety at the idea of them locked in the tiny room together.

For several moments there was a standoff of sorts. Mason persisted in his presence, and Ava worked to keep the shriek of unfounded fear from her voice. In the end, both agreed to a compromise that was, surprisingly, suggested by Sophia. Mason played trucks on the foot of Ava's bed, while Ava showered with the bathroom door open.

Nerves still perpetuated her system, and she rushed crazily through her routine, but she got it done. Once out of the towering granite stall, Ava wrapped herself in a soft white towel and proceeded to blow dry her hair. Remembering Finn's words about trauma leaking out in different ways, she wondered if perhaps his recommendation for therapy had been a good one. How her heart longed to tell him that he was right.

A wide swath of expensive new makeup lined the swirling granite counter top, all of the shades were a match to her light skin tone. Opening up the little boxes, Ava marveled at the quality of the products as they blended to perfection on her face. The occasional sound of a revving engine emanated from beyond the threshold of the bathroom door, causing Ava to smile. Mason drove his toy cars in a death-defying race, talking contentedly to himself. God how she had missed that.

Sophia had selected his clothes for dinner and he looked all too grown up in the pair of khaki colored slacks and green-checked button up shirt. It brought out the hazel mix of his eyes, so much like his father's. The Lockett family dressed up for their evening meals, so Ava walked to the closet and ran her hand along the selection of ultra-feminine attire. She settled on a simple grey dress, its long sleeves were in stark contrast to the short length of the skirt, but the blouse had a series of little buttons down one side that piqued her interest. Slipping into it, she couldn't help but appreciate the expensive fabric and excellent fit. It made her feel pretty and strong at a time where she was in actuality, immensely weak. Mason's eyes brightened when she twirled for him.

"Will you be my date?" Ava asked him.

"Yeah, Mommy." He grinned, taking her hand in his own.

The nanny stayed behind to eat her dinner in the common room alone. Sophia and Mason led Ava out of their wing of the estate and down a wide hallway. Their footfalls echoed off of the hand-scraped bamboo flooring. Rich modern art, sculptures on pedestals, and windows overlooking the ocean flanked their path. At the end was a set of double doors that stood open, the sound of male laughter drifted out hauntingly at their approach.

When they entered, Ava hesitated while Sophia passed through first. A massive stone table stretched almost the entire length of the room. Its austere imposing presence reflected that of its owner, the man positioned so carefully at its head. Robert Lockett stood when he saw his daughter, causing the other men in the room to do the same. He was shorter than Ava had imagined him, but every bit as severe as on his many videos. Even his smile seemed to slice.

"Welcome," he called.

Gesturing to several seats along the table, Robert bade them sit. A man used to power, he arranged their positions according to his own liking. Ava thought of Clay, he always did the same. Thankfully the chairs that surrounded the giant slab were not made of stone themselves, but instead of a sleek wood, hand carved and polished to a sheen. Mason sat between his two mothers, unusually quiet, making Ava stare down at him a beat. When he glanced up at her, his eyes held a strange sort of trepidation. Something had happened here, something that frightened him into silent submission. Ava bent to reassure him, whispering lovingly in his ear, but she received only a simple nod in return.

Straightening, she felt Michael take the seat on her other side which caused her to stiffen momentarily. He kept his gaze averted, focusing instead on his uncle. There were three other men in the room, all business associates of the LO. Ava was introduced as Mason's second mother and a round of indulgent chuckling ensued. Robert joked about keeping an open mind in modern culture. Sophia rolled her eyes then, which had Ava softening, at least this one individual showed no fear.

The room itself was lined with broad windows as opposed to paintings. Its position was jutted out from the surrounding structure to showcase an almost panoramic scene of the ocean. Darkness prevailed outside, but well-placed outdoor lights provided a view of the lawns and sloping sand. In the daylight, it would be breathtaking.

The meal service was extremely formal. It included servings of soup and a light salad before the main course of fresh fish. Ava wasn't a big seafood fan herself and expected Mason to balk at the dinner, but instead he sat solemnly, consuming the tiny pieces Sophia cut for him. Doing her best to be polite, Ava also swallowed testing bites, and soon discovered the fish to be flakey and mild. Normally she would have inquired as to the kind, but the men were so absorbed in conversation, that she dare not interrupt.

Sophia piped up every once in a while, however. Saying something sassy, she would make the men laugh, and her father frown. Ava got a glimpse of what had made her brother fall so hard for this particular woman. Occasionally, Michael leaned over and attempted to engage Ava in conversation but frostily she refused him. To his credit, he accepted her attitude with an unruffled manner.

Well over an hour had passed by the time Mason's nanny arrived to collect him from the dinner. Robert expected Ava to remain in place, but Mason refused to leave without her. The men fell silent and Sophia's expression grew nervous as she and the nanny tried to peel Mason from his chair. He began to whine and despite the increased pleading from the women, his noise level accelerated.

"Mason!" Robert slammed his palm down to smack against the stone table. "You will obey your mother!"

Immediately, Mason melted against Ava, as if trying desperately to disappear. His plaintive whimper reverberated against her side. Sophia and the nanny held their breath, while

Michael shifted, readying himself to intervene. So, this was the issue with dinner, Ava thought, Robert frightened her son like he'd never been before.

"With your permission, Robert." Ava steadied Mason with a reassuring hand. "I'd like to put Mason to bed tonight. After such a lovely dinner, I'd appreciate the opportunity to pull my weight around here."

"Of course." Robert calmed instantly, flashing a smile around the room. "Yes, go take care of my grandson."

"Thank you." Ava rose, clutching Mason's hand in her own. "It was nice meeting you gentleman."

The men echoed a similar sentiment as she followed the nanny out of the room. Just before they cleared the door, Robert instructed Michael to go after them and assist. Ava's insides rebelled but she hid any visible reaction.

Sweeping out into the hall, they walked in brisk silence until they reached the women's wing of the estate and were closed safely back inside. Mason raced ahead of Ava with his nanny in tow. Skipping and jumping along together, the nanny playfully got him to the bathroom and up on a stool to brush his teeth. After turning on the water, she began to sing a little song that had him giggling. The girl was good with him, he viewed her as a playmate.

Stopping short in the frame of the doorway, Ava whirled to confront Michael. The vehemence of her expression had him backing a step, but he reached out with both hands, as if about to stroke her arms. Hesitating at the last second, he seemed to think better of it and instead balled his fists at his side.

"So, your organization abuses women and children," Ava accused. "Your lovely uncle scares the shit out of my son."

"I regret the day that you were hit more than you know." Michael searched her eyes. "It was part of my job at the time and I allowed it without thinking. Will you ever be able to forgive me?"

"No." Ava stared at him, fury resonating. "Did Robert hit Mason?"

"He's a hard man," Michael acknowledged. "But for the most part, not overly cruel. As children, we learned how to avoid his temper early on. Unfortunately, Mason has had to do the same."

"You admit that he beat him?"

"I didn't let it get that far." Michael reached for her hand, but she snatched it away.

"Don't," Ava warned. "Don't touch me."

"I'm sorry. I won't."

"Uncle Mickey!"

Mason launched himself into his uncle's arms and was caught with ease. They joked together before Michael set him back on the ground and sent him to fetch his pajamas. Much to Ava's dismay, Mason had developed a bedtime routine that included his uncle. They tucked in the puppy, cuddled in bed together, and read a story. Just before Mason dropped into sleep, Michael slipped out, leaving a train car nightlight aglow.

It was clear that Mason trusted this man, maybe even saw him as a protector. Trying to think without bias, Ava had to admit that it was likely true that Michael had intervened in Robert's punishment. Crossing her arms in front of her chest, she walked with him to the wide French doors.

"I know that you're afraid of me," Michael began. "But it seems that we're going to be living together for a long, long time. I will never hurt Mason and I will never let anyone hurt you again. Maybe in time, you'll come to believe that. Goodnight."

Ava stood in the open doorway and watched his figure drift across the darkened courtyard. Chilly air swept in around her, raising goosebumps on the exposed length of her legs. Frowning, she waited for the light to flip on in his room across the way before slowly swinging the door shut.

"Night," she murmured under her breath.

TWENTY-ONE

en days passed, then a month, then two. Spring was upon them, and the peninsula flourished under a wave of warmer weather. Flowers blossomed, the ocean swirled, and sunlight heated the white sand between bare toes. Still, Clay did not come for them. Still, Ava pined for her brother and their failed plan. But her father had never raised his daughter to remain listless or idle for long. The compulsion to push forward, despite emotional obstacles, reigned supreme.

It was one value that both he and Robert Lockett apparently had in common. A value that was passed down to his own daughter, and had Ava admiring Sophia Lockett's rigid efficiency. The pace with which she ran Mason's homeschool program soon had him excelling in reading, science, and math. Ava witnessed it first hand, despite listening with increasing boredom to each lesson.

During the first several weeks, Mason was insistent on remaining in the same room with Ava. His anxiety from their months of separation made him prone to fits of rage which melted into fear whenever she attempted to leave. With nothing better to occupy her time, Ava did her best to remain supportive and understanding, even if that meant she had to use the toilet with the door open. Thankfully, after the initial month passed without her sudden disappearance, Mason's paranoia waned. There came a day when he didn't follow her to the bathroom, and then another when he played with Hank on the lawn by himself.

Despite these advances, each night he would wake and sneak into her room. He curled up beside her in bed, murmuring sleepily about having nightmares. Holding him tight, she rubbed his back, not minding the occasional bout of snoring that followed. Shortly after, there came a morning when Ava excused herself from his daily lessons. Confined to the estate, this change in schedule left her with a block of empty time during the day. So, like any good prepper, she took to wandering, testing the boundaries of the property, and memorizing the weaknesses.

The central house was a maze of corridors leading to locked doors that protected rooms she could only guess about. Michael seemed to occupy the wing directly across from them entirely by himself. The only possible exception was a room reserved for one or two of the security guards, she never did catch their names. Robert maintained a large section for his private use, but the hallway that led there was always blocked off. By contrast, the door leading to Michael's wing was consistently left open. Once or twice, Ava lingered in the hallway, but in the end, she dare not enter. Though her curiosity was piqued, she didn't want to give him the wrong impression, at least not yet.

Over the past few months, as her hopes of rescue had

begun to wane, Ava's mind plotted and planned in turn. Scenario after scenario played out in her head, but they all ended in disaster. The only way that she could escape with Mason would be with help. If not from her brother on the outside, then perhaps she could convince someone on the inside. Sophia had been unable to leave even before Ava came, so she was not a viable option. The nanny was useless, and Ava had been unable to befriend even a single guard.

That only left one person. One person with whom she interacted on almost a daily basis. One person who was certainly capable but would have to be willing to risk his very life. And that life had become precious to a certain little boy over the past few months. Mason simply adored his Uncle Mikey.

It was difficult for Ava to admit, but Michael had become the father figure that Mason craved. On most afternoons the three of them would swim together in the courtyard pool. It was heated and gave Sophia a much-needed break after hours of intensive schooling. If the weather was fine, they would take Hank for a walk along the shore or toss a baseball around on the lawn. Watching them interact was a sad sort of pain. Michael genuinely loved Mason, but he wasn't Clay, and that hurt.

When Robert and Michael were not in residence, the guard shift tripled. The only plus was that Ava got to wear actual pants for her daily jog down the beach. Running was the only activity that helped to stave off the unwelcome feeling of helplessness that plagued her. Just as Sophia had initially described, the massive homes along the shore were mostly unoccupied, save for visiting business associates or close friends. She had only ever seen one family, and that was several weeks ago. They had two little girls about Mason's age, but they spoke only French. The children quickly got over the language barrier, but Ava's tiniest hope of communicating with the other mother had been dashed.

Waking late one day, Ava rolled over in bed to find Mason had already gone for his morning lesson. For a moment, she stretched, then simply stared out the window at a sky gone cloudy grey. Glancing at the clock, she was surprised to see that it was well past ten in the morning. Grumbling to herself, she changed into her workout pants, then shrugged into a powder blue zip-up jacket. Lacing up her shoes, she proceeded out into the common room where Sophia read aloud to a squirming Mason. Doing her best not to make eye contact, Ava skirted around them, grabbing up a left-over piece of toast that lay untouched on the small dining table.

"Mommy! Mommy!" Mason had spotted her.

"Just going for a quick jog," Ava called over her shoulder with a wave. If she broke stride now, it would all be over.

Swallowing the bread in three big bites, Ava strode to the lawn where she stopped to stretch for several minutes. Bending this way and that, she glanced at Michael's quarters. They had been gone for over four days now. She wondered at the business errand that kept them away, then shook her head decidedly to clear it.

Breaking into a light jog, she warmed up, cruising almost casually down to the shore line. The peninsula itself wasn't terribly long but running in the sand made the short distance seem to stretch. Her boundaries were restricted to the ocean-facing side of the peninsula, but if she repeated the trip, it made for a decent workout. Breath puffing, she picked up the pace until her muscles burned and beads of sweat leaked from the line of her forehead. Altogether there were five large homes that lined the shore, with the Lockett estate established clearly in the middle. Veering to her left, she passed two of the empty homes before making a wide circle and doubling back.

The ocean was beautiful, with the sun burning behind mid-morning clouds. As she ran, rays struck the water, causing glitter to pop before a swift breeze pushed the shine back behind the cover. The last home was positioned at the end of the strip of land, and as Ava jogged past, the hair on her arms raised. All of the houses were empty, but the unmistakable sensation of being watched persisted. The LO monitored the beach using surveillance cameras, not guards, and despite the heat from her body, gooseflesh prickled. Craning her neck around, she surveyed the glinting windows of the darkened home, fully expecting to see someone standing on the wide wooden balcony.

There was no one.

Frowning, Ava turned on her heel and started back the way she had come. Footsteps thudding heavily along the uneven shore, she couldn't resist a last glance over her shoulder. Finding nothing out of place, she made a mental note. It was likely no big deal, but she would inform their guard detail anyway. The LO was a dangerous organization after all, and Mason's safety was her priority.

Making her way back, Ava's heart raced with the shot of adrenaline. Distracted with uncertain worry, she nearly ran over the man sitting at the edge of the lawn. Dress jacket tossed carelessly at his side, Michael's bare feet rested on the sand. Relief flooded her system, perhaps these were the eyes that had tracked her so far down the beach.

"Michael!" She laughed, breathless from running. "I thought that I felt someone watching me."

"Sorry." He smiled up into her face. "I know how you hate that."

"Mason is going to be so glad that you're back." Offering her hand, she helped him up.

"Only Mason?" He joked. "I still haven't swayed you yet?"

"Very funny, walk with me?"

"Sure."

"Is Robert back, too? I hope he doesn't see me in my pants," she mocked, as they walked cooling circles around the lawn.

"It is a silly rule." Michael strolled casually, one hand tucked in the pocket of his slacks. "Maybe I'll talk to him about it."

"No." Ava waved at him absently. "Save your protection for a day when I'll need it."

"Alright." He waited a beat, then shifted topics. "Hey, I've brought you something."

"Again? I thought we talked about this."

"I know, I know." Michael brought the small jewelry box out anyway. "But think of this as a gesture of friendship, no strings attached."

"Wow." Ava couldn't help her quick intake of breath as he produced a large tanzanite necklace.

"I thought you'd like this one."

His smile was broad as he held up the indigo colored gem, it's deep purplish hue shined invitingly. Of course she liked it, call it a female weakness. Ava brushed her fingertips over the surface of the jewel as it dangled from his hand. Every few weeks he would show up with a new box, and every few weeks she would turn him away. He was like a faithful retriever, constantly bringing her back prizes that she admired before returning.

Finn's words, spoken a lifetime ago from inside the cage, echoed in her mind. You could seduce him into helping you escape. She could hear him whisper it. There was no doubt that she could indeed seduce Michael. But the escape part might turn out to be a pretty long con and morality had her hesitating. Ava hadn't yet decided how far she was willing to go, and on top of that, Michael was turning out to be a fairly good guy. Sophia loved him and so did Mason, but it appeared that he was Ava's only chance at eventual freedom.

"I can't accept it." She sighed.

"I'm tired of stacking up bracelets, necklaces, and earrings on my dresser." Michael waved his hand tantalizingly side to side, making the gem dance. "If you wear this, it doesn't mean that you're going to sleep with me. You're a beautiful woman and this is a beautiful jewel, you deserve each other."

"Well-" Ava nibbled at her lip.

If he knew that she wasn't going to sleep with him, then what was the harm in wearing this one necklace? Seeing her conflict, he raised his eyebrows in question before shifting around behind her to loop the gem about her neck. As it settled into place on her chest, Ava grasped it in her hand. She had never worn anything this lovely in all her life.

Fastening the clasp, Michael was true to his word, as he always was. He didn't stroke her skin or rest his hands unnecessarily on her shoulders. Stepping back around, he gave her a quick nod of approval, before resuming his stroll towards the house. Suppressing a slight smile, Ava followed.

"Uncle Mikey!" Mason rocketed through the French doors, Hank yapping happily at his heels.

"Mason my man." Michael caught him up, twirling around once giddily before setting him in the deep grass. "What do you say we talk Mama Sophia into letting you out early? It is a Friday."

"Awesome!" Mason scooted back inside.

Sophia agreed to the change in schedule while Ava rinsed off, trading her pants for a comfy maxi skirt. Lately, even with Michael so close around, her panic attacks surrounding the shower had dissipated. Trauma was a tricky thing. Maybe it was getting to know Michael as a real person that had helped in the end. Ava couldn't be sure.

While the boys splashed in the pool, the women took lunch under the covered veranda. Sighing with pleasure, Ava munched contentedly on a chicken lettuce wrap.

"These are amazing." She moaned between bites.

"So is that necklace." Sophia's eyes twinkled knowingly. "I'm surprised you're wearing it."

"It's a symbol of our friendship." Ava choked back a laugh. "Truthfully, it's the most gorgeous thing that I've ever worn and I had to have it."

"I understand." Sophia bobbed her head as she sipped her iced tea. "I've got my share of blood diamonds, as they say. You know, my father has plans to see you marry Michael."

"Ugh." Ava rolled her eyes. "Why?"

"Well, Michael likes you for one." Sophia eyed her appraisingly. "And it would keep you bound to the household and family. My father doesn't care for loose ends."

"If being single makes me a loose end, then so are you."

"No running!" Sophia yelled at a racing Mason, then leaned back to avoid his splash. "Sure am, but that's why he's invited Mr. Iverson back."

"Mr. Iverson?"

"He's a long-time business associate of the LO," Sophia explained. "My father is having him over for dinner, again."

"Tonight?"

"I'm afraid so." Sophia traced lines in the condensation that collected on her glass. "Not that he isn't handsome, because he is, or rich, because he's that, too."

"So, what gives?"

"I don't know." Sophia shrugged.

"Maybe I'll see at dinner tonight," Ava ventured, curious.

"Maybe."

THAT EVENING, AVA SELECTED HER OUTFIT TO BEST accentuate her new jewel. Holding up first a black dress, then a soft silver, she bit her lip in concentration. The black was form-fitting, had cap sleeves and a short skirt. The neckline was high, leaving the tanzanite to wink with the material as a background. The silver dress shimmered with spaghetti thin straps. Flowing softly about her body, it ended abruptly above her knees. It's deep V-shaped neckline left the tanzanite pressed coolly against her skin and she kind of liked that.

"Which one?" Ava stomped into Sophia's room. "I can't decide."

"Um-" Sophia watched as Ava held up first one, then the other. "I like the silver."

"Me, too." Ava agreed. "You look stunning, by the way."

"I figured that I may as well make an effort, if you are." Sophia leaned close to her bathroom mirror, fitting a large diamond earring into her right lobe. The red dress she wore devastated and understated all at the same time.

"You're so classy," Ava commented. "How do you do it?"

"Please." Sophia winced. "Can you not remind me of your brother for one night?"

"Sorry." Ava watched the controlled exhale of the other woman.

"He always used to call me that," Sophia explained, flicking on her mascara. "Classy."

"You took off the ring. I guess that I just thought-"

"I didn't give it back to you, did I?"

"No." Ava patted an affectionate hand against Sophia's shoulder. She had come to really enjoy the other woman's company. "I guess you didn't."

"Okay." Sophia faced Ava, clasping her wrists tightly. "So, I can't have Clay and you can't have whoever it is that you're hung up on, right?"

"Right."

"We chose Mason, and that's the best choice."

"It is." Ava's mind wound slowly around, thinking of the next choice she should make.

"I put away the ring and you're wearing the necklace."

"I am."

"So, let's try to forget about what we can't have and just try to have fun instead. Agreed?"

"Agreed." Ava echoed.

MASON HAD BEEN EXCUSED FROM DINNER WITH THE ADULTS, having been offered a pajama party with his devoted nanny instead. It had seemed like a great deal at the time he made it, but when his mommies were all decked out and ready to leave, he appeared to change his mind. In true kid fashion, he clung, pleaded and whined, trying to convince them to stay.

His behavior only further solidified both of his mothers' desire for an adult only night. They kissed and hugged him in turn, then left him in the care of his nanny. Linking arms companionably, Ava and Sophia clicked off down the hallway. The feminine sound of their heels echoing off the corridor had them both flowing with confidence.

They were a few minutes late, but Sophia had been the one to insist on keeping the men waiting. It was a little trick that she had learned from her late mother. Her death was another thing that the two women had in common, although Sophia had lost her mom fairly early on in life.

Male voices drifted out of the open doors at the far end of the hall. Light laughter beckoned, causing Ava's insides to jump just a little. This may be the right time to start getting closer to Michael, she thought. Glancing at Sophia, they shared a sly smile. If she could commit to this, then freedom for Mason may not be so far off.

As they crested the threshold of the dining room, Michael greeted them warmly. An appreciative smile took over his face as his eyes fell on the necklace. Taking it as a sign, Ava dove in with both feet. Before she could change her mind, she gave him a kiss, then pulling back, she whispered a breathy thank you in his ear. Caught by surprise, Michael held her at arm's length, studying her a moment for confirmation. She did her best to give him an inviting expression, biting at her lip just a little before brushing her fingers over the tanzanite.

"You ladies look simply lovely." Robert offered from the far end of the room.

"Thank you, Daddy," Sophia responded, pushing past them to greet their guest.

"So, you like the necklace then." Michael beamed.

"Very much." Ava relaxed, letting herself drift into the new role.

Taking her by the hand, Michael guided her down the length of the table. The feel of his fingers as they twined with her own had new nerves pumping. On the opposite side, Sophia embraced another man.

In an instant, Ava's stomach dropped out completely.

His hair was highlighted, changing the dark locks into an almost sandy blonde, and he wore colored contacts, covering the brown with a striking shade of blue. But as the man stepped back from his familiar embrace with Sophia, his eyes blazed with a mutual recognition. It was Andrew Moore, Finn's brother.

Purposefully, Ava replaced her expression of momentary shock with one of polite interest. A quick glance around showed that Michael had been distracted by a request from Robert, who in turn had been focused on his empty drink. With Sophia's back to her, no one had noticed that anything was amiss.

"Ava." Sophia turned to make introductions. "This is Ryan Iverson. Ryan, this is Ava."

"It's a pleasure to meet you, Miss Ava." Andrew inclined his head as he reached for her hand, giving it a brief squeeze.

"It's nice to meet you as well." Ava smiled, but inside she wanted to throw up.

Having filled his uncle's drink from a nearby bottle of brandy, Michael pulled out Ava's chair, then sat beside her. The expansive stone table was set for five, with Robert settling into his place at the head. It was all Ava could do to keep from staring in Andrew's direction as he sat next to Sophia across the table.

"You put that necklace to shame." Michael whispered in Ava's ear. "You're so beautiful."

Nodding her head, Ava's heart pounded in her chest. She could feel Andrew's eyes upon her, assessing her interaction with this man that was not his brother. Hands trembling, she kept them carefully folded in her lap.

"Thank you," she managed, then worked hard to produce a bright smile.

"Robert, you mentioned an addition to your household." Andrew's voice lifted into the air. "But I was under the impression that it was a grandson, not a beautiful new woman."

"Well, Ava was part of that bargain." Robert raised his glass to her and she bowed her head in obedience. "She's Mason's second mother."

"Two mommies?" Andrew's eyebrows raised, then shifted to Sophia at his side. "Are you two together?"

"Oh, no." Sophia laughed easily. "It's not like that. Ava is-"

"It's a long story," Robert intervened, effectively cutting off the topic. "Ryan, why don't you tell us about your latest project in the Maldives?"

Andrew's eyes darted once to Ava, before swiveling back to lock with Robert's. His reluctance to detail business in front of her was apparent, but Robert brushed him off.

"You can talk with my family here," Robert assured him. "Besides, Ava's not going anywhere."

Painting a relaxed look on his face, Andrew complied with the request. As the wait staff drifted in and out, pouring ruby colored wine into sparkling goblets, Ava listened to Mr. Ryan Iverson's discussion on money laundering. He was an expert at it, having successfully serviced a multitude of clients over many years. Freelance photographer her ass.

In typical fashion, the meal was exquisite. Each course was matched with a glass of wine, which Sophia drained until her pupils were dilated, her giggles giddy. Ava, on the other hand, had sipped each glass with measured reserve, making certain never to finish one. Conveniently, as the next course arrived, so did a replacement goblet. If she could keep her head, there may come an opportunity to speak to Andrew alone. Even with only a few seconds, she may be able to send a message to Finn, and that could be her saving grace.

As the meal drew to a close, conversation slowed. Robert rose to leave the table, causing Andrew and Michael to stand as well. Excusing himself, he made to retire to bed, but encouraged the young men to continue entertaining the ladies. As Sophia had warned her earlier, Robert's intention to pair the couples was clear, and so was the fact that he always got what he wanted.

"Shall we take a walk down the beach?" Andrew suggested. "Catch some fresh air?"

"Sounds good." Michael eyed his cousin with mild concern, she was flighty and nearing drunk.

French doors swung wide onto the sweep of green lawn, admitting a cool nighttime breeze thick with moisture from the ocean. Andrew led Sophia out by the hand. Ava followed, the heat of Michael's palm spreading across her lower back. She didn't make it very far into the grass before the heels of her shoes sank deep into the lawn. Pausing, she steadied herself against Michael and slipped them off. Stumbling a bit ahead of them, Sophia stopped to do the same.

Barefoot now, the couples tottered down to stroll alongside the gentle lap of water as it licked at the shore. Andrew and Sophia walked together in front of them, arms linked, heads drawn in close. Occasionally, the sound of her laughter would float back to haunt Ava, whose stomach tumbled with a mix of hope and fear. Michael accepted her silence without question, content to hold onto her hand.

When they arrived at the last house, the one where Ava had felt someone watching her, the lights inside had been turned on. To her surprise, Andrew turned to walk up the narrow wooden staircase that led to the wide deck. When they entered, the fireplace in the main living area was blazing, making the open space welcoming and warm.

"You're staying here?" Ava questioned, before catching herself.

"Just for the night," Andrew replied. "I arrived this morning."

"Oh, you can't stay the weekend?" Sophia complained.

"Unfortunately, not." Andrew pulled his eyes from Ava. "I've got business. Maybe next time."

As Michael and the women took a seat by the fire, Andrew fetched yet another bottle of wine. Pouring for each of them, Ava watched him sip leisurely, letting the others be the ones to imbibe. Following his example, Ava drank sparingly and observed Andrew pass over her glass time and again. After several hours, Sophia was close to passing out, and even Michael showed signs of unsteadiness. Leaning back against the sofa, one arm slung around Sophia's sagging shoulders, Andrew blinked soberly at her. Michael's hand had drifted to rest on Ava's exposed thigh. Not wanting to stir things up, she didn't move away.

"Ava." Andrew began lazily. "I never did catch your last name."

"It's Montgomery," she answered.

"Any relation to Clay Montgomery?"

"He's my brother," Ava responded as Michael shifted uncomfortably.

"We've never met, but his reputation for business proceeds him these days," Andrew continued. "Any chance you could introduce us? Perhaps he's in need of my services?"

"No." Michael shook his head, frowning.

"I'm afraid not," Ava supplied quickly, taking advantage of Michael's foggy state. "I'm not allowed to contact him."

"Ava-" Michael warned, shaking her leg with his hand as if to jog her memory.

"Family trouble?" Andrew pressed.

"My father won't allow it," Sophia supplied. "You see, Clay is the father of my son."

Michael stood abruptly. "I'm sorry, but it's time I took you ladies home."

"Oh, calm down Mikey, it's only Ryan." Sophia laughed drunkenly.

"Of course," Andrew nodded. "Looks like you'll need some help."

Sophia cackled, head thrown back as she tried unsuccessfully to stand. Andrew reached to steady her, but Michael shook his head. Stepping between the pair, he swooped his cousin up without effort, tossing her over one shoulder.

"No offense, Ryan." Michael grunted. "But she's just a bit

too drunk, and my uncle would kill me if I didn't get her back myself."

"I understand, let me at least walk with you all."

"Sure."

Down the wooden steps, Michael hefted Sophia with ease. For a while she braced herself against his back, keeping her head up, but then melted down, hands swinging limply with his gait. Andrew and Ava followed a few steps behind but made sure to walk considerably slower. After only a few seconds, they were effectively alone.

"It was you watching me this morning," Ava whispered, the bottoms of her feet growing chill in the damp sand.

"Just snapping a few scenic photos." Andrew kept his voice low. "For work, you know."

"Freelance photography, yeah right," Ava hissed.

"A boring administrative assistant," Andrew countered. "I can't believe I fell for that, and the whole software engineer thing. Total crap."

"Finn told you?"

"Who do you think sent me here?" Andrew asked.

"Oh, thank God." Ava exhaled her relief. "Tell me we're getting out of here tonight."

"Not a chance." Andrew shook his head. "I did this because he cornered me and begged. I'm only here to locate you. When the FBI swoops in, Ryan Iverson will be long gone."

"So, Mr. Iverson isn't a cover?" Ava glanced up, making sure they were still isolated as they plodded along. "You really launder money for a living? For bad guys?"

"What I do and who I do it for is nobody's business, but because of you my brother now knows about me. That being said, Finn promised me that you could keep a secret… not ask too many questions."

"I see. Well, Ryan, I've spent my life keeping men's secrets." Ava nodded solemnly, catching his drift. "Trust me, no one will find out about you."

"Are you really sure that you want to leave this place?"

"Why would you ask that?"

"The allure of money can be a strong one." Andrew looked pointedly at her necklace. "That's a pretty jewel. Did Michael give it to you?"

"Listen what you saw earlier-"

"No need to explain." Andrew cut her off. "I'm only asking before I potentially blow my whole livelihood apart saving a girl that maybe doesn't want to be saved."

"I want out of here, but only if Mason goes too."

"Alright." Andrew paused. "Have you heard from your brother?"

"No, why?"

"Finn can't get a hold of him, but don't worry about it. I was supposed to ask just in case." Andrew stopped walking, the lights from the Lockett house shone down before them. "Keep as close to Mason as you can."

"I will."

"And, Ava-" Andrew whispered, making her turn to face him. "Stay away from Michael, don't break my brother's heart."

TWENTY-TWO

Ava followed the sounds of retching into Sophia's bathroom. The classy woman in the tiny red dress knelt on the travertine marble floor, face hovering just above the white porcelain toilet. Michael stood awkwardly, holding his cousin's hair in one hand, covering his nose with the other. Stifling a laugh, Ava leaned against the threshold, surveying the carnage of too much alcohol play out before her.

"Make it stop." Sophia moaned, hands clutching desperately at the seat.

"You want some water?" Michael asked. "I'll get you some water."

Releasing her hair, he turned to exit and spied Ava. Rolling his eyes, he kept his hand over his nose. Ava stepped back to let him through, and in that moment, realized that she felt no fear. Standing in a bathroom with Michael did not send the shivers of panic to stifle her breath as it once had.

"Why?" Sophia groaned, then heaved again.

Taking pity, Ava crouched down beside her, gathering the

other woman's long dark locks in her hands. As Sophia vomited repeatedly into the toilet, Ava turned her face away to stare at the blank wall. When Michael returned, he set a bottle of water on the floor next to the two women, then lingered just outside the door.

"It's okay." Ava waved him off. "I'll take care of her."

"Are you sure?" Michael questioned, shifting his weight from one foot to the other.

"Yeah, it's fine. Go get some sleep."

"Okay."

Bobbing his head in acceptance, Michael scooted away as Sophia began to choke and sputter once more. After another round of sickness, she slumped over and laid her head against the cold tile floor. Urging her to drink, Ava helped to lift Sophia's head slightly and pour a little water down her throat. This was so exactly like college, that Ava couldn't help but smirk.

"Ha, ha." Sophia squeezed her eyes shut.

"Sorry." Ava got up to fetch a cool wash cloth. "This reminds me of my college days. Takes me back."

"Me, too." Sophia sighed as Ava placed the damp towel over her forehead. "Only, it was Clay taking care of me then."

"How did you meet him?"

"At a bar on the coast. I was studying at Duke, and it wasn't a far drive to the shore."

"He was stationed in North Carolina for a while." Ava recalled.

"It was the first time in my life that I was out from under my father's thumb and the freedom felt, oh, so amazing." Sophia shifted onto her back, wedging herself awkwardly between the toilet and the wall. "A bunch of my girlfriends and I were out to have a good time, but Clay was just sitting at the bar, all by himself."

Ava tried to picture it in her mind. The smell of stale beer, the twist of old wooden barstools, and a sticky laminate countertop. At least that was the scene that she had always been partial to. If Clay had been drinking alone, that meant something heavy had been on his mind. She wondered if he was already having second thoughts about the Program.

"Oh, he looked good." Sophia ran her hands back through her tangle of hair. "He was fit, you know. Like you could see the definition in his shoulders through his shirt, and his hair had that military cut to it. But the way his eyes stared at me, I'll never forget it."

"Did he ask you to dance?"

"Clay?!" Sophia snorted, then sat up suddenly to vomit once more. Swiping her hand across her mouth she lay back down, then went on. "No way, he never even got up off his seat."

"So, what happened?"

"Well, I ignored him at first. My friends and I danced, then there was this guy, then another. Eventually, I made my way to the bar, but when I tried to pay, the bartender wouldn't accept my money."

"I don't understand."

"The bartender told me that Clay was paying for my drinks. All of them."

"All of them?"

"The whole night, no matter if another guy tried to buy them, it didn't matter. He was picking up my tab."

"Wow." Ava was impressed. "So, what did you do?"

"Well, I went over to talk to him, of course." Sophia smiled. "The rest was history. I wish I could go back to that night."

"Why did you leave them?" Ava watched the smile fade. "Why didn't you run with Clay and Mason when you had the chance?"

"Because I knew my father would never stop looking for me. Because I knew that no matter how far I went, or what color I dyed my hair, that the LO would catch up. I didn't want Mason to live like that. I didn't want my son to be a part of it."

"But he is anyway."

"Yeah." Sophia squeezed her eyes shut. "He is now."

"You should drink more water."

"Alright."

Ava helped Sophia to sit up, tipping the bottle to glug its contents into her mouth. The two women spent the next hour or more that way until eventually Sophia drifted off to sleep. Snoring slightly, she wrapped her hands around the base of the toilet, head propped under a bunched-up bathroom rug. Normally, drunk rules would have Ava leaving her there to sleep it off, but she felt guilty walking away now. Better to get her into bed.

Pacing around the large bedroom, Ava wondered if she would be able to drag Sophia's limp body all the way across the floor. Then there was the task of lifting the other woman up and onto the mattress. If only there was a helpful guy around to lift her up, then the job would only take a few seconds. Ava knew of just such a man but hesitated in disturbing him. Andrew had warned her to stay away from Michael, but it's not like she could jog down the beach at this hour and get him to do it.

Walking back into the bathroom, Ava wrapped both hands around Sophia's ankles and gave a good tug. The lifeless body came loose from its clutch around the porcelain throne. Leaning back with all of her weight, she was successful in dragging Sophia about twelve inches before waking her. With a cry, Sophia kicked out, sending Ava sprawling on her butt. Scrambling drunkenly back for the toilet, Sophia wrapped herself around its cold base, effectively undoing Ava's previous work.

"Screw it," Ava huffed, then stomped out.

At the end of Michael's hallway, the door stood open. The collection of rooms beyond were all dark. Ava lingered there, wringing her hands undecidedly before sucking in a breath and going inside. Moonlight filtered in through glass windows, lending a glow to the expansive central room. Walking past the furniture, Ava noted that this wing of the house was a mirror image of the one she had lived in for the past several months. There were five doors in a semi-circular pattern, all of which were closed.

Glancing down, Ava saw a trail of discarded clothing that littered the floor. A pair of dress shoes were tucked next to a leather chair, along with two balled up socks. Flung to one side was a dress jacket, then further on, a tie. Bare feet padding along the hardwood floor, Ava stepped over Michael's button up shirt, then found herself face to face with his bedroom door. Fingering the jewel at her neck lightly, she turned away, but after only a few steps, doubled back.

Sophia lay in a heap on her own floor and something inside Ava just couldn't leave her there. Knocking lightly at first, Ava held her breath, waiting. When nothing happened, she pressed her ear against the door. Silence. Reminding herself that Michael had been drinking too, she knocked harder this time until the sounds of rustling meant he was awake.

Stepping back, she hugged herself, running her hands over her arms while the sound of feet came to the door. He opened it wearing only boxer shorts, looking rumpled and half asleep. Running his hand through his brash red hair, it took a moment for his eyes to register recognition at her presence.

"Ava." Michael reached for her hands, drawing her gently inside. "You've come. I've waited for you to come, you don't know for how long."

"Michael, I-" Ava tried to speak, but his lips were taking her own, kissing her softly.

For a few moments, she let him, analyzing the feelings he generated inside her. As his hands cruised down her sides, Ava kissed him back, searching. But as he sought to increase the heat, she worked to cool things down. What she felt for him was care for a friend, not the thrill of a lover. Stepping away, she spread her palms wide over his chest.

"What is it?" He watched her.

"It's Sophia."

"Is she hurt? Is she okay?" His concern was genuine, the moment of their brief interaction shoved from his mind.

"She passed out on the bathroom floor," Ava explained. "And I can't move her."

"I'll come, just let me grab some pants."

Flicking on a light, Michael stooped to grab his dress slacks from the floor. He hoped on one foot, then the other, before pulling them on. Giving her a sheepish smile, he zipped up, then trailed behind her, back the way she had come in.

"She does this every time he sets her up on a date," Michael confided as they walked.

"Drink too much?"

"Drink until she throws up or passes out."

"Why?"

"Self-preservation," Michael commented. Opening the door to the women's quarters, he stepped aside to let her through first. "Uncle Robert has a way of making everyone's choices for them. If Sophia is seen as a drunk party girl who gets too wasted to put out, then she's definitely not marriage material."

"What about you?" The question popped from Ava's mouth, her sudden concern for him surprised even herself.

"Well, he likes to make my decisions, too," Michael admitted.

"How can you live like that?"

"I love him," Michael said simply. "I never knew my father, Uncle Robert raised me."

Ava stared at the side of his head as Michael surveyed the mess that was his snoring cousin crumpled on the floor before them. Grunting tiredly, he stooped low, half-lifting her up to move her out of the corner. His motions were practiced, he had removed her from this spot countless times before. Wriggling and crying out, Sophia batted at him absently.

Shushing her, he scooped her into his arms and within a few steps deposited her onto the mattress. When he looked back over his shoulder, Ava had a new understanding of the workings of this family. Michael and Sophia were more like brother and sister than cousins. They were raised together by the same man, with very little intervention from other family members.

If Ava's ultimate plan was to take Mason and Sophia with her, then she was going to have to recalculate. Sophia had run away from her father, and would likely do so willingly again, but loyalty to Michael might sway her to stay, or even return some day.

"I'll change her clothes and tuck her in," Ava volunteered.

"I just usually toss a blanket over her and walk out." Michael sighed. "Want me to wait for you?"

"No." Ava shook her head. "I'm pretty tired."

"Another time then." Michael smiled before giving her a kiss.

"Another time."

Ava bobbed her head, thinking what an asshole she was for leading him on. Rifling through Sophia's dresser, Ava selected a nightgown. With a sigh she worked to undress her friend, then clothe her in the more comfortable attire. By the time Ava meandered out of Sophia's room, and peeked in on Mason, it was coming on four o'clock in the morning. A groan of exhaustion escaped her lips as she changed into her own nightie and slipped into bed.

Her back ached from the combination of walking in high heels and kneeling on the hard bathroom floor. Rolling this way and that, the turmoil of the day's events kept replaying in her mind. Rescue was coming, her brother was missing, and no matter what way she looked at it, someone she cared about was going to get hurt. Despite her body's desperate plea for sleep, the precious commodity simply would not come.

With dawn approaching, Ava pushed aside the covers in a huff, grabbed a thick sweater and stomped out. In was still dark, but the gray fingers of a newborn sun were working their way into the horizon line. At the edge of the water, where the ocean lapped at the sandy bank, Ava stood. She had never seen the sunrise over the water. Perhaps the piercing rays would help to clear her cluttered mind and scrub at her troubled soul. It had never been so hard to tell if she was doing the right thing.

"Making your getaway?" Michael's voice was subdued behind her.

Un-startled by his sudden presence, she turned her head, smiling at him over her shoulder. He looked rumpled, again. Poor guy, undoubtedly she had dragged him out of bed once more. Cell phone flashing, he glanced down, tapping his finger to stop its persistent glow.

"How did you know I was down here?"

"Silent alarm." Michael held up the now vacant cell. "Ring, ring, wake up Mike."

"Hmmm, sorry about that, but if I wanted to escape, this wouldn't be the way." Ava backed a few steps until she stood next to him.

"Oh?" Michael laughed softly, taking a seat in the gritty sand. "How would you go about it?"

"I can't tell you that." Ava sat beside him, wrapping her arms around bare legs.

"You'd leave without saying goodbye?"

His playful tone had her chuckling. For a few moments, they sat together, watching the sun peek ever so steadily from the edge of the earth. Its light reached upwards in muted yellows and oranges. Soon the first inkling of warmth came to chase away the remaining darkness. Inhaling, Ava smelled the salt of the sea. Eyes cruised over the side of her face, she could feel Michael appraising her. Gently, his hand came to tilt her chin towards him. When he lay his lips against hers, the kiss was sweet, sad even.

"You don't love me," he whispered it, forehead bent to touch hers a moment before releasing his hold. "And that's okay."

"Is it?" Ava held his gaze, questioning. "I'm sorry, Michael."

Shrugging, he looked out over the water. When she lay her head against his shoulder, he looped his arm around her waist.

"You know," Michael murmured. "If you ever want to leave, all you have to do is tell me. I'll drop you back at your brother's doorstep, or anywhere else you want to go."

"I could never leave without Mason."

"I could never take Mason from Sophia, or my uncle, but you know that."

"Yeah, I know that."

"Listen, I'm going to be gone for a while on business. I want you to keep your head down and try to keep Mason under the radar, too."

"Robert's not going?"

"No. I've been allowed to stay longer than usual to help with the transition, but I can't avoid it anymore." Michael didn't shift his gaze from the shining water.

"Oh." Ava wasn't sure what else to say but noted that her insides pinched with worry.

"If my uncle asks you to do anything that you don't like, just agree to it, and we can deal with it together when I get back. Okay?"

"Okay." Ava was certain he had something particular in mind but wasn't sure what. Perhaps he had provided more protection than she had been aware of.

They sat there for a long while in companionable silence until her stomach grumbled with hunger and her eyes itched from lack of sleep. When he left, she had no idea that would be the last time she would see him for well over three weeks. In her mind, she thought that Finn and the full force of the FBI would come sweeping in the very next day. But that day came and went. So did another, then a week, and one after that.

Ava began to internally review and question her interactions with Andrew. Had he gotten cold feet? Felt he couldn't trust her with his true identity? Wringing her hands together, she was often distracted, withdrawn. Sophia was also stressed. Her father dogged her relentlessly, apparently having been embarrassed by her behavior in front of Mr. Iverson. Robert made frequent visits to observe Mason's homeschool, critiquing the lesson plans, manner of delivery, and even his grandson's performance.

Playtime without Michael presented its own set of challenges, Mason was sullen and not easily entertained. He drifted from activity to activity without much enthusiasm for anything. Ava found herself perpetually frustrated. Not a year ago she would have packed up and taken him to the park or had a playdate with a friend, but now that wasn't an option. Dinnertime was especially tense. Alcohol had been forbidden to Sophia, but as some sort of twisted punishment, it was pushed excessively on Ava.

Glass after glass was filled, with Robert insisting that Ava partake. As she drank, his eyes rested on her, calculating. Remembering Michael's words, Ava obeyed and even did her best to bribe Mason into silence, but occasionally that wouldn't work. When Robert would lose his temper, the entire table jumped in alarm. He had yet to strike anyone physically, but a fair number of dishes were thrown, sending food to splatter across their tight faces.

The latest evening left Ava's heart pounding in her throat as the three of them scurried back down the hallway to their rooms. Covered in angry slashes of Cabernet Sauvignon, their expensive dresses were ruined, and Mason's hair was sticky with the substance. When they crossed the threshold, the nanny clucked in concern and swooped in to maneuver Mason into the bathtub. Left alone, Ava blinked openly at Sophia, who after a moment, began to laugh.

"This is funny?" Ava's mouth was agape.

"I've never shared it with anyone." Sophia struggled to catch her breath. "Now I'm staring at you covered in wine and I see how ridiculous I've looked all these years."

"Ridiculous?" Ava frowned, perplexed. "Try horrified. This is so not normal and it's not good for Mason."

"You're right, of course you're right."

"Does Michael tolerate this?"

"Oh no." Sophia sobered instantly. "My father only does this to women. Michael doesn't know."

"Why haven't you told him?"

"I don't know, he loves my father. I don't want to hurt that."

"We have to get out of here, with Mason. We can't live like this."

"I've tried that, and I've failed every time."

A knock on the door startled them both. It swung open without either of the women's assent to admit one security guard with a chiseled chin and impassive face. Somberly, he informed Ava that she had been requested by Robert. He needed to speak with her and she was to come immediately. Sharing a look of concern, Sophia gripped Ava's elbow. This was the first time that Robert had ever made such a request. It was unusual, filling her with apprehension after the stunt he had pulled only half an hour before.

Ducking her head in acceptance, Ava gave Sophia a parting look as she followed the guard back into the hall. High heels clicking, she ran her hands over the wine stains that ran diagonally across her powder-blue dress. The satin material was stiff where the liquid had soaked in to dry. Expecting to be led back into the dining room, Ava's pulse quickened when instead the guard veered towards the entrance to Robert's private quarters. The heavy carved wooden door that she had wondered at for so many months was now held open for her.

Inside was a massive great room, its cathedral high ceilings towered overhead. Ornately carved furniture, statutes and works of art were positioned expertly to give the feeling of ultimate largess. She was dwarfed in comparison; that was the idea. Eyes darting about as they walked, Ava tried to keep her expression in check when she failed to see Robert anywhere. They passed rows of windows and alcoves until finally stopping at a pair of closed double doors. After a brief knock, she heard the sound of Robert's voice lifting in its superiority to admit them.

Hesitant, she stepped first one foot and then the other into his bedroom before the doors swung closed behind her. Relaxed, like a king on his throne, Robert glanced over at her. He was pouring himself a glass of brandy, the ice tinkled and cracked when it met with the liquid. Ava swallowed hard. He didn't offer her a place to sit.

"Ava." Robert faced her. "Pretty Ava, you've caught my nephew's eye."

"Michael is a good man." She nodded, twisting her fingers together behind her back.

"He's too soft in some respects, but yes, he does his job well. You're wearing the necklace he chose for you. I wonder, would you wear a ring?"

"I'm not sure I understand."

"I want Mason to go to private school, have the opportunity to interact with children his own age. Don't you?"

"Yes."

"I'd like to take him to the movies, to the zoo, have birthday parties, that sort of thing."

"That sounds great." Ava nodded eagerly.

"But none of that is possible-" Robert moved closer, watching her for a reaction. "Because of you."

"Why?"

"Because he'll get older, and you will convince him to give away his location."

"I won't do that."

"Stop." Robert shook his head. "Let's not pretend you won't. You're still a Montgomery. You're still loyal to your brother. I've tried to convince Michael of this, but he can't see past your charming face."

Robert closed the distance between them. Ava shivered but refused to look away. Severe eyes evaluated her as he raised his hand, still clutching the short crystal glass. Slowly, he ran his knuckles down the side of her cheek. Her voice evaporated in her throat.

"There aren't many options available to you." His words were ever so quiet. "Marry Michael, prove your loyalty by making a family with him. Have a few children, and then I'll know that you'll never leave. Or..."

He let the alternate scenarios permeate the air, unspoken. She could only guess at the exact details, but the threat of violence rang clear. There had been a time in her life when lying had been difficult for her, but that seemed long ago now. Back then there had been no secrets, no false names, or hidden children. Whoever that person had been, was gone.

"I'll marry him," Ava breathed it.

TWENTY-THREE

Robert's eyebrows shot up in surprise. She detected an element of disappointment there, but he didn't bother to hide it. Removing his hand from her face, he sipped his drink, appraising her over the rim of his glass. When a rapid knock sounded against his door, he pursed his lips.

"Uncle!" Michael called from the other side. "I'm back early."

"Come in." Robert turned away from Ava and strode to the other side of the room.

The dim lighting made it possible for Ava to watch the double doors swing open without turning around. Shadows formed against the dark hardwood of the bedroom floor as shafts of brighter light grew wide, then narrowed once more. Feeling Michael just behind her, she could sense his shock at seeing her there. It was in the energy that collected at her back, the sucked in breath, the offbeat of his halting steps.

"Ava." Michael grasped her shoulder, shifting around to

look at her. "What are you doing here? What's all over your dress?"

"We were just discussing your engagement," Robert interjected, drawing Michael's attention across the room with an upraised glass. "Shall we toast?"

"Engagement?" Michael's expression furrowed. "Uncle Robert, you promised that you would let me handle this my own way."

"You take too long." Robert's smile didn't reach his eyes. "Now I've done the hard part for you, and she's said yes. Isn't that cause for celebration?"

"Honestly, no." Michael's tone grew heated. "I've done everything else in my life the way that you've wanted. All I'm asking for is that this one thing be up to me. I'm sorry, Ava, but I'm going to have to withdraw any promise of marriage that my uncle has made."

"She's a loose end!" Robert's voice pitched with frustrated fury. "Either you marry her, or we phase her out."

"Mason loves her," Michael argued. "We won't be doing anything like that."

As the dispute grew, Michael moved forward, placing a protective arm across Ava. Pacing back and forth, Robert shouted and flailed, causing the brandy to splash out in spurts over the rim of his glass. When Michael stepped decidedly between them, a flashing light from his pocket caught Ava's eye. It was his cell phone, blinking its silent insistence. Completely absorbed in their fight, neither of the men noticed it.

Taking the opportunity to melt into the background, Ava inched tentative steps back until she bumped into the sealed doors. While her hand searched for the knob, her eyes were drawn once more to another flash. On the far dresser, Robert's cell blinked in alarm. This one drew Michael's attention as well.

Grabbing for his own phone, Michael swiped at the screen and held it up to his ear. Within seconds he had barked orders for all security to report to the beach. The fight forgotten, Robert scrambled in his nightstand for a weapon, his back to the broad windows that ran the length of one wall. In this position, he never saw it coming.

The sound of gunshots and shattering glass reverberated around the room, seeming to come from everywhere at once. Robert's body dropped limply to the floor. Michael screamed.

"No!" His voice was harsh with disbelief.

Making a low dash for his uncle's body, he checked frantically for a pulse. Finding none, he began to administer CPR, hands pumping downward into Robert's chest. For a moment, Ava watched in quiet horror. Glancing down at her dress, the wine stains morphed into Agent Palmer's blood. Mind swirling, it was hard to separate the man that now lay on the floor, from the other one she had seen shot mere inches from her face.

"Run, Ava!" Michael called to her before bending over to breathe oxygen into lifeless lungs.

Shaking her head, Ava forced herself to move. Hands trembling behind her, she searched blindly for the door handle once more, unable to rip her eyes from the scene. More glass shattered as a boot kicked out the remnants of a window. In one fluid movement, a soldier entered the room. At least he gave every appearance of being a soldier. Clothed in black, his face was partially hidden behind a half mask and his head was covered by a helmet. The way that he walked, though, and the eyes that beamed at her, were oh so familiar.

When he leveled a black handgun against the back of Michael's head, Ava's stomach dropped. He didn't have to say anything for Michael to stop CPR, raising his hands above his head in submission. Only, Ava knew that wouldn't be enough. Many months ago, she had had the opportunity to save a man's life but had hesitated. In those minutes of reluctance, Agent Palmer's time had run out. It wasn't something that she had recognized until that moment but the utter guilt of his death had etched lines of disgrace into her heart. She would not hesitate now.

Flying across the room, Ava skidded to a stop on her knees, facing Michael. Pressing her forehead to his, she lined her own head up with the gun. If the soldier pulled the trigger, he would certainly kill them both.

"Ava," Michael hissed. "What are you doing? Run, get Mason and go."

"You're not a bad man." Ava stared into his eyes, speaking not only to him. "You've protected me, and Sophia, and Mason. You don't deserve to be executed like this."

"Ava." Michael was positively shaking. "Get out of here, now."

"No." Ava reached her hands up, intertwining her fingers with Michaels as he held them above his head. "I've got you. We're just going to stay still right here. Let this man go back out the way he came."

The room was filled with harsh breathing. Time extended. Ava felt the sweat beads on Michael's forehead, absorbed the faint flick of his eyelashes. Then the handgun shifted away, and the soldier began to fade. Tears of relief flooded behind

Ava's eyes, but they never got a chance to brim. In that moment, Michael made his own decision, and it cost him.

Pushing Ava down with all of his might, Michael whirled, gripping the weapon concealed at his side. Before he could rotate fully around to fire, two more shots rang out. Blown back against the nightstand, he sagged, blood oozing from the wounds to his chest. Boots crunched broken glass as the soldier leapt back out the window frame and into the deepness of the night.

Scrambling up, Ava shrieked at Michael, holding her hands against the blood pumping from his body. Yanking him down to lie on the floor next to his uncle, Ava applied as much pressure to the wound as possible. The warm red flow soaked her hands, his clothes, the floor, her dress.

"Why?" Ava cried. "He was leaving!"

"You're so beautiful." Michael coughed, reaching up to touch her face, he left blood to smear.

"Damn it, don't you die."

"It's okay."

"It's not okay." Ava held her hands against the flow, but it kept coming. "It's not okay."

Suddenly, the double doors were blown wide, admitting man upon man to run in, weapons drawn. They barked orders, swirling and yelling, adding chaos to the death that hung heavily in the air. Ignoring them, she kept pressure, tears streaking, chest heaving.

"FBI! Hands up!" They shouted at her.

"Save him!" She screamed back. "He's been shot, he's dying!"

Glancing up, she saw that they looked nothing like the blacked-out soldier from minutes ago. These men all had vests that were clearly marked with FBI lettering, their faces were not covered, and they wore no helmets. Mouth dropping, Ava stared down the barrel of a gun, but refused to raise her hands for fear that Michael's heart would give up its last blood.

"That's her! Weapons down!" A voice called from behind her.

She felt an arm loop itself about her waist, jerking her back, breaking her grip. Hoisting her easily into the air, she thrashed about madly, eyes locked on Michael's as an FBI Agent bent to inspect his wounds. Was he already dead? He blinked at her once before she was hustled from the room.

"Help him!" She called.

Writhing in agony, she was carried away. Out through the great entrance room with all of its finery, down a hall, and through a side door. Thrust into sudden darkness, her screams gave way to sobs as the door shut firmly behind them. Flicking on a light, the man sat her on a toilet, and crouched low to inspect her.

"Are you injured?!" Finn's eyes darted over her body. "Is this your blood?! Ava! Answer me!"

"No," Ava whimpered, sorrow fresh. "It's Michael's blood, he's been shot. Is he dead?"

"I don't know." Finn pulled her down onto his lap, hugging her tightly against his chest. "Don't ever do that to me again. Don't ever disappear on me."

"Why did he do it? Why didn't he just hold still?" Ava mumbled into Finn's chest. "He was leaving."

"Who was leaving?" Finn asked. "Did you witness the shooting?"

"Yes." Ava covered her face in her hands. "What about Mason? Sophia?"

"They're fine, everyone's okay," Finn assured her. "There were no shots fired except in that room. What happened? Was it one of our guys?"

"I don't know." Ava's thoughts were scattered, but instinct and years of influence had her blurring the truth. "It was dark."

"We don't have much time." Finn set her up on the lid of the toilet. "As much as it kills me, I'm going to have to let you out of my sight."

Standing, he searched through the cabinets. Ava blinked, shock numbing her senses. When he located a case of tiny paper cups, Finn twisted the gold nob of the bathroom sink and filled it with water. Holding it to her lips, he watched her sip, worried brown eyes alight with concern.

"What comes next?"

"You and Mason are the subjects of a kidnapping investigation and now you've witnessed a shooting. The FBI will want to interview you."

"Can I refuse?"

"It will look suspicious."

"When will they do it?"

"Right away." Finn knelt in front of her once more, running his hands up her arms, over her shoulders. "When we leave this room, I am not your friend. Do you understand?"

A knock on the door had him jolting. The voice on the other side inquired about Ava, and what exactly they were doing in their together. Finn called out that she was feeling sick. Grabbing her up with one hand, he carefully lifted the lid, then whispered for her to gag. Faking a dry heave, she stood back and watched as he dumped the remaining contents of her water cup into the bowl with a splash. Stepping forward, he pulled the handle to flush.

"Be out in another minute!" Finn called to the stomp of retreating boots, the sound of vomiting had scared away the other agent.

Standing there together, Ava's body began to shake. It was slight at first, but the shock was beginning to wear off. Staring down at her own hands, she saw them stained up to the elbow with red blood. When she tried to wipe them off on her dress, she saw that it too was soaked. Finn's vest was black, but the long sleeve collared shirt he wore underneath had once been a stark white. It too bore the traces of crimson, imprinted here and there when he had embraced her. Looking finally up into his face, she felt the need to crumble, but he caught her half way to the floor.

"Ava." His whisper was strained. "When we walk out of this room, I am not your lover. I am not your friend. Nothing that I will say to you will be to help you. Can you remember that? Nothing that I say is to benefit you."

"I don't understand." She tilted her head up to peer into his face, saw distress clearly in his eyes.

"I'm the lead on this investigation. I'll be the one interrogating you."

"I see." It took everything she had to push away from him.

"When this is all over, promise me that you won't disappear." He gripped her elbow tightly in his hand, keeping her body close. "Just give me a chance to see you, explain things, do you remember the number?"

Nodding, she let him turn her to the door. They opened it onto a scene flooded with lights, sound, and personnel. Every inch of space was taken up by someone walking, taking photos, placing evidence placards, barking orders. No one noticed as Finn guided her out, keeping a careful grip on her upper arm. As he walked her out of the mansion, out of the sprawling Lockett estate, she felt the heat from his contact. Body positioned just behind hers, he used his hand to steer her out into the pitch of night. She felt the ocean's breath blow against them both.

When she had been brought to the house originally, she had been unconscious. Though she had been restricted to the rear of the home, she had spied the paved road that ran along the length of the peninsula through shuttered windows. Stepping onto the hard surface now, she didn't feel the relief that she had once imagined. Darks sedans lined the road, one on top of another. FBI Agents crawled back and forth like ants. To and fro from their vehicles they transported paper bags filled with items of evidence from the household. She supposed that she was just another item now, too large for a brown bag.

Sirens echoed faintly somewhere in the distance, she thought of Michael. Closing her eyes, she felt his forehead press against hers, heard the sound of his labored breathing. Then it was Palmer's eyes she looked into, his hot blood that splattered across her face. Shifting her head to the side, she vomited onto the pavement, for real this time.

"Little help over here!" Finn shouted, refusing to release his hold on her. "I need a medic to check her out, then an escort to the closest field office."

"On it." Another agent jogged over, taking her swiftly into his possession.

She knew the instant that Finn let go. Her arm throbbed

with the empty abandonment. If she had felt like an item of evidence before, the next several hours confirmed it. A medical technician inspected her. She was transported to a nearby field office. A forensic team photographed, cataloged, and took possession of her clothing.

Sitting alone, wearing nothing but a thin paper hospital gown, Ava shivered in the overpowering custody of the FBI. At least in the possession of the LO she had sweat pants. At least in the possession of the LO the cage that confined her had been visible. When the door opened, and Sophia stepped in, Ava burst into tears. The two women hugged, rocking slightly, holding on to one another.

"Are you okay?" Sophia choked.

"I'm so sorry," Ava moaned. "Have you heard anything?"

"They won't tell me how Michael is." Sophia's voice hitched. "But my dad is gone."

He had been an abusive controlling asshole, Ava thought, but he was still Sophia's father, and she had loved him. Stepping back slightly, Sophia wiped at her eyes, then produced a set of clothes for Ava.

"What have you told them?" Ava asked, slipping into the grey pencil skirt before shrugging into the sheer white blouse.

"Not a thing," Sophia whispered, helping Ava to adjust the clothes. "Mason is your son and I am your friend. I won't let them speak to him and we will wait here until you're finished."

"Thank you."

Standing up from the wooden chair, Ava slipped into the four-inch pumps that filled her with a sense of confidence she hadn't had in way too long. The blood had been washed from her hands and face, the dress stained with indignity had been removed. It was time to finish what had begun in an FBI interrogation room. It was time to face Agent Johnathan Finn.

When they showed her to the unassuming room just down the hall, she wasn't surprised to find it empty. Taking a seat at the vacant metal table, Ava folded her hands carefully in her lap, watching the closed door. Like Clay and Robert Lockett, choosing seats for every person at their table, this room was Agent Finn's territory. This was where he ruled supreme.

Keeping her waiting was all part of the game. The game of submission and catching one another off guard. But she had something on him that nobody did. When he pushed open the door, the curl in her belly reflected briefly in his eyes before he shaded them. Papers in hand, he took the seat across from her, then began.

"Miss Montgomery-" Finn's voice was casual, controlled. Everything they said was being recorded. "It is good to see you again on the outside of a cage, though I'm sorry for the circumstances."

"Yes." Ava nodded. "It's been a long time."

"You must be exhausted from your recent ordeal, but unfortunately the time to get the best witness accounts is right after an incident occurs. We appreciate your willingness to sit down and answer some questions."

"Of course." Ava caught his eye. "After what happened with your former partner, I'm happy to help you in any way that I am able."

"For the record." Finn glanced up to the corner of the room. "You are referring to a time where you, Agent Palmer, and myself were kidnapped and held for ransom by the Lockett Organization. During that time, Agent Palmer was executed, and even though you and I were not held in the same room, we were able to communicate from time to time. Is that right?"

"That's right." Ava crossed her legs underneath the table.

"It is my understanding that tonight you witnessed the shooting of both Robert Lockett and Michael Tamson, his nephew."

"How is Michael?" Ava leaned forward.

"I'm unable to provide you with an update at this time, can you please answer the question?"

"No." Ava shook her head. "I'm not going to tell you anything until you tell me how he is."

"Is that because you two are lovers?"

"What?"

"Is he your boyfriend?"

"No."

"Are you sure?" Finn's eyes were steady, piercing her as he produced a photograph of Michael and Ava kissing on the beach. "How do you explain this?"

Reaching across the table, she plucked the photo from his hand. Bringing it to her face, she studied the angle of the shot. This was the morning sunrise, the one when Michael had offered to return her to Clay. How she wished now that she had told him yes. Laying the picture gently on the table, she slid it back over in front of Finn. They both knew who had managed to get this particular shot, even so, he couldn't help but look down at it. Whatever feelings he may have were meticulously hidden.

"Tell me how he is." She watched Finn's jaw clench.

"He's alive," Finn conceded. "In surgery now."

"He's not my lover," Ava admitted, noting the slight shift in

Finn's shoulders as she spoke. "But he became a close friend. This picture was taken out of context."

"Give me the context."

"He protected me and my son, whenever possible."

"Did you need protection?"

"Yes."

"From whom?"

"Robert Lockett."

"Can you give me details?"

"No."

"Were you kidnapped and held against your will?"

"Who reported me as being kidnapped?"

"Your brother, Clay Montgomery."

"Are you in contact with him?" Ava's heart rapped against her rib cage.

"We were working closely with him for a time, but then he disappeared. When is the last time you spoke with him?"

"I couldn't say." Ava thought of the soldier, and what he had done.

"Let's circle back to the shooting," Finn redirected. "Why were you in Robert's bedroom?"

"He had me brought there. It was the first time."

"And Michael too?"

"No." Ava looked away. "He walked in later. He was supposed to be away on business."

"Let me get this straight. The man that isn't your lover, but who you were kissing, walked in on you and his uncle in a bedroom together? Did they fight over you?"

"I never slept with either one of them." Ava leveled her gaze at Finn, trying to remember that he was just doing his job. "They argued about me, but it wasn't how you're making it sound."

"Then clarify it for me."

"I can't."

"Did Michael and Robert shoot each other? Did you shoot them? What happened in that room, Ava?"

"Another man shot them both," Ava conceded, but would give no more.

"Who was it?"

"I don't know."

"Did you see him?"

"It was dark."

"Was it an FBI Agent?"

"It could have been."

"But you're not sure?"

"No."

Pausing, Finn shuffled through his papers, eyes scanning. Ava watched the calm reserve of his manner, the nonplussed movement of his hands. Did he still itch to touch her? Or was their stolen time together gone, like sand sinking through a sifter, leaving only a pile of soft memories behind.

"This is beginning to sound like a domestic dispute between powerful families," Finn commented, eyes shifting to lock with hers. "And now you're smack dab in the middle of a murder. If you know who committed this crime, but refuse to name him, then we can arrest you as an accomplice."

Rocking back in her chair, Ava folded her arms across her chest. Teeth clenching, she refused to look away, but remained silent.

"On the other hand-" Finn slid another photograph across the table. "We might be able to work something out if you could help us with this man. Any information about him would be welcome."

"What's his name?" Ava held her breath as she stared at a picture of Finn's brother, Andrew.

"Ryan Iverson." Finn didn't miss a beat, but slid another photo, then another to rest in front of her. "It appears that he has been a longtime associate of the LO, but we aren't sure what he does for them. Have you ever heard of him?"

"I don't know him." Ava uncrossed her arms, brushing the photos aside, and leaned over the table towards Finn. "But I think that I've had enough of your little games. I've answered all of your questions, and now it's time for me to go."

"Are you sure you want to do that?" Finn tilted his head up to watch as she rose to stand before him.

"Nearly one year ago, the FBI unlawfully took me into custody." Ava's voice raised, she wasn't just talking to Finn. "They subsequently allowed me to be kidnapped by the LO, where I was beaten and starved. As if that wasn't enough, tonight they raided a private residence at the same time that a murder took place, and I'm the one being accused of it?! If I so much as hear a breath of my name, or the name of my son, mentioned in any relation to what has gone on here tonight, then you can expect the biggest lawsuit that you've ever seen to land on your boss's desk the very next day. Goodbye to you Agent Finn, I wish you the best of luck in your investigation."

As she shoved out of the room, Ava called down the hall for Sophia and Mason. Collecting them up, she headed for the exit. There was nothing that Finn could do to stop her.

At the curb outside of the FBI building, her plans ceased. She had no cell phone, had been given no opportunity to place a call. Glancing at Sophia, the two women shared an uncertain expression. Neither one had planned this far ahead. Neither one had ever thought that they would be kicked out into the wind, with Mason in tow, able to go wherever the breeze blew them.

In the far corner of the parking lot, the headlights of a large navy-blue pickup truck came to life. Engine rumbling, it caught Ava's attention. After all, this was the middle of the night, and the lot was practically empty. Retreating a few steps, she brushed Mason behind her body as the driver guided the hulking vehicle to a stop before them. Ava was just about to turn back to the building entrance when the window rolled down and she spied a face that she recognized.

"David!" Ava cried with relief.

"Need a ride?" He asked, hitting the unlock button on the doors.

"You know him?" Sophia was tentative.

"Oh yeah." Ava nodded. "I know him."

Climbing inside, the three castaways settled into the wide cloth seats, felt the heat blasting from the vents. As they pulled into traffic, Ava glanced over her shoulder at Sophia and her son cuddled in the back.

"Hey Mason," Ava asked. "Want to meet your dad?"

TWENTY-FOUR

"What's next?" Clay sighed as Ava handed him another folder.

"This one contains the projected budget for that next level training course you wanted to set up."

Ava swiveled around in the brown leather office chair while he flipped through the printed pages. Rifling through a nearby file cabinet, she carefully replaced the previous packets in their proper spots. They had been settled into the new house for over a month, but only now was she beginning to feel like their shared office space was coming together.

Set back on a twenty-acre parcel of land, the large two-story home had been the perfect fit for their blended family of four. Sophia had insisted on painting the outside white with blue shutters, saying that she'd always liked the farmhouse look. Although Clay grumbled about doing the work himself, he was forced to admit that it looked good.

Giving up his apartment in the hotel hadn't been a difficult decision. Working from home, however, had been an adjustment for him. With the understanding that it would be temporary, they had all agreed that Clay being around a lot would help with Mason's transition into yet another family structure. All of the adults involved hoped that this one would be permanent.

"Have you called him, yet?" Clay knew the answer but asked anyway.

"Who?" Ava busied herself with the next folder.

"You know who. It's been five weeks, don't you think you've punished the man enough?"

"Why? Did he call you again?"

"Only every few days." Clay waved off the next stack of papers Ava placed in front of him. "What's your deal?"

"I'm still settling in." The excuse was getting tired, but she used it anyway.

"Mason's back in school and Sophia's playing home-room mom, everyone else has adjusted already."

"Yeah, it didn't take her long to move into your bedroom now that I think of it," Ava teased, trying to throw him off balance.

"I don't know what you're talking about." Clay smiled, tilting back in his chair.

"The next item we have to review is the property for the survivalist training center." Ava tapped her finger on the folder in front of Clay. "Did you look at the photos that David sent over?"

"Yes." Clay flipped through without concentrating. "It looks okay."

"Okay?" Ava scoffed. "You are the biggest pouty pain in the ass. It looks perfect, you couldn't find another like it in that price range."

"I'm just used to being able to see it for myself." Clay shrugged. "But you're right, let's buy it."

"Great." She swapped folders once more.

"I'm tired of running interference for you, Ava." Clay circled back to the personal. "I'm not going to do it much longer."

"Just do me a favor and let it go. Stop answering his calls." Ava shuffled papers angrily, the mention of Finn caused conflicting emotions to rush through her system.

"Now wait a second." Clay leaned forward in his chair. "What did he do that's made you drop him like this? He put his ass on the line to get you back, not to mention Mason and Sophia."

"And what about you?" Ava glared at her brother's indignation. "What about your little rogue murder mission? Was Finn in on that?"

"Hey!" Clay pointed an accusing finger at her. "Don't tell me that Robert Lockett didn't have it coming."

"And Michael?"

"Oh, here we go again." Clay huffed a breath, rolling his eyes. "He survived, didn't he?! I could have shot him in the head, but he recovered just fine. And that reminds me, don't you ever pull a stunt like that again. What if my finger had slipped? I could have killed you."

"Your finger never slips." Ava gritted her teeth. "Are you ever going to tell Sophia that you killed her father?"

"No." Clay paused. "Are you?"

"No." Ava lowered her voice even though they were alone in the house. "Do you think anyone suspects you?"

"Maybe Johnny." Clay fiddled with a blue pen, tracing

doodles on the papers before him. "And maybe Michael, but he doesn't want a war."

"Mason misses him," Ava commented. "Sophia, too."

"What, you want me to invite him over for dinner? You're out of your mind."

"Mason has a birthday coming up," Ava suggested. "What could it hurt?"

"I'll think about it." Clay paused in his writing, peering down at his phone as it buzzed. "Tell me about John, Ava. Tell me before I put the guy out of his misery."

"I don't know who he is." Ava watched Clay silence the call. "Is he the guy that I was locked in a cage with? Is he the guy that I spent months on the run with? Is he the FBI Agent who interrogated me? What comes first for him? I don't know."

"Do you think that it's easy for him? Do you think it's easy to have to walk that thin of a line? One slip from Johnny, and people get arrested, maybe even die. He had to act like you were nothing to him. If there was even a hint of a connection between you, then it would put you, Mason, Sophia, me, everything in jeopardy."

Crossing her arms over her chest, Ava felt a rush of heat flood her cheeks. Part of her ached to see Finn again, the one who helped repair his father's rental houses, not the agent. How could she explain that to Clay without giving away the Moore family? She couldn't, and the difficult part was reconciling the two identities. Try as she might, she just couldn't see a spot in this house for him.

He was still in the Program, he was still with the FBI. He couldn't very well live with the two people who ran the Militia. There could be no trust between them. In the end, she didn't want to see him again because she knew it could never work. If he looked at her with those eyes, held her in his arms, then she'd want to try. Better to end it now, instead of breaking both their hearts over and over.

"You don't know him," Ava murmured. "Not really."

"I know what comes first." Clay pointed his pen at her, then nodded soberly. "Let me tell you a little story about Johnny Finn. When you called him that last day, to tell him that you loved him…"

Ava's eyes darted up to her brothers, a slight frown filling her face.

"Oh yes." Clay nodded. "I know about that. You see, when your call dropped out, I was the next person that Johnny contacted. Unfortunately, by the time I picked up, Michael had already taken you away. We expected them to find the first tracker, so when I pulled its path up on the computer, I wasn't concerned that it had been destroyed within the first hour. Johnny freaked. He demanded that I involve him in the plan, but I refused. Don't ask me how he did it, but he showed up at the hotel the next day. For a while he just stood out front, but finally I figured it would be best to work with him so he wouldn't report the whole mess to the FBI, or worse, the Program."

"You took a risk," Ava commented.

"Life is about taking risks." Clay's phone buzzed once more, and again he silenced it. "So the original plan was to turn the second tracker on within ten days, right? Not good enough for Johnny. He wanted to track you right away but I convinced him to wait three days. I don't think either of us slept during that time."

"It had already been destroyed by that time," Ava supplied.

"No." Clay shook his head. "It had been removed, not destroyed. When we turned it on, the damn thing sent us a signal. I've never felt so superior in all my life. My plan had worked, or so I thought. We mobilized a team, got prepped, then checked the location, and you still hadn't moved. My gut sank just a little, that tracker is accurate to about a ten-foot radius. It was scary to think about why you hadn't moved more than ten feet in several hours, but maybe you were being held in a room, or another cage. That's when Johnny stopped eating."

Ava looked away from Clay's steady gaze as he spoke, visualizing the turmoil they must have felt. By then she had been in the comfort of the Lockett estate, reunited with Mason, alive and safe. But they hadn't known that, and it must have been awful.

"The tracker was somewhere in Mexico, just south of the border. We drove all night to get there. When we pulled up to the spot, there wasn't any house, or even a building. It was a tiny graveyard with a fresh mound of dirt four rows in. Ava, they made us think that they killed you and buried you there. They even left one shovel to dig with. Do you know how long it takes to dig up a grave with only one shovel?"

"I'm so sorry." Ava's hand covered her mouth.

"When it was my turn to dig, Johnny pushed out dirt with his bare hands. We kept two men to guard, then sent two more to find more shovels, but that took hours. I'll never forget the look on his face when we hit that coffin. It was surreal prying open the box, expecting to see you lying there. When we found the tracker instead, Johnny cried like a baby. But you see, where he felt relief, I felt nothing but death. So, you'll have to excuse me for putting Robert Lockett in the ground next."

"I didn't know." Ava shook her head.

"Well, I do know. I know how Johnny looked when he thought you were dead, and I know how he looked when he found out that you weren't. If you want to know what comes first for him, then that's easy for me to answer. It's you."

Exhaling, Ava rose to her feet, crossing to the unobstructed bay window. Before her stretched their winding dirt driveway, stands of mature oaks offered shade on the far side of open fields. This new information about Finn did not help her, if anything it made her decision even more difficult. Clay's cell began to vibrate once more, pushing up from his desk, he answered it this time. After a few brief sentences, he strolled to the doorway, but paused to turn on his heel and stare at her back. She could see his reflection in the window pane.

"Look, I've got somewhere to be, but you really need to give him a call." Clay shoved a hand casually in his pocket. "He's still suffering."

Outside, the day appeared fine. Spring was giving way to summer, with a soft warmth and a hint of humidity on the horizon. Hank lolled in the shade of his dog run, perking up only to yip at Clay as he strode by. Ava watched her brother get into his black SUV, backing expertly around before zooming in a cloud of dust down the driveway. She hated dark SUVs. She hated dark sedans too, for that matter.

Puffing out a frustrated breath, she shoved back from the window and surveyed the room. Was she still in love with Finn? Yes. Was he still in love with her? It seemed so, but so were Clay and Sophia, and look at the disaster that had followed them. Sometimes being in love didn't mean that you ended up together, she coached herself. Of course, Clay and Sophia were together now, but the path that led there was littered with dead bodies. Admittedly, their circumstances were very different, but also had some similarities.

Ava went around and around with herself as she had almost every day since she'd last seen Finn. Keeping her hands busy, she tidied up the office space, still covered with file folders, papers, boxes and endless to-do lists. Distracted, she listened absent-mindedly to the rumble of an engine signaling Clay's return.

Glancing at her phone, she noted the time, thinking that Mason and Sophia wouldn't be home for another three hours or so. It gave her a chance to review a few more items with Clay before starting dinner. Since it was her turn to cook, Ava thought spaghetti sounded pretty good, and easy. With her back to the door, she called over her shoulder, listening to Clay's footfalls climb the wooden stairs.

"I'm thinking that I'll make spaghetti tonight." Ava smiled triumphantly before adding. "But it's your turn to do the dishes."

Busy arranging the last few documents on his desk, Ava sensed him fill the doorway and stop short. He was always crabby when it was his turn to clean up, but so far Sophia hadn't let him skip a turn. Good woman, Ava thought to herself.

"I've got a few more things here for you to-" Ava glanced over her shoulder, sentence drying up on her tongue. It wasn't Clay come home early after all.

It was like him not to say anything. It was like him just to wait, dark hair slightly mussed, brown eyes tracking. Finn stood silently before her in worn denim jeans, his collared shirt untucked. The short sleeves revealed his toned arms, but she didn't need reminding about what lay underneath.

"Finn." She turned away from him in an effort to hide the tremor in her hands. "What are you doing here?"

"Clay said I could come." He shifted his weight, causing the floor boards to creak. "I had to see you. I wanted to explain the interrogation and make sure you were alright."

Bracing her hands against the edge of the desk, Ava caught his eye in the reflection of the bay window. A low pull inside her began to spread, so she quickly bowed her head, avoiding his look.

"Can't you even face me?" Finn asked.

"No."

"I'm sorry if it felt like I abandoned you after Michael was shot." He approached her slowly while he spoke. "But I couldn't be seen coddling you through processing."

"I know."

"It killed me to leave you at the scene." His fingers reached out, tracing light lines down her arms.

"Stop." Jerking away, she whirled to face him, back pressed up against the desk. "Don't touch me."

The hurt was clear in his eyes as he held his hands up in defense. Her words had come out harsher than she had intended. If she let him hold her now, then there was no telling how far it would go. A part of her yearned for it.

"And I'm sorry that I accused you of shooting Robert and Michael," Finn continued, brows raised, eyes steady. "If I didn't pursue it, then they'd wonder why. I couldn't go easy on you."

"What about making it sound like I was sleeping with both of them?" Ava couldn't help the anger that crept into her tone.

"It had to be asked." Finn was cautious, choosing his words carefully. "We were given a photo of you kissing Michael, and you were in Robert's bedroom when they were both shot. On top of that, you were extremely upset about Michael's shooting and kept insisting on knowing if he was okay."

"We both know where you got that photo," she seethed.

"It was emailed anonymously along with your coordinates; the whole team saw it."

"It was taken out of context."

"Was it?" His voice sharpened, emotion creeping in.

"How dare you?!" Ava shoved past him, stopping a few steps away to turn. "You don't know what I've been through. You don't know what it was like there."

"How could I? You won't talk to me. You won't even let me call you," Finn accused. "Is it like Andrew said? Did you fall for him? The lifestyle? The jewelry and the money?"

"Screw you, Finn," Ava spat.

"Do you want him?"

"No."

"Did you just play along with him to save yourself? Was it that way with me? Because I could have sworn that you were the one welcoming me into your bed. Did you ever actually want to be with me?"

"Want you?!" Ava yelled, fury vibrating within her chest. "I can't have you! Don't you get it? This can never work."

"Is that what this is all about?!" His chest heaved, hands running in frustrated fists through his hair. "You figured it couldn't work between us, so we don't even get to try?!"

"Look around you, Johnny." Ava gestured to the wide

room. "Does this house look like a place where an FBI Agent can live? You're standing in the heart of the Constitutional Militia."

"Tell me one thing." Finn's voice was low, body creeping steadily closer. "Are you in love with me?"

"Stop, John." Ava backed a step at his approach.

"Why are you calling me that?" Finn kept moving forward, eyes locked with Ava's. "I'm not him."

"You are, though." Ava bumped into a filing cabinet, forcing her to stop.

"You know better." Finn halted inches away. Raising his hand, he ran his fingers haltingly through her hair. "Do you love me?"

"Finn," she breathed it, need for him releasing to run thickly through her blood stream.

"Do you?" He lay his lips against hers, kissing softly before pulling back to watch. "Because I'm in love with you, Ava."

Biting at her lower lip, she tilted her head up, looking into his eyes that hunted for answers. Tentatively, she let her palms spread across his chest, then cruise up to his shoulders. When he kissed her again, the softness had gone, but his whispered question remained unchanged.

"Do you love me? Do you love me?" He asked, lips brushing down the side of her neck, fingers curling tightly in her hair.

Tingles bloomed everywhere he touched, there was no more fighting him. No more fighting the feeling he created inside her, no more fighting with herself. Breathing ragged, eyes fluttering, she gave up; true words dropping uncontrolled from her lips.

"Yes," she whispered back. "I'm in love with you."

Small red suitcase flung open on her bed, Ava pulled clothing from the hangars in her closet, tossing them carelessly into the luggage. Her brother watched her, reclining casually, one elbow propping him up on her mattress. Outside, the ground was covered in a thick layer of snow. Its white blanket reflected the bits of sunlight that peeked occasionally from behind stormy clouds.

"It's not like I don't know where you're going," Clay complained.

"You have no idea where I'm going," Ava countered, not breaking stride in her packing.

"Do you have to leave every two weeks? Can't he come here once in a while?"

"It's been eight months, Clay." Ava strode into her bathroom, collecting toiletries. "You all do great while I'm gone."

"How long do you plan on living like this?" Clay sat up as she came back into the room.

"It would be easier if you didn't have someone follow me

to the bus station every time I leave." Ava began to zip up the bag.

"Why even bother packing?" Clay helped her to compress the bulging case as she struggled with the last few inches of the zipper. "I know that you leave it in your car."

"Appearances are everything." Ava smiled.

"So that means you have a whole wardrobe at his house," Clay reasoned. "Must be getting pretty serious."

"Hmmm." Ava refused to answer, dragging the heavy suitcase by the handle off the bed, it gave a loud thump as it hit the hardwood floor.

"I heard he got an annulment from Stephanie." Clay raised his eyebrows, testing the waters.

"How'd you hear about that?" Ava frowned, then brushed it off. "Never mind, I don't care."

"What does the Program have to say about it?"

"If you must know, he's trying to withdraw from the Program."

"Well." Clay stood, following her out the doorway. "All the more reason why he should come here sometimes."

"He's still in the FBI." Ava let her voice bounce off the walls, Clay stomping just behind her.

"Yeah, I know." Clay grabbed her bag to carry it down the stairs. "But he got transferred to the missing persons unit in Texas. He's close. I'll bet you guys have a little house not more than an hour from here."

"Nice guess." Ava laughed. "But no."

Clay did this every time that she packed. He peppered her with questions, constantly pursuing the location of her alternate life. It didn't matter that he knew she would be spending the time away with Finn. It didn't matter that he trusted the other man, liked him even. What mattered to Clay was the puzzle. It drove him crazy not knowing where his sister went. As siblings will do, the fact that it bothered Clay, made it all the more pleasurable for Ava to keep it from him.

Boots crunching in the scattered snow, Ava stomped down the freshly shoveled driveway to her SUV. It was silver, she had a rule against black vehicles. Loading her suitcase in the back, Clay slammed the trunk compartment, then walked around to her window. Rolling it down, she let the vehicle idle while her brother said his goodbyes.

Ava flashed him a triumphant smile before retreating down the driveway. Hands clutching the leather of the steering wheel, she could almost feel the warmth of the desert stroking against her skin. Three short bus rides, and one storage facility later, she would be firing off that same old Jeep. Rambling down the road, she would aim it for Lake Havasu, where Finn would already be waiting. Closing her eyes for the briefest moment, Ava could feel the wrap of his arms around her, gathering her close. She could taste his kiss on her lips, see the smile spread across his face.

That's how they blended their very different lives. For two weeks at a time, they stole a piece of reality with each other. It didn't matter who they worked for, or what secrets they carried. All that mattered was that they got to be together, and that kind of love was enough.

A word from the author:

Want more of Ava and Finn?
They make appearances in - The Captive Series
Check out Book One now…
THE CAPTIVE BORN

Try my UNPUTDOWNABLE new series…
OUTLASTING AFTER - Book One (Post Apocalyptic
Romance)

Want to know when the next book is ready?
Sign up for an email notification here…
LK MAGILL NEWSLETTER

Reviews, pretty please…
Each and every positive review makes a huge difference.
Please leave one with the retailer from whom you purchased
this book.
Thank you and I hope to see you in the future.

Websites:
www.lkmagill.com

Like me on Facebook:
https://fb.me/LKMagill1
Follow me on Instagram:
https://www.instagram.com/lk.magill.author
Check me out on Amazon:
http://amazon.com/author/lkmagill

ALSO BY LK MAGILL

Standalone novels:

VANISH ME

The Captive Series:

THE CAPTIVE BORN - Book One
THE CAPTIVE MISSING - Book Two
THE CAPTIVE RISING - Book Three

Outlasting Series:

OUTLASTING AFTER - Book One
CHASING TRUTH - Book Two
SURVIVING THE WALL - Book Three
BREAKING BEFORE - Book Four
TAKING TOMORROW - Book Five
FINDING FOREVER - Book Six